GRACE AWAKENING

DREAMS & POWER

GRACE AWAKENING

DREAMS & POWER

**The first two books of the
Grace Awakening series
in one volume**

Shawn L. Bird

ISBN 978-0-9877296-2-0
1. Teenagers — Juvenile Fiction 2. Mythology, Greek — Juvenile Fiction
3. Fantasy

Lintusen Press
Ste. 148 Bag 9000
190B Trans Canada Hwy NE
Salmon Arm BC Canada V1E 1S3

Cover art & design:
Mareike Klem
The Urban Think Tank

For John:
The music from your man cave
always fills my heart with joy

For Charlotte and Nicholas:
Your mother loves you!

In fond memory of Lloyd Milton

BOOK ONE:

GRACE
AWAKENING
DREAMS

PROLOGUE

FEARFUL ANTICIPATION WAS WAKING

Light from Olympus is flashing, thundering power from Zeus.
Bolts that are flashing unerringly, ending their destiny's long truce.
Moirae are steadfastly calling them, summoning love from the old myths.
Lovers awaken to start again, called to renew ancient trysts.

"She's not going to escape me this time," the tall blond declared, his mouth set in a firm line. He was handsome and muscular in the manner of ancient Greek statues. "No matter what tricks he pulls, I'm going to be there." He looked at his two companions as they leaned languidly against the cedar trees, and began pacing between them.

The dark one shook his curly hair as his eyes followed the pacing. Twilight was dissolving into night, and there was menace in the air. "You aren't strong enough to defend her yourself, O. You're going to need help."

The third, a bronzed angel, thick with corded muscles, nodded in agreement. "Mars is right. The enemy is determined to destroy her, O, and his determination is lethal. There's no way you'll be able to protect her, considering... well. You know."

"So what can I do?" O asked quietly.

Mars shrugged his shoulders. "So we help."

He looked meaningfully over to the bronze one who shook his head in response. "Not me. I have other things to do."

"Get over yourself, Xandros. You haven't had anything this serious to do for over two thousand years. This is war. You have a responsibility."

"Not to O, I don't."

9

They turned to him then, their brows down.

"What do you mean?" O demanded. "Are you working for…?"

"Of course not. But my priorities are at odds with yours." Xandros smirked and lifted his eyebrows suggestively. "If I'm there, she will want me. I know I'll want her. What I want is mine. You understand that she won't be able to resist me?" He swelled his chest unconsciously. He was massive.

Xandros and O stared at each other for a minute or two before O shook his head. "You can't have her."

Xandros cocked an eyebrow. "We'll see."

A rumble in the distance drew all three gazes to the dark clouds gathering on the horizon.

Mars observed, "He's watching."

"Yes." O was unable to stop the tremor in his voice, "They're all watching."

"Are you ready?" asked Xandros in sudden seriousness.

"I have to be. Will you help?"

Xandros shrugged and glanced away.

O turned away from him, "Mars?"

They studied each other for a while before Mars responded with a nod of his head. "If necessary I will help keep her safe. I'm not doing it for you, though. I'm in it because of the fight. I know perfectly well that you're asking me because I'm the only one who has ever defeated him. But be aware, if she falls for me, I'm keeping her as my prize. I'm not fighting to give her to either of you. Understand?" He glanced over at Xandros with a challenge in his eyes.

Xandros only smirked again.

"We'll worry about that another time," O grimaced.

Lightning flashed and the horizon filled with brilliant light.

A thundering growl echoed through the sky and declared, "It has begun!"

The three men exchanged glances. O inhaled deeply. "I have to go now. She's going to need me." He looked between the other men with command. "Keep watching."

The other two nodded.

Mars wished, "Good luck."

As O vanished into the blackness Xandros added, "You'll need it." He chuckled languidly, "He's doomed, Mars."

Mars clenched his jaw. "We're all probably doomed if we join this fight."

Xandros clapped him on the shoulder. "Makes it much more interesting, doesn't it?"

<u>Sonnet for Grace</u>

I fear, my love, for what they plan this time,
What power have I to keep thee close to me,
Except the power of love I have for thee,
To rise above the tricks that leave thee blind?
I would not seek to win thee with my rhymes,
If thou wert not the only one I see,
Whene'er I close my eyes and sleep brings dreams,
And so I'll fight to prove that thou art mine.
It matters not if they will storm and rage,
Thy love is mine and I will hold thy heart.
Love sings thy praise my Grace and so I choose,
To follow thee throughout the coming age;
Thy love brings joy and beauty to my art;
Grace is my verse, my light, my only muse.

<u>CHAPTER ONE</u>

THIS IS POTENT STUFF

Truthful Mnemosyne whispering; Orpheus plucking a golden lyre.
Lethe is veiling sweet Charis. Tender heart trembling requires
Healing elixir from Parthenon; Kind Asklepios has gifted.
Charis revived to see destiny; lovingly caution's uplifted.

      The first time I saw Ben Butler in this lifetime, I was in grade ten. He was in grade twelve. I had just settled on the floor in the band room to do my math, waiting for Christie to finish her thirty minutes of flute practice time. It was Friday after school, and we were going to go shopping and see a movie when she was done. She'd just started playing her scales when I heard rolling laughter as he walked into the room, still chuckling over something someone had just said to him in the hall.

      "Hey Ben," said Mr. Johnson, glancing up from a box of music folios, "I switched you to room three today. The keyboard from room two is out for repairs, so I let the flute in there. Can you just use the piano today?"

      "Sure thing!" he'd called across to the teacher, "I just have a motif I want to work up." He walked into the practice room without a second look, actually not even a first look, at me with my binder and text book spread out on the grey carpet just left of the door. Glancing up from my books as he went by, I had just enough of a glimpse of him to register an average height, average looking guy with boring light brown hair as he opened the door into the small practice room I was leaning against. Nothing extraordinary at all. Nothing worth noticing in the least. Just another band geek in a plaid shirt to pass in the halls.

      Until the music started.

He had played one rapid set of scales up and down and then my happy little high school world inextricably changed forever. My back against the wall of his practice room was absorbing the waves of sound as his fingers flew up and down the keys of the old upright piano. I could suddenly visualize… what? Everything. Expansiveness. Eternity. I felt myself being pulled away from the world of math into a swirling vortex of sound.

The music was somehow weaving a story, and it was as if a movie started playing in my head. I saw silhouettes of a couple running along a beach, talking in a car, rolling down a hillside, dining at a restaurant… I began to get dizzy from the racing images, my head rolling with the swirling music. I remember wondering vaguely if the chicken burger I'd had in the cafeteria at lunch might have been off; my whole body seemed to be shivering and convulsing. I was drowning in music.

"Grace? Grace! Are you okay?"

Christie's concerned voice pulled me back to the world. I blinked at the bright lights and sudden change in my vision. "I… Yeah... I…" I couldn't seem to form words. I just looked up at her blankly; feeling suspiciously like someone had pulled me out of a lake, like I was fighting for air.

Christie looked behind her and called out across the room, "Mr J! Something's wrong with Grace!"

I groaned. Nothing was wrong with me. Well, I didn't *think* anything was wrong with me, but then again, I wasn't exactly feeling like my body and brain were cohabitating, either.

Mr. Johnson hurried over looking alarmed. "What's wrong? What happened to her?"

Christie shook her head, "I don't know. I finished my practice time and when I came out of the room, there she was looking like, like…" words seemed to fail her, "…like *this*!" she finished, sweeping her hand toward me in a rather overly-dramatic motion.

Mr. J seemed quite undecided about what he should do about this strange quivering creature at his feet, but at that moment, I was released. I inhaled deeply and instantly felt my head clearing.

What had changed? There was only the sound of breathing. Then I realised that the music from the piano had stopped.

I smiled up at them with an apologetic smile and discovered I had my voice again. "I'm okay; I just had a dizzy spell. It must have been something I ate." My mind clicked in alarm as I spoke: Christie had *finished* her practice time? Where had I been for half an hour?! I looked at my math. I'd written two questions on the page. The second one wasn't

13

finished.

Neither Christie nor Mr J looked particularly convinced that I was really okay. They seemed to be deliberating about their next course of action when Ben opened the door of the practice room.

"Is everything all right? What's going on?" He looked at them and then down to me. When he registered me, he did a double take and his eyes narrowed slightly.

What was that about?

I looked up into his shockingly blue eyes and felt the world spin again.

"It's Grace," Christie waved her arm dramatically again in wordless distress.

Ben studied me clinically for a moment before he nodded. "Ah. I see. Here Grace," he said, reaching his hand out to me, "can you stand up?" He said my name with familiarity, like we'd been friends for years.

I looked at the hand and back to his face in confusion. While his eyes seemed outwardly as concerned as Christie and Mr J, behind the concern I saw something else. Was that a twinkle of amusement there? His mouth twitched just a little and I saw he was definitely fighting a smirk. Damn him. He *was* amused! Who was he to laugh at me? I looked away with the thought that his hand was the last one I'd ever use to help me stand, and attempted to heave myself up on my own. Damn musicians! My mother was right, nothing but trouble! I wobbled and both Mr J and Christie moved as if to catch me. Before they could reach me I felt a firm grip on my elbows, as Ben said, "Whoa there, Sweetie. Gotcha! Stand up slowly." Mr. J and Christie relaxed their posture and Mr. J unstacked a sturdy blue band chair and set it near me.

"Sit down Grace, and put your head between your legs."

Ben gently guided me down onto the chair. As he settled me down, he was between the others and me. He leaned in ever so slightly, whispering softly into my right ear, "I'm sorry, Grace."

Sorry?

Sorry for what? Sorry for offering his hand? Sorry for being amused at my expense? Sorry for my obvious mortification? Sorry for drowning me in music? My head was between my knees in a most undignified way, but when I tilted my head, I met his eyes again. He was squatting beside me, watching me carefully, and trying to read something in my expression.

What was going on here?

His eyes were clear and calm, but they seemed troubled. There was no amusement lurking in their depths any more, but there was definitely a concern well out of proportion to what I thought he should show a dizzy girl he didn't even know. As that thought passed through my mind, I saw something else flicker behind his eyes.

Someone he didn't even know?

But he did know me, didn't he?

For at that moment had the craziest sensation that I did know Ben Butler, and that I'd known him forever. Why? I looked into his eyes again searching for some explanation. Instantly I was drowning once more, this time not in the music, but in the clear blue of his eyes, and as I stared, the awareness was right there. I recognized him from…where? Just as I was within reach of the knowledge, everything went black.

From the blackness a voice spoke, echoing as if it was speaking from within a cavern. "Well hello, girl. So you're finally waking up? You've been slow this time. It was hard to find you. But there you are. They're supposed to be protecting you, but I see they've left a rather large opening for me. Amusing really. You'll be quite entertaining to kill. I'm looking forward to it."

When I woke up, it was to find myself face to face with a paramedic, calmly repeating my name with a professional detachment, "Grace. Grace. Come on, Grace." As my eyes flickered open he smiled, "Ah, here you are. Welcome back." His was not the voice I'd heard.

I saw the paramedic's face in the centre of my vision: everything around the edges was still black. I was wearing an oxygen mask, and I reached to pull it off, feeling claustrophobic.

His hand touched mine gently, "No, you'll need to leave that on for a few minutes." He smiled again, "Just breathe normally as we get you stabilized."

I tried to move my legs, but realized they were strapped onto a stretcher. Without moving my head, I glanced around the band room to see who was a witness to my mortification. Just Mr. J and Christie. Through my haze, it occurred to me that something or someone was missing. I tried to concentrate on what it was. I recalled the sensation of trying to reach for some important thing in my brain just before everything had disappeared, and then I remembered. Right. Ben. Where was *he*? I glanced toward the practice room and back to Christie. She turned, following my eyes and then looked back to me. I saw her grasp my question, but then another look crossed her face. One I didn't understand. She gave a little shake.

The paramedic spoke gently, "All right, we're just going to load you up and let them have a look at you at the hospital to make sure that everything is okay. Are you ready?" Then the stretcher rose to waist level and I was being rolled down the halls, into the elevator, and out to the ambulance. I kept my eyes closed and prayed to all the gods of heaven that this long after the end of classes, there would be no one in the halls to see me. How embarrassing. How beyond embarrassing.

Christie was following along behind me. I heard the tap of her shoes quick stepping to keep up with the paramedics' swift marching, the swish of the doors opening, and then I felt the bump as the stretcher went over the threshold. The rush of fresh air caressed me as we thumped along the sidewalk toward the waiting ambulance. As they loaded me into the ambulance Christie called, "Grace?"

I looked up and found her worried face. I tried to look reassuring, but I don't think I was very convincing.

"I'll meet you at the hospital, okay? Your Mom is supposed to be meeting us there." Mr. J stood behind her jiggling his keys.

The ride to Rockyview Hospital seemed very short. As the ambulance wove through the street, I closed my eyes, and I was reminded of that horrible voice I'd heard in the blackness. It was so cruel and threatening. I'd never heard voices before. Just the memory made my shoulders tighten in fear. That was stupid. Who's afraid of imaginary voices?

When they slid me out of the ambulance and pushed through the doors into emergency, my mom was already there, waiting for me. I wondered how she'd gotten there so quickly.

She reached for my hand as I went by, and the paramedics stopped to let her talk to me. Obviously, they weren't in a rush, which probably meant that I wasn't dying. That was a small consolation.

"Grace! Are you okay?"

I smiled at her, but it seemed to make her more upset, because she turned to the paramedic and asked him somewhat frantically, "Is she okay?"

The paramedic assured her, "She seems stable now," as he rolled the stretcher into a curtained room and with the other paramedic and two nurses, unstrapped me from the stretcher and manoeuvred me onto a bed. He glanced at me as he left the room, and called back, "Bye Grace. Hope I don't see you under these circumstances again!"

Dr. Kyle had been my doctor ever since I could remember, so it was remarkably convenient that he was on duty. He came into my curtained corner and joked with my mom while he took my blood pressure, listened to my heart, and looked into my eyes and ears. His was a comfortable safe presence, and it was very calming to have him in the room.

Christie sat on a chair, out of the way, watching everything solemnly.

While he poked at me, mom watched us with worried eyes.

Finally, he said, "So what exactly happened?" He looked from me to my mom. She shook her head. I just stared at him blankly. He turned to look at Christie.

She stood up and came beside the bed, resting her hand on a railing. "We think she fainted twice."

Dr. Kyle's eyebrows twitched upward, "Twice?"

"We were in the band room."

I closed my eyes as she told him the story. When she finished, I opened my eyes to see him staring at me with an appraising look and then he turned to my mom. "Do you remember the medication we used the last time?"

Mom nodded.

"I think we should probably go that route again. I suspect this malady might be related."

"Is there any available? I thought it was hard to come by?" she asked.

"After the trouble last time, I made sure to keep a store of the ingredients on hand in case Grace needed it again. I have everything in my office. I'll go compound them. It won't take long."

I was intrigued. He wasn't writing me a prescription because he had something that had been brought in years ago just for me? I tried to remember another time when I'd been ill and required medication. I couldn't. I watched Dr. Kyle leave the room, thinking that something was not quite normal about this whole process.

"Mom?" I croaked it. It sounded more like a crackle than a word when it came out of my mouth, but with her mom super powers she understood.

"Yes?"

I mimed writing, and she rummaged in her purse for a pen and scrap of paper, handing them to me on a magazine for stability.

Am I going to be okay?

She patted my arm, "I'm sure it'll be fine, Sweetheart. We'll just have to be patient."

That wasn't very re-assuring.

I leaned back in my bed and closed my eyes. Out in the hall I heard the nurse calling, "Dr. Kyle, this young man would like to speak to you."

I could make out a vaguely familiar voice, but I couldn't make out his words. Whoever he was, he sounded worried. I heard him say something about blood. His voice was breaking, as if he was fighting back tears.

Dr. Kyle's response was calm and soothing.

They murmured back and forth until Dr. Kyle's comforting tones finally seemed to have reassured the poor guy.

A few minutes later Dr. Kyle pushed back the curtain. He was holding a small, old-fashioned looking cut glass vial with a glass stopper. It looked like something from an apothecary shop in another century. The liquid inside was transparent, with just a hint of a golden tint. He smiled at me as he unstopped the vial, "Well Grace, I hope this will do the trick again." He grinned confidently. "It's potent stuff. Just swallow the whole thing."

I was prepared for something foul, but as I tipped the contents into my mouth, I was pleasantly surprised. It was really cold on my tongue, like liquid ice, but it was sweet with a vague hint of fruit and honey. It was quite nice. As it flowed down my throat, the ice became fire and the flavours intensified; my eyes popped a little. It wasn't painful, but it was a very strange sensation.

Dr. Kyle caught the look on my face and laughed out loud. "Oh sorry, Grace! I forgot to warn you about the temperature sensation! It's quite something, isn't it?" He chuckled as I nodded in agreement.

"We'll just have you rest here for a bit, Grace, while my magic elixir does its job," he grinned a little at his joke, "then we should be able to send you home. I'll go see some other patients, but I'll be back in an hour or so to check on you, all right?"

I nodded.

"OK. Don't try to talk or move, just let the elixir do its thing while you completely relax. If you can fall asleep, that'd be even better. I'll be back in a bit." He smiled, and stepped through the curtain surrounding the bed.

My mom looked at me. "Is it feeling better?"

I closed my eyes and concentrated. Was I still dizzy? Yes. As dizzy? No. Did my body feel like it was my own? I wiggled my toes and tightened my abs. Yes! Everything was listening. I opened my eyes to smile at her and nod.

Her worried look relaxed a little. "Good." She glanced over to Christie, sitting so quietly in the corner of my curtained room. "Christie, would you get me a magazine at the gift store, and pick up something to eat at the cafeteria? It's almost seven o'clock and I'm hungry, so I'm sure you must be." She rummaged in her purse and handed Christie a twenty-dollar bill.

Christie eased up stiffly; I'm not sure she'd moved an inch since she'd sat down several hours ago. "Sure Mrs. Severin," she said, taking the bill and stepping through the curtain.

My mom took my hand. "Close your eyes, Grace, and let the medicine work. Your complexion is already looking a bit better." She took my hand and gave it a squeeze. "Remember that time three summers ago when we were in Greece? Do you remember lying on the gravel beach? Can you remember how blue the water was?" Her voice trailed off. I recognized that she was using a visualization technique to make me relax, but it was working, so I didn't fight it. I could feel the warmth of the sun as I lay on that beach. I could hear the lapping of the waves and the faint calls of the fishermen. One of the fishermen's voices sounded strangely like Christie's; another sounded like the worried boy who'd been talking to Dr. Kyle in the hall. I let myself drift off on the turquoise waves of my memory until it faded into darkness.

"She is to be mine," insisted the deep voice out of the blackness.

"She will never be yours," responded a familiar voice. Where had I heard that voice before?

The evil voice laughed as it echoed away. "We shall see!"

"I will keep you safe, Grace. He will never have you." The voice was warm and urgent. "I will not let him have you," he said again, but the desperate tone of his determination made me doubt him, whoever he was.

The next thing I knew, Dr. Kyle was bending over me grinning, "Well! You look much better!" I didn't feel better. I felt strangely anxious.

He handed me a Styrofoam cup of water. "Have a sip of this now to clear your throat."

I sipped obediently.

He took back the water and smiled encouragingly, "How is that? Are you feeling better now?"

"Yes." It came out very faintly, but at least it was audible. I smiled in relief, and saw my feeling echoed by the rest of the faces around the bed.

"Well, I'm feeling good about this improvement.

He looked thoughtful as he wrote on the clipboard. "That's good. I would like to see if we can pinpoint the trigger. I think we'll get some blood tests done, and I'll book a scan for her head," Dr. Kyle said to my mom. "Just to see if there is anything going on."

Christie cleared her throat from where she was sitting. Dr. Kyle looked over at her as she hesitantly remarked, "Um. I think it had something to do with the music."

Dr. Kyle looked at her thoughtfully, then his eyes flicked over to mom who raised her eyebrows. "Music?"

Christie nodded, "I think the trigger could have been the music."

"But Grace listens to music all the time, don't you?" my mom said.

I nodded. I knew what Christie was getting at. "Yeah, but there was something strange about it. It made me dizzy."

Dr. Kyle's brows were down, but he pursed his lips and remarked, "Well, that could be, I suppose. We'll see what the tests say, in the meantime." He muttered to himself, jotting down another note on his clipboard, "Music, eh?" He glanced at my mom and she nodded once. He bobbed his head thoughtfully and scribbled as I settled back onto the bed. "I'm going to discharge you, Grace. You'll need to go down to the lab for the blood work before you leave. The hospital will call with your appointment for the scan. Take it easy today, but be sure to eat, to drink lots of water, and to walk around the house. If you wake up feeling fine tomorrow, you can go back to school."

"Tomorrow is Saturday, Dr. Kyle."

He laughed at me, shaking his head. "Is it already? Okay, you don't have to go to school tomorrow even if you feel great." He reached out to shake my hand and then my mom's. He looked me in the eyes and said seriously, "If anything like this happens again or if you have *any* concerns, I want you to call me right away. Okay?" He looked at me intently to emphasize his seriousness.

I nodded. "Yes, of course. Thanks, Dr. Kyle."

He nodded to my mom, "Bye Blythe," and disappeared through the curtain.

CHAPTER TWO

IT'S INEVITABLE

Erinys finds she's defeated, grudging e'en more after conflict.
Truth from Apollo's hushed prophecy through the confusion can't predict
Danger approaching her quietly, planning a deadly endeavour.
Love has been hidden by Lethe: love that's existed forever.

Mom drove us home, with the plan to drop Christie off along the way. I leaned back in my seat with my eyes closed, feeling their concern floating in the stale air. I knew that if I cracked my eye open even the tiniest bit, I'd catch them both wearing identical, worried expressions, so I concentrated on keeping my eyes tightly closed and saved us all from the agony.

When Christie got out of the car, she whispered, "Good bye," as if she was at a funeral.

"I'm *not dead* Christie."

She gave me a rueful glance, "Yeah. Sorry. I'll message you later, okay?"

I nodded to her as mom pulled away from the curb.

We pulled up at our house a few minutes later, and for just a moment, I didn't recognize it. It was the same grey split-level, set on the same urban lot in Calgary, but it seemed different somehow.

"Here we are, home at last." The word *home* brought an image of marble columns to my mind. My house didn't have marble columns. It was disorienting.

Mom caught the perplexed look on my face and asked with alarm, "Grace? Is anything wrong?"

I shook my head and ignored the strange sensation. "I'm *fine*, Mom.

Let's go in." I wanted nothing more than to crawl into a hot bath with a good book and drift away from all this surrealism.

She hovered at my elbow, but I was able to make my way into the house on my own power without any stumbles or pauses. It was that most of all, I think, that finally soothed her. Momentum is powerful.

I kept my feet steady and light as I climbed the half flight of stairs to the bedroom level and went into my room. I smiled brightly at her as I shut my bedroom door, but as soon as the door clicked shut, I crumpled. I tried to take a step to get to the bed, but I was folding like origami. Thankfully, I had the sense to do it quietly. I collapsed to the floor of my bedroom. I contemplated calling my parents, but they had worried enough already. I sat on the floor on my thick purple rug and I thought grateful thoughts to my Auntie Bright who had knit this cozy thing for my birthday coming next week. Christie had thought a rug was an odd fifteenth birthday present, but I thought it was wonderful. Bright had an uncanny way of knowing the perfect thing.

As usual, my bed wasn't made. I leaned up against it. When the room was tidy, it was really gorgeous with the white matelassé cover on the bed and the robin's egg blue walls. My bulletin board was covered with photos and postcards. My desk was buried in paper and my laptop was interred beneath. My bookshelf was stuffed and overflowing. I could reach it from where I sat, so I grabbed a book. I was just opening it when mom opened the door without knocking. I hated when she did that.

She stared at me sitting on the floor and there was the obvious question in her eyes.

The best defence is a strong offence, they say. I glared up at her, "How many times have I asked you to knock before you come into my room?"

It worked. She took a step back, looking embarrassed.

I added, "I'm just getting a book to read in the bath. If that's okay with you?"

She winced, so I tried again more gently, "Did you want anything?"

She shook her head. "No, just checking. Have a good bath." She turned and added, "Hang up the wet towels and take your dirty clothes back into your room when you're done, please."

I wouldn't, of course. She'd think I was seriously sick if I did something that out of character.

"Grace!"

I turned in the school hall to see the swarthy complexion and black hair of Lloyd Isaac pushing through the crowds to reach me. He'd been around since elementary school, and he'd kept Christie and me laughing through all the drama of junior high. "Hi, Lloyd."

"Are you okay? I heard what happened Friday."

I grimaced. Terrific. Just what I needed: the entire school to know.

Lloyd seemed to read my mind because he added, "I was talking to Christie last night. I don't think anyone else knows…"

I appreciated his intuition. "Good. I'd like to keep it quiet. It's so embarrassing…" My voice trailed off. I thought that Lloyd must be really concerned about me, because he hadn't made a pun yet.

"You're feeling all right, then?" His dark brown eyes were worried as we walked down the hall side by side. "Christie was pretty freaked out."

I nodded, "Yeah, as far as I know I'm completely back to normal. I have to go have a few tests to try to figure out what caused it, but I feel fine now."

Suddenly there was a loud crash and I was tackled from behind.

As I fell hard into the lockers lining the wall, I heard the unmistakeable sound of Ben's voice calling authoritatively, "Hey! Cool down there! You're going to hurt somebody!"

Rubbing my smashed shoulder, I straightened up and turned to see a sullen boy from my English class glower at Ben as he continued down the hall away from us, swinging his shoulders somewhat aggressively. An irritated blonde girl was on the floor scowling after him.

Ben walked up, staring blackly at the girl. He nodded vaguely in my direction.

The girl fought for a moment to clear the irritation from her face before she called out with saccharine sweetness, "Ben! Help me up!" as she stretched her arm up to him. Did boys always fall for that fake helplessness?

He sighed and stepped forward to grab her arm and haul her to a standing position. "Careful Meg," he said curtly, "I don't want to see anyone get hurt." He was staring into her eyes as if he was conveying secret messages.

She shrugged her shoulders and pranced down the hall with a coy glance back to him. He didn't see it because he was looking at me like he was about to say something. There was an angry flash in her eyes when she realised her flirting wasn't having the desired effect.

Before he'd uttered a word to me though, the bell rang. When it stopped, he asked quietly, "You okay?"

I nodded, but I wasn't okay. Suddenly my head was spinning again. *Through a black fog an eery voice echoed, "I'm waiting for you, girl! You will be on my altar soon!"*

Evil laughter faded as I blinked back to the present.

Ben pursed his lips for a moment and murmured, "Really? You don't look all right."

"I'm perfectly fine, Ben. You can go to class."

His brows wrinkled, but with a sigh he finally said, "Okay then. See you later."

I watched him head down the hall with that familiar sense of confusion.

Lloyd brought me back to the present when he calmly remarked, "You know, I once had a similar experience at a baseball game..."

"Huh?" I shut my locker and we started off to class.

"Yeah, I was just sitting watching the game when I started wondering why the ball was getting larger and larger, but then it hit me." He paused for a moment waiting for some response from me. Finally, he added, "The *ball hit me.* Kind of like Josh just hit you?"

I groaned and muttered, "Ha ha, Lloyd."

He smirked and then asked, "Want to take bets on how long Josh Dagan is going to last before he gets himself suspended again?"

I rubbed my sore shoulder. I was going to have a bruise there.

"He's in my home room, so I hear the lectures every time he misses a class; I thought he was getting turfed out the first week of school he'd missed so many." He shook his head in bemusement. "You have to wonder why he bothers to come at all."

The day progressed normally without any relapse of the dizziness, which was a relief. Against my better judgment, I was inclined to agree with Christie's hypothesis that it had something to do with the music, even while I knew that didn't really make much sense. Of course, whatever was causing the dizziness probably was behind the weird voices, as well. It made me uncomfortable to think about the whole incident. I just wanted to forget the whole thing. It'd be nice if the voices would let me. I had the most persistent feeling of dread, as if a dark cloud was following me.

Christie and Lloyd had a lunchtime practice so I ate with Bonnie and Taylor. Bonnie was a slender, curly headed blonde with huge brown eyes. She'd been dating Taylor since the first year of junior high. He was just slightly taller than she was now, having grown about six inches in the last year. He had light brown hair that was quite wavy when it was long. At the moment he'd shaved it really short for some sport thing. They were very comfortable to hang around as a couple.

Neither of them knew anything about the hospital incident, so I felt pleasantly free while I was with them. It was nice not being stared at with stressed out eyes, or being asked how I was. Such freedom wouldn't last though, because Christie and Lloyd were in my English class.

Sure enough, when I arrived in class, Christie accosted me the moment I crossed the threshold. "Still fine?"

I sighed, "Yeah, no relapse." I didn't mention anything about the evil voices.

"Have you heard any music today?"

I looped a thumb around the cord of my earphones running up through the inside of my shirt. "Of course."

"No reaction?"

"Nope."

"Hmm. It must have to be a specific kind of music. There were piano and flute playing when you had the attack, right?"

"Yeah," I said with an undisguised air of irritation. I really didn't want to have this conversation with her.

"Do you have any flute or piano on there?

"Just leave it Christie, okay?"

I glowered at her, but then my vision went black as someone covered my eyes and whispered a deeply menacing, "Guess who?"

No guess necessary. I shook my shoulders in annoyance, reaching up to pull off the hands, "Cut it out Lloyd, I'm not in the mood."

He backed off with his hands stretched out defensively. "Sorry, sorry! I didn't mean to start a war!" He sat down and I saw him exchange a look with Christie that clearly indicated that they though I was being far too touchy.

I changed the focus away from myself by asking the question that had been bothering me since Friday. "Who is this Ben Butler guy anyway, Christie? What do you know about him?"

She seemed glad I was not sounding as upset. "He's awesome, Grace. He is really into music and drama. You heard him play: he's amazingly talented."

I nodded. That much was obvious.

She continued, "He also has been really involved in the student leadership program. My brother was in the yearbook and debating clubs with him back when Shane was in grade twelve and Ben was our age. I think I heard that their team was in the provincial finals, so Ben must have some skills at persuasion. He's a really nice guy who gets along with everyone. My brother said he was 'nauseatingly perfect,' but I think he was just jealous."

Mr. Moore came into the room at that moment and called the class to order. I was able to ignore Lloyd and Christie for a while. I couldn't help but think about Ben. Mr. Nauseatingly Perfect. Who played piano like an extension of his soul. Who made me dizzy. I tried to focus on the lecture without much success. I was going to have to get someone else's notes to make any sense of it at all.

At the end of class, Christie leaned across her desk and asked, "So do you want to walk home with me after concert band or are you leaving right away?"

"I'll wait. I'll go get started on this essay he just assigned."

She smiled, relieved that I was back to myself. I was beginning to be afraid, but I didn't want her to know that. The sense of dread that the voices left was digging deeper into me.

As we separated at the library door, Lloyd commented, "Have fun with the bard!"

Yeah, lots of fun. I opened the library door and headed to a table.

The library was a haven when I felt like my world was tilting off its axis. Mrs. Hart, the librarian, believed in the library as an oasis from the insanity of the halls and intensity of the classrooms. She had big, comfortable chairs in the corners, tall plants releasing fresh oxygen, and a small waterfall on her desk. In the quiet of scratching pens and turning pages, the sound of the falling water was very calming. Some days she even dimmed the lights. I spread out my books on a table in the brighter area to work on the essay for Mr. Moore: "How friends impact relationships in Shakespeare's *Much Ado About Nothing*." I pondered where to begin. Pen in hand, I was vaguely thinking about Beatrice and Benedict and their contrasting passionate feelings. Their initial hatred for each other was so easily turned to love. Busybody friends were interfering in their relationship, but it all worked out for Beatrice and Benedict. Benedict. Ben. Many thoughts bumped around in my brain, and my pen took off. I wasn't thinking consciously of the words I was writing. They almost seemed to be appearing on the page of their own accord even though I was holding the pen. As my hand moved across the paper, I was hearing Ben's music in my head, like a soundtrack to my essay. It made me remember the feeling of the sound waves travelling through my body as I'd leaned against the wall outside Ben's practice room. What had happened to me?

I was startled by someone's muffled giggle in the corner, and glanced over to see a couple of grade eleven girls sneaking something into a plant while surreptitiously glancing to Mrs. Hart's office to ensure that she didn't see them. I looked down at my coil bound notebook and was somewhat surprised to see a whole poem there in my own handwriting. Weird how the subconscious mind worked; I didn't recall thinking any of it let alone writing it.

> When I look at you
> I see sunshine in darkness
> Passion through naïveté
>
> I think that we were lovers once
> In another life
> You and I belonged
> And that is why we were drawn
>
> That is why I love you so much
> And why your name
> Brings happiness through sorrow
>
> A wisp of a smile
> When day dies
> I remember you and I smile
>
> You are my day and my night
> Your face is a memory
> That time cannot erase,
> And someday
> In another life
> We will be lovers
> Once again

Whoa. I felt a wave roll through my head. Nausea threatened to overwhelm me. I closed my eyes. Ben's face swam behind my eyelids, but he wasn't the same. What was different about him? Was he older? His clothes weren't quite right. The look on his face in this vision was the most astonishing thing. He was smiling in a way that made my knees weak. I concentrated on him, trying to figure out what I was seeing. I felt the world spinning as I strained to see… what?

"What's this Grace? Copying poetry?" I hadn't heard anyone come up behind me and I snatched the notebook to my chest as Ben dropped into the chair beside me. His hushed voice was unnerving.

"It's nothing." I sounded breathless.

Shawn L. Bird

"Hmm." He looked at me carefully. "Are you okay?"

"I'm fine. Go away." I said it before I thought it. It sounded very rude.

"You know what?" he said with a twinkle in his eye, "I think we need to start again. Let's just pretend you have never seen me before, and I'll pretend I've just noticed this lovely girl sitting all alone in the library. What do you say?"

I looked at him feeling more than slightly nauseous with nerves. I didn't answer him.

He stuck out his hand, and sounding more than a little like an actor on a kids' TV show he said, "Hi there, young lady. I'm Ben. Who are you?"

I closed my eyes. He was a completely average boy and yet he seemed to be having a crazy effect on my equilibrium. Pictures were swirling in my head, making me dizzy again. This was ridiculous. I breathed deeply, opening my eyes and nodding to him. "Hello Ben. I'm Grace. I enjoyed your music the other day." 'Enjoyed' seemed a little mild for my experience.

"Nice to meet you, Grace," he said solemnly. "Your name is as lovely as you are."

I blushed.

He fought to maintain his serious expression, but one side of his mouth tilted up and his eyes twinkled. He liked that he was making me uncomfortable, the jerk. He glanced at my notebook again and remarked, "So you like poetry, eh? Can I see?"

I tightened my grip and shook my head.

"Come on, Grace," he whispered, pulling his chair far too closely beside me. "Let me see. That top one looked familiar." He had put out his hand, like he expected me to hand him the book.

I held on obstinately, flushing scarlet. "I don't think so." He'd seen some of it. OMG OMG OMG. What did he mean it looked *familiar*? Why would he have seen this before? His hand was still outstretched, but somehow I knew that he wouldn't try to take it without my permission, so I just clung to it and tried to hold myself together. My heart thundered in my chest. The last thing I needed was him reading this emotional outburst of confused thoughts that I'd apparently just put on paper. He'd think I was some stupid little lovesick girl and I didn't even remember writing it. The shock of this realisation left me gasping. I *had* written that poem. I'd written it about *Ben*. I felt as if I was going to choke.

The giggling grade elevens were looking coquettishly over at Ben. It looked like Christie was right. For some reason, everyone seemed to know and to like Ben. He was a grade twelve, though and grade twelves

28

had very little to do with the grade tens. I could almost hear their bafflement about why he was in friendly conversation with me. I could certainly feel my own bafflement.

He sighed. "Grace, you are such a silly girl."

My chin went up defensively. "What do you mean by that?"

He shook his head in mock remorse, "You don't trust me at all, do you?"

Hmm. Did I? Actually, the greater part of me felt like I would trust him with my life and should follow him around the world for the rest of eternity. But one small, very noisy part was shouting, *Run! Run for your life!* like I was in an old monster movie. I sat silently staring at the table, swallowing as waves of embarrassment, anger, frustration and confusion coursed through me.

"Ben! Are you going to come practise with the ensemble or not?" shouted a stunning blonde girl from the door of the library. Mrs. Hart leaned out of her office with her brows down and shook her finger at the loud interruption. The girl scowled at her and waved her arms at Ben. She was the one who'd been on the floor behind me after the tackle this morning.

"Looks like you have somewhere to be. You'd better go." I said quietly.

He looked down at me and did not conceal his aggravation. "Yeah." He leaned in closely and whispered, "It's okay. I'm perfectly safe you know."

I met his eyes looking past my reflection into the blue depths. I shook my head and returned his whisper, "I don't think I am."

No. I did not feel safe at all.

"BEN!" The blonde was getting annoyed.

He looked over his shoulder at her with a glare, "I'm *coming* Meg!" He glanced apologetically toward Mrs. Hart's office.

Meg glared back at him and then at me. I was making an enemy, it seemed.

Ben turned back to me, clearly frustrated.

I looked away.

He sighed and stood up. He touched his hand to my shoulder and repeated, "You're safe, Grace."

I did not like the feeling that he was causing in me. I felt like I was on the verge of being attacked. Why was I feeling so anxious? What was wrong with me?

I watched him as he walked out of the library. He glanced over his shoulder and met my eyes before I could look away. He had an oddly warm expression as he walked through the door to join Meg, who grabbed him rather possessively by the elbow and marched him down the hall past the library windows. Meg was a barracuda. Poor Ben. I felt sorry for him in spite of myself.

Breathing deeply, I tried to focus on my essay, but every time I wrote 'Benedict' it led my thoughts back to Ben. Ben. Ben. Ben. A wave overtook me again and I put my head down on the table. I was so dizzy. Why did thinking about him make me so dizzy?

I spun into a vortex of colour until I was surrounded by red. There was a shrieking from behind me, "Let me have her! I've got it!" The female voice was strident, but as cruel as the deep male voice that kept coming back. Sure enough, it spoke next. "Keep the idiot busy. I have plans for them. Have fun. The girl is too stupid to understand yet the power that surrounds her. She does not know that her doom approaches."

I don't know how long I was lying there. I could hear the quiet library noises now: pens, pages, the beep of the computer signing books in and out, the thump of books falling into the bin from the hall. Steps. A chair pulling out beside me. Someone sitting down. I held my breath.

"Hey Grace. I've been looking for you all over the place."

Just Christie. Thank heaven.

I raised my head and tried to look coherent. "Hi Christie."

"Were you sleeping?"

Apparently, I hadn't succeeded at my ploy of feigning coherence after all. "No. Trying to write my *Much Ado* essay."

"Looks like it's pretty boring if it puts you to sleep while you're writing it!"

I smiled absently in response. "Yeah, I guess." I looked at the row of false starts down the page. Every sentence ended in "Ben…" She glanced over at the paper, and I quickly shut the binder. "I'm giving up on this for now. What did you want me for?"

She paused, a glimmer of concern in her eyes. "Are you okay, Grace? First you faint in the band room, now you're falling asleep in the library…" her voice trailed off.

"Yeah, it's weird, eh?" I shook my head. "I don't know, Christie. Maybe I'm coming down with something. I keep feeling really dizzy." After I've been around Ben, I added to myself as I glanced at the clock. School had been over for an hour already.

"Hmm." She studied me carefully. "Are you up to a walk to get something at Tims?"

"Sure. I could use some fresh air, I think." I gathered up my books, and moments later I stashed them in our locker and we were heading toward the back door of the school.

30

We passed the band room just as the senior vocal ensemble was leaving their practice. I saw Ben immediately, and tried ever so casually to hide behind Christie so he wouldn't notice me. She looked at me a little quizzically as I moved away from her side. From the corner of my eye, I saw him spot us. His head turned and his arm started up in our direction as if to wave us down. For a moment, it looked like he was going to try to push through the crowd to catch up with us, but then Meg grabbed his arm insistently and with a wrinkled brow and a final frustrated glance at us, he turned to talk to her. Go Meg. Saving me again.

It was a couple of weeks later in English class when Bonnie came rushing over to me. I'd known Bonnie since about grade three. She was perky, tiny, and very intense. You never had to worry about pretensions or underhanded motivations around Bonnie. She was always completely, unabashedly honest, for better or worse. Whatever she was thinking she said aloud. This was quite often a terrifying proposition, because she was also very intuitive, and she had an annoying habit of figuring out some essential truth that you were just discovering and blurting it out to the entire world. Seeing Bonnie head straight to me, I felt a stab of fear and I looked over at Christie with some sense of panic. Christie smiled in sympathy.

"Grace!" Bonnie shouted. Every one in the room turned to look at her. I felt my cheeks turning red. "Ben Butler likes you! *Ben Butler, Grace!*"

I tried to hide my face in my hands in mortification.

Bonnie would not respect my embarrassment and leave me alone. Oh, no. Apparently, she needed me to squirm in front of the whole class. "Isn't that fantastic, Grace?"

Behind me, Lloyd perked up in interest. "What's this?"

Bonnie barely glanced at him as she stared intently at me and remarked emphatically, "This is more than fantastic! This is *fantabulous!*"

Christie looked as confused as I did when she asked, "Why?"

Bonnie looked at Christie as if she was some kind of idiot, "Ben Butler, Christie. Ben."

"Ah. Right."

I interjected, "He's just another band geek, Bonnie."

Bonnie's eyes grew absolutely huge. She practically shrieked, "Ben Butler is not a *band geek*! He's going to be famous some day soon."

Christie scoffed and Bonnie turned on her, "Ben is writing music for Grace and she's going to make him famous!" She whirled back to me with

31

a rather terrifying excitement and wagging a finger at my chest she announced, "*You*'re going to make him famous, Grace!"

This was so ridiculous that it wasn't even worthy of comment. I had never heard Bonnie make a crazy pronouncement like this, but even as I thought, she was a fool, even as I outwardly scoffed, somewhere deep inside something prickled.

Lloyd studied Bonnie, and then looked at me thoughtfully. I felt as if I was under a microscope. "Ben Butler, Grace," he said with mocking sincerity, "I'm sure you know that the butler always does it. He's bound to be incredibly successful, and imagine, it'll all be because of you."

I gave him what I hoped was a withering look. He laughed.

Mr. Moore stood at the front of the class, looking over at us. He had not missed Bonnie's noisy pronouncement. "If you're done trying to find converts for the Ben Butler Fan Club, Bonnie, can you please take your seat?"

She grinned at him, "Sure thing Mr. Moore!" and headed for her desk. Thankfully, she sat on the other side of the room from us. I looked at Christie with a grimace and she chuckled as she opened up her binder.

Josh Dagan came running into the room, laughing uproariously as he shouted, "Yo! Here I am, you lucky people!" As he went past me, I could smell the reek of cigarettes off his brown leather jacket, so he'd just been out at the smoke pit.

Christie leaned over me, "I think Bonnie's right you know. It does seem as if Ben likes you."

"Well," I whispered back, glancing up to be sure Mr. Moore was distracted with Josh the Troublemaker in the back corner, "something is definitely going on, but why would he say anything to Bonnie? He's not a kid who would ask 'Find out if she likes me!'"

"He probably didn't, but she could have overheard him talking to someone else, couldn't she?"

"Yeah, I suppose, but why would he be talking about me?"

Lloyd piped up, "How he could he resist?"

Mr. Moore shot us a warning glance, and we shushed up while he began the next Shakespeare lesson.

At the end of the class, Bonnie caught up with us as we were heading into the hall. "So don't you want to know *how* I know he likes you?" she demanded.

Part of me thought that this was a very immature, but the other part of me was too curious to tell her I didn't want to know because I did.

She laughed at me, grasping my dilemma. "My locker is outside the theatre, and while I was getting everything ready this morning, The Scary Twins and Meg were there."

I could picture the scene. I knew just the twins she meant. They *were* very intimidating. They had black hair: one wore hers short and spiky, the other wore hers straight to her waist, and they usually dressed in black. They weren't exactly Goth, but they were tall, very fair and in all the black, they looked suspiciously like stereotypical vampires. They added to the look by glowering most of the time. The Scary Twins. Funny.

Bonnie carried on, "Meg was grumbling about how she'd had this plan to get Ben to ask her out, and it wasn't going so well because he seems to be obsessed with this grade ten girl." She glanced meaningfully at me.

"How do you know she means Grace, though?" Christie asked, saving me from having to ask the question myself. "There are a lot of us in grade ten."

"Well obviously, I didn't know at the time, but then I was outside the band room between classes when Meg accosted Ben." She laughed at the memory. "He was at his locker and he was talking to another guy about this composition that he was really excited about. Meg butted right in and asked him why he was ignoring her, and what was going on with 'that grade ten chick.' He looked at her as if she was something disgusting he'd found on the bottom of his shoe and said, 'Meg, what does it matter to you to whom I speak?' She was embarrassed then, because the way she'd asked the question, she'd shown pretty obviously that she was jealous, and he was showing pretty clearly that he didn't share her feelings. It is good to see snotty little miss perfect model girls put in their place, isn't it?" She sighed happily. Trust Bonnie.

She continued, "Meg was *really* mad then, so she made some slur about grade twelve boys slumming with grade ten girls, and that made *him* really angry. He looked at her with eyes like icebergs and I swear the frigidity of his voice should have frozen her solid. He just said, 'I like Grace, and she's good for my music. Leave her alone, and leave *me* alone Meg.' Then he turned and walked away with his friend, leaving her positively sputtering she was so ticked off." She laughed again, and then sighed happily, "It was wonderful!" She looked meaningfully over to me. "That's when I had the vision of him being famous because he's composing for you." She grinned. "I think it's terribly romantic. Will you go out with him?" We had reached the locker I shared with Christie, so we paused while Christie put her stuff onto her shelf and then we traded places while I put my binders away.

Bonnie was looking at me expectantly. I looked over to Christie for some help, but she just grinned at me, waiting for the answer. Traitor.

I swallowed. "Umm. I don't know. It isn't... I mean... Bonnie! He hasn't asked me."

Bonnie nodded. "He will though." She looked over to Christie, "right?"

Christie nodded back, "Yes, I'd say it's an inevitability."

Lloyd groaned. "You girls are such saps. You're making me ill. See you tomorrow." He marched down the hall.

"What does he care about this?"

Bonnie giggled, "I think he's been hoping to cultivate a little romance of his own. He isn't likely pleased to be run over by the inevitability of Grace's great love."

I sighed deeply looking from one to the other. "Inevitable?"

"Yup." They both nodded.

Bonnie glanced down the hall and smiled impishly as she whispered, "Speak of the devil."

I glanced up and there was Ben, about sixteen feet away and beaming at me. I swallowed nervously again.

Bonnie looked over at Christie and remarked, "Maybe we should give her some privacy."

"No!" I shrieked, and grabbed their arms. I whispered frantically, "Don't leave me!" like I was some crazy person. At that moment, Ben arrived, so I dropped my hands from their arms, blushing guiltily.

He looked around our circle, smiling. I had the uncomfortable feeling he knew exactly what was going on. "Hi Grace," he said calmly.

"Hi." My voice sounded funny. I'd squeaked a bit.

"How are you feeling today?"

It was quite remarkable how his very innocent words were making me feel like my legs were jelly and my voice didn't work. My heart was pounding, and I could feel my ears tingling, which meant they were probably turning scarlet.

"I'm okay, thanks."

He nodded, "Good, I'm glad to hear it. That whole fainting thing was a little scary, wasn't it?" He looked over at Christie for confirmation. She nodded dutifully.

He pointed to a poster on the bulletin board. "Are you guys coming to the Term End Band Concert?" He glanced at Christie and Bonnie too, but it felt like he was really only asking me.

Bonnie glanced at the poster to check the date and shook her head, "No, I have to work every Thursday."

He looked at Christie and then chuckled, "Oh. I guess you have to be there, don't you? You play flute, right?" When she nodded, he asked, "Which bands are you playing with?"

34

"Junior concert band and Junior jazz band."

"Good for you! I've heard you play, then." That left me to ask, and as he turned to me, his eyes melted mine, oh so casually. I gulped and then coughed as I started choking on my spit. Why did I do this kind of stupid stuff around him?

Christie whacked me on the back, and I reached into our locker to grab my water bottle as the coughing subsided. "I'm okay. It's okay." Now my whole face was scarlet, not just my ears. I sipped gratefully, trying to hide my face behind the locker door.

Ben smiled again, a strangely affectionate smile. He was creeping me out. Why did he do that?

"So are you coming, Grace?" he asked.

I shrugged my shoulders. "I'm not really sure yet. Maybe. Why?"

He grinned, "It'll be good. We're a talented bunch." Then he chuckled and added, "Seriously, the bands and choirs here are extremely good. However, if you're there in the audience, we'll be even better, I promise."

"Oh, really?" I couldn't keep the sarcasm from my voice. That was a little snotty of me.

He was serious all of a sudden. His eyes were solemn as he said emphatically, "Yes. *Really.*" He looked at Christie and Bonnie, as he took a step back. "Well, I guess I should let you guys get to your lunch." He looked meaningfully back at me, "You should come, Grace. You'll enjoy it." Then he stepped out into the stream of people in the hall and disappeared.

Bonnie was positively bouncing with triumph. "See! See, I told you! He *likes* you!" She was beaming.

Christie nodded in agreement and as we headed down to the lunchroom, she whispered in my ear, "Inevitable..."

CHAPTER THREE

HE'S A PLAYER

Music of Orpheus playing her, slowly awakening lost love.
History's longing for future, memories imagined and dreamed of.
Discord is spreading her poison; doubt will arise in beginnings.
Venom can infiltrate secretly; strife will appear to be winning.

As I walked home that afternoon by myself, I thought about Ben. He was starting to monopolize my thinking in an annoyingly obsessive way. I couldn't shake the feeling not just that I knew him, but that I'd known him for a really long time, and yet at the same time I was equally certain I hadn't met him before that day in the band room when I'd fainted.

It was just too confusing to deal with, so I decided the best solution was *not* to deal with it. He would be graduating in seven months. If I could just avoid him for that time, he'd be gone from my life and I wouldn't have to worry about it, right? Maybe I wouldn't have to try even that long. Maybe if I avoided him for a week or two he'd get the message that I wanted to be left alone?

Still, part of me wanted to know more about him. A very traitorous part of me wanted to chase him down and throw myself into his arms. It was rather disconcerting. I didn't like feeling overwhelmed whenever I was around Ben.

After I'd begged her to help, Christie was grudgingly in on the plan, helping to shield me or checking around corners for me with the air of a martyr.

I found a far more enthusiastic ally in Lloyd, however. He was overjoyed to help, and was very good at appearing at my elbow with a bad pun between every class. Since he was a head and a half taller than I was, he had a much better viewpoint to observe potential Ben interceptions. I was a little suspicious that he faked a few of the sightings just to ensure we shared a very long walk to class even when my classrooms were almost next to each other. It wasn't so horrible, because I was always either laughing or gritting my teeth at his puns. I tried not to feel too guilty for using him, particularly considering the ever more obvious way he was showing that he had a romantic interest in me.

I managed to keep away from Ben for the rest of the week. Whenever I caught a glimpse of someone who might be him I spun around and went in the opposite direction or I froze where I stood, angling my face toward the closest wall. I ended up taking inconvenient stairwells and hiding in the girls' washrooms a lot. This meant I was frequently late to my classes, which didn't make me popular with my teachers.

Still, it was worth it, because I hadn't bumped into him accidentally. I hadn't had him sneak up on me in a hall. I hadn't been accosted in the library. I'd been gloriously Ben-free. Well, physically, at least. Because of course, as I so *studiously* avoided him, he filled almost every thought.

I was completely obsessing; eyes glued for any head that might be him. It hadn't taken long before I knew his schedule, his regular routes, and the locations of all his friends' lockers. In order to avoid him, I learned his preferred lunch eating spot and where he liked to sit in the library. I became a reverse stalker. Despite Lloyd's joyful attitude toward the endeavour, by the end of the week I was emotionally exhausted.

I was walking home alone after school on Friday, thankful for a chance to enjoy the fresh air and have my head clear. Lloyd and Christie had stayed for band practice, but I didn't want to waste the sunshine. I was mulling over my almost finished *Much Ado* essay. I felt smug that I'd avoided Ben all week, but I had still caught myself humming the tune Ben had been playing in the practice room a couple of times. It was irritating to find him sneaking stealthily into my brain when I was trying so diligently to escape him.

Gravel crunched behind me as a car pulled up and stopped slightly ahead of me. The passenger window opened. "Grace!"

Ben. My breath stopped. Damn. Damn. Damn. I kept walking, staring straight ahead. My heart was pounding.

He drove slowly alongside. "Grace, can I give you a ride?"

"No thank you. I'm enjoying my walk." I could feel the fog invading my brain and I attempted to fight it off with deep breaths. In: one, two, three. Out: one, two, three. It occurred to me that there had once been a time when I didn't have to *think* about breathing nearly as hard as

I'd had to lately.

The car pulled ahead and stopped. Ben unfolded himself from the driver's seat and went to stand in the middle of the sidewalk facing me.

I stopped about six feet away from him, fighting to control the pictures that started spinning in my head.

Suddenly, he looked alarmed and jumped toward me, as I crumpled onto the concrete.

"Welcome back," said the dark voice. "Strange, isn't it, how the more desperate he is to keep you from me, the more he drives you closer." In a quiet whisper he added, "You'll be mine very soon, girl."

The next thing I remember, I was sitting beside Ben in the passenger seat of his car. I closed my eyes to try to make sense of the words and pictures that I'd seen through the fog in my head. That evil voice made my skin crawl. I remembered the sensation of being lifted and carried into the car, the sound of the door opening, being set into the seat, and the gentle whispers of "cara gratia, cara gratia" which sounded strangely like a prayer, the words that had pulled me back to consciousness. What was that?

How annoying this was. How embarrassing. Here I was again passed out, and once again, Ben was rescuing me. This was an irritating pattern. I didn't want to be fainting in front of him. I didn't have any of Dr. Kyle's mysterious medicine.

"Grace? Please tell me you're okay."

I sighed. "Yes. I'm okay." His face was so close to mine I had to fight not to faint. "Um. How are you?"

He laughed then, a ringing, musical laugh that couldn't help but make me smile in response. He leaned back in his seat. "I'm fabulous now that you're conscious." I looked into his blue eyes and blinked as the dizziness threatened again.

"You make me dizzy, Ben." It slipped out before I had a chance to think. The colour rose on my cheeks and I closed my eyes again.

He smelled of peppermint and musk. Very nice. He smelled comfortable. Homey.

His warm chortle was close to my ear, and his breath wafted across my face. "Do you know why?"

Why? I opened my eyes again. His eyes were only a few inches away; his lips were oh so close to mine. I suddenly imagined him kissing me and I blushed again, turning my head slightly away to avoid both his eyes and his lips. Where had that thought come from? "No, I don't know why you make me dizzy. Why do you think it is?"

"Love at first sight," he chuckled again, "obviously."

"Oh." He was joking, wasn't he? But perhaps the joke held an element of truth. I felt momentarily mortified, but then with a moment of shocking clarity I realized that the small piece of missing knowledge I'd been seeking had just clicked into place. I blinked up at him, meeting his eyes without blushing for once. He looked back frankly. He wasn't laughing now. I considered the depths of his eyes, but I didn't fall into their blue pools this time. I studied him. Well, this was interesting. When I finally spoke, it was calmly. "You think so, do you?"

"Definitely."

"Hmm. And you? Are you suffering from the pangs of love at first sight?"

What was going on with me that I kept saying stuff like this? Sure, I had said it lightly, like I was teasing, but I wasn't. Worse than knowing, that I was serious was the fact that I was pretty sure that he knew it, too. The blush raced back into my cheeks while I held my breath and waited for his response. If he hadn't figured it out before, then the panic in my eyes gave it away. His eyes glowed close to mine.

"Nope." He spoke in an intimate whisper.

His no sounded like a yes. What did he mean? I stuttered, "Ah, well, how unfortunate for you to have missed the experience."

He smiled very gently while his eyes glowed at me. "Oh, I didn't miss a thing." He paused to let the words sink in before he leaned closer to me and added, "I think I've been in love with you pretty much forever, Grace." His eyes were smouldering inches from mine, intensifying his words.

Such a statement didn't *need* any intensifying.

I just sat there, blinking at him in complete astonishment. His words had such a tone of genuine sincerity that I couldn't help but think he really believed them. But I had known Ben Butler for little more than a month, and it was completely illogical that this popular, talented boy, no this *man*, actually thought he was in love with *me*. It was crazy. Insane! Besides, even if he actually *thought* it, what fool would actually chase down a girl who was plainly avoiding him, to *tell* her that he loved her? Ben didn't seem that stupid.

The cynical part of me, the regular every day teenager part of me, was completely, totally and absolutely creeped out. Part of me thought that this was the absolutely most romantic thing anyone could ever say to another human, but it was stalker creepy. I shivered.

He watched my face. "Oops. Over kill, eh? Sorry. I didn't mean to freak you out."

I chewed on the inside of my lip, thinking *too late!*

He read that in my eyes too. "Oh damn. I *did* freak you out, didn't I?"

I turned slowly and met his eyes. They were not deep pools of azure today; they were darker, like blue grey smoke, but again they oozed apprehension. I sighed. "Yup. You did." I turned away and shook my head, muttering under my breath. "You *definitely* did."

We sat there in his car in silence, each of us just staring ahead into nothingness. Oddly, despite his insane declaration, my head was now quite clear, and I realized that I didn't want to get out of the car. In spite of the weirdness of this conversation, it actually felt nice to be with him, now that he was sitting quietly instead of saying creepy things, at least. It was a very companionable silence. This was a new feeling with him, and yet it felt like it was right—like it was the way it was supposed to be.

"Grace?" he said, finally breaking the silence. His voice was quiet and very calm—no mushy intonations at all. "Can I play you something?" He was reaching for the dials on his car stereo. "Listen to this tune."

A piano melody began. Parts of it were quite lovely, but other parts seemed strained. It was on its way to being something interesting but it didn't seem complete. It was kind of painful to listen to actually. I kept hoping for some improvement, but it didn't happen.

"What do you think of that?" he asked, as the music died away.

"Um...Did you write it?"

He smiled with chagrin, "Yeah, but don't let that hold you back from answering honestly."

I pondered what I should say. Did he *really* want an honest response, or should I just be kind? I glanced up at him and met his even gaze. Okay. Honesty, then. I decided to put on my music teacher voice. Mrs. Clark, the scary piano teacher of my childhood, came to mind with her pompous air that was so inappropriate for teaching young children. I cleared my throat like the queen about to give a speech and said, "It seems to want to go somewhere, but it seems lost. The motif is promising, but the development is missing something. It's not as good as the one you were playing in the practice room last week." I hoped the fake voice would lessen the severity of the comment. The words were true. It felt odd to be articulating so clearly something so subjective. What did I know about music? I wasn't sure I'd ever made that kind of an analysis before, but he seemed to be fine with my observations, even in Mrs. Clark's voice.

He nodded. "Exactly so. Thank you for being honest. Now, how about this one?" He pushed 'play' again and another tune started. No, not another tune. The same tune, but this time the melody was dancing and the harmonies were full and lush. It was achingly, hauntingly beautiful.

My eyes welled up with unbidden tears, and I glanced over to him in amazement.

"Is that the same song?" I gasped.

He nodded again, smiling faintly. "Yes."

"Wow, what a difference….You wrote both versions?"

"Yes."

"Wow." It was the only word to capture my awe. I shook my head in stunned silence. The second one proved what my band room experience had hinted at: he was incredibly talented. Dauntingly talented.

"Grace, I wanted you to hear those for a reason."

"Oh?" Was he fishing for compliments?

"You know how horrible the first piece was?" He looked at me for confirmation. I nodded regretfully and he continued, "I'd been working on that piece for a month. It was going nowhere. You heard it: it was crap."

"It wasn't *that*…"

He interrupted my comment firmly, "Yes, it was *that bad*. Grace, you don't have to be gentle with me. I don't ever want to lose my perspective about my music. I need to hear it for what it is, good, bad or ugly. *That* one was both bad AND ugly." He snickered. "I had a vision in my mind of what I wanted it to be, but it just wasn't getting there. It sucked."

I chuckled to hear him use the term, though he was right. That first one really was awful. "But the second piece…"

He tilted his head, "Yes?"

I shook my head. "The second one was wonderful. Full of joy and brilliance. It was…"

He interrupted, finishing my sentence with an assured whisper, "It was full of *grace*." He looked at me meaningfully.

"Grace?"

"Grace."

"What do you mean, 'grace'?"

He laughed. "*You* don't know the definition? Grace; noun; a pleasing quality; beauty in form and movement…"

My eyes grew large. "Oh!" I heard the tune in my head again, lush, full and mesmerising. "You're right. It *is*." That was interesting.

"The first one you heard was the Thursday version. I'd recorded it the day before I met you in the band room. I started it again on Monday, and everything had changed. You heard the difference. Can you guess why it's so much better now?"

"Why what?"

"Why it's *full of grace*?" he smiled encouragingly, as if he wanted

41

me to guess a secret.

He was being weird again. I figured that he was going to somehow connect my name to this, and suddenly I was feeling more than a little awkward. What was it with Ben Butler? Did he have no sense of boundaries? He was looking at me expectantly. "Okay Ben. Yes, I want to know. Why is it so pleasing and beautiful in form and movement?" and then I added, "But don't be weird, Ben. You're starting to creep me out again."

He chuckled softly again. "You are very difficult to have a serious conversation with, you know."

I harrumphed, crossing my arms across my chest and looking out of the window. I vaguely considered escaping.

He laughed. "Fine, then. I won't tell you. You can just let it eat you up with curiosity." He turned away from me and put his hand on the ignition keys. "Can I drop you off somewhere?"

"No, it's okay. I'll just walk." I reached to open the door, but he put his arm across my shoulders.

"Grace." He paused to ensure I was paying attention and I had to turn toward him before he continued, "It wasn't actually a question, Sweetie. You just passed out on the sidewalk. What kind of guy would I be to let you walk home after that? I'll take you home."

His tone had become intimate again, and it was making it hard for me to breathe. I was about to argue when I caught the real concern in his eyes.

"Please, Grace?"

I sighed. "All right, fine. Take me home." I gave him the directions, and he drove without speaking. He'd played the second tune over again while we drove and the music had soothed away some of my irritation by the time he pulled up at my door. The piece was breathtakingly beautiful. I got out of the car carefully, pausing on my way up to a standing position to make sure I wasn't going to have another dizzy attack. I didn't. "Thanks for the drive Ben, and for sharing your music. I enjoyed it."

"Sure thing. Any time," he said as I shut the passenger door.

He waited while I walked to the front door of the house, so after I opened it I turned to wave. He waved back before he put the car into gear and pulled away from the curb. I shut the door behind me and leaned against it, breathing deeply and counting again. Calm breath in… Calm breath out… That was so strange. What was going on in his head? *Full of grace*. Seriously.

Mom walked by and stopped, watching me as I leaned against the door. This was not a regular way for me to come into the house. Her brows went up. "Grace? What's up? Are you okay?"

"I'm fine, Mom." I sounded breathless. I most definitely didn't sound fine. Damn.

"Who was that who drove you home?"

"Ben Butler."

Her eyes got wide.

Not her too. Did *everyone* know him?

She didn't comment, though. She just watched me as I stepped away from the door and headed down the hall to my room before she called, "Dinner will be ready in half an hour, Hon!"

I tossed my pack over by my desk and flopped onto the bed. Theoretically, I didn't believe in love at first sight. I thought it was a silly myth, touted by fools and romantics. I didn't consider myself either a fool or a romantic, but there was no denying that Ben had completely unsettled my world. His presence overwhelmed everything. The scent of him intoxicated me. His music turned me inside out. Was this love? I didn't really know anything about him. How could I have fallen in love with someone before I knew his favourite colour or the names of his parents? He was insane if he thought he was in love with me. This couldn't be love.

Could it?

I thought about my parents and my aunts and uncles. What had they been like when they'd first met each other? Had they played silly games to try to attract each other's attention? Had they been dizzy and confused like I felt around Ben? Had they fawned over each other and giggled into the night?

What was love, anyway?

How could Ben possibly be in love with me after a month and claim it was forever?

What about those weird voices I heard whenever I fainted? Thinking about the evil voice brought a quiver up my spine. Who were they? Or perhaps, *what* were they?

I picked a novel off my shelf and went to have a long bath. I needed to escape into fictional drama, although I suspected the book wasn't going to be nearly as dramatic as my life was at the moment.

The next few days at school were warfare in my mind. Ben seemed to genuinely like me. He'd sought me out repeatedly. It made no sense to me that someone like him would be interested in me. Somehow being around him was nerve-wracking and disconcerting. I wasn't ready to deal with the way my head spun when I was around him. I couldn't handle the intensity of his eyes. So. If I ran into him, fine, I'd be pleasant, but I wasn't going out of my way to be anywhere that he was. The key to sanity was avoiding over-exposure to him. Simple.

One glitch: the Term End Concert.

Not only would Ben be there, he'd be playing his music. That seemed needlessly dangerous for me.

It made perfect sense not to go, except for one small detail: I would have gone to see Christie perform if Ben hadn't been the one to suggest that I go. That wasn't exactly fair to Christie. She was my best friend. I should be there to support my best friend doing what she loved. Damn Ben, making my life so miserably complicated. Christie or Ben? Pride and loyalty battled for days, but eventually loyalty won and I decided I had to go. I was afraid. What if his music made me collapse again? This time I'd be in an auditorium full of people. There'd be no place to hide.

Christie would never know the risk I was taking for her.

On the night of the concert, Christie and I walked to the school together. The November air was cold, but there wasn't any snow at the moment. We had our hands deep in our pockets and our chins buried into the collars of our jackets. Neither of us was inclined to talk—Christie because of performance nerves, me because of fear. She had to be there a little early, so I had a book in my purse to kill time out in the audience while she and the rest of the bands were getting ready back stage.

Our school had a really nice theatre that the community shared. There were several hundred comfortable padded seats arranged on a slant toward the stage. Below, all the chairs for the bands were set up on the stage. Risers for the choir were arranged on the left. I glanced at the program as I found a seat in the middle of the auditorium that had good views of everything. The sound was slightly better a little higher up, but I liked this perspective best. The junior bands were performing in the first half, so if Christie was willing to, we could leave at the break. I wouldn't have to be there to see Ben perform. That would be a perfect solution for me, but I suspected it would not work out that way. Even as I had the thought of sneaking out, I knew that Christie would want to stay to the end to see the senior classes perform. She would say that it would be a valuable learning experience or something like that. I would give in rather than let her walk home alone, so I was going to lose. No point asking in the first place. I sighed to myself. Ben was winning again, and he didn't even know he was in the fight. It was so unfair that I had so little power!

Suddenly the air around me seemed to vibrate ominously, and I twisted around to see that Bonnie's 'scary twins' had seated themselves behind me. I was somewhat surprised to notice that they weren't dressed in black tonight. Eris, the one with the short hair, was in a lavender dress, and the one with the long hair was in a denim skirt with a pretty pink blouse. They didn't look nearly as spooky when they had on nice clothes. The theatre was practically empty, so they needn't have chosen to sit quite so intimidatingly close to me, but I had chosen my seat because it afforded the best view, so they probably just shared my thinking. I tried to ignore them and I pulled out my book. Their voices distracted me before I got through a page. They were obviously continuing a conversation they'd been having before they'd sat down.

"I think Meg is right. Obviously something has gone off in his brain if he's even thinking about some dimwitted little grade ten," said one.

The other replied, "Personally, I think he's playing a game with her. He's probably doing what he did with that girl last year, Colby's sister, what was her name?"

"Oh yeah. I'd forgotten about that. Rae-Ann wasn't it?"

"Yes, Rae-Ann! Remember how he was always talking to her, flirting outrageously, and then once she was totally into him, he just laughed her off?"

"Yeah. Remember how she was at that dance? He had her in tears on the dance floor and she just ran out of the gym bawling."

They laughed at the memory, and I cringed for the unknown Rae-Ann. Bad enough to have such a humiliating experience, but to be laughed at for your agony—that was really awful. These weren't just scary twins, they were evil twins.

"Remember how he laughed and told everyone she was just a little confused, and then he'd wrapped his arms around Meg and they'd danced every dance afterwards?"

The other one laughed viciously, "Yeah. They were practically making out on the dance floor."

"I haven't seen Her Nerdiness this year."

"Didn't she transfer out?"

"I heard she tried to kill herself and that he laughed when he heard."

"He's a player."

I had thought when they first started talking that they were talking about Ben and me, but obviously, this didn't fit. Ben didn't seem like a player. Christie said he was well liked. They couldn't be talking about Ben, and if they weren't talking about Ben, then obviously they weren't talking about me. I relaxed a little and tried to focus on my reading as they continued, unaware that I was eavesdropping on their conversation, but speaking so loudly it was impossible not to when I was sitting right in front of them.

The other laughed. "Definitely a player, but Meg can handle him. Remember all the nights she spent at his house this summer? He would do anything she asks. Meg knows how to play him pretty well herself."

"Didn't he and Ryan have a bet that he could break a girl's heart?"

"Something like that. I heard that Rae-Ann was picked because she was the nerdiest girl in the room at the time. I heard Ryan had to pay Ben a hundred bucks when he lost."

Pay *Ben*? There was only one Ben. My heart hit the floor.

"Imagine the little nerd imagining someone like Ben would actually be interested in someone like her. Rae-Ann deserved it for being so stupid."

"I think he and Meg are probably doing the same thing this time."

"Well, whoever this little grade ten is, I think she'd better watch herself, because there is trouble ahead for her. Ben Butler is going to make mincemeat of her, and she'll be a pathetic cadaver by the time he's done."

"Yeah. Meg will enjoy watching him torment some naïve little girl." They chuckled sinisterly, and I had the sense again that they would enjoy sucking the blood out of someone, even if they looked more approachable in girly clothes.

At that moment, Mr. J walked onto the stage, and the audience of students and parents applauded him enthusiastically. My own claps were not energetic. So Ben was playing me, was he? That actually made sense. I *knew* it wasn't possible for someone to fall in love like that. This explained everything. I had known instinctively that no one was *that* nice. He was a great musician; obviously, he was a great actor as well. He could play all he wanted. I wasn't going to be his next victim. I wasn't stupid. I would heed the warning the twins had inadvertently given me. They didn't know that I was the one who needed to hear this information, but it was very convenient that they'd sat behind me. I was extremely thankful for the warning.

Although I did not want to agree with anything he said, I had to admit that Ben had been right. From what I was able to catch when the music burst through my fog, each of the bands was good. The Senior Jazz Band with Ben at the keyboards was astonishingly good, but I was distracted by the waves of relief, anger, and confusion. I was also battling a small little flurry of doubt. I fought the doubt the hardest. No one could be as wonderful as Christie had painted Ben to be. Everyone has a flaw. Ben's flaw apparently was that he found it amusing to humiliate girls by pretending that he liked them. He was lucky that he was a good enough actor that people still managed to believe that he was a nice guy despite this extraordinarily nasty side of him. My anger somehow seemed to inoculate me from the usual effects of his music, because it didn't make me dizzy to hear him tonight. It made me fume.

CHAPTER FOUR

A LITTLE RETRIBUTION IS A GOOD THING

Goddess of war rouses misery; Kharon is pushing his boat off.
Sacred elixir is drawn again, Charis is questioning motives;
She is defensive but powerful, crushing her foe with a hard strike.
Finding support from a rougher man, kindness endangers her this night.

"Here." Christie said as she handed me an empty tray.

"Thanks. What's the special today?" I couldn't see the menu board over the huge kid standing in front of me.

"Chicken Caesar"

"Mm. Good day for us."

Lloyd ran up to us with a vaguely apologetic grin to the people behind us in line. "Christie, here's some money; can you get me a cheeseburger? I'll go grab us a table."

"Sure." She watched him weave his way toward a table at the back and then looked at me muttering, "Lloyd is making me crazy."

As our turn came to order I giggled, "Hasn't he always made you crazy?" I handed my cash to the cafeteria worker at the till and requested, "Special, please."

She gave me my change while another student put the huge salad with a mound of diced chicken onto my tray. I wasn't paying much attention since I was still waiting for Christie's reaction.

"Enjoy," the line worker said with a paradoxically aggressive tone that was out of place in a food line.

"Ah, thanks," I said, glancing up guardedly. Then I did a double take. It was the longhaired twin, Enyo, her hair pulled back into a ponytail with a net over it and a white apron covering her skintight black t-shirt and

48

jeans. The black eye-liner and scarlet lips were the same as usual, as was the brooding stare. She was probably the last person I ever expected to see working in the cafeteria. Her scowl was enough to make you lose your appetite.

Her brows came down as I stared and she growled, "Move along little girl, you're holding up the line."

I looked behind me at the three students who didn't look at all impatient and back at her with confusion. She glared again until I said, "Sorry," and turned to follow Christie as she wove through the tables to the back of the room with her own tray of salad. Little girl. Ouch.

As we sat down Christie handed Lloyd his burger and remarked casually, "Friendly service, eh?"

"Mmm," I agreed as I dug into my salad. The food was good here. I usually tried to remember a sandwich for my lunch, but I was glad to have other options some days. Sandwiches got boring.

Between bites of his burger Lloyd commented, "Strange that they named a salad after a military coward, isn't it?"

"Huh?"

"You know, a chicken Caesar…"

I groaned, but Christie piped up, "It's not named after a Roman Caesar anyway. It was some chef in Mexico whose first name was Caesar."

"Quit spoiling my jokes, Christie," he chuckled.

As we finished I asked, "Does anyone want to come to the library with me? I have to get a new silent reading book for English."

Ben walked past and smiled at me.

I turned studiously away from him, but saw Christie's sympathetic grin in his direction.

"Christie!"

She looked back to me guiltily.

"Are you coming? To the library?" I reiterated.

"Um…no," she looked over at Lloyd. "I need to get something in the band room."

"Oh yeah," said Lloyd, reading something in her expression, "me, too."

I felt left out of a secret. I muttered, "Fine then. I'll see you in English." I headed up the stairs feeling decidedly grumpy with both of them. It had not escaped my notice that Ben seemed to be heading toward the band room as well. Wonderful. Stupid musicians. They all stick together.

I entered the library and was immediately enfolded by the calm. I loved this library. I tossed my book into the return slot and checked the shelves for the next book in the series. I was pleasantly surprised to find it was there. As I set it on the desk to check it out, Mrs. Hart looked at me oddly.

"Are you feeling all right dear? You're looking a little pasty."

Now I look sick. Great. I sighed, "I'm just a little tired. Busy week, you know."

She nodded in understanding and handed the book back to me. "Are you enjoying this series?"

I nodded, "Yes. I love these characters."

She smiled. "I agree. Good characters make you feel like you have new friends, don't they? You have to re-read the books just to visit with them again."

I laughed faintly. "Very true." I glanced around the room. One of the big comfortable reading chairs was empty and I headed there. Kicking off my shoes and pulling up my feet, I leaned back and closed my eyes. I felt kind of queasy.

I listened to the soothing sound of the miniature fountain on Mrs. Hart's desk, the whir of the computer fans and the hum of the lights. It was hypnotic and restful. I lost myself in the sounds, breathing deeply, focusing hard to ignore the waves in my belly.

The next thing I knew I was wandering down a dark corridor alone.

I came to a fork and turned right. Deep in the gloom there arose a frozen creature standing half again as tall as me. It had sallow skin and dark hair that hung to its knees. It wore a tattered white gown. Its eyes were closed; it didn't seem to know I was there. I backed up cautiously and went to go up the left fork instead. Blocking my way was another pale, frozen creature. The corridor seemed to be shrinking around me. I backed quietly to the point between the forks and went to inch back the way I'd come. Another creature was there though, this one taller, burlier, and clad in armour. It was awake. It stared ahead at me menacingly, but did not move a muscle.

I considered whether I could sneak past one of the sleeping creatures since I wasn't going to be able to go by this armoured giant, but as I looked up the forks, each of the gowned creatures was now watching me with the same cruel stare that I could feel burrowing into me from behind. I pivoted slowly around as all three creatures simultaneously raised their right arms to shoulder height like they were aiming at me, and then the air was full of streams of light pouring from their finger tips.

I let out a howl of pain and found myself rolling in agony on the floor of the library.

My belly was on fire.

I couldn't stop screaming.

Mrs. Hart came flying over from the desk. "Grace! Grace! What's wrong?"

I grabbed my stomach, groaning. It was if I was being stabbed repeatedly in the belly by a dull knife.

Then the nausea hit.

I clamped my hand over my mouth and raised my eyebrows in panic. She recognized the universal distress signal and grabbed the nearest garbage can. Thankfully, it wasn't a big hallway one, just a small rectangular office one. I would never have been able to raise myself enough to reach the tall one.

As it was, I eased up into a sitting position and wrapped myself around the can as if it were a life preserver. I was clinging precariously to the edge as I lost my lunch amid waves of pain that rolled from my toes to my nose. My face was tingling. I was shaking. I couldn't see for the tears in my eyes, and I couldn't imagine how I was going to hold myself together much longer.

Then suddenly, Ben was there. His hands firmly supported my shoulders as he eased himself down behind me, leaning his chest against my back and absorbing all my weight, leaving me free to focus on vomiting rather than staying upright. As angry as I was with him, he was salvation at this moment. I didn't care if he was Genghis Khan.

I couldn't mutter my gratitude (or mortification) while he whispered soothingly in my ears. I had no idea what he was saying, but the hushed tones seemed to reach inside me, comforting the myriad agonies that added up to this overwhelming sensation of excruciating pain. Now it was possible to endure.

I drew a quivering breath and melted into him. He didn't speak, but pulled me closer to him. He simply rubbed his hands gently up and down my arms, leaving a trail of lightness behind. The agony diminished.

Mrs. Hart was staring at us.

Ben leaned down and whispered in my ear, "Better now?"

I nodded, without turning to face him. I was nestled into his lap, and so long as I didn't turn around, I could simply savour the comfort without facing the repercussions.

"Mrs. Hart, can you get the water bottle out of my pack there?" He indicated where he'd dropped his bag in his hurry to come to my rescue.

She pulled the stainless steel bottle out and handed it to him silently.

"Thanks." He undid the cap and handed it to me. "Sip slowly."

My arm was shaking as I raised the bottle to my lips.

I don't know how long I sat there on the floor with Ben wrapped around me. It seemed like forever. I sipped gingerly at the water and felt my head clearing and my stomach settling. After the third or fourth sip, I realized that I was experiencing something similar to the frozen fire I remembered from the hospital. That was suspicious. I craned my neck around to look at Ben, "Did you get this from Dr. Kyle?"

"What?"

"This drink. It tastes like the medicine my doctor gave me after the band room incident."

"Oh?" He smiled softly. Whether the fluid was water or not, I didn't really care. The pain seemed to flow away through the heat against my back.

Mrs. Hart said quietly, "Can you stand now, Grace?"

I nodded, "Yes, I think so."

Ben stood first, and then reached out for my hand, pulling me up slowly. "Wait for a minute before you move," he said gently as I stood rocking from side to side while the room swayed around me. "You need to get your equilibrium back."

"Mm." I agreed. Slowly the room stopped moving. I looked up at him and smiled weakly.

He didn't smile back, but his eyes were glowing with intimate warmth. "Let me take you to the sick room."

"I don't want…" I tried to say, but he interrupted with a chuckle.

"Of course you don't. But you will go anyway. Come on, Sweetheart." He wrapped his arm securely around my waist and guided me down the hall. I was irritated that he was so sure of my compliance, but I was too weak to protest.

"You're sure you've got her, Ben?" Mrs. Hart called. I had the distinct feeling that she was glad to see me out of her formerly pristine library that was now tainted with an unpleasantly sour smell.

"Yeah, I'll get her there, don't worry."

"All right, I'll call down to the office and tell them you're coming."

We padded along so slowly that we were only half way to the office when we heard the page for Mr. Swan, the teacher who looked after first aid, and by the time we arrived at the office, he was already there.

I was embarrassed, but too feeble to object while he did a cursory exam, checking my pulse and blood pressure.

"So you were nauseous?" he asked.

"Yes."

"What did you eat at lunch?"

"I had the special at the cafeteria." I shot a look over at Ben who was still there, watching quietly. "Is it food poisoning? Did anyone else get sick?"

Mr. Swan shook his head, "You're the first. It does look like that's what it might be though. Let's hope there aren't many of you."

In my mind, I could see Enyo's evil glare at me in the line and wondered if she would do something like that deliberately. I thought she probably wouldn't be too troubled by the idea of poisoning most of the student body, even if she had a single target. Could it be that I was her target? I shivered a little. Being the object of Enyo's malevolent focus was a scary prospect.

"Just stay here Grace; we've called your mom and she's on her way. Will you wait with her, Ben, or do you need to get back to class?" asked the secretary.

Ben looked at me for a moment and seemed to ponder before he said, "I'll go back to class. She'll be fine now."

I nodded in agreement, but I felt strangely bereft at the idea of him disappearing again. To trust or not to trust: that is the question, I sighed to myself.

"Ben?"

He turned around at the doorway, "Yes?"

"What was in that bottle?"

"Why?"

"It was the same stuff, wasn't it?"

He tilted his head in a vague assent, but then stood up. "I need to get to class."

"Ben. Thank you. I appreciate your kindness. I didn't think I was going to survive for a moment there." I wasn't sure I was ready to trust him, but he had been amazing in the library.

He smiled that warm smile again. "You're welcome. Recover quickly, okay? I'll see you around."

"Yeah. Bye."

I watched him until he disappeared around the corner, and I was astonished at the empty feeling in my belly that didn't seem to simply be the result of the nasty vomiting session.

I couldn't figure out what I thought about Ben. On one hand, he had rescued me repeatedly like some gallant knight. On the other hand, my brain was full of thoughts about the poor Rae-Ann and what had happened to her. I'd casually mentioned, "Colby's sister" to a couple of people. Both times heads had shaken sadly and a comment had been made about how sad it was. That settled it. Even though I appreciated his help in the library, and picking me up off the street after I'd fainted, this was all too suspicious. There could be no good reason for his attention. I was going to go back to the best strategy and I was going to avoid him.

A week went by. Then two. I was successfully keeping out of his way, but it was hard work.

As I got to English last block on Friday, it was a relief to have reached the end of the day. I'd managed to see no more of him today than the top of the back of his head on two occasions. That was more than enough of him. It was still enough to leave me anxious. As we sat with our open books doing silent reading Christie tapped me on the arm, whispering faintly, "Are you okay?"

I shook my head.

She waited.

I turned the last page of my book and looked around the room. It was very quiet. Even Josh the troublemaker was quiet. Why was that? I checked out his corner, and looked right into his eyes. As I continued to look at him, he actually flushed and looked down at his desk. What was *that* all about?

I reached down to get my binder that was leaning against the leg of my desk and felt a rush of air over my head. I saw a paper airplane crash into the back of the projector. I looked at Christie and she flicked her head in Josh's direction. I turned to stare him down, and he smirked as he innocently pretended to read his novel. Good grief. Was I going to be his next spitball target? This I did not need. I got up quietly and approached Mr. Moore's desk.

"Sir? I've just finished my novel. May I go to the library to return it and get another?" He nodded, fishing out a library pass and filling it out for me. I thanked him and left the room with a sense of freedom.

I didn't really need to go to the library. I had another book in my binder since I'd known I'd finish this one today, but I just had to get out of the room. I felt antsy and irritated and I wanted to walk. I decided to take a creative route to the library via the bathrooms on the second floor.

I left the bathroom five minutes later and walked quietly down the corridor by Mr. Moore's room. I hoped his door was still closed so he wouldn't see me coming from the wrong direction, still carrying the novel I was supposed to be returning.

Before I got to the corner, Josh came around it. He was slinking backwards. I took it that he was sneaking out of class without permission. He twisted to face the direction he was travelling and met my eyes. I watched irritation, guilt and bravado cross his face. Bravado won. He stood up taller and puffed out his chest, adding a little sway to his walk as he sauntered up to me.

"Hey," he said with a flick of his chin.

It felt vaguely like being in a gangster movie. I tried to look composed, and not quite as disdainful as I felt. "Hey."

"You going to say anything?"

"Huh?"

"About me. You going to tell him?" he asked, tilting his head toward the classroom door.

I looked at him with my eyebrows raised, "Why would I have to tell him anything? He's probably already noticed the quiet in the room."

He grinned at me, clearly deciding that we were co-conspirators. He called, "Thanks!" as he sprinted down the hall.

Now there was a higher likelihood that Mr. Moore would be poking his head out the door. I walked more quickly.

I peeked gingerly around the corner. The hall way was empty, and unbelievably, my classroom door was closed. It was my lucky day.

I was just past the door and feeling safe when someone came up behind me. I heard an eerily low, "Don't move!" and something tickled behind my ear.

I responded with instincts that I didn't know I had. With an alarmingly aggressive growl, I swung my elbow high and hard. I was surprised to have heard such a sound coming out of me, and rather shocked at the way my body had reacted. My arm connected with my attacker much sooner than I'd expected. I heard a definite crunch as my arm contacted flesh.

"Oof! Ouch!" The voice was muffled

I turned to see whom I'd nailed. I expected to see Josh, but to my surprise, Ben was behind me, his hands cupped around his nose, which was gushing blood. "Crap Grace! You trying to kill me?" His eyes were huge as he crossed the hall to the nearest garbage can.

I was too annoyed with him to feel very sorry for him, so I glared at him instead of answering. His face was swelling up as I watched. He leaned over the garbage can, took his hands off his nose and blood poured into the can.

At that moment, Mr. Moore opened his door. He took one look at Ben and said, "Let's get you to the office, young man." He leaned back into the classroom and ordered firmly, "Keep reading!" Then he shut the door behind him and came up to us. He picked up the garbage can, holding it under Ben's face. Ben wrapped his arms around it, endeavouring to hold with his wrists and keep his bloody hands away, as Mr. Moore put his arm gently around Ben's shoulder, and guided him down the hall to the office. Ben looked at me balefully over the can, so I followed along. Mr. Moore studied Ben's face as they walked. "Looks like that nose might be broken. What happened?"

Ben just shook his head.

"Not talking, eh? Afraid to have him come after you again?"

Ben grinned a little sheepishly.

Mr. Moore laughed, "Well, we'll let Mrs. Nemeth get to the bottom of it after we've got the bleeding under control." He steered Ben into the medical room and indicated that I should sit in the chairs outside the room. "Will you wait here with him, Grace?"

I nodded.

The teacher who was the school's first aid person came rushing in and started bustling around. I heard the murmur of voices while he quizzed Ben and received very brief, apparently unsatisfactory, answers in return. A secretary came in with a cold pack. Her voice joined Mr. Swan's as I sat with my elbows on my knees, my head resting on my hands, staring at the floor.

I sat outside the medical room waiting for ages. I heard the secretary calling Ben's mom to tell her to come get him, because they were pretty sure he'd broken his nose. Terrific. My luck had certainly changed quickly.

Eventually Mr. Swan left, but Ben stayed in the first aid room while he waited for his mom. He waited inside. I waited outside. Waited and waited. Finally, I couldn't stand it any more. I looked around, and since no one was paying close enough attention to tell me not to, I slipped into the room. Ben was sitting on a cot with the compress over his nose. He had an ice cream bucket under his chin catching drips of blood. It wasn't flowing quite as quickly as it had been coming down the hall, but there was still quite a puddle in the bucket. His eyes were closed, partially covered by the cold compress.

I cleared my throat. "Ech hem."

Without opening his eyes he responded quietly, "Yes, Grace?"

Of course, he knew it was me. I sighed. My voice was small. "Sorry."

I saw his cheeks puff out a bit, and knew he was smiling. "You have a very impressive swing there."

"Yeah. Sorry. I didn't know it was you."

"Would it have mattered if you had? I have gotten the impression lately that you don't like me very much at all."

I didn't know what to say to that. He was right.

"I suspect if you'd actually known it was me, you might just have put even *more* force behind that swing, and put my nose right through to the back of my head." He sounded understandably discouraged. I couldn't disagree with him, because he was partially right. I hadn't known

56

I was such a violent person. It was unnerving.

I sat down on the cot next to him. He seemed very sad and very innocent of any of the evils the twins had accused him of. I thought for a moment.

"Ben?" I asked quietly.

"Yes?"

"Do you know Rae-Ann?"

He sighed deeply, and it sounded very melancholy. Was that guilt? There was a long pause. "Everyone knew Rae-Ann"

"Knew? She didn't *die*, did she?"

"No, 'knew' because the girl she was doesn't exist any more." He shook his head gingerly, holding his compress, his eyes still closed. "That was a really horrible thing." His voice trailed off.

At least he was acknowledging that much.

"Where is she now?"

"Last I heard she'd been sent to the mental health facility in Ponoka. It was very hard on her family. I was good friends with her brother Colby for a few years, so I knew her quite well. I hope she recovers." He paused, and then said in a hushed voice, "She was a very sweet girl."

The anger boiled and I felt my ears turning red. My blood pressure was going up. What kind of jerk was he to have done this to 'a very sweet girl' and then be able to speak of it so calmly? My fury overwhelmed me and I stood up. I fought the urge to pound his nose through the back of his head as he'd suggested. "You are disgusting." I spat the words at him.

"Excuse me?" He said innocently. He opened his eyes; they were swelling up too. "What did I do?"

My fingers curled and uncurled in my fists. My nails were cutting into my palm. Poor, undefended Rae-Ann. My eyes flashed as I whispered venomously, "You know very well what you did! You are SCUM!" I turned on my heels and left the room before I really did injure him more. I was defiantly overjoyed to have at least caused the damage I had. Smashed nose. Excellent. He'd received a little retribution for the pain he'd caused Rae-Ann, at least. I stalked out of the school. I was sure that I'd be hearing from administration tomorrow for skipping out, and I would probably be suspended for breaking Ben's nose, even if it was just an accident and hadn't happened in anger. I had enough anger now to warrant the suspension. I deserved it.

I stomped away from the school, heading furiously away without a direction in mind. A light snow was falling. I was lost in my angry thoughts when I heard faint footfalls behind me. Someone was running after me. Damn Ben. I whirled around ready to deck him again and stopped in shock. It was Josh Dagan.

He bent over panting as he looked up at me gasping, "You are freakishly fast, you know that?"

"What do you want?" I sounded harsher than I intended to, but I was too angry with Ben to be very nice.

"You look upset. I thought…" he shrugged his shoulders. He came up beside me, still breathing heavily. He reeked of smoke. No doubt about what he'd been doing while skipping class.

It was very weird to be standing here beside Josh the troublemaker, with him feeling sympathy for me. I hadn't thought him capable of that much emotional depth. I just stared at him fuming.

His voice was tenderly persuasive when he spoke next, "Come on, I'll take you out for coffee and you can tell me all about it." He smiled then, and tapping me gently on my sleeve, he led me down the street at a more relaxed pace.

I followed along in spite of myself. I told myself that it was the direction I'd been walking already, so it would be weird if I refused to go. As we walked along, I found my anger replaced by bafflement as I tried to figure out what Josh was thinking. Why this sudden Good Samaritan act? Very odd.

I studied him through my lashes. He was slightly built with sandy brown hair that was in need of a hair cut under his ever present brown ball cap. His jeans were grubby and the crotch hung half way to his knees. He was wearing a much worn leather jacket that I'd never seen him without. I wondered if he wore it in PE, and chuckled at the picture that came to my mind.

He glanced over at me, "What?"

I shook my head, embarrassed. "It's nothing."

His lips curled at the corners slightly, not quite a grin. "You feeling better yet?"

I exhaled a puff of air through my nose while I considered it. Huh. Another surprise. "Yeah, I am."

He nodded. "Good."

We reached the coffee shop. He stepped ahead of me and opened the door, gallantly motioning me inside. He was full of surprises.

As we joined the line to the counter, he pulled out a silver square, and opened it up. I realized I was looking at his wallet.

"Is that duct tape?"

He grinned, opening it up and showing me, "Yeah. We made them in shop last year. Cool, eh?"

I nodded, impressed. That *was* cool.

"So what would you like?"

"It's okay Josh; I can get my own."

He shook his head. "No, no, none of that. I was the one who invited you, remember? Besides," he smirked conspiratorially, "I happen to be flush right now." He tilted the wallet at me, running his thumb across the top to fan a wad of bills.

I tried not to show it on my face, but the amount of money was a little disturbing. "Pay day?" I asked, as indifferently as I could.

He smirked, "Yeah. You could say that." He laughed in a way that made me even more nervous about the origins of his windfall.

We had reached the counter and the cashier looked at us expectantly. She looked like a happy grandma. "Hi there, what can I get for you today?" I wondered idly how many times she said that phrase in a day.

Josh replied, "Large double double for me." He looked expectantly over at me and I gave in.

"Large hot chocolate please, with topping."

He nodded, satisfied that I was being reasonable. I stood there feeling awkward while our drinks were prepared. What was I doing here? The cashier put the drinks on the tray and Josh picked it up. He looked the cashier in the eyes and smiled pleasantly at her as he said, "Thanks." Apparently, out of school he was more polite to adults. Looking toward me he tilted his head to a table for two tucked into the corner. "Over there?"

"Sure."

He set the tray down and took the seat against the wall. He could study the room from that spot.

"So," he said taking a deep swig of his steaming coffee, "you don't seem to be having a very good day, eh?"

I wondered why his tongue wasn't burning off. My tentative sip of hot chocolate had been way too hot to drink yet. "No. Not the best day of my life." I agreed.

"Would it help to talk about it?"

I was surprised again by how concerned he seemed, but I wasn't up to sharing. I shook my head. "No, I don't think so."

He shrugged his shoulders. "You're good in English." It was a statement, not a question.

"Ah. Yeah." His change of subject threw me off.

He nodded. "I don't get the grammar, and I don't get why anyone would want to study that Shakespeare dude, but sometimes I like the books."

"You read?" It was out before I could stop it. "Oh, I'm sorry.

That was rude."

He laughed. "Nah, it's okay. I guess I don't look like the type. My grandma used read to me all the time when I was a little kid. Kinda got me hooked, you know?" He didn't look upset. "I don't much like school; I really only come for the...uh...*social* connections, you know?"

I could see that. "Did your grandma live near your parents?"

"No, I lived with her for a couple of years around the time I was in kindergarten. My dad was in jail and my mom was in rehab." He was matter of fact about this information. "I liked living with Gram. She was a good cook and she seemed to actually like me."

I digested that. He didn't say it bitterly and there was something even sadder about how unemotional he was about it.

"Do you get to see her at all now?"

"No." Now he did look sad. "She died when I was in grade five. I would go to stay with her in the summers until she died though. It was always the best part of my year."

"You must really miss her."

He had his hands wrapped around the cup, staring into the coffee as he nodded slowly. "Yeah. I really do." We sat in silence for a while until he looked up. "What about you? What's your family like?"

I was a little embarrassed to tell him. I shrugged my shoulders, "Oh you know, the standard issue two parents."

"Both your birth parents?"

I nodded.

"You're lucky, you know. That's becoming less and less common."

I thought of all my friends and the many variations of family groupings that they had. "Yeah. I know."

"So what's the best summer vacation you ever had? You do the Disneyland thing and all that?" he asked, studying my eyes.

"No, not Disneyland, but my mom is Greek, so we go back there to see her family every couple of years."

"Greece, eh?" When I nodded he added, "I've seen pictures. It looks pretty beautiful with the blue sky and white buildings. It is really like that?"

"Yes, in the villages and smaller islands particularly. It's like another world. On some islands, donkeys are still the main mode of transportation. The light is amazing, and the smells..." I trailed off thinking of markets and donkeys and sweat.

"Smells?"

I smiled. "Wonderful smells. Salt, fish, animals, fresh air, and ocean. It doesn't smell *anything* like Calgary. "

He laughed. "I guess not!"

We sat there, companionably sipping our drinks, each of us thinking our own thoughts.

So," he asked casually after a few minutes, "do you skip class often?"

I laughed. "No, this is the first time."

He nodded. "Thought so. Good thing I caught up to you so I could help you do it properly." He grinned. "So what caused you to break with habit and take off today, to spend this time with me?"

I chuckled at him. "Oh, I had a bit of a temper tantrum in the hall. I figured it was safer for the school community if I took it outside."

He laughed. "Very civic minded of you. Do you usually have temper tantrums in the halls?"

I shook my head in mock severity, "No, that was a first, too."

"It seems to be your day for firsts."

That was an understatement. "Indeed."

At that moment, his cell phone rang and he smiled apologetically, reaching into his pocket, and flipping it open with a snap. It looked very new and very expensive. "Yeah?" He listened. "Yeah okay." He glanced up to the coffee shop clock. "Yup. Bye." He folded the phone up and put it into his pocket again. "Sorry Grace, I've got to go." He seemed genuinely sorry. "Another time perhaps?" And before I had a chance to swallow my mouthful of hot chocolate and say good-bye, he was gone.

I remained at the table, swirling the dregs of my hot chocolate and pondering my day. If someone had told me this morning that I'd have broken someone's nose and then gone for coffee with Josh Dagan I would have said she was crazy. I *was* crazy. I lifted the mug to my lips and chugged back the last of the chocolate. Adding my cup to Josh's on the tray, I picked it up and set it over on the garbage stand. A worker washing tabletops smiled over at me, "Have a good day!" I smiled back and headed out the door.

Have a good day? That was funny.

Something woke me. I lay quietly in the darkness of my room listening to the occasional rumble of a passing car out on the road and watching the trail of its headlights squeezing through the cracks of my blinds. Slowly the blur of a distant voice came to me. I glanced at my closed door and noticed a glint of light. Someone else was awake in the night. I listened through my stupor and recognized my mom's voice.

"No, it's definitely started again." Long pause. "He's trying, but would you believe Aglaea," she laughed, "that she broke his nose?" More laughter. Was mom's sister laughing at me all the way from Greece? That explained the late call. It would be early afternoon there. Wait. How did mom know I'd broken Ben's nose? Or was she talking about someone else? Could someone else have a broken nose? I lay there in the haze of half sleep, semi-consciously listening to the one-sided conversation that didn't make too much sense, waiting for sleep to reclaim me.

"Obviously he's not having quite as much success as he's had previously." She listened to the reply for a long time before responding again. Through the fog of sleep, I thought she said, "Well, ask Dad if he has any ideas. I don't know what to do about this one. I'd thought it would take longer for him to find her here." She paused again, "She's fifteen; she just had her birthday." Another long wait and my eyes were heavy as I drifted more fully back to sleep. "Yes, that's true. Maybe the punch is a good thing and this time she won't fall for him, but to be honest, I'm not holding my breath; the attraction has been strong enough to keep them finding each other for more than two thousand years, after all." A vague confusion touched my brain, but I was back to sleep before I was able to thoroughly register it.

Xandros was laughing gleefully, without even the vaguest sense of decorum. Mars watched him with disapproval.

"Control yourself, Xandros. It isn't funny."

"It's hilarious, Mars, and you know it. He's so worried about this poor, helpless, little girl, but she is holding her own. She's far too spirited to be attracted to him. She's worthy of me!"

"She's worthy of the one who loves her the most. That's not you."

"It could be me."

Mars shook his head. "Be prepared. He's getting closer. She's going to need all the power she can develop to be ready."

"I'm watching."

"Good."

CHAPTER FIVE

DO I LOOK LIKE AN IDIOT?

Lovers for eons, but loneliness taunts her with fears of belonging.
Apple of discord is tossed again. Innocents suffering wrongly.
Roughly she's warned of the menaces. Coming toward her is danger;
Can he be trusted implicitly? Is he a deadly arranger?

When Ben showed up at school on Monday with a splint on his nose and two black eyes, it spread through the school like wildfire. Gossip was rife on all sides as people speculated about who'd beaten him up. My face was perennially red, as I expected at any moment to be called into the office, but the day passed without a principal appearing at the classroom door, beckoning me to come meet my fate.

At lunch, I'd passed Meg and the twins in the hall. I heard Meg mention Ben's name as she went by. She had smirked at one of the twins, who'd grinned back smugly.

By the end of the day, it had become clear that Ben hadn't told anyone in the office what had really happened. Mr. Moore obviously knew that I'd been with Ben at the time, but even he didn't seem to think that I could be violent enough to have broken anyone's nose. He didn't even acknowledge me when I came into English class. I'd waited all day for discipline, but I hadn't even been called to the office to be a witness to the event, and that was confusing too, since Mr. Moore should have explained to administration that I'd been there. If Ben wasn't talking, wouldn't they seek out the only other person who'd been there to try to get the story from *some* source?

"What's up with you today?" Christie asked in a whisper. "You look like you're expecting to be called up in front of a firing squad or something."

The metaphor was so appropriate that I guffawed, which made her eyes widen. She was even more surprised when I said, "I am."

"Why? What happened?"

My voice dropped to a whisper and I leaned close to her so no one would overhear. "Did you see Ben?"

"Of course."

I raised my eyebrows meaningfully.

She looked confused for a moment, then her eyes got huge and her mouth dropped open. She pointed at me and mouthed, "You?" I nodded. She grinned. "Wow! Heavy hitter!" I cringed as she added, "Did it happen at school?" I nodded. Her brows furrowed and she asked quietly, "Why haven't you been suspended?"

I shrugged my shoulders and grimaced, "That's the question, isn't it?" Perhaps no one cared about students being punched in school, but that seemed pretty unlikely. Nonetheless, I had waited through the day with no sign of trouble coming my way, until I finally began to relax in this last period. It was ironic that Christie thought I looked like I was waiting for a firing squad now, because I was much less worried now than I had been earlier in the day. "By the way, thanks for taking my books back to the locker Friday. Did Mr. Moore say anything?"

She shook her head, "No. I wondered why you hadn't come back to class, but figured I'd better not draw it to his attention in case he hadn't noticed."

"Thanks." I had no idea where Mr. Moore had expected that I'd gone, but it was good that he hadn't been reminded that I should have come back to his class.

Mr. Moore started his lesson, so Christie and I focused. Well, I *pretended* to focus, but really, I was contemplating what the administration would consider logical consequences for assault.

The video had barely started when Josh had sauntered in, loudly proclaiming, "Sorry I'm late! Did you miss me?" He didn't sound very sorry.

Sighing, Mr. Moore calmly remarked, "Just take your seat, Josh."

As he walked past my desk, Josh gave me a very distinct wink.

I nodded as slightly as possible and then caught Christie's expression. Subtle as I thought I'd been, she hadn't missed it.

She hissed, "What is *that* about!"

I shook my head as Mr. Moore cleared his throat conspicuously and I obediently turned to watch the video. From the corner of my eye, I could see Christie was still watching me with a baffled expression. I studiously ignored her. She wouldn't believe me if I told her.

After the video, as we were dividing into groups to work on performances, Mr. Moore appeared at my side and very quietly asked, "Grace, can I see you outside for a moment?"

My heart dropped. Ah. This was it. Finally. I glanced over at Christie on the way to her group across the room, and she met my eyes with a note of concern. I followed Mr. Moore out his door fatalistically. As I passed Josh's group working by the door, he gave me an appraising look. I was hoping I looked nonchalant and guiltless. My ears were burning again.

"So Grace, I wanted to talk to you about Ben's nose," Mr. Moore began casually.

"Ah. Okay." I did not meet his eyes. I admired his black tassel loafers. Very classy. You'd never see those on a PE teacher. Probably not on a Science teacher either. I wondered vaguely if Mr. Moore was planning to go into Administration.

He continued, "I wondered if you saw anyone else in the halls before the incident on Friday, besides yourself and Ben, of course."

"I passed a few people…" my voice trailed off.

"Specifically in the hallway where Ben was hurt, did you see anyone?"

I could answer that one honestly enough. I looked up at him, "No, I only saw Ben."

"Nobody else?"

"Not a soul."

"Huh," he mused. "Really? That's interesting."

I waited for him to come to the logical conclusion of that statement: if there were only two people in the halls at the time, one would be the hitter and the other would be the hittee. If Ben was the hittee, that made me the hitter. Come on Mr. Moore! You can do it! He shook his head, then looked at me and said, "Okay then. Thanks for your time." He swept out his arm to indicate I should return to the class, and then followed me in.

He was not a stupid man. Could he honestly not figure out that *obviously* I was the one who had punched Ben? Maybe I'd succeeded in my desire to look guiltless and nonchalant? Maybe I was such a wimp no one figured I had the physical prowess to break a nose? I wondered if I should just stand on a desk and announce to the class that it'd been me so that the tension would finally be over and I'd be able to stop looking over my shoulder, waiting for doom. Perhaps I should pick up his phone and hit the page button to tell the whole school, "Attention Redman High, this

is Grace Severin confessing to the brutal beating of Ben Butler yesterday!"
Yeah right. I'd be lynched.

At least it'd be over.

I rejoined my group and caught up on the planning about who would
bring which costumes and props to use in our performance. Apparently,
the tension hadn't completely left me though, because when the bell rang, I
jumped as if I'd been shot. Christie looked over at me with sympathy.

We gathered our books and called, "See you Mr. Moore!" over our
shoulders as we left the class. I'd actually made it through the day without
confrontation. Thank heavens. I breathed a sigh of relief.

Unfortunately, my relief was completely unwarranted, because
when we reached our locker, we found Ben sitting on the floor leaning
against it, waiting for us.

"Hello Grace," he said evenly, hardly glancing up from the floor.

I matched his quiet tone, nodding cordially. "Hello Ben. Can we
get into our locker, please?"

His voice remained calm and coolly polite. "Not just yet, if you
don't mind. I'd like a word with you when the crowd clears."

Ah. He shifted his body from one side to the other while our locker
neighbours came, glanced at him curiously, loaded books and removed
coats. As they slammed locker doors and chatted, I hoped Meg would
show up and demand that Ben head off with her, but no Meg appeared.

Josh walked by and I saw him pause as he looked from Ben to
Christie and back to me. He met my eyes and grinned.

I frowned and looked away.

According to the clock, it only took four minutes for the crush of
bodies to clear, but it seemed like an hour. There were still people around,
but there was lots of room around our locker now. Ben slid over so
Christie could open it, and patted the floor beside him with his hand.
"Have a seat, Grace."

I sighed, but settled next to him on the ground, handing my English
binder to Christie on the way down. She set it on my shelf, and then took
out her flute and music folder. "I'll be in the music room, okay Grace?
I'll do my flute time. Meet me there?"

I nodded at her, and then glanced over at Ben. He was staring
straight ahead at the wall across the hall. I focused there too and said,
"Well?"

He didn't reply. We just sat there side by side, legs sticking out into
the hall, backs against the lockers, staring ahead of us. He seemed calm.
I'd felt expectant and tense at first, but gradually my turmoil settled into
even breathing and the wait felt strangely comfortable. Weird how nice it
was just to sit beside him like this. Even when he was such a jerk. Even

when he was bruised and broken because of my violence.

Finally, he spoke. "I am not sure what to do about you, Grace." He still didn't look at me. "I don't know what is wrong this time... I mean..." He thought for a second before he clarified, "I don't know what I've done to make you so angry with me."

"I didn't hit you because I was angry." I glanced over at him, and then returned to studying the wall opposite.

I saw him nod in my peripheral vision. "I know. You just lashed out because I surprised you."

I nodded.

"But still, you *were* angry afterwards. You called me 'scum.'" His voice had gotten very quiet.

I didn't answer. Continuing to look across the hall, I waited for him to carry on, but he didn't. He seemed to want me to reply. I didn't. The second hand on the clock made two rotations of the face.

"Grace?" he whispered with an aching tone, "What have I ever done to you that would make you think I'm scum?"

I still didn't reply. We sat silently for a long time. Finally, he turned and looked at me. I pivoted my head to meet his eyes. I was feeling a confusing mix of defiance and sheepishness.

He continued to look at me, waiting for my reply. I knew that he would not go anywhere until I answered, so I sighed and said, just as quietly, "You didn't do anything to *me*."

"I don't get it, Grace." He shook his head. He looked absolutely pathetic with his sad, puffy, black eyes over the splinted nose. A nose splint is a ridiculous implement. It's hard not to feel sorry for someone who looks that idiotic.

I decided to put him out of his misery. Perhaps this would settle things one way or another. Once he knew that I knew about the bet, perhaps he'd leave me alone to get on with my life without having him cornering me all the time. I could be free to take direct routes to class again. I sighed and said, "It's what happened with Rae-Ann."

"Rae-Ann?"

I wondered how he could possibly be so obtuse. My temper flared, so I answered sharply, "Yes. Did you think I'd be okay with that? That I'd volunteer to be next? Do I *look* like an idiot?"

He shook his head, but said with an exasperated tone, "No, but you *sound* like one."

My eyebrows came down and I went to stand up, but he put his arm on my shoulder, weighing me down. "No wait. I'm sorry Grace. Stay. That was uncalled for." He shook his head, "I just don't understand what

67

you have to do with Rae-Ann."

I glared at him and spoke very slowly, staring into his eyes to make it as clear as possible, "I. Don't. Want. To. Be. The. Next. Rae-Ann."

"Who would? What do you *mean* Grace?"

"Damn it, Ben," I snarled. "I'm not going to be some pawn in your game! I am not going to give you the power to break me!"

He looked at me quizzically and then I saw a glimmer of an idea come into his brain. He tilted his head slightly to the side, thinking a moment before he said slowly, "Grace, you know that Rae-Ann has schizophrenia, right?"

Schizophrenia? I thought about that for a moment. Cause or effect? Did Ben trigger a psychosis when he led her on and then mocked her at the dance? Was he lying to me? Or was there something I was missing?

I stood up as I saw Christie coming down the hall. I looked down at him and said coolly, "Whatever, Ben."

He shook his head with a sad sort of sigh. He remained sitting on the floor, but he tucked his legs up, wrapped his arms around them, and rested his chin on his knees.

As Christie reached the locker, he slid over and watched me as I waited silently for her to gather her things. She glanced at down at him curiously but didn't comment.

We left without a backwards look at him. As we went through the front doors, Christie asked with studied casualness, "Do you want to talk about it?"

I shook my head, and we walked home in silence.

A couple days later, it was icy and the wind was blowing the dry snow into my eyes as I huddled into my hood on my walk home.

"Hey there!" Heavy footfalls clomped up beside me.

I had to turn my whole body to see who was there and was surprised to see Josh's tell tale brown leather jacket. He had a grey hoodie pulled up over his head from beneath the jacket and, his bare hands were stuffed in his pockets. He was slouched over, shivering a bit. "Oh, hi."

"We need a Chinook," he said grimly.

I laughed, "Yes, we definitely do." Weather was one of the strangest things about living in Calgary. A blizzard could blow in and close the highways with a dump of snow any month of the year. Conversely, in the middle of winter you could walk to school in minus twenty degrees, bundled up so only your eyes showed, and in the afternoon a Chinook wind could blow in and it could be plus twenty degrees on the walk home. It was hard on plants, but it was pretty great for people.

Josh stomped his feet hard, and I noticed he was just wearing running shoes. "You realize it's minus twenty-six degrees out, right?

"Yeah. I didn't go home last night, so I didn't get my boots."

"Is that jacket warm enough?"

He chuckled with a sheepish look, "Not really. Stand closer. I need you to block the wind." As I laughed he added, "Come into Tims with me for a coffee. I need to warm up."

I followed him through the door to the coffee shop, wondering why I wasn't even thinking about refusing. Josh was trouble. I knew that. I had the very clear sensation that hanging out with him could only lead to bad things coming my way, and yet I had to admit that I liked being with him. I liked his dry humour. I liked how he said what he was thinking and didn't seem to care too much one way or other how I reacted to it. And— this was the hardest thing to admit to myself—I liked how he had chosen me to be the 'normal' person that he talked to. I'd never seen him hanging out with anyone who wasn't a regular at the smoke pit; I felt strangely honoured that he wanted to talk to me, that he chose me to tell about his grandmother. Was I just stupid?

"Large double double and a large hot chocolate with whipped topping."

I was brought back to the present as he placed the order, "Oh hey, I can pay for that."

"Nah, I got it. Hot chocolate is good again?"

"Yeah. Thanks." I was strangely touched that he'd remembered.

"Go pick a table, I've got this."

I found a place for two in a corner away from the doors. I stood there for a moment assessing the air. Josh came up to me carrying the tray. I sat down, "I think this is the warmest table."

He grinned. "Excellent choice, then." He cupped his hands around the coffee and breathed in the steam. "Mmmm. I love my caffeine, and I love to be warm. This is the best of both worlds." He took a large sip of the scalding brew and then looked over to me, "So. Hit anybody lately?"

I stopped my first tentative sip of hot chocolate and looked over the cup at him. How did he know about that? I forced my voice to be calm and steady, "Not today, no. Why do you ask?"

He just smirked and stared into my eyes without responding.

I held his gaze steadily. He had very pretty eyes: light brown but flecked with grey, gold and green.

"It was a good strong punch to have broken his nose."

I continued to look at him unflinchingly, while my mind turned over my options. So far, nobody knew except Christie (and she had probably told Lloyd). I wondered if Josh had overheard something, or whether he'd just put two and two together after our last coffee break together.

He raised his eyebrows, waiting for my comment.

I shrugged my shoulders and looked down at my hot chocolate. I sipped too much and burnt my tongue, but kept my face blank.

"All right, then," he whispered.

I looked up at him.

"I get it," he pursed his lips and nodded. "You're not talking. It's probably a good idea not to let the word get out. You don't want something like that on your record." He paused, as if waiting for me to respond before he shrugged and continued. "Did you know that he's not talking either?" He studied me carefully and he pondered thoughtfully, "I wonder why that is? You'd think he'd tell them when they're nagging him so much about it, wouldn't you? Unless of course he's fallen for his attacker, or if, say, perhaps it was a lovers' tiff?"

I snorted in disgust.

Josh smirked again and leaned further back into his chair with his right leg crossed above his left knee. "Yeah. I'd say he probably has it bad. Not that I don't see the attraction, of course." He fluttered his eyebrows suggestively and his smirk changed darkly. He leaned across the table. "Do you go for that clean cut type or do you like your guys a little rebellious?"

I laughed at him. I couldn't help it.

He leaned back again and his grin became light hearted once more. "He has a reputation, you know, for being a little unethical with the ladies. I'd tell you to watch yourself around him, but you look like you've got it under control."

I blushed a little and looked into my drink. Where Ben was concerned, I didn't feel like anything was under control.

He chuckled. "I like you Grace. You've got a face and a figure, as well as a brain and some guts." He studied me appreciatively. "I think you'd be good in a crisis, and around me there is always a crisis. What do you think? Do you think a girl like you and a guy like me could have any future together?"

"Are you serious?" I did not attempt to remove the incredulous tone from my voice.

He smiled with his mouth, but his eyes narrowed. "Yeah, actually, I am." He leaned forward again, tilting his head. "What do you say? Would you go out with me sometime?"

I knew I should say no. There was no one I knew who would think twice about saying no, but somehow the idea of getting to know him more intrigued me. I tilted my head to mirror his and studied him quizzically for a moment before I finally replied hesitantly, "Maybe."

He grinned. "Maybe, huh?"

"Yeah. Maybe."

"What exactly is the condition that would change 'maybe' to 'yes'?" He had angled himself to the back of his chair again, and was looking very curious.

I considered that for a while before I finally shrugged. "I'm not sure. I guess it would depend on what we would be doing."

He nodded. "That sounds reasonable. Let's see. We have lots of options. We could go to a movie, or a concert, or bowling, or golfing, or skiing, or tobogganing, or skating, or perhaps," he grinned, "we could make out in the back room at a party." He leered a little at my renewed blush before he added, "Any of those catch your interest?"

I imagined him kissing me and felt the flame in my cheeks travel through my body in a rush of heat. I looked up at him nervously.

He waited patiently for my response, lifting an eyebrow as we looked at each other.

Finally, I whispered, "Maybe."

"You're not being very helpful here, you know."

I sighed. "I know. Sorry. I just can't really *imagine* going anywhere with you, though I'm not particularly opposed to going somewhere, you know?" It was only a little lie. I fought down the image of his mouth on mine, his arms traveling down my body…

He grinned again. "Yeah. I get it." His phone rang then, and he flipped it open with a quick glance at the number that produced a scowl. "Yeah? Yeah. No. Okay. Yup. Yeah, bye." He snapped the phone shut and pocketed it.

"Profound conversations you have."

He chuckled without comment.

"Do you have to go?"

He smiled openly at me. He knew my suspicions, but he didn't care. "Not right now." He stared blankly into the distance for a minute, and then blurted out, "Hey, you want a doughnut?"

"Huh?"

"It's a doughnut shop, Grace. Do you want one before we go?"

"No. Too many calories."

"Oh get serious, you're not fat." He looked annoyed.

"Yes, I know. But I'm not fat because I don't have doughnuts every day." I laughed at his shocked face. "I'll have one another time. If you want one, feel free. It won't bother me if you're eating and I'm not."

"Now I feel guilty about wanting one."

"You're just looking for excuses to stay inside and keep warm."

He laughed, "Yes. Definitely." Then his eyes got all soft and mushy and he added, "and stay with you, of course."

"Of course. But sadly, I have to leave now or I will be late getting home." I stood up, "Thanks for the hot chocolate."

"Yeah."

"Next time I'm buying."

He shook his head. "No you're not."

"Don't be silly, Josh." I added teasingly, "I'll even buy you a doughnut."

He laughed. "Well, if you're going to bribe me."

"See ya."

"Bye, Grace." He was just sitting in his chair looking kind of lost.

"Josh?" I didn't want to leave if he was upset about something.

"*Bye* Grace. See you in English class."

I was dismissed. So he wasn't letting me in on whatever he was trying to hide. I shrugged in defeat, "Yeah, okay." I walked out of the restaurant, but glanced back, feeling more than a little worried about whatever was bothering him. He could be involved in all sorts of dangerous stuff. What was he doing? I saw Josh pull out his phone as I pulled my hood up a little more securely and focused on moving quickly enough to generate some heat to keep me warm. If I let my imagination go, I knew that I would have plenty of heat, but that was a dangerous thing. A very dangerous thing. I had just agreed in principle to date Josh Dagan. What on earth was I thinking?

The snow was thick outside and it was thirty below, so the student body was staying inside during the breaks. School was crowded. The gym was open for intramurals and that kept the athletic types, and those Lloyd laughingly called 'the athletic supporters' busy. The cafeteria was packed so tightly the noise seemed like a solid thing. There was room in the library, if you wanted to study, but there was no eating in the library, so Christie and I were sitting on the floor by our locker eating our lunches, wondering where Lloyd was as we watched water dripping out of the locker doors from the stashed snowy boots.

"Was he in band today?" I asked.

"No, but he always lets one of us know that he's going to be away, so it's really weird. I wonder if he's sick?" she mused.

The twins walked past, looking down their noses at us with curled lips. I watched them frankly, as they turned into the chemistry room, thinking it was a shame they always looked as if they were smelling something rotten; they could be quite attractive if they could learn to reflect a pleasant thought or two on their faces.

Ben walked past with Meg trailing after him. She was grabbing his arm possessively and he was looking exasperated. He didn't seem to notice me down on the floor, but as she pouted up at him with what I guess she imagined was a flirtatious look I heard her say, "But Ben Sweetie, you have to come! Simply *everyone* is going to come!" He gave an emphatically negative shake of his head in response. His ugly scowl for her showed me the other side of the sweet boy he was trying to be around me. That was definitely the expression of a boy who would deliberately make a girl crazy for his own entertainment. That sneer cut through to the heart of me. Right. His reputation was deserved, no matter how sweet he was trying to persuade me he was. I was having nothing to do with him.

I was stuffing the sandwich container and juice box back into my lunch bag when a cold presence manifested itself beside us. A puffy navy blue coat and minus forty rated work boots stood beside our locker emitting frigid air. I looked up as puffy navy gloves appeared from invisible slit pockets and began to unwrap a hand knit red scarf that I recognized. "Hi Lloyd. Cold enough for ya?"

He shook the snow from his coat onto us and made us squeal and shiver, then innocently apologized. Shoving the cold gear into his locker he remarked, "It's cold enough out there that I think Toronto might actually have a chance at the Stanley Cup this year."

"Huh?" said Christie quizzically.

I smirked. "Hell freezing over?"

He nodded with a serious expression. 'Yes. I think so." He plopped down beside us and asked Christie, "Anything exciting happen in band?"

She shook her head. "No, but don't forget you have trumpet sectionals after school. He'll freak if you miss it after missing class." She studied him curiously, "So where were you? Were you skipping?"

He laughed. "Yeah right. I skipped to go hang out at the beach. No. Nothing exciting, just a dental cleaning. Mom had forgotten and told me this morning just as I was walking out the door."

I was looking at him as he talked, but my peripheral vision caught sight of Eris, the spiky haired twin, leaning out of the chem. room, glancing down the hall where we were sitting and then vanishing again. I was pretty sure she hadn't seen me noticing her. Without explanation, I had a glimmer of an image flash in my head, and simultaneously I had a strange feeling in my belly—a sense of dread that made my stomach churn and bile rise in my throat. I stood up with the wild look in my eye reflected in Christie's glasses. "Let's go!" I said urgently as I pulled Christie's arm until she was standing. "Quickly! Come now!" Lloyd rose with her as if attached on an umbilical cord, "Grab your coat, Lloyd!"

"What? Where are...?"

"Don't ask questions! Just come! Something is going to happen, come!"

I started pushing my way through the crowded hallway, panic making me strong and determined. I looked back over my shoulder to see Christie and Lloyd exchange looks that suggested they thought I was insane, but at least they followed me without argument and Lloyd had his coat over his arm. Looking past them, I saw what I'd seen in my vision: an arm reached out of the classroom and a golden sphere rolled down the floor of the hallway. When it came to rest precisely where we'd been sitting, it began to smoke.

Faster, get behind here!" I shouted and pulled Christie past me as I released the door at the top of the stairs. They must have caught a whiff of the smoke then, because their speed increased and we tore down the stairwell.

Above our heads, we could hear the shouts and coughing of the other students, and then there was an explosion that rattled the windows and set off the fire alarms.

"Did they think we were STUPID?" I shouted at no one in particular. "Did they think we were going to just sit there while that thing smoked in front of us and wait for it to explode?" We could hear the sirens coming as students streamed past us. It was thirty below and we were evacuating the school. Those twins were idiots!

Ms. Martindale was calling students, "Stay close together to conserve warmth! Quickly, let's get to the marshalling area at the elementary school; come along every one!"

It was pandemonium. As we walked away from the school shivering, our breath clouding around us, I was grateful at least to be wearing a hoodie. Some girls were in tank tops, and the students who'd been playing intramurals were all in shorts. Their sweat was going to chill them dangerously quickly. Thankfully, the elementary school was within sight.

Lloyd wiggled in between Christie and me and threw his coat over our shoulders, squishing us all together like a six-legged, three-headed monster.

Mr. Moore was already at the elementary school and holding the exterior gym doors open for us as the student body flooded into the building. He must have driven over. We squished as closely as we could to try to steal each other's heat, but everyone was so cold there wasn't much to steal yet. With Christie and I crushed up closely against us, Lloyd sighed a little too happily. I ignored him.

Christie tilted in to my ear and asked over the din, "Who did it?"

I shook my head, "I didn't see exactly, but it was one of the twins. I can't believe either of them is this inconsiderate or this stupid. What on earth were they trying to prove?"

"What did you mean back there when you asked if they thought we were stupid enough to sit there?"

"Just that."

"I don't get it. What happened?" asked Christie.

"Someone threw a bomb down the hall. It landed as precisely as a curling rock at the Tournament of Hearts right where we were sitting. I don't think that was a coincidence, Christie."

Lloyd looked stunned. "You think they were trying to hurt us?"

I shook my head. "No. I think they were trying to hurt *me*."

Obviously, classes were cancelled for the rest of the day. Word went out on local radio that we were waiting for rides home, and some of the parents showed up with coats and boots and picked people up. It was quite well organized as far as that went. I was kind of surprised.

Since we had Lloyd's big coat, we walked to Christie's house six legged, and then I borrowed an old coat of hers to walk home. When I came through the door, my mom was freaking out. She rushed the door and threw her arms around me as if I'd come back from the dead.

"Mom! Ow! Hey! What's going on?" I grunted as she squeezed the breath out of me.

"I was so worried when I heard the news on the radio!" she gushed. "I sent your father to go find you!"

"Why?" My mother was not prone to hysteria. The over-reaction was very odd.

She stared at me for a moment, taking a slow, deep breath. She stepped back and with determined calm remarked, "Oh, no particular reason—besides *a bomb* going off in your school, I guess."

"It was just a glorified stink-bomb, Mom."

"Yeah. I heard that. It wasn't anywhere near you, right?" she asked hopefully.

I didn't want to answer that question. "Um. Well." I met her eyes and shrugged, trying to be nonchalant, "Actually, if I hadn't decided in a hurry to get out of the hall, it would have been on my lap."

She swallowed slowly while emotions battled behind her eyes. "Oh? What made you move?"

I pursed my lips and shrugged again, "I don't know. Just a feeling."
She studied me thoughtfully. "Ah. That's good."
"Good?"
"Convenient, at least. Some people have strong survival instincts.
It would be handy if you did."
"Right. Because my life is so incredibly dangerous." I giggled.
She inhaled deeply and nodded, "Yes."
What? I tilted my head and met her eyes. "Mom, I was *joking*."
"Oh. Oh right." She was completely flustered. Finally, she waved
her arms toward the stairs and insisted, "Well, go have a bath and warm
up. I'll get dinner started." She turned and walked into the kitchen while I
stared after her in confusion. Why did she think my life was dangerous all
of a sudden?

*Smoke filled the sky. "Watch out!" shouted Mars from off in the
distance. "Here comes another one!"*
An explosion scattered dirt.
"I've got it!" O hollered,
*A black bearded man roared up the hill in a black chariot. Flames
flared behind him as his horse huffed and tossed its mane. "Come on, you
coward!" he shouted at O. "I'm ready for you!"*
*Xandros appeared from out of the smoke, a spear in his hand. He
flung it powerfully and the bearded man shrieked as it ripped through his
bi-cep.*
*Mars jabbed his own spear into the wheels of the advancing chariot.
It stopped rolling, and flipped over, dragged by the racing horses. The
bearded man was dumped onto the ground.*
*O raced over with his sword, but before he could reach him, the
bearded man, his chariot and his horses disappeared in a flash and
crackle of light.*

Because the bomb scare had happened on a Friday, there were a
couple days for them to clean out the air ducts and things, so school was in
session as usual on Monday. While the school had been empty for the
weekend, haz-mat crews had gone through the building and assessed the
damage. On Saturday, the media reported it as a particularly powerful
stink bomb made in the chemistry labs and reported that a student had
been put on suspension for it. I wondered which one of the twins was
getting a holiday.
As Christie and I walked to school Monday morning, we wondered

what kind of shape our locker would be in, since it'd been at Ground Zero. To our surprise, besides the lingering odour of smoke on our coats, everything was fine.

I watched curiously for the twins, but didn't see either of them. Two for one peace of mind. Meg was around, though, I saw her grumbling with someone that afternoon.

Though I watched warily for him, wondering when he was going to ask me out, I only saw Josh in passing. Aside from a nod of acknowledgment when I met his eyes in the hall, he seemed to be ignoring me. It was a little irritating to have been bold enough to agree to go out with him, and then to have him change his mind and decide I wasn't actually good enough for him after all.

Ben became a spectre. I passed him in the hall and he gave me the strangest look, as if he was ill. Apparently, I was nauseating *him* now. I had turned away with a flush of irritation that overwhelmed me. I made a point to stay away from him after that.

When I went into English class the following Friday, I couldn't help but glance over to Josh's corner when I sat down. He caught my eyes but turned away without acknowledging me. I pursed my lips in aggravation and flopped unceremoniously into my chair. Lloyd studied me thoughtfully.

"Got plans for a biker tattoo, Grace?" he sounded as irritated as I felt.

"Huh?

"Well, if you're going to flirt with the rebels and drug dealers, you're going to end up a biker's moll or hanging in a crack house, aren't you?

I glared at him. "Shut up, Lloyd."

He glowered back. "I'm not kidding, Grace. He is going to end up dead or in jail; you don't want to mix yourself up with that crap."

I fought the urge to hit him and turned away.

Christie came into class then and looked from Lloyd to me in our mutual postures of annoyance. I stared straight ahead, ignoring her, but couldn't help notice her questioning look at Lloyd, his head jerk to Josh's corner and her answering flash of understanding. She sat down beside me and murmured a quiet, "Hi."

I grunted in response, staring resolutely at Mr. Moore. Christie just settled in her seat, deciding in her infinite wisdom not to pry. However, although I was assuming the posture of complete attention to the lesson and even keeping up with the notes, half my brain was absorbed in processing my anger. It wasn't really fair to be angry with Lloyd for articulating exactly what I'd already admitted to myself. I knew Josh was dangerous, but he also seemed to need me somehow, and how could I abandon him when he was reaching out to me? Perhaps I was the key to bring him out of the cycle of addiction and violence he'd been born into? How could I ignore him?

The bell rang and I was jolted out of my stupor. Where had the hour gone? The page in front of me was covered in notes. I hoped I'd be able to make some sense of them, because I didn't remember writing a word of it. I glanced back at Lloyd and he met my eyes cautiously. I took a deep breath as I gathered my books and admitted, "You're right, Lloyd. I know you're right."

Christie looked back and forth between us again. "Is it okay, Grace?"

I was getting really tired of having people wondering how I was doing all the time. "I'm absolutely fine, Christie. Go to band. I'm walking home now."

"Okay. I'll call you tonight?"

"Yeah."

Lloyd went to follow her out of the room, but hesitated. He reached out and rested his hand on my arm. "Grace. Be careful. We don't want you to get hurt."

"Yeah, I know. You'd better go, and what'd you say? 'Make like Bizet…'"

He laughed a little grimly, trying to match my attempt to lighten the mood as unsuccessfully as I was. "Bye, Grace." His eyes were still concerned.

"Bye. See you."

I started to follow them out of the room. I'd resolved to make a decision of self-preservation. I would decline when Josh asked me out. I was pretty sure that he wouldn't be completely surprised.

I gathered my books at my locker and suddenly felt a presence behind me. I turned slowly, knowing very well who was behind me. It was creepy how he had snuck into my awareness when I didn't want any connections to him.

"Hello Grace." Ben sounded strained.

I scowled and turned away.

"Don't be like that, Grace." He sounded almost hurt. What a good actor he was.

"Don't be like *that*, Ben." I didn't like the sensations warring in me. I felt entangled in a web of emotions.

"What am I being like?" he sounded genuinely confused.

I couldn't have anything to do with him. He had power to crush me, I could feel it. I sneered at him in disgust, "Don't be an idiot chasing after someone who isn't interested in you. Leave me alone. I don't want to *talk* to you. I don't want to *walk* with you. I don't want to be with you in *any* way. Leave. Me. Alone." There. Even someone as stubborn as Ben could not possibly misinterpret that. I turned and marched down the hall, focused on moving forward without a glance behind me. I was surprised that he hadn't made any response. Maybe he had, finally, actually *heard* me.

My eye burned. A single tear travelled down my cheek and dripped off my chin.

CHAPTER SIX

SO MUCH FOR OUR PLEASANTLY INNOCENT DAY

Voyagers joyfully travelling, shocked by festivity ended,
Caused by a moment of terror, cushioned and safely defended.
Charis has reasons for doubting him, yet still she opens her young heart
Seizing a chance that astounds her, he overwhelms like a braggart

The hoped for Chinook had come and there was no need for a winter coat. It had blown in while we slept and Thursday morning we awoke to spring-like conditions as the snow dripped noisily off the roof. I put my headphones on and pulled my hoodie over my head, stomping up the road in time with the music thumping in my brain. I wasn't paying any attention to my surroundings when I was grabbed from behind.

Despite what had happened with Ben's nose, I reacted exactly the same way. Without a conscious thought in my head, my body turned and my fist crashed forward with full power, but this time there was nothing there but air and my momentum pulled me around and made me stumble. Before I could regain my footing, I was enfolded by brown leather clad arms, and the earphone was being removed from my left ear by Josh's teeth.

"Hi, Beautiful."

I growled at him. Literally growled. Like an angry dog.

He laughed. "You're slipping. Or else I'm just a better fighter than Ben Butler."

I glared at him.

My anger just seemed to roll off him like gumballs tipping out of a broken machine. He grinned benignly. "So Grace, I think it's time to schedule our big date."

I looked at him incredulously for a few minutes. I was tired of males treating me like I didn't have my own opinions. I was just plain tired of *males*, actually. Ben. Josh. Lloyd. I didn't want those mushy looks that made it too difficult to concentrate on anything else. I didn't need any of this. My eyebrows lowered and I shook my head, "No Josh. I'm sorry; I've decided I am not going out with you."

He smiled more widely. "Of course you are. I am picking you up Saturday at six and we're going out for Italian. You'll dress up. Wear a skirt. Be sure you look sophisticated, because it isn't a burger joint I'm taking you to, all right?"

I just stared at him in disbelief.

He turned to walk off in the other direction.

I turned after him, "Josh!"

He kept walking away from school.

"JOSH!" I wanted to chase after him and give him that punch that had missed earlier. "JOSH! I AM *NOT* GOING OUT WITH YOU!"

He waved a hand behind him dismissively.

Sputtering with anger, I stomped the rest of the way to school.

I made it through the day on a simmering burn. I glared at Lloyd. I glared at the empty corner of the English class that Josh usually occupied. I walked home by myself instead of waiting for band rehearsal to release Christie. I was foul company today. No point inflicting myself on anyone else.

When Christie called me that evening I was still too angry to want to talk to her about it. I was frustrated that I didn't have his phone number or know where he lived. I just had to hope he had taken my refusal seriously. I was pretty sure that he hadn't.

I figured I'd distract Christie from talk of my mood at school or the males who had caused it with band class gossip or shopping trip scheduling.

She short-circuited my plans when she casually remarked, "You know what, Grace, I think what we need is a day of carefree, childish innocence."

Wasn't that the truth. "Yeah. I really wouldn't mind a trip back in time when things were a little less complicated."

"Okay then. This Saturday?"

"What? Do you have a time machine booked?"

"Yes. I do."

"Christie, are you insane?"

She laughed. "Not at all. Do you remember all those Saturdays that we spent at the Calgary Zoo as kids? How great that was?"

I giggled. "How many photos do we have behind the 'World's Most Dangerous Predator' cage, do you think?"

"Exactly. Time for another one. What do you think? Good idea?"

"Awesome idea. What time shall I meet you?"

"Ten o'clock at the C-Train station?"

"Perfect. Too bad we couldn't skip school tomorrow to go."

She laughed, "You're becoming quite the little rebel, aren't you?"

She started to say something else, but I replied before she could utter it, "Fine, we'll be good. See you tomorrow."

I could hear her snickering as I hung up the phone with a feeling of optimism I hadn't felt in weeks. The zoo was a wonderful place to spend time re-living our happy days as kids. Christie was a genius. I crawled into bed that night and I drifted off to sleep remembering the bristly feel of elephant hide and giggling as I recalled the slime left behind when a giraffe wraps its tongue around your arm up to the elbow to take something off your hand.

We were so glad to see the snow melted away by the Chinook, that most of the school was outside at lunch the next day. We were sitting on our coats on the damp grass, soaking up whatever vitamin D was coming down. Christie had flute sectional practice, so Lloyd and I were outside together sitting back to back against each other with our eyes closed, my head on his shoulder, his head on mine, faces pointed upwards, enjoying the insipid sun.

I was trying to be civil to him. He'd been my friend a long time. He couldn't help that his boy hormones had detected that I was a girl. I sighed just as a chill of shadow came between the feeble warmth and us.

"Grace, can I talk to you?" said a familiar voice, and I looked up to see Josh standing in my sun, his ball cap low on his forehead with his tousled brown hair poking like a fringe beneath, his leather jacket unzipped in a tribute to the sunny day.

I bit back my angry thought when I saw that he looked really worried about something. "Ah. Yeah. Sure. What do you want?"

"Can I speak to you *privately*?"

Lloyd looked at him suspiciously.

I sighed, "Fine," and unfolded myself from the ground.

"Grace?" Lloyd's voice was apprehensive.

I glanced over at him and shook my head. "It's fine Lloyd." I stood up and followed Josh off a little ways. As we went by, a few people looked at us curiously. "What?"

Josh gnawed on his lip for a moment before he said, "I've been hearing some rumours in the smoke pit."

"Yeah, so?"

"Rumours about you."

"Oh?"

He looked at me without speaking.

"Are you going to tell me what they are or just keep staring at me?"

He shook his head as if he was sorting out some puzzle. "Grace, it's not good."

"I'm sure whatever it is it's just a lie. I'm not worried."

"You *should* be worried, Grace. Trouble is coming."

I sighed. I didn't need this kind of melodrama. "Don't be silly Josh."

His eyes were kind of freaky as he stared hard, as if he was trying to convey something profound. "I'm not being silly. I'm trying to warn you. You need to be careful."

I glanced back to where Lloyd was watching us vigilantly.

"Yeah. Okay. Thanks for the warning."

"You're not taking this seriously enough, Grace."

I saluted smartly and intoned, "I'm taking your warning under advisement, sir. I will 'be careful' as per your request. Josh sir!"

"Good." He was still staring at me; I could tell he didn't really believe that I was hearing what he was trying to convey.

I rolled my eyes. "What exactly does 'being careful' look like to you, Josh?"

He breathed deeply. "Watch. When your gut warns you of trouble, listen. Stay with people you trust. Just…" he shrugged he shoulders, "…be *careful*."

I felt a rush of tenderness for him. It was so sweet that he was distressed on my behalf. I reached out and put my hand on his arm. "Thanks Josh. I appreciate your concern. Really." Thinking about the bomb scare I added, "I am actually really good at listening to my instincts."

"Good." He glanced over my head. "Your friend is getting worried. You'd better go back before he comes over to attack me or something." He flexed his biceps with unconscious menace.

"Yeah. Okay. See you in English?"

"Probably not today. But I'll see you Saturday." He gave me another intense look. "Be *careful*."

"Yeah. I got it. Watch. Listen." I glanced over to Lloyd who was starting to stand up and looked like he was going to come over. I lowered my voice, "I was serious, Josh, I am not going out with you tomorrow."

He stepped away with a grin. He didn't argue, but only because obviously he wasn't considering my opinion. "See ya, Grace."

I sighed again, "Bye, Josh." This was so weird. Josh was giving me warnings. It didn't make any sense. Was this some ploy to ensure I'd go out with him?

Lloyd materialized at my side. "What was that about?"

I shrugged. "Nothing in particular."

"Do you *really* want to get mixed up with Josh Dagan?" There was a distinctly jealous tone in his words.

I turned to look him in the eyes, narrowing mine as I said purposely, "Leave it, Lloyd."

His lips tightened but he didn't say anything as the buzz of the warning bell called us back into classes.

"See you in English?" I offered penitently. Lloyd didn't mean to be a jerk; I knew he was just looking out for me.

"Yeah. See you."

The Light Rail Transit system was a fast and convenient way to travel from one end of Calgary to the other. We could get on only a few blocks from home, and get off at the Memorial station to walk across the swinging bridge to the zoo. It was a quick trip, and then we'd be in another world, winding along the river. I loved going to the zoo.

"Hey!" called Christie as she came up the stairs onto the C-Train platform. Taking full advantage of the warm spell brought by the Chinook, she was wearing a long layered skirt and a puffy white blouse with big hoop earrings. She looked like a gypsy. Her bright, woven purse was slung across her chest, bulging from the coat stuffed inside, just in case the weather turned.

I smiled. "Hi. Cute outfit!"

She laughed. "I felt like a hippy this morning." She looked at me appraisingly and remarked, "You, on the other hand, look like a warrior princess today."

"What?"

"Black boots, black jeans like some tough guy and then a girly top and that wild hair?" She laughed. "Definitely a warrior princess."

I didn't know what to say to that so I just shook my head.

Christie glanced at the platform, "When was the last train here?"

I understood her question. "There should be one here any time. I'm looking forward to this. It's been ages since I spent a day at the zoo. I love watching all the little kids. Even the ones who are crying are so funny."

"You're weird, Grace."

A distant hum informed us that the train was about to arrive, and we stepped closer to the track. I glanced at my fellow passengers. Beside us, there was a young family, balancing a couple of toddlers and a stroller. There was a baby in a pack strapped to the dad's stomach. Next to them was a businessman or at least a man in a nice navy pinstriped suit with a pale blue shirt and a rather eye-catching black and turquoise tie. Beside him was a boy about my age with greasy hair and very dirty jeans. On the other side of us were a couple of women chattering quietly in a language I didn't recognize.

The train arrived in a whoosh of air, bells sounded, and the doors opened. A few people got out. I helped the young family get their stroller in and the mom smiled gratefully as she pulled one wayward toddler into the car. He seemed determined to stay on the platform. I grinned up at Christie. The people-watching was entertaining already. The family took the last seat, so Christie and I stood close together, our hips against a seat, our arms gripping a pole. The businessman smiled at me lazily as he took up a spot standing next to me, his left hand gripping the horizontal bar above our heads. On the other side of us, the greasy teen-ager stared sullenly out the window, one hand supporting a tall skateboard he had balanced on the top of his foot.

Christie grinned and remarked conversationally, "I keep waiting for you to tell me, but after almost two weeks, I've given up. What happened with Ben after school? Was he mad?"

I stiffened. The air around me felt oppressive suddenly, vibrating like taut piano strings. I glanced around me in search of the source. Was it Christie's question? Someone around me? I studied the businessman staring off into space and the teen. No one looked menacing. I looked at Christie who was watching me expectantly. She looked calm and expectant as she waited for me to respond, so plainly she didn't feel the tension. A shiver rippled down my back and I shook myself free of the eerie feeling while I met her baffled eyes. "No, he wasn't mad at all. Weird, eh?" I shook my head. "He was just really sad about something that I had said to him in the office."

"What did you say?"

I sighed deeply. "Well, um," I avoided her eyes. "I called him scum. He, um, didn't think it was appropriate."

"Why did you say it?"

"Because it's true." The businessman was listening with interest, though he was obviously pretending not to.

"What did he do?" Christie looked confused. Apparently, this didn't seem to fit with her vision of Ben. It was time to ensure that she was better informed.

"Did you know Rae-Ann? Colby's sister?" I asked.

"Yeah..." she looked thoughtful, but still confused.

"Were you at the dance when she flipped out?"

"No." She looked at me carefully, and then I saw a light bulb click on inside her head. "Oh. Right. I'd forgotten about all that."

"What?"

"That she had been so obsessed with Ben and had made a huge scene at the spring dance last year. Poor Ben."

"Poor Ben? Don't you mean Poor Rae-Ann?"

"Well, that too, of course, but it was horrible for Ben. He felt so awful."

"He *should* have felt awful," I declared vehemently.

She looked at me blankly. "Why do you say it like that?"

I looked at her, stunned that she could even ask.

She met my incredulous eyes and explained, "It wasn't his fault that she imagined there was more to their relationship than there was. He was mortified when she freaked out at him when he was dancing with someone else."

"Was he dancing with Meg?" My eyes narrowed.

"Yeah, I think they were going out at the time, so probably."

"Ah ha." I was so right, and she was so wrong...

At that moment, three things happened simultaneously. First, the train slowed down for the next stop, so everyone standing was jostled together. Secondly, I looked up to see Ben entering our carriage with a look of acute anxiety, and thirdly, while quickly looking away from Ben, I saw that the businessman had reached into an inner pocket of his suit jacket, and had surreptitiously taken out a small, lethal looking knife. It was all metal, very slim, and no longer than five inches. The blade was about two inches wide by the short handle, but it curved into a vicious looking point. His eyes narrowed as he glanced toward my belly.

So the ominous sensation was legitimate. Here was the threat. I gasped involuntarily and he met my eyes, slipping the knife toward me as he took a step back. He bumped the skater. The skateboard that was gripped loosely in the greasy teenager's hands thudded to the floor. As the kid bent over to reach for it, the carriage jolted again and his shoulders rammed into the businessman's hips, tipping him off balance as well.

I don't know what I was thinking, but some crazy instinct took over. As he stumbled forward, I stepped behind him and I pushed my heel with all my strength into the back of his knee. He wasn't expecting that, I guess. As he doubled over, I stepped forward again and rammed my elbow hard into his neck, just below his ear. He slumped to the floor of the train.

It had all happened so quickly that it felt like I'd imagined it all. I hadn't made a sound and it occurred to me I should have been yelling, "He has a knife!" or something, so that others could help or at least get out of the way. Now there he was, sprawled on the floor in his pinstriped suit and it probably looked like I'd attacked him without cause. Oops. First rule of defence, get the witnesses on your side. Too late now.

The people around me gasped and stared at me with horrified expressions.

I swallowed hard. I meant to shout, but it came out as barely more than a whisper, "He had a knife! He was going to stab me!" Adrenaline was coursing through me, making all the lights brighter, all the sounds louder, and all the sensations more intense. Christie was staring at me with wide eyes.

The train had stopped at the station. Someone reached up and hit the emergency cord. People tried to come onto the train, but a guy from further down the carriage had moved forward and blocked the entrance near us. He shouted authoritatively, "Stay back! A man has been hurt!"

As the people around me stared, Ben materialized beside me. "Are you okay?" he asked urgently.

"Yeah." I was starting to shake. "He has a knife," I repeated.

The transit driver appeared next to us, and glancing up I could see uniformed men running down the platform toward the train. That was fast.

The driver demanded, "What happened?"

A lady beside us said, "This girl attacked that man. She *says* he had a knife." Her doubt was plain on her face.

Ben looked her in the eye and said, "If she said it, it's true." He unceremoniously rolled the man over. The pinstripe suit jacket was open. There was the knife, all right.

Unfortunately, all that was visible was the thin handle sticking out of his belly as a scarlet stain spread across his blue shirt and dripped into a carmine pool beneath him.

So much for our pleasantly innocent day at the zoo.

Of course we were hauled down to the police station for questioning, and I was sure we would be locked up for the next twenty years, but to my surprise about four hours later both Christie and I were sent home with our frantic parents. The police had identified the businessman as a runner for a biker gang. He was well known to them.

They'd asked me many questions, but obviously, they'd eventually decided I wasn't the girlfriend of a rival gang member or anything. The constable had shaken his head, "Must have been a case of mistaken identity. You're lucky you took self-defence training. It saved your life today."

I decided not to tell him it was fluky instinct alone that had guided my actions. Who knows? Maybe I'd absorbed my dad's hokey martial arts film moves by osmosis?

We walked into the house at five o'clock and dad went straight to the answering machine while mom followed me up the stairs looking worried.'

"It's fine, Mom. Nothing happened."

"But it could have." Her voice quivered with anxiety.

"Mom, anyone *could* get struck by lightning or hit by a bus any time. Years have gone by without any lightning coming after us or any buses running us down, haven't they?"

"Yes, but…"

She was interrupted by dad shouting up the stairs, "Grace, did you forget you have a date tonight?"

"What?" Oh no.

"That was a phone message from a young man reminding you that he'll be here at six o'clock. That's less than an hour away." He sounded happy. Weren't fathers supposed to be upset when boys came calling on their daughters?

Mom argued, "David, she shouldn't be going anywhere after today."

"She needs a positive experience to distract her from the trauma. It'll be good for her."

I shouted down the stairs, "I don't really want to go!"

"See, David?"

"Grace," he called up to me, "you need to do something fun. Go with this boy tonight, and have a nice time together!"

I didn't want to, but what could I do? I was too emotionally exhausted to be angry with Josh, now. I was too exhausted to argue with him about going on a date. I was probably too tired to be on a date either, but at least I wouldn't be alone with my thoughts. Suddenly my memory filled with red and I shivered. I would keep my promise and I'd go out with him *one* time. If I could convince him to let me pay for my own meal, that'd be even better. That wouldn't actually be a date. I went upstairs to take a bath and get ready.

The hot water had turned my skin a glowing red, but even immersed to my neck I was still shivering uncontrollably and my teeth were chattering. If I closed my eyes, I kept seeing that pool of blood spreading over blue. The pulse behind my eyes pounded the beat for throbbing, ever-widening concentric circles of scarlet. It filled my vision until it felt like it was filling the world. Neptune's ocean was incarnadine. I forced myself out of the tub, but the change in posture brought a wave of nausea, and I vomited up the red vision, praying that I wouldn't be tortured by nightmares.

What company was I going to be for Josh with my churning stomach and my scarlet visions? That was probably a good thing. Maybe I'd throw up on him. That'd ensure he'd never ask me out again. My body shook as I looked through my cupboards for the warmest dressy outfit I could put together.

The doorbell rang promptly at six o'clock. Somehow, I hadn't expected Josh to be so punctual when he was usually at least ten minutes late for English class. I wasn't ready yet, so I didn't have time to beat my parents to the door. I heard Dad say, "Hello there. You're here for Grace?"

"Yes sir. I'm Joshua Wyatt Ames Dagan."

Joshua? I'd never heard him ever referred to as anything but Josh. Where had the Wyatt Ames come from? Was he actually giving my parents his middle names? I chuckled, imagining him nervously facing my father like the boys in the movies.

My dad was continuing, "I'm afraid Grace has had a bit of a shock today."

Good. Perhaps he'd get me out of this stupid date. There was a murmur of talk. I felt embarrassed for Josh, but from what I could hear, he seemed to be managing just fine. I don't know why it still amazed me that he could be so self-controlled and courteous outside of school. I'm not sure why he needed a tough mask at school, but it was obviously the way he coped with his life. I wondered if he could get beyond it, or if it would always influence his decisions.

I stepped onto the landing and did a double take. My casual, "Hi," took on an astonished tone. Josh was... well, there was no other word for it... he was *gorgeous*. His unruly mop of hair was without its usual ball cap; styled back into tousled curls it was glossy and...oh my...really *sexy*. He was wearing grey flannel dress pants that fit in all the right places and a skintight black sweater. His leather jacket was clean and today it looked classic rather than worn out as if it usually did. Had he had it cleaned? His shoes were black leather oxfords instead of his usual grimy skate shoes, and they'd been polished to a high gloss. He looked like he was walking off the pages of GQ. I was speechless.

Josh looked up at me and time slowed down. A smile spread slowly across his face and his eyes twinkled as he drawled, "Well helllllloooo there, Beautiful."

Despite my thick sweater dress, I felt naked under his appreciative gaze. I glanced nervously over to my father, but Dad just grinned at me. I wondered if he knew that he was supposed to be more protective than this?

Josh reached behind him for the doorknob and ushered me out of the house calling, "Nice to meet you, Mr. and Mrs. Severin!" in a suspiciously sincere voice.

My dad just waved as he headed toward the kitchen.

I kept staring at Josh and trying to remember to stop moving my mouth like a shocked goldfish as the astonishment caught me over and over again. Who was this stunning replacement for the kid who looked like he slept in his baggy clothes and hadn't bathed in weeks?

He opened the door to a blue sedan and I was taken aback, "You have a car?"

"My mom's."

"Yeah, but, I mean, we're in grade ten. Are you old enough to drive?"

He laughed. "I failed two grades. I'm seventeen, Grace. It's not really something to brag about, but it comes in handy."

"You never drive to school."

"Well, no. My mom is a little protective about the car. She doesn't even really like to drive it herself to be honest, so I generally walk or take transit, unless it's some special occasion and I need to chauffeur a beautiful lady…" He grinned that lascivious look at me again.

"Do you do that a lot?"

"Oh yes. Several times a month. I like variety, so I rarely escort the same one twice." He smirked as he climbed into the driver's seat. "I say that so that you don't get any ideas. I'm not the kind of guy who is fond of commitment."

"Ah. Thanks for the warning." Good. Love 'em and leave 'em. That's exactly what I wanted from him.

"Just keeping it real." He said with a chortle.

The drive to the restaurant was companionable. Josh seemed to be making an effort not to tick me off again.

When we were seated in front of the fireplace at the restaurant and studying our menus he asked, "So am I forgiven yet?"

I sighed. "I'm thinking about it."

He smiled warmly and just offered a firm, "Good," before changing the topic to local sports.

The food was wonderful when it arrived and we ate enthusiastically. "This is a great restaurant Josh, how did you know about it?"

"Oh, I come here often. A cougar brought me here on our first date, and I've been coming ever since."

"A cougar?"

He grinned, "Yeah, you know, the ferociously powerful preying on the innocent boys..." His voice trailed off. I didn't know whether he was serious or not. I didn't know if I wanted to know.

He sensed my discomfort and changed the subject to English class. As he clearly intended by deliberately being light hearted and amusing, I relaxed. He was companionable. I realised I was enjoying him again. Maybe this wasn't so bad. Perhaps I could date someone like Josh, especially considering how well he cleaned up. I sighed as I set down my fork.

He smiled. "Grace," he said in a hushed tone, "Thanks for coming out with me, even though you didn't want to."

I smiled back. I was glad I'd come now, too.

"I wanted to let you know that I'm going to have to disappear for awhile." He watched my reaction carefully.

I just looked at him without replying. Was that why he'd been behaving oddly all week?

"I'm not sure how long I'll be gone, but when I come back, I would really like to see you again. Having you for a friend is the best thing about this town."

"*Are* we friends, Josh?"

He looked a little hurt. "Yes, Grace. We're friends. We talk together. We walk together." He smirked over at me. Ah, so he'd overheard my argument with Ben. That explained a lot. I still didn't reply, so he added, "I wouldn't even bother to come back if it wasn't for you."

What could I say to that? I was his one voice of sanity. How could I deny him? He could see me weaken.

"I will call you then. We'll go out for dinner again, okay?"

I nodded, watching him carefully. "Are you going to be all right? Where are you going?"

He shook his head. "Need to know, Grace, need to know. Trust me, not only don't you *need* to know, you don't *want* to know."

He was scaring me. I could imagine mafia wars and gang hits and crack addicts attacking him from all sides. Whatever he was doing, I was sure that it was dangerous. "Josh," my voice was plaintive, "don't do anything stupid, all right? Keep away from illegal stuff. Stay safe." I got a little daring in my distress because I added, "Stay here with me so we can explore our friendship." As soon as the words were out of my mouth, I regretted them. I knew very well that I wasn't going to be able to explore anything with Josh Dagan.

He laughed and his suddenly sexy smile made my heart pound. "Now that *does* sound tempting, but I really don't have any choice. I'll be back though." He got a gleam in his eye again as he lowered the pitch of his voice to a sultry purr and added, "Until then, I should give you a little something to remember me by, something to keep you warm at night."

"I…I d-don't think that's a good idea," I stuttered. My hands balled into fists on the table.

Josh reached over and placed his hands over my fists. "Grace, chill out. Everything is great! No worries." As he spoke, he leaned across the table staring into my eyes like a snake mesmerizing its prey. I was frozen. My heart was pounding in my chest and a warm flush raced through me. My head told me to pull back, but my body couldn't respond before he had rested his lips smoothly against mine, held them there a moment, and then pulled back slowly as I remained frozen. My jaw dropped and my eyes grew large as he collapsed back into his chair with a confident smirk. His hands slid off mine and rested on the edge of the table for a moment before he crossed his leg. It felt like a very seductive move even if it was moving away from me. His eyes hadn't left mine, and I could feel heat rising from my toes. I shut my gaping mouth; my eyes still locked by his. My thoughts and my heartbeats were racing each other. With great effort, I turned my head away from his gaze and attempted to focus on something, anything, by looking outside the window.

A body came into focus, then its face with its mouth agape just as mine had been, with an expression of shock etched into the eyes. I looked at it blankly for almost a full minute before recognition hit. I gasped as Lloyd dropped his eyes, turned away, and almost ran off down the street. Oh dear. Poor Lloyd. What was he going to read into that 'kiss' he'd just witnessed?

I heard a wry chuckle behind me and I turned back to Josh whose sardonic grin was almost a leer.

I grabbed my purse and went to stand, but Josh grabbed my arm. "Stay." It was a command.

I wrenched my arm away from him and attempted to glare at him. Commands again. What was it with these men always trying to tell me what to do? My heart was still pounding as I said as firmly as I could manage, "Leave me alone Josh." The adrenaline that had pounded through my system on the LRT was roaring through me again. I felt dark and dangerous.

He laughed as if I was a hissing kitten, "What? No thanks for dinner?"

Stepping away from his reach, I pulled out my wallet and tossed a twenty-dollar bill onto the table. "There. We're even."

As he boomed out another laugh behind me, I turned and stomped out of the restaurant, feeling like I had run a marathon. Suddenly running seemed like a very good idea, and although I didn't actually break out into a sprint, I did put on a burst of speed.

I raced around the corner and was stopped abruptly as I collided into someone with an "Oomph!" that knocked the breath out of me. My shoulders were gripped by strong arms that steadied us both. "Oh! I'm sorry!" I exclaimed, looking up apologetically at the stranger I'd attempted to mow down. Then I gasped again, "Oh!"

Ben looked grim, but he recovered quickly and smiled at me reassuringly. "Hi," he said softly. "You all right?"

"Yeah. I'm fine. "Did I hurt you?"

He laughed. "No I'm fine." He looked me up and down, noting my high colour and fast breath. He glanced over my head, "What are you running from?"

I glanced back behind me to where he was looking, wondering if Josh was coming after me. The street was empty. I glanced at the sidewalk before I answered. "Nothing."

"Grace?"

I took a deep breath, but stared determinedly at the sidewalk. I didn't answer him.

He reached down and tenderly lifted my chin.

I kept my eyes down.

"Grace, look at me please."

With a shuddering sigh, I raised my eyes to meet his. He studied me carefully, his hands resting gently on my shoulders. This felt uncomfortably intimate, and somehow very different from the feelings I had around Josh. Ben studied my eyes and then nodded.

"So who is he? What did he do?"

"Wha-? What?" I stuttered out.

He smiled knowingly, and then looked up suddenly, his eyebrows lowering and his face hardening. "Ah."

I followed his gaze, and met the sardonically amused smirk on Josh's face as he stood nonchalantly under the restaurant awning watching us.

Ben whispered, but his voice was commanding, "This way. Don't look back." He wrapped his arm around my shoulder in a deceptively casual way, and started walking the way he'd come. I could feel the tension in his body: his muscles flexing in his arm, his chest, and his thigh all pressed tightly against me as we strode purposely down the street. He looked so lanky and thin I wouldn't have expected him to feel like a body builder. Suddenly he stopped, and pushing gently on my shoulder he said firmly, "Get in the car." He turned and watched down the road, as I slipped into the passenger seat. He shut the door beside me, and almost instantly had his own door open and was sitting beside me. The ignition roared to life rather powerfully for such a beaten up old car.

He drove silently, occasionally glancing in the rear view mirror or over to me. A hundred questions were chasing each other through my brain, but I stared resolutely ahead. I'd been so angry with him for so long, but at the moment, I was just glad to be away from Josh. Was I over-reacting? I couldn't tell. I wasn't mad at Ben either. I didn't have room in my confused head to worry about Rae-Ann. I could sort this out later.

I had been so lost in thought that I hadn't noticed where we were driving, so I was surprised when he pulled up in front of Christie's house. "Here. Christie is expecting you."

"Huh?"

"Just go in. Everything is okay."

I continued to sit in the seat beside him looking like an idiot. Why wouldn't things be okay? He didn't know that Josh had just kissed me. Did he?

He smiled again in that scarily tender way and brushed my cheek with the back of his finger. "You did great today, Grace. It's all fine. Go hang out with Christie. Watch a movie or something in her basement."

"But…"

"Go." He stepped out of the car and came around to open my door. "Out you go, Sweetie. I have places to go and people to see. You can't sit in my car all night."

"Oh. Right." I got slowly and rather shakily out of the car at the same moment that Christie opened her front door.

"Hey Grace!" She didn't seem surprised to see me getting out of Ben's car. I wondered why, until Lloyd appeared behind her, watching with an odd expression on his face. Hmm. Maybe Ben did know about the kiss after all. How had Lloyd gotten here so quickly? Had Ben come for me? Why would he care who was kissing me? Even as I thought the question, I knew that he wouldn't want anyone but himself kissing me. A tingle ran up my spine.

I turned to him, "Um." What should I say? Here we were again. Finally, I settled on the most benign thing, "Thanks for the ride."

He laughed as he climbed back into his car. "You're welcome. See you around." He started up the engine and pulled away. The roar didn't seem as impressive from outside the car as he chugged off down the street. I watched him go, feeling more baffled than usual.

"Come in Grace!" Christie called out. "It's freezing out here!"

She was right. With a deep breath and an exhalation that rose in a puff around my head, I turned and headed up her walk.

Christie enveloped me in a hug. "I'm getting worried about you, kid."

"I'm fine."

"After what happened this afternoon, there's no way you're fine. I'm freaking out, and he didn't try to stab *me*. Why would you go out with Josh after a traumatic afternoon like that?"

"I didn't have much choice, actually."

Christie put her hands on her hips and frowned at me. "We always have a choice in how we react to things, Grace. It's the only thing we can control in our lives, actually."

"Yeah," Lloyd interjected, "You made a choice to let him kiss you."

Christie snorted. "Grace. You have someone like Ben interested in you, and you are being kissed by a low-life like Josh. You need to sort out your priorities."

"I'm walking home." I didn't need this.

Lloyd and Christie blocked the door. "Nope. If you're going home, you're calling your mom. Ben said you weren't to leave alone." Christie handed me the phone, but I dialled my dad. I wasn't doing anything that they suggested.

CHAPTER SEVEN

SOMEONE ALWAYS PAYS FOR HER VANITY

Mountains are gathering leaders in, deadly automaton powers
Forcing a terrible trial there, cradled below rocky towers.
Charis is facing awareness of love that has triumphed through ages.
Orpheus finally touches her; wisdom has come from the sages.

> The three warriors stood under ominously dark clouds. O paced furiously back and forth.
> "That was close. Do you want our help yet?" Mars asked.
> Xandros' sword clinked at his side and he smirked, "Yeah. I'm eager to get my reward." He wiggled his eyebrows suggestively and O's lips tightened.
> As Xandros laughed, Mars gave him a withering look. "Don't be an ass, Xandros."
> "Like you aren't waiting to join the fight just so you can get her for yourself."
> O shivered. "He was close, but it's still under control. I don't need you."
> Mars shook his head. "You definitely need us, kid. You're risking the world with this jealousy. Don't lose her again, just because of your possessiveness."
> O turned with a snarl, "You're a war god, too. Are you helping him?"
> "O, you know better than that. I have nothing to do with Ares' bloodthirsty, irrational approach to war. That's why I replaced him. I do my job efficiently, with the fewest casualties. We need to keep emotion out of this. You *need to keep emotion out of this.*"

O's eyes hardened. "I will not lose her and I'm not giving her to either of you. I have waited too long. I will defend her alone."
Mars shrugged. "Fine. It's on your head if Ares hurts her."
"Or kills her." added Xandros.

I'd seen the posters about the upcoming youth leadership conference in Banff, but I didn't belong to Leadership, so I didn't pay much attention to them. I was surprised when Ms. Martindale came up to me in the hall on Wednesday afternoon a couple weeks after Christmas break. She was a heavy lady with a booming laugh and a slightly eccentric enthusiasm that students laughed at behind her back, but were nonetheless genuinely infected by. She was a favourite teacher for her good humour and her willingness to listen to 'her kids.' There always seemed to be a group in her room, gathered around her chatting, or just using her tables for games at lunch while she marked. I hadn't known that she even knew who I was, so I was a little confused when she bounced up to me in the halls and boomed out happily, "Grace Severin! Just who I wanted to see!" She beamed at me as if I was her long lost puppy or something.

"Hi, Ms. Martindale," I answered somewhat quizzically.

She got right to the point and announced, "Grace, your name came up at the last student leadership class meeting as someone who would be a fabulous addition to our team. Several class members were ebullient in their praise over your accomplishments, so I would like to invite you to join the group and come with us to the youth leadership conference in March. What do you say?"

She had spoken so quickly that it took me a moment for my brain to catch up and absorb what she'd said. Ebullient. I wondered whether that was a compliment. "Um."

"Wonderful!" she replied enthusiastically. Apparently 'um' meant yes in her world.

"No, I mean, Ms. Martindale," I sputtered, "I don't know what it is, or why I would go, and what I would have to do back at school once I'd been…" I felt like I was letting her down by having questions, but she waved away my concerns.

"Not a problem Grace! Come to the class tomorrow at lunch, and all your questions will be answered." She grinned at me, as if sure of my agreement. "It'll be great having you in the class!" Then she turned and went chasing off down the hall after another student.

I felt breathless just watching her go. Where did she get all that energy from? She was wasted in high school. She was needed in a junior high. Grinning to myself, I headed off to class.

I went to the meeting, of course. The leadership class was full of familiar faces. There were students from all the grades there, and there was an air of expectation about them. I wasn't sure whether they had absorbed this energy from Ms. Martindale, or whether the positive kids were the ones who gravitated to leadership class. These were the kids who arranged spirit days, organized the school dances, and raised money for special projects. These were the students who made a difference in the school. They were the ones who planned to make a difference in the world, too. It was an interesting mix of athletic, artistic and studious types. The only group not really in evidence was the stoners, and that didn't surprise me. I always figured those kids were really only in the building to find out when and where the parties were. They didn't have enough energy to actually experience their own lives, let alone help out anyone else. I figured they were too busy escaping life, blowing it out in smoke or burning it out through their veins. I thought about Josh. He was a perfect example. He was always late, reeked of smoke that didn't smell like tobacco, and didn't really seem to care about anything. If he wasn't so irritating in the way he was constantly disturbing the class, I could almost feel sorry for him.

A small voice in the back of my mind interrupted my condemnation, reminding me that Josh did seem to care about at least one thing. I thought about his kiss at the restaurant and flushed again as I sat down.

Christie came through the door and grinned when she spotted me, "Hey! You came!"

I laughed. "Ah ha. So you're the one I can thank for my invitation?"

She giggled mischievously. "Oh no. I got dragged in, too.' She glanced at the door at the same moment Lloyd bounced through it.

"Yeah, Grace!" he shouted enthusiastically. I could guess who my nominator was. "I knew you'd come! This is awesome! Oh, and you too, Christie."

"So are you going to this conference thing?" I asked them.

Lloyd grinned, "It's going to be fabulous. It's at this amazing facility in Banff. We'll take all these workshops with other leadership classes from across Alberta and B.C. We'll come home pumped, and full of great ideas to try here. You *have* to come, Grace!"

"Have to, huh?"

"Have to. It'll be the event of the year." His eyes seemed to get darker, "Please come, Grace. It won't be the same without you.'

I glanced at Christie. She was looking away, her lips tight. Damn. This was a complication I didn't need.

"All right everyone!" called Ms. Martindale, "settle down!" She set everyone into groups sitting at tables with sheets of chart paper and lots of coloured markers, and got us talking about various projects within the school. Christie was pulled into another group, but Lloyd had manoeuvred himself into mine. He talked animatedly and kept trying to catch my eye. He made me uncomfortable. I liked him a lot, but I didn't want to endanger my relationship with my best friend. I breathed deeply. Someone was going to get hurt whichever way this went. A group of grade twelves was working across the room near the door. I watched them under my lashes, checking surreptitiously to see if Ben was with them. I was pretty sure I would have sensed him if he'd been in the room, but I checked anyway. Leadership was definitely something that he would be involved with, and it was weird that he wasn't here. I wondered whether he was just not at this meeting, or if he really didn't belong to the class. If I was being honest, Ben was the reason I was hesitant to commit to joining. I would actually love to be part of this group, but if Ben was at meetings, I wasn't sure whether I'd be able to stand it. I couldn't function in his proximity. It was too embarrassing to imagine trying to organize an event with him, or to meet his eyes, or... I had the strangest vision of Ben and me rolling down a hill together laughing. I shivered to shake it off.

"You cold?" Lloyd asked, "Can I give you my jacket?" He was already reaching behind his chair for it.

"No, no it's okay Lloyd." I lied. "It was a no source shiver. *I am fine!*" I hissed. "Put your jacket back." I glanced over to Christie's table, hoping she hadn't seen. Her hair was bouncing in a way that suggested her head had just turned, but she wasn't looking now. This was getting problematic.

"Maybe someone just walked over your grave, eh?" he suggested.

Thanks Lloyd, I thought, grimacing. *That* makes me feel *so* much better. I scowled at him in what I hoped was a very menacing way. Obviously he didn't take me very seriously because he laughed as he arranged his jacket neatly again on the back of his chair.

He settled back into his seat setting a penny on the table in front of me. "Here Grace, I *cents* you are getting annoyed with me..." he grinned while wiggling his eyebrows at me. "Penny in and I'll behave, I promise."

I smirked back at him in spite of myself. "Penny in?"

"Okay, it's not my best, like 'pen me in,' get it?"

I groaned. How could I be mad at such a goof? It probably wasn't going to make things smoother with Christie, but what was I supposed to do?

The rest of the class passed quickly as our group came up with all sorts of ideas.

"All right everyone," called Ms. Martindale, "that's all our time for today! If you can please bring your charts and stack them on the desk here, we'll go over them next meeting. I saw some really great ideas coming along, so I'm looking forward to some wonderful events! Don't forget to pick up your permission forms if you're planning to come to the conference in Banff during Spring Break. Good work today people! You have about ten minutes until the warning bell. See you!"

Students dribbled out of the doors in pairs and trios chatting and giggling. As I added our chart to the pile Ms. Martindale seemed to have materialized out of thin air. "So Grace, have you given any thought to joining us in Banff? We'd sure love to have you." She smiled winningly at me.

"Well, um…" I thought again of Ben. I really didn't want to continue if he was going to be around, but how rude would it be for me to say that? "Umm. Is this everyone in the class?"

She smiled even more widely. "Yes, we have a great group this year, and you seemed to fit right in, didn't you?"

I could see I'd have to be a little more specific in my hinting, so I asked, "Was there anyone missing today?"

"Oh, there's always someone missing. I don't recall anyone in particular though." She narrowed her eyes and looked at me quizzically. "Why?"

I blushed a little. I didn't want to admit anything. "It just seems like there are already so many people in Leadership, I can't imagine that you need me there as well."

Her smile became beatifical, "Oh Grace, a new perspective is always helpful, and always very much appreciated. I do hope you will come again to the next meeting and that you'll join us in Banff as well." She looked at me expectantly.

I didn't want to commit yet, but I could feel her sense of hopeful encouragement. "I had a good time today, Ms. Martindale. I think I'll come to the next meeting, but I'm not sure yet about Banff."

She tilted her head, "Fair enough. See you, then! You'd better hurry," she added glancing toward her clock; "the warning bell is about to go." No sooner were the words uttered then the bell sounded.

I laughed. "Freaky."

She laughed and turned to her desk. "See you, Grace."

After school, Christie met me at our locker looking flushed. "Did you hear?"

"Hear what?" I replied, stuffing my homework in my pack, and flipping it onto my shoulders.

"About Josh."

My heart stopped. I fought to keep my expression neutral. "What about him?" Inside I was screaming. He'd said that had to go away. I was sure it was some stupid drug run or something. What if he was hurt? Dead? I struggled to keep my breath even.

Christie shouldered her own pack and shut the locker door. She started walking down the hall. I kept step with her, waiting with increasing alarm for her to continue. She didn't say anything.

"Christie! What happened?"

"Hush Grace," she cautioned. "Just wait until we're outside. You don't want us to be overheard."

Now I was really nervous. My brain was churning.

"Hi Ben." Christie called out.

I looked up to see him standing by the office, talking to one of his friends. He glanced up in response to Christie's call and waved at her. He looked over at me and nodded his greeting to me. My lips tightened and I gave him just a hint of a nod in return. I didn't have room in my brain to be worrying about what was going on with Ben when I was so worried about Josh. I sped up, pushing through the doors. We waded through the crowd of kids waiting for buses and pushed through to the sidewalk. Once we were finally by ourselves, she started right away. "He's suspended."

I exhaled. Was that all? Josh was probably suspended twice a month. A rush of relief flooded me. "Oh? What for, this time?"

"For punching Ben." She looked over at me.

"Punching Ben?" I thought back to Ben standing in the hallway moments before; he'd looked fine to me. "When did he punch Ben?"

She looked at me incredulously, "He *didn't*, Grace."

"Well then why...?" I didn't have the question fully articulated before I knew the answer. "No."

"Oh, yes."

"How is that possible? Ben knew it was me who hit him." I shook my head. "I'm sure Josh knew. Why wouldn't he turn me in if they were coming after him?" This didn't make any sense.

"I was in the office when one of Josh's little stoner friends came out of Ms. Nemeth's office. She thanked him 'for coming forward' and actually shook his hand. A couple minutes later Josh was paged to the office. I heard later from Stephenie that he'd confessed to everything. Apparently, he was screaming at Nemeth that Ben had seen him in the halls and threatened to turn him in for skipping. They're going to send him to a district hearing to decide whether he should even be allowed back in school."

I could imagine exactly how this had all played out, but what was he thinking? Why would he confess when he knew perfectly well that it was me who'd punched Ben? Why was he covering for me? I knew that screaming at Mrs. Nemeth was an act. When he was angry Josh became deathly quiet; I'd seen it in class often enough. That was a performance in Mrs. Nemeth's office, not a confession. He was throwing away his education for nothing. Even if Josh had some crazy noble idea of protecting me, why didn't Ben come forward to tell Mrs. Nemeth that it was me, not Josh, who'd punched him?

Boys. I didn't get them at all.

I was glad to have reached Friday at last. There was just one more week before the Spring Break. I desperately needed a break. The bell rang and I headed for the stairs, rummaging through the paper in my binder for some project notes Christie needed. Josh had said he had to go away. Was the confession part of some plan?

I glanced down to make sure of the first step and then glanced back into my papers, my thoughts still churning.

Eris and Enyo were coming up the stairs laughing. As they were about to pass me I looked down and saw Lloyd on the landing. I nodded a hello to him but then did a double take as a look of horror crossed his face at the exact same moment that my left shin rammed into something. My left leg had stopped moving, but my right leg kept going, stepping blindly into nothingness, and then I was flying through the air, arms windmilling as I fought to grab something, anything, to arrest my descent.

My binder and papers flew everywhere. Several voices shouted out. Lloyd yelled, "Grace!" and like he was a homing beacon, I seemed to be travelling straight at him. He threw out his arms and I crash-landed directly on top of him.

He crumpled like a blown up paper bag with an expulsion of air that alarmed me, and then the two of us were on the floor in an untidy pile. He was lying perfectly still.

People were gathering around us shouting. I heard only a babble of sound. I felt Lloyd beneath me though, so I knew I hadn't broken my neck at least. I tried to move and to my joy, my legs actually responded. I rolled gingerly off Lloyd, until I was lying beside him on the floor, eyes closed, panting. I hurt all over.

"Lloyd." I whispered. He didn't respond. I opened my eyes and howled, "Lloyd!" If I had killed Lloyd because I was some clumsy idiot, I would never be able to forgive myself. "Lloyd!"

Mr. Swan pushed through the crowd then and met my eyes, "Are you okay Grace? Someone said you fell down the stairs?"

"I fell on Lloyd," I sputtered out, tears pouring down my face, "I think he's dead." I couldn't see through the tears pouring down my face as I whispered, "I killed him." He had saved my life, and I'd killed him.

Mr. Swan had been teaching for years, and he was good in a crisis. His authoritative voice rang out, "Clear back people, let's give them some air." Kids immediately obeyed by stepping back a step or two, but no one broke the circle around us. Light filtered down from the windows and a beam set a halo around Lloyd's head. I gasped. He was being sainted in front of my eyes for his sacrifice. I drew a shuddering breath and sniffed. Dear sweet funny Lloyd. What would we do without his laughter?

Mr. Swan leaned over Lloyd and put his fingers on the jugular. He looked over and said, "He's not dead, Grace."

"Oh thank God." I felt faint from the relief, but one relief only opened up the opportunity for greater pain. I had to ask, "Did I break his back?"

Before Mr. Swan could answer, Mr. Moore came running down the stairs with Mrs. Nemeth clattering right behind in her high heels. Mr. Swan asked if the paramedics were coming and she nodded, "Yes, they're on their way.'

"Check Grace, Dwight. She's the one who pitched head first down the stairs."

Mr. Moore came up to me then and had me move my legs and arms, wiggle my toes and fingers, before he finally allowed me to cautiously ease up into a sitting position. My eyes never left Mr. Swan and Lloyd. I was watching for the slightest sign of movement when Ben pushed through the crowd and knelt beside me.

He didn't say anything, but he put his arm around my shoulders and held me, while the tears continued to drip off my chin and onto my lap.

I whispered, "I thought I killed him, but they say he's got a pulse."

He nodded solemnly; watching Lloyd with me, he asked quietly, "You fell?"

I stared blankly at Lloyd for a while before I took a deep breath and replied, "I think... I think that I was *tripped*, actually."

He turned his head and studied my swollen eyes. "Oh?"

"Something hit me at mid-shin, and then I was flying. I didn't slip or anything.'

"Hmm" he muttered, nodding.

I cuddled deeper into his embrace as we sat watching the teachers trying to get some response from Lloyd.

The paramedics arrived at the same moment that Christie pushed through screaming like a banshee, "NO! Lloyd." Her agony pierced me. I had caused this pain. I would never, never be able to forgive myself.

The paramedics worked on him while I watched for any sign of life.

"His nose twitched!" I slapped my arm down on Ben's thigh. "His nose twitched!" Christie's howls hid my voice from the others.

Ben nodded, placing his hand over mine. "Yes. I saw it, too."

We stared as Lloyd's eyelids fluttered and a groan escaped his lips. "Oh, Lloyd!"

His head turned at my voice and unbelievably he actually smirked. "Grace."

"I'm so sorry."

He shook his head and said, "Grace, I've got to say—your take off was amazing, but girl, you *really* need to work on your landings!"

I couldn't help the little smile that quivered through the tears. The crowd erupted in nervous twitters of laughter. Leave it to Lloyd to be the clown even when being strapped to a backboard with his neck in a brace.

The paramedics levered him onto the gurney and Christie reached out and took his hand. "Be okay Lloyd."

Lloyd smiled at her fondly. "Well, all right, if you say so."

Ben pulled me up to standing and we watched them go. I felt okay. I knew I was going to hurt all over tomorrow, but that would be nothing. Guilt was pulsing through my veins. Ben squeezed my shoulders. "I am pretty sure he's going to be all right Grace."

"You can't know that."

He looked down into my eyes and then looked over at Christie who was staring at him as well. "I am pretty sure, Grace. We'll go see him at the hospital later. But I think it'll be okay."

I was shaking, so I guess I was going into shock. Again. I sighed, irritated that my body was freaking out on me again. Ben tightened his lips and his grip on my shoulder. He spoke quietly but authoritatively, "Come on love, I'll take you to the office. I think you should sign out for the rest of the day and get to the hospital yourself so they can make sure everything is fine with you."

"I'm okay."

He exhaled a chortle. "Yes dear, but let's go anyway."

I nodded weakly, and he led me down the hall.

At the hospital, my mom was far calmer this time, which was something to be thankful for. It did all feel like déjà vu though, as Christie sat on one chair and mom sat on the other while I lay in the bed waiting for Dr. Kyle. We'd been there a couple of hours when he finally pulled back the curtain and announced with a smile, "Grace, we've got to stop meeting like his!"

I grimaced. "Yeah, tell me about it. I feel fine though. I'm more concerned about my friend Lloyd. He's the one who absorbed the impact of my fall."

As he read my chart and listened to my heart through his stethoscope, he remarked, "They're giving him a bunch of tests at the moment. It's looking all right Grace, I think you both survived this battle and will live to fight again another day."

He smirked over at my mother, who was gazing at him gravely. "Seriously Blythe, she looks fine. The boy took the brunt of the damage, but he'll be walking out of here too. Everyone is fine."

Mom scowled. "I don't like what's going on here."

He nodded, "Of course not, but you knew it was going to happen, didn't you?"

She tightened her lips angrily while I looked over at Christie in confusion.

"Mom?" I asked, "What on earth are you two talking about?"

She transferred her scowl to me and muttered, "Never mind."

Dr. Kyle patted me on the shoulder in a very fatherly way and said, "Your mom doesn't like the fact that I'm seeing so much of you, that's all. You're free to go. I'll give you a call in a couple of days to check that we didn't miss anything, but I think you'll be fine." He signed my chart with a flourish and looked over at Mom again. "Blythe, this is just …"

She stood up abruptly and said, "Collier, I'd like to see you outside, if you don't mind?"

They stepped outside the curtain, and I suppose they moved a little ways away, but not far enough that we couldn't make out their voices. Mom was hissing in an aggressive whisper that was carrying easily down the hall. His responding whisper was not as loud, but his calm words were still clear. It was obvious that she was not being soothed.

"They're targeting her," Mom hissed

"Yes, but we knew it would happen, Blythe."

"It wasn't supposed to happen this quickly."

"Blythe, she is going to be able to handle it. Do you see how well she weathered this one? Not even a scratch!"

"Eventually they're going to be successful. So far, they've tried to poison her and stab her. They set off a bomb near her, and now they've pitched her down a flight of stairs. I think Lloyd foiled a kidnapping attempt the other day. She's not going to make it."

"I don't think so. She's strong Blythe, stronger than you and me."

"Stronger than Bright?"

He laughed. "No one is stronger than Bright. Let her be. It will all unfold as it's supposed to unfold."

"Ben should have been there. He is not proving himself a worthy guardian."

"He did his job, Blythe. His second was there. Don't make this into something it's not. She has to grow. She has to train. Let it happen."

"I don't like it."

"Of course not, this time you're a mother. That's a different perspective entirely. She'll make it through, Blythe."

I could visualize the grimace on Mom's face when she sighed at him.

"Fine. I'll bring her to your office on Wednesday to check that everything is all right."

"Fine," he echoed. "See you then."

Christie and I exchanged baffled glances as Mom pushed back the curtain and announced, "We're going now, Grace. Come on."

I didn't get to go back to see Lloyd, but Christie did. She phoned when she got home and exhaled her relief into my ear.

"He's actually going to be okay. I can't believe it. I was sure he was dead."

I visualized his crumpled form on the landing beside me and said, "Yes, I know. Me, too. What was the verdict? Did he break anything?"

"Just two cracked ribs, can you believe it? Apparently he'll be out tomorrow and he can go back to school right away if he wants, although they think that he'll be too sore to go for a couple of days."

"Yeah, I think I may be in the same position." I was stiffening up and longing for a hot bath with Epsom salts to soothe my muscles before I headed to bed.

That seemed to remind Christie that Lloyd wasn't the only one who'd been to the hospital. "So how are *you* doing?"

"Oh, I'm sore and getting sorer, but it's a small price to pay for Lloyd to be okay."

"Yeah. Hey, he said he saw what happened. What made you fall, I mean."

"Oh?" I remembered the look of horror on his face as I tipped forward. "What was it?"

"He said that Eris dropped something and Enyo leaned down to pick it up for her. She was leaning right across your path and you weren't watching, so your one leg ran into her and down you went."

"Huh." Interesting. "How come she didn't fall?"

"No idea. I guess she was lucky. Maybe Eris grabbed her or something."

"Yeah. Maybe." I replied doubtfully.

A voice hummed in the background on Christie's end and she remarked, "Sorry Grace, I've got to go. Do you think you'll be in class on Monday?"

"I doubt it."

"Okay. Take lots of pain killers and muscle relaxants, so you can come back soon!" I laughed in reply and she chuckled back. "I'll call you tomorrow."

"Bye Christie."

This was all too suspicious. Did Lloyd know who was behind all these attacks? Did Christie? Mom thought someone was trying to kidnap me. Did she mean Josh? I lay awake wondering, but I couldn't make any sense of it.

Lloyd wasn't back at school until Wednesday. He moved a little tentatively, but he was there. As we sat in the cafeteria, I looked at him goofing around with Christie and I was more thankful than I'd ever been in my life.

I hadn't spoken to Ben since he dropped me off at Christie's after that horrible 'date' with Josh—the date my mom seemed to think was a kidnapping attempt. That didn't make any sense.

I was so confused about my feelings. I couldn't believe how natural it had felt to lean into Ben's comfort. How right it felt to be with him. He was so kind to me whenever I had one of the crazy crises that were haunting me this year, but it *wasn't* right. It couldn't be. There was no reason for him to be so attentive unless he had an ulterior motive. Rae-Ann hovered above my head like a malevolent spectre.

Spring Break was coming and it was time for the Leadership Conference. I'd been to three Leadership class meetings so far and I was enjoying the mix of goofiness and hard work that seemed to be the hallmark of Leadership Class. I kept expecting Ben to show up, but inexplicably he didn't seem to belong to the class, so I handed in my forms and joined officially. Ms. Martindale threw her arms around me in a bear hug of joy when I did. It was a little weird how fervent she was, but kind of nice, too.

Friday after school we were gathered in front of the school with our sleeping bags and back packs waiting to load up the bus for the trip to Banff. Everyone was laughing and chatting enthusiastically. The bus driver called us to line up in pairs with our stuff. When I got to the front of the line I went to put my bag into the hold, but suddenly it was out of my hands.

"I've got it Grace, that's fine."

I stared at Ben.

He grinned and flicked his head toward the door of the bus. "Load on in."

"I... um... ah... thanks..." I mumbled as I stumbled toward the door. Christie was right behind me.

"Christie! Is Ben coming on this trip?"

She chewed on her lips guiltily, feigning innocence. "I don't know. Maybe.'

Maybe nothing. He wasn't just helping with the loading. I was sure he was coming. Damn. Damn. Damn. How was I going to avoid him now?

Lloyd came onto the bus then, and settled into the window seat behind us. He was jauntily humming "She'll be coming around the mountain when she comes" as if we were off to summer camp.

Christie and I knelt on our seats, leaning over the backs to talk to Lloyd and Riley, his seatmate. I was in the aisle seat. Suddenly, someone going down the aisle dragged a finger from my shoulder, down my arm, and wrapped my hand momentarily before carrying on to the back of the bus. It was an intensely intimate touch, and I felt heat rising. He hadn't turned to look at me as he'd passed, hand dragging behind him, but I recognized Ben's back. I took a quivering breath.

Lloyd had been immersed in his conversation with Christie and hadn't noticed anything, but he heard my uneven breath. "Are you nervous about the trip, Grace?"

I almost had a hysterical outburst. I fought it down with a choking gasp.

Christie looked over in alarm.

I glared over at her, and she glanced down the bus to where Ben was sitting with Paul, chatting easily. She met my eyes guiltily but quickly looked away toward Lloyd who frowned before he made a joke and reclaimed Christie's eager focus.

I looked down the bus, drawn against my will to Ben's eyes. He smiled across ten bobbing heads and it was suddenly as if everyone else on the bus had fallen away. It was a warm seductive smile, different from any that he'd given me before. I felt the rush of blood coursing through my system, and tore my gaze away as his look changed from seduction to gentle amusement. I had the uneasy feeling that he knew exactly what he was doing to me.

Banff is nestled in the Rocky Mountains in the national park that bears its name. The crown of the town is the glamorous old Banff Springs Hotel. It watches over the town like a European castle. Between conference events, we could hike, take a gondola up to the peak at Sulphur Mountain, or spend time lazing in the hot pools. The air was crisp and cold, blanketed in white, and the streets were crowded with tourists, bundled thickly in winter coats. Some were there to take photos, others to ski or to climb the ice.

On Saturday afternoon, we were divided into groups who didn't know each other, and sent through the town on a photo safari. We had to take a variety of group photos: beside Bow Falls, with an elk, next to a grizzly bear, next to a horse, with someone from Japan, with someone under five years old, with a senior citizen, with a Banff Springs Hotel doorman, among others. There were twenty-five different pictures required with only two hours to comb the town to get them.

My group of six was a mix of both provinces. There were four from Alberta: Rob from a school on the other side of Calgary, Kris from "Poland via Red Deer," and Tomiko from Canmore. There were two from BC: Surjeet from Vancouver and Claire from Salmon Arm. We were an efficient team. Canmore is so close to Banff, that Tomiko knew the town really well, and she was able to direct us around to find all sorts of places that the rest of us would never have been able to find. We tore around Banff, giggling as we posed goofily with the objects, animals or people we were required to capture for posterity. Finally, we were left with five minutes to go, and one last photo to get— the one with the grizzly. We were getting desperate when Surjeet remembered he'd seen a restaurant with grizzly in the name on the way to the Banff Springs. We raced down the road, spotted the restaurant and sprinted across the road hoping to find a stuffed bear to pose with.

The boys were all ahead and had already reached the other side of the road with Tomiko on their heels. Claire and I were neck and neck, laughing as we sped up to catch them. I grabbed at a stitch in my side and howled as I ran. Suddenly there was a squeal of tires and a huge car with blackened side windows came barrelling around the corner, aiming straight for us. I looked up in terror and stared through the windshield at the determined face of the driver. I gasped in shocked recognition. Claire put on a burst of speed, stretched back to grab my arm and heaved me toward her. The car raced past. It missed me by a hairsbreadth.

I heard Kris shouting what I presumed were Polish curses. Surjeet shouted "Get the licence number!" and Rob appeared at our sides as Claire and I collapsed on the sidewalk, hearts pounding, lungs burning.

"Holy shit!" Rob shouted. "Are you guys okay?"

I could just lay on the ground panting and trying to get my head around the face I had seen in the driver's seat. Could it be possible?

Claire spoke. "Yeah. I'm okay. Grace? How about you?"

Before I had a chance to answer, I heard a shout and racing feet. In a moment, Ben was on his knees at my side, his face right against mine, staring into my eyes. I was shocked to see that he was almost sobbing, "Grace! Grace!" I still didn't have enough breath to speak, but I reached out, wrapped my hand around his forearm, and smiled unsteadily to indicate that I was okay.

He was shaking as he bent over and rested his forehead on my shoulder. "Oh, God. Oh, Grace. I am so sorry."

I found my voice. "What are you sorry about *now*?"

He shook his head without lifting it off me and muttered, "I was supposed to be watching you. Oh crap, oh crap, oh crap."

"Ben. Stop it. I'm okay. I'm fine." I tried to sit up, but the weight of his head held me down. "Ben, get a grip on yourself. Seriously. Now. Get *off* me." My firm voice seemed to get through to him at last.

He moved, and I sat up. The rest of my team was looking at me in confusion. Ben's eyes were glistening with tears.

"Ah. Yeah. Well." I took a deep breath. "Kris, Rob, Tomiko, Surjeet and Claire meet Ben, my erstwhile protector. He goes to my school." They all nodded and attempted halfhearted smiles at him as I named them. Ben's strange emotional state was making everyone feel rather uncomfortable.

I glanced at my watch. "Well, time's up. Only twenty-four pictures on our safari."

I could see Ben gathering himself together. He dabbed at his eyes with his shirt cuffs, and then glanced at me, "Seriously? Twenty-four?"

Kris nodded, "Yeah. How many did your team get?"

Ben shook his head in clear astonishment. "I don't think we got more than fifteen. Wow. Twenty-four. That's impressive."

We started walking back to the conference centre. Ben started by walking closely at my side, but we weren't very far down the street before he raised an arm with studied casualness and dropped it across my shoulders. It wasn't romantic. It was clearly protective.

I didn't know what to think of this. I debated shrugging him off. I didn't want to give him the impression that I had forgiven him or anything, but even as I thought that, the vision of the car zeroing in on me came into my mind and I shivered. Ben's grip tightened and I snuggled into him, despite my misgivings.

At the banquet that evening, our team was declared the winner of the photo safari challenge. The next closest team had only nineteen pictures. We whooped joyfully and danced up to the stage to raucous applause. I think all six of us should have earned Best Actor nominations for the way we ignored the day's trauma.

Christie and Lloyd sat all through dinner looking worried. They'd been talking together in the lobby when my team came in, Ben's arm still draped across my shoulder. Lloyd raised an eyebrow as he observed Ben's black look, but Christie was the one to ask what was wrong. Both she and Lloyd gasped in alarm when they'd heard, but I scowled at them, and told them to leave it alone. To my surprise, they had. Sort of.

All evening Christie snuck me concerned looks. I was trying to be light and enjoy the festivities, but I kept seeing the car coming toward me, kept seeing that cold, determined face, and so I knew that shadows were crossing my face despite my best efforts.

Finally, the evening was over and we were sent up to our rooms. I couldn't relax. The room was closing in around me. I wanted to be outside, breathing fresh air and letting it clear my clouded thinking. I was picturing that face over and over again. I needed clarity. The room was too small for all the thoughts filling my brain.

"I'm going out," I announced to Christie.

"You can't go out. Curfew is in four minutes."

"I *have* to go out." I felt a call in the back of my head. I couldn't stay indoors.

"You'll get us into trouble, Grace."

"I won't get caught."

My hand was on the doorknob when Christie asked, "When will you be back?"

I shook my head. "I don't know. In a couple of hours maybe. Don't worry Christie, I'll be careful." I slipped out of the room, and crept out of the hotel through a side entry. Outside, the air was crisp and cold. I headed off down the road, my head churning.

I wandered around town, aimlessly watching the mountaineers and tourists coming in and out of restaurants and pubs. I wasn't really planning to go anywhere; I just needed to be moving, but an hour later, I stood at a viewpoint watching the moon and Mount Rundle with a tingling sense of awe. The glow of the faint light and the twinkling stars above the silhouetted Rockies left me without breath. I didn't need to move or to think. I just stood feeling the awesome enormity of nature exposed on a grand scale. There were no subtleties evident here: this was power, breadth, expansiveness. I felt very, very small.

There was a crunch in the snow behind me and I listened cautiously. It occurred to me that it had been perhaps a *bit* stupid coming out by myself. The wilderness was right on the doorstep of the hotel. While elk and deer were relatively benign wild visitors, cougars, bears or wolves were just as likely to wander the town at night. I suppose the bears were all still hibernating. Wolves and cougars would just be more hungry. I focused carefully on the sound. It was a light step: two footfalls. That meant it wasn't either a bear or an elk. There could be two footed predators out at night as well. The vision of the car careening toward me generated a momentary gush of panic, but then I felt a wave of serenity wash over me and I didn't bother to look back to see who was approaching. I studied the sky, trying to pick out the constellations above my head.

"It's pretty amazing isn't it?" he said quietly from beside me.

"Uh huh." I could feel that my pulse had quickened, but I concentrated on ignoring it. The wave of serenity around him was doing wonders for the wild convention of thoughts in my head. Peace was erasing my anxiety.

"Can you see Cassiopeia?" he asked conversationally.

"Huh?"

Ben chortled, "Cassiopeia, the constellation. It's that little zigzag of stars there." I followed where he pointed, but couldn't find a pattern in the twinkling above our heads. "Here, just a second." He pulled out a flashlight and made a slanted W with the light beam toward the northeast. There. Do you see?"

I glanced at him incredulously. "You carry a flashlight around in your pocket?"

"Of course. It's dark out, why wouldn't I?"

I shook my head and studied the sky. He was such a nerd. Sensible to carry a flashlight of course, but who did?

He drew the W again. "Do you see it now?

"Oh yes!" Suddenly the pattern seemed very clear.

We stood there quietly for a while before he commented casually, "Cassiopeia kind of reminds me of Meg."

"What do you mean? Because Meg thinks she's a star?"

He laughed softly. "Yeah, that too." He paused for a moment, looking at the stars. "The story is that Cassiopeia was an Ethiopian queen. She was really vain. She announced that she was more beautiful than the Nereids of the sea, who were famous for their beauty. Needless to say, the Nereids were completely unimpressed, and told the powerful sea god Poseidon about it. He forced Cassiopeia's husband to sacrifice their

112

daughter to a sea monster by tying her on a rock in the ocean in punishment. That's what reminds me of Meg the most. Someone else always pays for her vanity."

"What do you mean?" I turned to face him, curious now.

He gazed intently at me in the starlight. "Someone always pays when things don't go the way Meg wants them to. Last year it was Rae-Ann. This year it's you."

I watched the frosty puffs of his warm breath in the cold air without responding. I felt a little tug at my heart. I could hear the sincerity in his voice, and I realized that he hadn't lied to me. Someone had, though. I'd been deliberately manipulated. I remembered Meg and the twins smirking at me in the halls, and a rush of irritation with myself flushed through me. How stupid was I to believe them, instead of Ben?

He continued in the same quiet voice, tinged with what I took to be a mix of exasperation, embarrassment and annoyance, "Meg has a thing for me. I don't really understand why she keeps trying when I've been pretty clear that I don't have any romantic interest in her. I guess she believes persistence must always pay off. She hasn't figured out yet that her petty desperation is extra-ordinarily unattractive."

"I heard you were dating her last year."

"No. I never dated Meg. I danced with her occasionally at school dances because we have always been in musical theatre together and know some fun moves and routines, but I *never* dated her." He was unequivocal. I believed him.

"Did you date Rae-Ann?" I asked it quietly. I was afraid of the answer.

I noticed his lips tighten, and he stared without speaking for an interminable time. Finally, he nodded and said very softly. "Yes."

Something tightened in my throat and I felt my stomach give a little jolt. I swallowed, fighting back a wave of nausea that took me completely by surprise. I had never expected to be jealous of the mysterious Rae-Ann. I waited for him to continue while I willed my body to calm down.

He stared at the stars for a long time. I watched his face, realising that he wasn't an average, ordinary looking little band geek at all. Was it something in the night air that made him look older, taller and stronger? He was actually handsome. Very handsome. His face was carved and his cheekbones were high. His shoulders were broad. Why had I thought he was average? How had I missed this golden god in the bright lights of the school hallways?

Finally, he spoke very slowly, his eyes still on the twinkling lights above us. His discomfort was obvious. "Rae-Ann was the kind of girl that captured a lot of interest in the male population. She was very pretty, in a fresh sort of way. She was also a little quirky, which made her interesting." He paused for a moment before he sighed and explained, "I wanted to get to know her, figure out what was going on in her head. You know, figure out where she came up with the goofy little things she said." He shook his head, and finally turned to look at me. "What I found out eventually was that there was something very *wrong* going on in her head. She wasn't joking when she said odd things; she actually believed she had voices talking to her. By the time I'd gotten close enough to her to realize that she was ill, she had opened up her secret world more to me than anyone else. When I tried to step back, her voices," he sighed deeply, "objected." He paused again, remembering something. "I imagine you heard what happened at the dance?"

I nodded. "I heard something about it."

"Her worlds collided and it was horrible for everyone who saw it. I'm pretty sure that everyone who was there will remember it for the rest of his or her life." He grimaced, and looked at me intently. "It wasn't my fault, but I still feel rather guilty. I shouldn't have dated her, but she was sweet and fun and my curiosity led me to convince myself there was no harm in a friendship while I waited for you." He looked at me with agonized eyes, "I'm so sorry, Grace. I should just have waited."

I swallowed, staring at him as I whispered, "You didn't know me. How could you wait for *me*?"

He shook his head whispering insistently, "No Grace. I knew you. I've known you forever. I've been waiting here for you for years." He stepped to the side, leaned to me and wrapped his arms around me, pulling me close. He rested his head against mine, and I felt his lips brush against my forehead.

I didn't look up, because I knew that if I did, those lips would be brushing against my lips and I wasn't ready for that yet. His words didn't make any sense, but in spite of that, I couldn't find it in myself to doubt them. He obviously believed that he'd been waiting for me. Perhaps Rae-Ann wasn't the only one with voices of delusion in her head.

Somehow, it didn't matter. Right now, it just felt right to be in his arms. I wrapped my arms around his waist and nestled closer into his chest. He sighed with a mingled air of happiness and sadness, and kissed my head again. He murmured huskily into my hair, "Welcome home, *Amata mia*."

Ben and I snuck back into the hotel through a service door at the back door when an employee took some garbage to the bins. We didn't see anyone in the halls as we separated and made our ways to our floors. It was just after midnight. Christie was bouncing on her bed in her pyjamas as I snuck back into the room. She grinned broadly. "I saved your butt tonight," she announced melodramatically after I had almost silently shut the door behind me.

"Oh?"

"Ms. Martindale came by for room check at 11:00."

I blanched and gasped. "What did you do?"

Christie smiled, "I heard her next door, so I turned on the taps and told her you were having a bath."

"Wow. Good thinking. She bought that?"

"I think she was a little suspicious, but she didn't try to talk to you through the door or anything."

"Good thinking. Thanks."

Christie just smirked while she filed her nails and asked with nonchalance, "So, did you know that you can see the Rundle viewpoint from our window?"

I looked over at her doubtfully.

"That was quite a clinch you two had up there..." she said suggestively.

"You didn't really see anything. Nice try."

"Oh? Come look." She pulled the curtain open and gestured.

Hmm. She wasn't lying. You could see the viewpoint perfectly. Crap. "Is Ms. Martindale's room on this side of the building?"

She shook her head. "Nope, she faces the town side. Even if she had seen you, from here you could only see silhouettes. She wouldn't have known it was you and Ben."

"Then how did *you* know it was me and Ben?"

She lifted her eyebrows as if I was stupid. "Who else would come find you like that?"

I tilted my head thoughtfully. A few faces passed through my head, but I blocked them out.

"So did you two get everything sorted out?"

I nodded, sitting down on the bed and slipping off my pants.

"Are you going out with him now?"

I shrugged. "I don't know. It didn't come up."

"But you're not angry with him anymore?"

"No."

"And you like him?"

I climbed into the bed as I answered, "Yes."

"A lot?"

115

"Yeah." I smiled softly to myself.

"So he's probably going to ask you out."

I sighed, "I guess it's inevitable."

Christie laughed from under her own covers. "That's what we kept telling you."

CHAPTER EIGHT

INVISIBILITY IS QUITE PEACEFUL

Close to the heart of the music, Charis finds love between grace notes.
Orpheus carries her skyward, while the Hesperides trace hopes
Glowing and golden in air above; smoking explosion throws them down.
Stepping into an abyss of black, quickly descending toward ground.

We returned to school and gave our report to the rest of the Leadership class about the conference. None of us mentioned the most profound thing that had happened and I avoided it, too. We had reported the incident to the Banff RCMP, of course. Between them Surjeet and Kris had figured out the licence plate and the make of the car, but I hadn't told anyone what I knew. No. What I feared.

As we'd been clearing out of the conference centre, Claire had come over to me with a warm smile. "Hey Grace, how're you doing? Had any other near death experiences since yesterday?"

"No, have you saved anyone since me?"

She laughed. "No, but the day's just begun. Give me time."

Ms. Martindale's voice boomed out over the chatter of the students mingling in the lobby over their farewells, "Redman students! Our bus departs in five minutes!"

I looked at Claire. "'That's me."

"Oh okay. Well, listen Grace. You said that you sometimes get to the Shuswap, right?"

"Yeah," I nodded, "my aunt lives in Salmon Arm so we usually get there for a week every year."

She shoved a slip of paper into my hand. "Here are my email address and phone number. Get in touch with me when you come, and we can get together, okay?"

I smiled at her as Ms. Martindale put her hand on my shoulder, "Time to go Grace."

"Right. Bye Claire. Thanks again for the rescue."

She waved as I was ushered to the bus. Ben was waiting at the door for me. He grinned, giving me his hand to guide me up the stairs and whispered, "Save me a seat."

I nodded.

Back at school, everything was different now. Thanks to my intimate knowledge of Ben's schedule, it was easy to ensure I was in the right hallway between every class, if only just to share airspace. Sometimes we did nothing more than look at each other as we passed, but the looks were deep and warm. Sometimes one of us reached out a hand, and we touched briefly as we passed. On those days, I would walk into class tingling to my toes, and would find it almost impossible to concentrate on whatever the lesson was that day.

Sometimes I hated that Ben, Christie and Lloyd were involved in so many school music programs, because their lunch hours were always being taken with group, sectional or solo practice time. Today it was jazz band and jazz choirs practicing together for the Big Band Dance, so none of them was around. I ate my lunch with Bonnie and Taylor again, feeling a little out of sorts. Bonnie was her usual self, and embarrassed me by asking about my blossoming relationship with Ben. I just blushed and studied the floor, which she seemed to find terribly amusing. I managed to flee with about ten minutes left before start of afternoon classes, and stood for way too long at my locker pretending I actually had stuff to look at as I took out various binders and leafed through them.

"Hey." Ben smiled as he came and stood beside my locker. Strange how a simple syllable had the ability to melt my heart into mush.

"Hey." I closed the binder I was leafing through and pushed it back onto the shelf, feeling heat emanating from my chest and burning through my body.

"Are you free after school?"

Hope flared and then died. Crap. I wasn't. I said sadly, "I have to work on some science stuff that's due tomorrow." I was wishing I wasn't such a procrastinator now.

"Hmm. That should be okay. I was just wondering if you'd come into the band room while I work on a piece. I could use some inspiration. You don't have to do anything, so you can bring your homework into the studio and do it while I'm working."

"You just want me *there*?"

His smile curled around my heart and started purring. "Yes."

"Sure." He was making me breathless. "Shall I meet you there?"

"We'll find each other."

"Yeah, okay. See you then," I replied airily as the warning bell sounded. This would be my first time back in the band room after the unceremonious and rather traumatic trip to the hospital in September. I had been superstitiously avoiding it, mostly since it was the place I was most likely to come across Ben, and of course, up until lately, I had been masterfully avoiding him. I couldn't help but wonder what was going to happen when I heard his music again. Did he still have the power to play me into unconsciousness? Should I ask the office to put an ambulance on stand by?

I fretted about it all afternoon, giving only part of my attention to the teachers and my class work.

I met Christie at the end of the day at our locker. Why do you look so worried?"

Damn. I tried to look casual, "Do I?"

"Yeah, you look like you expect to be mowed over by a truck any moment. What's up?"

"Ben asked me to come listen to him compose."

"Oh yeah? That's nice." She was shelving her books into the locker and only half listening. She turned at my silence and I grimaced at her. Her brows lowered in confusion. "Isn't it? Why are you looking like that?"

"Christie, remember what happened the *last* time I was in the band room listening to his music?"

She exhaled a deep "ohhhh" of understanding. "Right. I hadn't thought about that. Hmm." She looked at me carefully for a moment. "Do you want me to come along, just in case something happens again?"

"I think he'll be able to handle it if I pass out again, but I am more worried about what the ramifications of fainting would be. I don't want to have to go to the hospital after every visit to the band room." I sighed with a melodramatic air. I didn't want Ben to feel guilty over making me faint.

"I see your point. I'm coming."

"Christie, you don't have to…"

"Nope. I'm coming. Let me grab my flute." She looked over my head and smirked. "Looks like he was worried you weren't going to show."

I glanced behind to see Ben strolling up the hall.

He waved, "Hi. You coming?"

"Yes, we're on our way. Christie is going to do her flute practice at the same time."

He nodded. "There were still a couple of practice rooms free when I left just now." He stopped beside me. "Can I take your binder for you?"

"Um. Sure." He was carrying my books for me. How cute. I smirked in spite of myself.

"Is there a problem?" he queried, his brow wrinkling adorably.

"No, everything is good." I smiled to myself then glanced at Christie asking, "Do you need anything else?" She shook her head, and I shut the locker up. I smiled at Ben. "Ready."

"Good." He reached out and took my hand.

I felt my face burning as we walked down the hall. Even though there was hardly anyone around now, I was sure that this would attract attention. Sure enough, as we passed Ms. Martindale on her way to the office she glanced at our hands first before she looked up to our eyes and said with a significant smile, "Well *hello* Grace. Ben."

I blushed as Ben gave my hand a squeeze, and glanced at Christie to see if she'd heard the same tone of amusement that I'd interpreted.

Christie smirked back at me.

There was still one practice room free, so Christie headed straight for it, while Ben led me into the room he used the most. The recording studio was arrayed with three keyboards of various types, a drum machine, a microphone, a mixer and various other complicated devices that were all boxes and knobs and dials.

He indicated a corner where I could spread out my books.

"Um, Ben?"

"Yeah?"

"Isn't it going to be a noise problem if I'm writing, turning pages and breathing while you're recording?"

He smiled. "No, not today. I'm doing digital recording so it goes from one machine to the other directly. If I was singing or on the acoustic piano you'd have to leave, but for this kind of work you can make as much noise as you like. I'll be wearing headphones as well, so you won't even hear anything I'm doing." Then a thought must have crossed his mind because he added, "Do you mind? You might have been expecting to listen?"

"No, I don't mind." I didn't mind at all. I was still marvelling at the idea that he just wanted me close while he was working. That was insane.

He gave me a smile as he sat down on his wheeled stool, but once he'd put on his earphones it was like the rest of the world dropped away for him. I heard the keys of the synthesizer tapping, saw his whole body following his hands, watched him tweak dials and push the sliding knobs, but not once did he turn around and acknowledge my presence in the room. He had said he just wanted me there, but it was weird to be so thoroughly ignored.

I worked on my science, but I kept looking up at him, hoping to catch him checking on me. Nothing. It was as if I didn't exist.

Finally, from the corner of my eye I saw him reach up to remove his earphones and I lifted my head as he beamed down at me. "That was fabulous," he grinned. "You were a big help. Thanks."

"Oh, come on." I countered, "How was I a help?"

"Ah Grace. You were the inspiration I needed. That's been a particularly uncooperative section and it's been an irritation for a week. Now, it's perfect because you were here."

"You're crazy." I observed as I closed my binder.

He laughed, reaching his hand down to pull me up. "Nope," he said, pulling me close to him and whispering with his lips against mine, "just in love."

I caught my breath and leaned back, "I think that's the same thing."

He touched my cheek as he looked into my eyes with the depths of the oceans sparkling at me. We stared at each other for a moment before he said, "Come, I'll drive you home."

"What about Christie?"

"Oh, right." He turned behind him to look out the studio window. "She's probably ready to go as well."

We walked out, my hand in his again, and looked into the practice rooms. They were all empty, but when we turned around there was a note on the white board, "Grace: 4:30. Walking home. Call you later! Christie."

"Looks like we're on our own. She left this note at four thirty? What time is it now?"

"Five thirty."

"Oh, no! My parents are going to kill me."

"Calm down Grace, I'll go in and explain. I'm sure it'll be all right."

We shut the door to the band room behind us and Ben called down the hallway, "Good night, George!"

There was a faint murmur of response in the distance as the outside door closed with a thunk.

As we walked out to his car, I asked, "Why do they let you stay in the school so late?"

"The janitors don't lock up until seven."

"So? They let kids just hang out until they leave?" I asked

121

incredulously.

He shrugged his shoulders as he opened the passenger door for me, "Mr. J arranged it back when I was in grade ten. Before they leave, they check that I'm out. Usually I let them know when I'm going. Sometimes I would work all night if they didn't kick me out. It'll be nice to have my own studio someday so I can stay up all night working if I want."

"Sounds like an awful thing working twenty-four hours a day." I couldn't imagine it.

He laughed. "Well Grace, if you love what you do it isn't really *work* is it?"

When we pulled up at my house my mom's car was gone. I hoped she wasn't out combing the streets for me.

Ben followed me up the walk. "Dad?" I called as we stepped into the entry. "Anyone home?"

"Downstairs, Grace!" Dad called back.

I went to the top of the stairs and asked, "Where's Mom?"

"She went off to hear a poetry recital up at the university. Do you need her for anything? She's probably got her cell with her." He sounded decidedly nervous.

"No, I'm good. When did she leave?"

"Early. Four o'clock or something, why?"

"Just curious. What are you doing down there, Dad?"

"I'll be up in a minute."

I smiled at Ben. "Looks like no one noticed I wasn't here. So you can go if you like."

"Or I could stay for awhile," he took a step forward.

"Yes but…" But what? Hmm. There was no real reason for him not to stay, except that I didn't think that my Mom trusted him. Come to think, after the tone of voice he'd just used, I didn't trust him either. I stepped back in confusion as he chuckled behind me.

"Ah Grace, you're priceless."

Dad appeared at the top of the stairs, wiping his hands on a towel. He looked up with surprise when he saw Ben standing beside me. "Ah. Uh. Hello there. Ben, right? Good to meet you."

"Thank you sir," Ben replied, confidently extending his right hand for Dad to shake.

Dad indicated the towel, looking over at me. "I'm trying to make a gift for your mother. I'm not sure it's going very well, but we'll see how it turns out in the end. Don't mention anything; I want it to be a secret."

I laughed, "Sure thing."

Watching Ben, he asked, "So you kids have plans for the evening?"

"Ah…" He sounded like he wanted us out of the house. I stuttered, "Not really."

Ben recognized an opportunity when he heard it, though. "I would like to take Grace out for dinner and a movie, if you don't mind? I can have her back by around midnight if that's all right with you?"

Dad leapt at it. "Sounds great!" He turned around and headed back toward the basement stairs without bothering to ask where we were going, what we were going to see, or precisely when we'd be back as Mom would have.

I glanced at Ben, who stood looking pleased and amused. He raised an eyebrow and said, "Well, Grace, are you going to go get ready?"

"Um, yeah, I guess so…" I shrugged my shoulders as he chuckled behind me. I went up the stairs feeling rather shell-shocked.

I had been staring into my closet for a minute or two when I felt his eyes behind me. I turned and he was smiling in the open door way.

"Nice room," he said with a grin as he poked his head in. "Can I come in?"

"Ah, yeah. Sure"

He stepped in and stood behind me, looking into the closet too. "Girls' closets are always so interesting."

"Oh? Are you in the habit of exploring girls' closets?"

He laughed. "I'm just saying."

"Yeah, yeah. So where are we going? Should I be formal or casual?"

"Here," he said, reaching in and taking a low cut royal blue wrap dress off the rod. Holding the curl of hanger he arranged the dress in front of me and leaned back until his arm was outstretched, sweeping his slightly squinted eyes up and down appraising the potential. "Yup. I vote for this one."

"Really?" I'd bought it to wear at a family wedding last year. I don't think I'd even looked at it since.

He laughed that warm chuckle that melted me every time, and I just reached out my hand for the hanger, defeated. "Go downstairs. I'll be down in ten minutes."

"Sure. I'll phone around and see where we can get reservations."

It was clear that this wasn't going to be a casual evening.

Nine minutes later, I stood at the top of the stairs showing more cleavage than I was used to showing and feeling more than a little precarious on my three-inch heels. I took a deep breath and Ben looked up with a gaze that swept me up and down as his smile slowly spread wider and wider. He glanced at his watch and cavalierly remarked, "Wow.

Impressive, a woman who's ready on time!"

I stuck my tongue at him and he laughed good-naturedly.

"Now *that* totally spoils that sophisticated look, and you were really rocking it for a minute."

"Yeah yeah. Whatever. Did you get reservations?"

"Yup. We have lots of time, but let's get on the road."

"Where are we going?" I asked as he opened the passenger door for me.

He smiled coyly. "Wait and see."

I waited. He drove down Deerfoot Trail and was only passed by two cars doing over 150 down the freeway for once. At Memorial Drive, he turned and headed into the downtown core. "Where...?"

"Shhh. Close your eyes." I shut them obediently as he drove on. He slowed and turned a few times, and then stopped. "Eyes still closed?"

"Yes."

Gently guiding my elbow, he helped me ease out of the car and set down onto concrete. "Just a sec.," he said, opening a car door again, and then shutting it. "Okay, let's go."

"Where are we?"

"You'll see." He chuckled and guided me into a building. I tried to peek through my lashes, but we were in a parkade, and there was nothing to see. I heard an elevator open and we stepped inside. "Here," he said as the elevator door closed, "You can open your eyes now."

At that moment, a disembodied voice announced, "Welcome to the Calgary Tower" and began a spirited recitation of the history and elevation as we ascended. My stomach was still at ground level.

"I've never actually been up here before," I said queasily, looking around the spacious elevator. It looked like it could have held twenty people, but we were the only ones in it. I watched Ben as he stretched out his arm, slipping into a jacket. "Hey, where'd you get a suit jacket?"

"Conveniently, it was in the back seat of the car." He grinned, as he pulled a tie out of the pocket and wrapped it around his neck.

We were moving quickly. A minute of travel and we'd rise almost two hundred metres, according to the voice coming out of the ceiling. No wonder my stomach was surging. Ben looked relaxed. "This speed doesn't bother you?" I asked.

He smirked as he tugged the knot and tucked his tie inside the jacket, "Not this slow speed! We have reservations at the restaurant for seven thirty, so we have time to go out onto the observation deck first."

By the time the elevator door opened, Ben had been transformed. For some reason he looked taller in his suit, and his boring brown hair appeared golden again in the evening light. His dark grey jacket was cut to broaden his shoulders somehow. I looked at him surreptitiously from under my lashes as he walked ahead of me and wondered what had made him suddenly so much better looking. It was freaky how much he changed from moment to moment. Normal people didn't do that.

We walked around the deck, looking through the mounted telescopes at the familiar landmarks and watching the sun as it inched across the prairie toward the Rockies.

"Can you see your house over there?" he asked, one arm draped across my shoulder, the other gesturing into the distance.

"Don't be silly, you can't see my house from here."

He laughed, "Sure you can: it's right there." He pointed off to the southwest.

"You're an idiot."

"You think I'm joking? Look, follow the roads; there's Elbow Drive... Do you see the school? Now a little to the left? Can you see your neighbour's big tree? Then the red roof next to it? That's your house."

"The little red dot by the green dot waaaay over there?"

He laughed, "Yeah."

"I'm totally freaked out that you know where my house is from this far away." I said, lifting my head from the binoculars and looking at him with wide eyes.

"Oh I know." He grinned and met my eyes frankly, "You're not the only stalker..."

"Hey!" I exclaimed with mock anger, "I'm *not* a stalker." I was mortified. I felt a blush rising.

He chuckled, "Stalker, reverse stalker. Whatever. It all adds up to the same thing in the end." I could feel the pulse in my ears and knew they were flaming red. How did he know this? He smiled fondly and changed the subject in a not so subtle distraction from my humiliation, "Come here, you should try this."

"What?"

"Glass floor—it's quite freaky to walk on!" He stayed on terra firma, but swung me out onto the transparent floor.

It was as if I'd stepped into nothingness. My head spun a little as my brain noticed I was in the sky, though my feet were definitely on something firm. My stomach turned again. "Yeah. This is *interesting...*" I said, reaching to the bar along the window to touch some security. It was dizzying.

He laughed, stepping out to join me in the air. "Look how the tower looks like it bends away—cool eh?"

It was a little too visceral to be cool, actually. "Um. Can we go to the regular floor now?" I asked, staring longingly at the abstract art woven into the carpet just four feet away.

He laughed, thoroughly enjoying my discomfort. "Sure." I closed my eyes to eliminate the dizzy sensation of walking on air as he took my elbow and led me off the glass. "Here we are, and," he glanced at his watch, "it's time for us to go down to dinner." He offered me an elbow like court dancer and intoned, "Come along, my darling."

My darling. Sheesh. I tried to breathe deeply enough to keep the blush from my face as we took the curving stairs down to the restaurant. As we walked into the warmly decorated room glowing with the beams of the almost horizontal setting sun, he said casually, "So Grace, fair warning, this is a *revolving* restaurant. I don't want you to be alarmed if you notice it moving…"

"Moving!" Oh my. Now that he mentioned it, I could feel a vague rumbling beneath my feet.

Ben smiled at the hostess, who took his name, checked it off in the reservations book and then walked us along the curved path. I could see the sun almost at the horizon line above the mountains as we walked to a huge semi-circular booth. "Here you go sir, ma'am," she said, with a sweep of the arm.

Fifteen years old and already, I was a 'ma'am.' I didn't think I looked *that* old. We slid into the booth and Ben stayed close beside me. The shape of the booth arced, open to the city beneath us.

"It's going to be a gorgeous sunset tonight," he remarked casually as he looked up from the menu. "Do you have any idea what you'd like to order?"

I stared at the mouth-watering selections in combinations of items that I'd never heard of. I sighed, "No idea. Everything looks amazing."

"Are you really hungry?"

I considered the way my stomach was heaving, "No, not terribly."

"How would you like to share this game platter?" He pointed to it on the menu. "It's a monstrous meal for one, but between us it should be comfortable, and still leave us room for dessert."

I read the description and raised my eyebrows, "Oh my."

He laughed again, "It's highly recommended."

"Well then," I said, thinking with a smirk that Lloyd would be proud of me for this, "I guess I'm *game* for it."

He groaned with a grin, and looked up for the waiter, who appeared immediately to take our order.

"Excellent choice," he observed as he headed back to the kitchen.

Ben and I sat in our booth looking out over the flat prairie as the skyline began to twinkle. It was twilight: the lights below us made a magical sparkling carpet. The arterial roads leading south were glowing with parallel white and red streamers of light. The mountain horizon was drawing closer as the sky began to blush. Our silence was comfortable again. I could sense the slight motion of the rotating floor and it made me feel vaguely nauseous.

"So Grace, what do you think your father is doing that he was so desperate to get us out of the house?" he asked curiously.

I giggled. "No idea. That was weird, eh? I've never seen him so nervous and distracted."

"Does he have a wood shop in the basement?"

"No, just his home office."

"Hmm."

At that moment, the food arrived and I stared in amazement at the huge platter of dried meats, pickles and breads. "What kinds of meats are these?"

He pointed to the items, "Trout, buffalo, venison, duck… just a little representation from air, forest, plains and water…"

We sat and ate, caught in a magical world as the sky around us glowed in pearlescent rose, fuchsia, and daffodil, above the jagged silhouette of the Rocky Mountains. My mouth was surprised with each new taste while my eyes were assaulted by beauty stretched before me.

"No one would believe these colours could exist in sky if they didn't see it themselves," he observed softly.

"I know. It's like some god splattered paint all over the whole sky."

He smiled. "In Greek mythology they say that the sunset comes from the reflection of golden apples carried by the Hesperides, but that doesn't explain all the pinks and reds, does it?"

"Maybe they've been given some red apples since then?"

He laughed, "Right, a delivery of Spartans from B.C. eh?"

Our companionable chuckles were interrupted by a sneering face, "Well, Ben, imagine seeing you here, looking so cozy and romantic with a *little girl.*"

"Hello, Meg," he said emotionlessly, sliding slightly closer beside me. I looked down at the table and tried to force my suddenly pounding heart to relax. "Are you here on a date as well?" he added significantly.

Her sneer deepened, "No."

"Meg? Who is this?" asked middle-aged woman beside her.

Meg turned to her and started to walk away from us, glancing over her shoulder with another glare, "Oh, no one. Just some people from school."

"Wow. Meg looks like her mom, eh?" I muttered.

Ben's eyes were following her with a thoughtful expression.

"Ben?"

"What?" he queried from far away.

"Meg looks like her mom," I repeated staring at him.

"Oh. Yeah, she does." He looked at me, glanced up to the curve around which Meg had disappeared, and then at our diminishing food platter. He smiled distractedly, slid over until our thighs were touching, and then wrapped his right arm around my shoulder so he had to eat with his left hand.

"That's talented," I observed.

"What is?"

"Ambidextrous dining."

He chuckled. "It helps my love life."

"Oh, does it?" I asked, and attempted to slide to the right. He dropped his arm and clamped his hand at my waist, locking me into position.

"Yes, it *does*." He smiled again, and flicked his chin at the mountain silhouette; the sunset was changing again. "Enjoy the view Grace, while I enjoy the company."

"Ben?"

"Mm?" he answered while he chewed.

"Did you ever bring Meg up here? Is that why she's so angry? Does she feel like I'm invading her special place?"

He shook his head and swallowed, "I don't know what Meg's problem is. I told you: we didn't go out. I never went on a single date with her, let alone shared a magical evening like this with her. You are the only one who makes me long to share earth and sky…"

I started to blush as he broke off, pulled his arm from behind me and frantically rummaged in his jacket pocket. "Shoot. Grace? Do you happen to have a pen?"

"Uh, yeah." I remarked in confusion, unzipping my purse and slipping my pen out of its slot. "Here."

"Thanks," he said, as he started writing on the napkin. The scribbles were a mix of words and staff lines. He began to hum while he scribbled and dotted. I leaned back, watching him. Every once in awhile he gazed up, as the mountains slipped behind us and the skyscrapers of the downtown core sparkled in front of us, but he didn't speak. The bus-girl came to clear the table and left again without a word. I sat just watching Ben or the view. It was like being in the school studio, though I had a better sense of the motif from his humming than I had been able to make out from the tapping of the keyboard. I was invisible, but it was okay.

128

Invisibility is quite peaceful.

Our waiter appeared and asked, "So, can I interest you in a dessert?"

Ben glanced up from his napkin, now hardly showing any white space, "Yes, a couple of Coffee and Doughnuts please."

The waiter smiled, "Excellent choice, sir" as he turned.

"Coffee and doughnuts?"

"Wait and see," he said, as he gingerly folded the napkin and tucked it inside his jacket.

The waiter was back within moments with two dessert plates, each set with a small bowl and adorned with little cinnamon doughnuts. I looked at Ben, who smirked.

"It's like a mocha pudding with the doughnuts for dipping. You'll like it."

The creamy texture and contrasting cinnamon flavour made my taste buds dance as I savoured the rich dessert.

Darkness had enveloped the sky, and as the tower rotated steadily past the downtown core, we were looking out to the east. Blackness revealed the path of the Bow River. Everywhere else showed grounded stars.

I set the spoon down and licked my lips. "Can you excuse me for a moment?"

He nodded.

"Um. Did you see the rest room go past recently?" This rotating thing was weird. I wondered how the servers could keep track of where their tables were when they kept moving.

He chuckled, "No, so I think if you head counter-clockwise you should find it fairly quickly."

He was right; it was just a little ways up. I used the facilities and as I stood at the mirror washing, my hands I couldn't help but notice the sparkle in my eyes. My skin looked brighter. Ben brought out the best in me.

The door opened, and I glanced up as I reached for the towel to dry my hands.

"Well, if it isn't Ben's little girlie."

I tried to keep my voice even and pleasant, "Hello Meg."

She stepped determinedly toward me until I was against the counter. "Listen," she said ominously, "you need to know that Ben is *mine*."

I shrugged. "He doesn't seem to share your opinion." It was an effort to appear nonchalant.

She glared at me with a look of loathing that almost shot flames.

I stepped to the side with a casual, "Excuse me."

She hissed, "He won't stay with you. Haven't you heard about Rae-Ann?"

I turned around, and smiled sweetly at her, "Yes, I did. Terrible thing to have to deal with a mental illness when so young."

Her brows lowered and her eyes narrowed, but she didn't say anything in response. As I swept out of the rest room with studied casualness, I could feel her glaring eyes burning a hole in my back.

When I stepped out of the room, our booth was right in front of me. I slid in next to Ben. He read my expression and asked with whispered alarm. "What happened?"

I whispered shakily back, "Meg."

Without a pause he looked up, met the eyes of our waiter several tables away, raised his hand and called, "Cheque!"

I gathered my purse and coat as the waiter arrived to put the little folder with the bill on the table. "I'll pay at the till," Ben told him. We stood and headed around the restaurant to the door.

Meg's family was sitting close to the till. She wasn't back from the bathroom yet apparently. Her mother looked up at us with a vague interest, watching as Ben paid the bill. His arm was draped protectively over my shoulder.

As he held me tightly against himself, we walked to the elevator and pushed the button. Ben was looking around at the others waiting with such determined casualness that I could tell he was on full alert, watching for any sign of trouble. Suddenly, there was a strange hissing from behind the elevator. Without hesitation, Ben pivoted us around and headed toward the stairs whispering urgently, "This way Grace."

"Are you crazy?" I whispered frantically as I stumbled a bit on my high heels, "There've got to be a thousand steps down to street level!"

We stepped into the stairwell, as the hiss grew louder above our head, culminating in a deafening pop that shook the Tower and plunged the stairwell into darkness.

"Not a thousand," Ben said calmly as the door shut behind us, "just seven hundred and sixty two." He had reached into his pocket and fished out the little flashlight he'd had in Banff. He held it in his left hand, my left hand in his right, and pulled me along behind him. "Come on Grace, we need to hurry."

Above our heads, others were now leaving the decks and coming into the stairwell as well. Emergency lights had flickered on, and the stairs were bathed with an eerie red glow. We could hear steps methodically sounding behind us, but Ben was almost racing down. My chest was aching. "Ben, stop. I have to take off my shoes before I kill myself."

He paused just long enough for me to slip them off and loop the backs over my wrist, and then started down again.

Awhile later, I stopped again, panting. My bare feet were killing me, raw from the cement steps.

"Come on, Grace. We're half way there."

"How can you tell?" I breathed out.

"I'm counting. This is four hundred."

"You're not counting." I muttered in disbelief, my knees starting to hurt like they never had before. It occurred to me to be thankful that I wasn't climbing *up* these steps.

"Four hundred thirty two," he replied.

I would have made some sort of exasperated noise, but I couldn't; I was too busy trying to catch my breath and control my aching legs that were moving up and down like un-oiled pistons. I tried to count steps but soon lost track. We could hear voices above us, some slightly hysterical, some laughing, some singing, but the distance was spreading. Down, down, down. Step, step, step. My legs were on fire.

"How much farther?" I panted.

"Almost there, we're coming onto seven hundred." For a band geek, he was remarkably fit. He wasn't panting at all.

"Good."

A door thumped open below us and a bright light filled the space. Uniformed fire fighters with their headlamps glowing brightly pushed past us on their way up hauling gear on their backs. Poor guys. I wondered if anyone was hurt up above.

Ben opened the door, holding me behind him. He looked in all directions and then pulled me out after him. "To the car, Grace."

"Does this mean we're not going to a movie?"

He laughed as we found the car and he opened the door. "Good guess."

"Yeah," I replied evenly as I collapsed into the seat, my legs burning, "I'm really getting the hang of the near death experience thing."

He started the ignition and looked over to me as I clicked into my seat belt.

"You're wonderful, Grace. It constantly amazes me how calmly you take all of this, *Amata.*"

Oh really? Hmm. We drove out of the parkade and headed south.

"What does that mean?"

"Amata?"

I nodded.

"It's Italian for 'darling.'"

"Why give me an Italian nick-name?" I didn't want to call it an endearment.

He laughed. "Italian is terribly romantic, don't you think? And beautiful, like you are."

"So does that mean there's a chance you might actually tell me what's going on?"

He laughed then, a ringing sound that was a mix of relief and joy and amusement. He reached over and patted my hand as he smirked and said, "Not a chance, *Amata*, not a chance."

"So

I puckered my lips thoughtfully. "Why did I know you were going to say that?"

By the time we got home, my legs had frozen into position. As I tried to climb out of the car my calves, thighs and buttocks blazed. I limped into the house.

Ben opened the door for me, smiling with sympathy. "Take a hot bath with Epsom salts and a muscle relaxant. You're going to really feel it tomorrow."

I massaged my butt. "Oh, I know…"

Mom and Dad were sitting in the living room. Mom looked rather blissful, and Dad looked completely proud of himself. Apparently, his surprise went well, whatever it was.

"Hi Grace," Mom called, and then frowned as she noticed Ben behind me. Dad gave her a glance of reproof and smiled at us both.

"Hello kids, how was dinner and the show?"

I laughed, "Dinner was great, but the show was just a really long descent."

"Huh?"

Ben looked at them calmly and said, in a way that seemed to suggest a lot more than he was actually saying, "There was some sort of explosion at the Calgary Tower, so we had to take the stairs down from the restaurant."

Dad's eyes were wide with alarm, "You took the stairs?"

I grimaced. "Yes. All seven hundred and sixty two of them. I'm going to hurt for a week."

Mom stared at Ben accusingly, as if it was all his fault, "Where were you when the explosion hit?"

He stared back emotionlessly and told her, "In the stairwell."

She looked at him for a minute, considering his words, and then nodded curtly. "Fine." She looked over at Dad.

Fine? What?

Dad stood up and extended his hand to Ben. As they shook he

remarked, "Well thank you Ben for keeping such a good watch on our daughter." He was guiding Ben to the door, but he glanced back at Mom as if challenging her to disagree with him.

"You're welcome, sir," Ben replied. "It was my pleasure." Dad was trying to hustle him out of the house. It was a little embarrassing that he was so obvious about it.

Ben smirked at me.

"Bye Ben. See you at school tomorrow." I had gotten to the door and Dad stepped back respectfully.

Ben kissed me on the top of the head, "See you. Thanks for a lovely evening, Grace."

"Thank *you*. It was quite an amazing dinner." I grinned mischievously as I added, "The free work out was entertaining, too."

He laughed as the door shut behind him.

I turned to see both of my parents looking at me oddly. Great. "Um. I'm going to go have a bath. Good night." I attempted to sprint up the stairs, but I'm sure I looked a little awkward since I couldn't unbend my legs.

Christie looked at me in surprise as I hobbled into school the next day. "Why do you look like you were run over by a truck?" Christie was always direct.

I answered grimly, "I took the stairs down from the Calgary Tower last night. I'm just a *little* stiff today…" I tried to keep the sarcasm out of my voice, but I wasn't even slightly successful.

"No! Were you there when they had that explosion in the kitchen? I heard about it on the news this morning."

"Yup. There was a hissing and then a bang and then Ben made me take the stairs down."

"Ben?" She tried unsuccessfully to hide her grin. "So does that mean it's official now?"

I smiled. "Yeah. I guess it's *official* now."

"Yay!" she shouted and raised her hand for a high five. People turned and stared as I blushed.

CHAPTER NINE

SOMETHING SLIGHTLY ODD ABOUT THE WHOLE AFFAIR

Visiting green spaces, Orpheus fears, for Eurydice haunts him;
Death by the asp's poison flowing, memory's agonies taunt him.
Harmony joined by Concordia, bonding the music and muse, so
Orpheus reaches for consciousness; she doesn't welcome the news though.

It was a very warm spring day a couple weeks later, when Ben and I pulled into the parking lot at Fish Creek Park. I looked around curiously at the trees and hills. "Why did you bring me here?"

He laughed mysteriously and raised an eyebrow in amusement, "You'll see."

I shook my head as we got out of the car, settling my purse across my body. He reached into the trunk and pulled out a pack of his own, slipping it onto his back with a smile. It was big and it looked heavy.

"Are we going to be spending a few days here?" I asked with a laugh. It was a rather large pack for a day in a small provincial park on the edge of a city. He just grinned in reply, reaching for my hand and leading me onto the trail. It was an unseasonably warm day for April, in our fleece jackets we were toasty warm.

We walked casually, keeping our hands together, occasionally walking single file when we met anyone else on the trail. We didn't speak, but Ben hummed and whistled the latest tune he was working on. It was the typical comfortable silence we shared that was always so wonderful and so strange.

Suddenly Ben gasped and threw himself in front of me with terror flashing in his eyes. "Watch the snake!" he shouted as he threw himself in front of me.

I glanced past him to see a little garter snake wiggling its way across our path. I laughed, stepping out and bending down to look at it more closely, "It's just a garter snake, Ben. They're cute, and perfectly harmless to humans."

He was shaking, "No! Don't touch it, Grace, please."

There was genuine fear in his eyes. "Fine. Okay." I stood up. "They don't eat anything larger than a mouse, you know, but if you're really…" I trailed off at Ben's determined stare down at the little thing. "Oh, whatever."

He grabbed my hand as the snake reached the tall grass and disappeared. He pulled me past the spot as if expecting the tiny creature to rush out and take off my leg. I shook my head in bemusement as we continued along.

"Step off here," said Ben after a few minutes as he indicated a small side path.

"Where are we going?" I asked again.

He simply grinned and pulled me along behind him, back to tuneful humming.

We climbed an incline that gave us a lovely view at the creek winding below us, until we reached a flat area with a stunning view that was sheltered beneath an overhang of earth, like a grass-roofed house. Ben stopped and pulled his backpack off. "Here we are."

"What a lovely spot," I remarked as I studied the creek meandering below us, the trees and dried grasses blowing slightly in the wind, and the tiny people walking on the main path below us. I glanced back at Ben to see that he had pulled out a red plaid blanket, and was busy setting up a picnic. "Ah Ben! What a good idea!" I grinned at him.

He returned my grin with a happy smile of his own, as he set dishes down. He settled himself on the blanket, and pointing to the other side, said, "Come along, Love. Sit down and enjoy all my hard work!"

He had lain out thick slabs of sliced chicken, potato salad, a green salad, and what looked like a bottle of wine. A small square closed container of dessert. My mouth started to water. He had real china, metal cutlery, and wine glasses.

"You brought wine?"

"No," he laughed, "sparkling pear juice, so we don't get arrested. Close enough?"

I nodded with a giggle and I sat down where he suggested, remarking, "This is very impressive."

"Thank you. Today is a special occasion."

"An occasion?"

He nodded solemnly. "Yes. Today is the anniversary of the day back in 1327 that Francesco Petrarca first saw Laure…"

"Who?"

He smiled softly, "You know: Petrarch, the poet."

"Petrarchan sonnets, Petrarch?"

He grinned. "Yup, that's the one. When he first set eyes on Laure in church in 1327 he started writing her sonnets."

"You're a goof."

"Hey. He was a romantic kind of guy, just like me!" I laughed. "He inspired Spenser and Shakespeare. He was an unstoppable force of sonnet writing, all due the incredible fascination he had for his lady love, Laure." He grinned as he added, "I understand *exactly* what could have inspired him to have written three hundred sixty six sonnets to her…" He looked at me meaningfully.

I blushed, looking at the view below us, unable to meet his eyes, until I heard him dishing up his offerings onto my plate. He smiled at me as he passed me a plate, and we ate in companionable silence. Everything smelled so good, and in the fresh air stirred by a gentle breeze, it all tasted better than it would have indoors.

As he set down his fork, he smiled and informed me, "Today is also the day in *this* year that I would like to reveal a new composition created in your honour."

He rummaged in his pack and pulled out his MP3 player and a paper. Smiling, he handed me the paper. It was no surprise, given the lead up, that it was a Petrarchan sonnet. Next, he handed me a pair of earbuds; he had a splitter on the end and he put a set in his own ears as well. "You want them loose," he remarked enigmatically. When I was set up, watching him curiously, he pushed the play button with a smile.

Once again, he surprised me, because as the introduction played in my ears, he reached into his pack and pulled out a wooden recorder. Smiling at my confused expression, he put the recorder to his lips, and then he joined the lush orchestral music in my head. Sometimes the recorder took the melody and some times it had a descant, but as his solo part wove in and out of music I found myself feeling quite melancholy as I read the lines of the poem accompanied by his song:

Canzoniere 61

Most blessèd be the day, the month, the year,
And blessèd be the hour, the moment when,
I found this place, and saw my sweet torment.
Her lovely eyes completely tied me here.

So blessèd was her breath as I came near,
That Love entangled me within her scent,
Against his arrows left me impotent,
And bound my heart to hers. So, thus endeared,

Sweet blessèd voices call my lady's name,
And weave her glorious beauty in my verse.
My sighs, my tears, and my desires contained,

Most blessèd are the papers I disperse,
To share the thoughts that bring me fame,
The thoughts of her that are my blissful curse.

As the music died with a minor chord in my headphone and a gentle trill of Ben's recorder, I sighed happily.

Ben set down the recorder, watching me carefully. "It's more beautiful in the original Italian," he said quietly.

"Ah. It must be *very* beautiful then."

He chuckled softly, "I thought your Italian might be just a little rusty."

I played along, nodding teasingly, "Mmm. Just a little."

His eyes were beginning to smoulder as he moved closer to me, "It rhymes more complexly in Italian, of course."

"Of course." I tried to reply calmly, but my heart was beginning to thud in my ears. I wondered if he could hear it. I didn't see how he could not. My brain hunted for some neutral topic of conversation. "Did Laure hurt him?"

He smiled sadly; I couldn't decide if he was acting or not. "Of course. She was married and remained faithful to her husband, like a dutiful wife. It was his agony."

"Did he ever speak to her?"

He shrugged his shoulders. "History doesn't mention much of the specifics, so I probably shouldn't make any comment."

Like he would know more than history had recorded. "Did he make a fool of himself chasing after a woman who was trying to avoid him?" My tone was mischievous. I was beginning to relate a bit of Laure's experience to my own.

He laughed, knowing exactly what I was hinting at, and the booming sound of his laughter echoed back at us from the hill. "She was buried with one of his sonnets, so someone knew."

"*Really?*" I pondered for a moment. "I wonder what her husband thought of *that?*"

Ben's eyes clouded, "I'm sure *he* was never told."

"I wonder how someone managed to sneak a poem into her coffin. Do you think Petrarch did it himself somehow?"

"No. He was out of town at the time." His voice trailed off. "You know, she died twenty-one years to the day and even the hour in which he'd first seen her." He looked at me with melancholy eyes.

What a sad coincidence. I shook my head slowly, pondering the dedication of such a long chivalrous love. "That's a very tragic love story."

Ben's eyes glowed next to mine, "But look at all the beauty that came of the tragedy: three hundred and sixty six beautiful sonnets."

"It seems as if all great poetic loves come to tragedy." I was suddenly feeling very dismal. I stared off blindly, not really thinking, but feeling with every inch of me. It was as if a series of unnamed losses were coming to consciousness: loss after loss rippling just below awareness. Tears started to flow down my cheek. I realised I was grieving for a couple who'd been dead for almost six hundred years.

Ben didn't seem surprised at this. He reached up, a knuckle gently wiping away a tear.

His beautiful blue eyes, so tender and kind, met mine and he whispered, "Poor Laure."

"Poor Petrarch."

He nodded solemnly, "We all die eventually, Grace. Whether love lasts a short time or a long time it is still a precious gift. It shouldn't make us sad. We should celebrate the joy it brings."

I shook my head and sniffled. "I know that in my head, but in my heart, I feel like I just watched my own true love disappear time after time." That sounded stupid, but it was the only way to describe the aching sensation crushing my heart.

"I'm sorry, Grace."

Through my sniffle I swallowed and nodded, "It's okay Ben. It's not your fault I'm crying."

He smiled sadly, "Of course it is, I rem… I told you the story." He reached into the front pocket of his pack, and pulled out a little box. "I have another little gift for you."

I studied the little box suspiciously. I looked like a ring box. I hadn't even known him a year. Was he going to be absolutely ridiculous and propose or something?

He saw the worried look on my face and laughed at me. "It's okay Grace; it's not an engagement ring."

I reached my arm up and swiped it across my forehead in a large pantomime gesture of relief, flicking imaginary sweat off my fingers. I was surprised to realize, contrarily, that his friendly re-assurance made me feel a little sad. Did a part of me actually *want* him to propose to me? At my age? What an alarming thought. "What's the occasion?" I asked suspiciously.

"I told you. The anniversary of Petrarch's first vision of Laure." He chuckled as I raised my eyebrow sceptically. "Come now, Grace, isn't that enough?"

He set the box on the blanket and handed me a wine glass. He opened the sparkling pear juice as I stared at the innocuous little box, all wrapped in pretty metallic paper and topped with a golden fabric bow. It looked expensive. Ben filled our glasses, and then he raised his in a toast and said with energy, "To Laure and to Grace, my muse and my delight." He sipped looking into my eyes; I sipped my juice, feeling the bubbles tingle on my tongue, feeling distinctly awkward about this whole thing. Again.

He then nodded to the box, grinning at me, "Go ahead. Open it."

I reached for the box tentatively, as if it was going to bite me. My hand was shaking as I caught my thumbnail on the paper and ripped carefully. What was he thinking? A ring box fell into my palm. I looked up at him with accusation in my eyes. He laughed again, rolling his hand in a gesture that encouraged me to keep opening. I gingerly lifted the lid and caught my breath.

There, nestled in black velvet was a wide silver band, carved all the way around in an ornate floral pattern. It was absolutely beautiful. It looked old; I had never seen anything even vaguely like it before.

I reached into the box and pulled the ring out of the little slot. As I held it up, I noticed there was writing on the inside; I looked closely at the deeply engraved capital letters that encircled the whole interior from edge to edge. They were blackened and very clear: BENEDICTA GRATIA.

"Ben, it's absolutely beautiful." I turned it over in my hand admiring the intricate workmanship and the way the light caught on the raised edges, highlighting the carving. "I've never seen anything like it." I shook my head in amazement, then studied the engraved words again, "What does it mean?"

He smiled, "It can be interpreted a few ways." He glanced at me before he continued, "It's Latin. *Benedicta* means blessings, and *gratia* is usually translated as kindness or friendship. So it's something like 'blessed friendship.'" He watched me studying the ring. "It sounds like us, doesn't it?"

139

I nodded, still turning the ring over.

"Are you going to put it on?"

I shook my head; I was still too busy admiring the amazing craftsmanship of the carving and engraving. Had he found it in an antique store? Was it a family heirloom? "Is it old?"

A smile twitched in the corners of his mouth, but his face remained serious. "No. It's a reproduction. The style is called a poesy ring. They were common in the Middle Ages for couples. Usually an epigram about love was engraved on them, but I thought this sentiment was more appropriate for us."

I nodded, "Yes. It's cool that there are the first three letters of your name in one word and the first three of mine in the other."

He grinned. "Yes."

He watched me with a bemused expression as I continued to study the ring, until his impatience got the better of him. "Come on Grace, put it on. See if it fits."

I laughed finally, and slipped the ring onto the third finger of my left hand. I stretched my arm to admire it. It was so beautiful. "It fits perfectly."

"Yes." His voice sounded like he was choking or something.

I looked up. There was a very odd expression on his face. "What's wrong?"

I watched the battle on his face as he fought with his thoughts before finally bursting out, "I like that you put it on your left hand."

"Why?" I hadn't thought of any significance.

"Wearing it on the left suggests love and commitment, even if it's *not* an engagement ring..." He sounded far happier than he should.

"Ben, I..." I didn't know where to go with my thoughts. I didn't know what to say. I liked him so much, and yet it was so silly to consider commitment at fifteen. This was a new relationship. Did he consider this ring a sign of his commitment to me? What was he presuming about me if I accepted it? What did I know about commitment?

What I knew was that Ben was crazy because he seemed to think it was okay for him to chase me all over creation. Crazy because he was saying things that just were so inappropriate for a couple of kids who'd known each other so briefly. Yes, I liked him, more than liked him, actually, but this just seemed...weird. Again. I sighed. This just couldn't be a good thing. Ben was obsessive. It wasn't appropriate for him to be so overbearing with his obvious affection. I looked at him without adding any more to my sputtering start, but apparently, I didn't need to. I guess my eyes showed what I was thinking, just as his eyes showed me how he was feeling at my turmoil.

"Ah, Grace." He shook his head, and his eyes actually brimmed with tears. "You're not making this easy."

Now *my* eyes filled with tears. Damn it. I needed a clear head. I didn't want to hurt him; I had the odd sensation that I'd already done that enough. I met his eyes and we sat on the blanket staring at each other. The tears overflowed and still we stared, our faces dripping onto the blanket. I thought vaguely that to anyone just walking by on the path we probably looked a picture of romance, glasses raised, eyes all teary, lost in each other's gaze, but it was something bigger than that. I felt the moment was a freeze frame. Many similar pictures flashed through my mind. It was like the first time I'd heard him play all over again. I swallowed and looked away first as the dizzy kaleidoscope of images threatened to overwhelm me again. I took a deep breath.

"Ben, I..." I reached for the ring. If he was going to imagine some crazy commitment, I had to give it back to him before this got any stranger.

Ben interrupted, placing his finger across my lips. "No." He shook his head, looking deeply into my eyes as he set down his glass and picked up my left hand. "No, Grace. This is us. Leave the ring where it is." He smiled at me with such tenderness that all discomfort left me. That inexplicable sense of belonging was back. He stared deep into my eyes until I was lost in his blue pools. "I love you Grace. I'm sorry you're finding it awkward." He tilted his head on an angle and studied me for a moment before he added, "I confess, I am a little confused about why that is, since I'm pretty certain that you have very profound feelings for me yourself."

I swallowed again. I considered that for a while. Everything to do with Ben seemed somehow profound. I nodded my reluctant affirmation of his observation.

He held up my left hand, smiling at the ring. "I'm not asking you to marry me, though of course, if we were a few years older, I would be." He grinned mischievously at the deep inhalation I needed at that point. "I am just saying, I'm here. Your friend," he met my eyes as he whispered emphatically, "forever." Then he grinned even wider and said, "Keep me in your heart and in your mind, *blessed friend*." He picked up my right hand and held the two hands together in his, shaking them gently for emphasis. "Gratia Benedicta. Is that okay? Can you live with that?"

I nodded and breathed out a whispery, "Yes." Suddenly, looking into his eyes, I was feeling something new. No longer lost and confused, I felt...*found*. This wasn't that annoying dizziness. It was overwhelming warmth emanating from the pit of my stomach. It was making my body tingle.

"Good." He lowered our hands into my lap and leaned across, kissing me on the tip of my nose.

I closed my eyes, breathing deeply, trying to analyze the strange sensation that was taking over my body.

He chuckled softly and asked, "Shall we go?"

I opened my eyes and looked around, feeling as if I was coming up for air after diving. The view below us suddenly seemed surreal. The colours were different. He was gathering the remains of our picnic and loading them into his bag. I handed him things to load in, then stood as he gathered up the blanket. Kind, gentle, sweet, affectionate Ben. Of course, I would keep him in my heart and in my mind. There was never really any other option, was there?

Ben reached for my hand. We made our way back to the car in quiet companionship. He hummed the same tune he'd been humming on the way up, but this time I knew the ancient words. He seemed far more relaxed than I felt. My brain was still trying to sort out competing thoughts. This relationship was insane. This was the most natural thing in the world. We reached the main path, and he pulled me close, dropping my hand and wrapping his left arm around my waist. I wrapped my right arm around his. I rested my head on his arm as we walked, feeling completely at home. It always felt so complicated around him, but so comfortable. A blessed friendship... forever. I smiled and glanced down at my ring. He noticed and leaned down to kiss the top of my head. He was right. I did have profound feelings for him. Despite all the confusion, all the crazy weirdness battling in my brain, I realized that there was really no mystery about how I felt in my heart. I had finally recognized the sensation from poetry, songs, and stories. How could I have missed it? It was a simple one: I loved him. I loved him purely, complexly, and absolutely entirely. I stopped as we reached the parking lot. Turning toward Ben I rested my left hand on his waist.

He matched my position and standing there, face to face, wrapped in each other I looked up at him for a moment before I was able to articulate the words. With the surprise of my discovery still plain in my voice I whispered, "I...I *love* you."

His eyes began to glow as his smile stretched slowly across his face until it reached both ears. He leaned over to kiss the tip of my nose, and then he threw his head back, his voice booming and his eyes beaming with laughter as he exclaimed, "At last!" He pulled me closer to him, bending his head, and as his lips reached mine a light filled me; there was no longer any doubt in my mind that he was my destiny.

Spring was my favourite season. Everything seemed so new. With Ben at my side, I looked with even newer eyes.

A knock at the door brought me rushing downstairs to beat my parents to the door. Too slow though, because my dad was already there.

"Hello, Ben" Dad said cordially, reaching out to shake his hand.

"Hello, sir."

My mom appeared in her office doorway: glancing up at me briefly, she turned to Ben. From the side of her face I could see her mouthing something; he shook his head with a serious expression. Then he looked up at me and a smile reached across his face and stretched to mine.

"Hi." He whispered it.

I don't think he meant it to sound seductive.

It did.

My mother glowered at him, but dad touched her on the shoulder with a quiet, "Blythe." She walked back into her office, her displeasure clear in her posture. I didn't know why she was so annoyed with him all the time.

"Got your walking shoes on, Grace?"

"Why? We walking somewhere today?"

He laughed. "Excellent deduction, Sherlock."

I grabbed my jacket out of the hall closet asking, "Where are we going?"

"You'll see."

"Ben…" laughter rolled off him, as he took my hand and swung it down the sidewalk.

I glanced up at the sky. "Is that going to be rain?"

"Maybe. It'll be okay though."

I chuckled, "I'm not worried that I'm going to melt or anything."

He squeezed my hand. "Good."

We walked along comfortably without speaking, hands swinging until I was sure that his whole purpose in going for a walk was to be wandering aimlessly. Then we stopped.

"Here we are."

I looked around at the houses. It was just a regular neighbourhood. Nothing exciting here. "Come on, I want you to meet someone."

Curious, I let him lead me up a pathway to the front step of a brick bungalow. He opened the door without knocking, calling out, "We're here!"

I met his eyes as he smirked and pulled me into the living room.

"It's about time," said a confident voice through a quiver. It was gruff, but feminine at the same time.

"Connie, here's Grace. Grace, this is Connie Iugo."

"Hello, ma'am" I said, reaching out my hand to shake hers. Her eyes were crinkly and sparkling. Her hair was curly and a curious silvery gold.

"Oh, none of that, girlie," she said, reaching up for my shoulders and swinging me right then left, touching her cheeks to mine like Aglaea would. "This is a proper greeting."

I smiled warmly at her. "How do you know Ben?"

"Bah!" she said waving her arm. "He's a fixture."

That was cryptic. I looked helplessly at Ben, wondering who this tiny old lady was, and what we were doing here, but he just smiled, his eyes twinkling fondly at both of us.

Connie fluttered her hand and said "Stand up straighter Grace; let me get a look at you." I obeyed, feeling a little awkward. She drew a little circle in the air with her finger so I turned obediently. As I came around to face her again she asked, "Let me see that ring, Grace."

I stretched out my hand and she took it in hers, studying the ring carefully, then she looked at Ben. "From you?"

He nodded.

She smiled at me again. "Do you love him?"

I blushed, but nodded.

At that, Ben grinned at Connie and asked, "Well?"

She nodded, "Oh yes."

"Good."

Connie unfolded from her chair. Reaching into a large bowl on the table, she stirred the air in the empty vessel, and then she came and stood in front of us. She placed her right hand on Ben's head and her left on mine. She faced us with her eyes closed and murmured musically over us for a moment, and then with her eyes still closed she crossed her arms so now I had her right hand on my head and Ben had her left. Ben closed his eyes and smiled with a happy sigh. Connie uncrossed her arms, still murmuring, and replaced her hands again. Her voice changed to a definite hum for a minute or so before she opened her eyes, and met my gaze with a happy smile, then she proceeded to smack us lightly on the tops of our heads and stepped back.

She turned to Ben. "It's done."

His answering smile was so bright it was almost reflective. As I looked at him suspiciously, he reached out and pulled Connie into a bear hug that swallowed her completely. He whispered huskily into her ear, but I couldn't make out his words.

When he let her go, Connie moved slowly to the door. "Off you go, then." She touched me on the arm and then smiled over at Ben. "Definitely yes."

Ben nodded, "I thought so." He reached for my elbow and steered me back to the door. "Bye, Connie."

"Bye, Ben, Grace. Enjoy your connections!" As he went to close the door behind us she added with a giggle, "Whatever you do, don't tell Blythe!'"

Ben shut the door behind us with a chuckle and took my hand again, turning back the way we'd come. He began to whistle. Another composition was on the way.

"What was all that about?" I asked.

He just smirked. "She's cute, eh?"

"Yeah." I would not be diverted, "What was all that with the hands and why aren't we allowed to tell my mother?"

He grinned mysteriously and said, "Isn't it great having a secret?"

Right. He thought that would save him this time? This time I actually had leverage. I cleared my throat. "You really should tell me what's going on, because you wouldn't want me to accidentally let anything slip around my mom..." I let the insinuation drip off my tongue like melting ice cream.

He froze, and then turned to face me with wide eyes. "No, Grace, seriously. You shouldn't say anything." That was definitely a panicked look.

"Oh? And why not?"

"Because if your mother hears about what happened, she will never let you see me again."

"Be serious." He was over-reacting. He had to be.

"Grace, I am deadly serious here. You can't say *a thing* to your mom."

"Why would she care?"

He sighed. "Grace. Can't you just trust me?"

I stared back at him, studying the anxious lines around his eyes. "You know I trust you, but you shouldn't be forcing me to have secrets from my parents. Isn't that like..." (Was I going to play this card? Hmm. Yes.) "Isn't that the first thing that *abusive* boyfriends do?"

"Grace!" His eyes were tortured. "Do you *honestly* believe I'm an abusive boyfriend?"

Oh dear. Had I gone too far? I shrugged. "Nope. *That* is why I'm so astonished that you want me to keep secrets from my parents."

He sighed. "You can tell your dad if you want, but you *can't* say anything to your mom. Your dad will understand, but your mom will be angrier than you have ever seen her in your life."

I put my hands on my hips and glared at him. A part of me was joking, but a part of me was actually annoyed. "Why would you do something that you knew would make my mother angry with me? That is not fair to me, Ben. It's also disrespectful of both my mother and me. What were you thinking?"

As if to punctuate my words, it started raining then. Huge great drops that seemed like something out of a movie fell like meteors, splashing onto the sidewalk with loud smacks like miniature bombs raining down on us.

His eyes had been mournful as he listened to me, now with the rain soaking us; he grabbed my hand more tightly. He started walking silently, but with breathless speed, pulling me down the street. He didn't meet my eyes when he finally decided to answer my question. "She wouldn't be angry with *you*, she'd be angry with *me*." He paused for another block, thinking. "You're right, of course. I didn't think that you'd feel that way. I was just so glad to have found a solution I didn't consider that you might disagree with it. I was sure you'd want to."

"Want to *what*? Solve *what* problem? If I actually *knew* what just happened, I would actually be in a position to tell you whether I would have wanted to or not!" I growled in frustration, "Just *tell* me already!"

He shook his head and stopped. We were back in front of my house. He spoke in a voice so quiet that I could barely make out the words over the percussion of the mutant raindrops, "I'm sorry. I thought you'd want to. Just don't tell your mom, please?" He was begging. "I promise it was nothing bad, and I promise I won't ever do anything again without asking you."

"Ben, just tell me…"

He interrupted the exasperated rant I was planning by dragging me into his chest. He kissed me with such passion that stars erupted behind my eyelids and I began to feel faint. When he let me up for air, I'd forgotten whatever it was we were arguing about.

"Bye, Grace," he said, as I stood there swaying woozily on the sidewalk. "Love you."

"Yeah," I managed, "uh, me too."

Chuckling softly, he climbed into his car and pulled away with a wave to me through the back window.

I stood watching the road through the watery veil long after the car had disappeared, trying to remember why I might possibly care about Connie's musical murmurs. Ben's humming started to fill my brain and I found I couldn't imagine anything even slightly odd about the whole affair.

CHAPTER TEN

EVENTUALLY THERE WILL BE PAIN

Gathering daily and listening, melodies weaving 'round Charis;
Mousai are dancing around but Dark Epialtes has flared up.
Gates tell the truth of the vision: horn or through ivory traveled?
Evil arrives with a vengeance and Charis' life is unravelled.

It began to be a habit. Every day after school, I'd sit in the studio with Ben while he clicked at the keys of his synthesizer and I did homework or read a novel. If I couldn't come for some reason, he would watch me go off alone with a melancholy smile. I knew that I deserved to have my own life and I shouldn't feel bad for doing whatever I needed to do. I knew, but I still felt guilty.

Christie and I were sitting in English class when she surprised me. Out of the blue, she remarked, "Did you know that on days when you're not there, Ben won't even compose?"

"What? You're kidding."

"No. I would see him through the glass before you started coming regularly and he could work consistently. Now when you're there in the room with him, it's as if he's on fire. But on the days you're not in the studio, he doesn't even try. He just cleans up the room or sits listening to music through the headphones. I don't even know if it's his own work that he's listening to. I know that he never lays new tracks any more if you're not there."

"Terrific. Now I feel even worse for not being able to go every day." It felt like a weight was pushing on my head.

"I don't think it *bothers* him," Christie clarified. "He doesn't pressure you to come or anything, does he?"

"No, but he always looks so pathetically sad when I'm not free. It's like I'm torturing him. It makes me feel awful. Now you tell me he can't even compose without me. That's appalling."

"Sorry. I didn't mean to upset you." She looked contrite. "I actually thought it was kind of romantic how bereft he is without you."

I sighed and slid to the floor with my lunch bag on my lap. This wasn't good at all. I didn't want him bereft. I wanted him confident, strong and... what? I was going to say 'committed' but the way he was going he could end up committed to a mental health facility. Commitment wasn't his failing. If anything, he was *too* committed. What was I going to do with him?

Lloyd arrived then to get into his own locker. As Christie sat down beside me with her lunch, he looked at us curiously. "Good mourning."

"Good morning," I replied distractedly.

"No, *mourning*, with a 'u'. Am I being too subtle for you these days?"

I rolled my eyes in response and he tried again.

"Why so stricken?"

"Because..." Oh, good grief. What was I going to say?

He waited for me to answer, and when I didn't, he looked over at Christie. I pulled out my novel. I didn't want to talk about this; I needed to work out how I felt.

She shrugged, "She's just upset that Ben isn't productive when she's not there," she looked at me like she thought I was being stupid, "but I think it's nice."

"Well she's right. It's *not* good if his music is dependent on someone else."

Christie looked at him doubtfully. "Isn't that the whole point of the word? By definition, isn't *music* supposed to come from the inspiration of a *muse*? Doesn't it make *sense* that he needs her?"

"Oh." He looked impressed with her reasoning. "That's a *very* good point, but," he glanced over at my sullen expression as I pretended to ignore them, "it doesn't mean it's a good thing if you're the one feeling the pressure to be the muse."

"So where's the pressure? She just has to *be*; she doesn't have to *do* anything."

"Except to put whatever she wants on hold to be where he needs her to be." He shook his head, glancing at me sympathetically.

"But he doesn't ask her to do anything. He doesn't complain if she has her own stuff to do."

"And yet she *feels* the pressure, doesn't she? Look at her. She's totally stressing out—feeling responsible for whether he works or not. That's not right Christie. It's not fair." He sat down beside her glumly.

Christie was being stubborn. "It's like it's her job, Lloyd. Sometimes it's inconvenient, but it's not exactly a *hard* thing that she has to do."

He shook his head again, "It's still not right."

They both turned then, and studied me as if I was an interesting biology specimen.

Finally, I snapped the book shut and looked from one to the other. "You guys realize that I'm sitting right here, right? That I'm not deaf?"

They looked a little embarrassed at least.

"I'm going to class." I stood up too quickly and wobbled from the head rush.

"Grace! Are you okay?" Christie asked with concern, while I swayed a little above her head.

Arg. I hated how everyone thought I needed to be babied. "I'm fine. I just stood up too quickly. I'll see you in English."

I stomped off to Socials 10 feeling mightily irritated with everything and everybody. Of course, the classroom door was still locked because there were still fifteen minutes of lunch hour left, so I slumped onto the floor outside the door and put my head on my knees while I waited. Breathe. Relax.

Lloyd was right. It wasn't right and it wasn't fair.

Christie was right. It just *was*.

I didn't understand the bond I had with Ben; it felt bigger than the universe, but I was still a free person. I loved him, but I wasn't *in love* with him in a goofy infatuated way. It was deeper than that, but because of its depth, it freed me somehow. I could almost feel the ropes of our entwined destinies looped around me giving me support. A million unspoken words floated around us.

It made me happy to know that I brought his music out of him, that he found the best of what he was creating when I was around. I was proud to know that I had a role in his skill. There was no doubt that he considered me a muse. What a horrendous responsibility. I was fighting the sense of obligation weighing on me.

Didn't muses depart, sucking all the creativity away from the artist who'd relied on them? Didn't departure leave the poor artists dried, withered shells of the glory they'd dreamt of? Was I doomed to crush Ben? How could I do that to him? Already it was an anguish to know that he depended on me. Already I wanted to escape him, even when his expectations were barely anything. I was horrible. I was going to destroy him. I felt the tears stinging in my eyes as I stared ahead.

A warm body slid down the wall and joined me on the floor. I looked up to see a fond smile. "Hey, Love."

"Hey, Ben," I whispered.

"I don't like that sad face. Are those tears? What's up?"

I sighed. This wasn't anything I wanted to talk to him about. I looked at him with agonized eyes as my thoughts crushed me, but I didn't speak. How could I articulate this?

He waited, watching me. "Ah." His smile was tender and understanding. "It's a hard job, Grace, but someone has to do it."

"Yeah." I whispered. How did he know?

"I love you."

"I know."

"It'll be all right, Grace. It's always all right in the end."

"I don't ever want to hurt you."

He reached his arm behind me and hugged me close to him. "I know."

I snuggled my head against his chest as I confessed in a hushed voice, "I'm afraid I'm going to end up hurting you really badly."

He nodded matter of factly. "Yes, I expect you will. That's all right."

"How is that *all right*? It won't be right for you."

"That's the thing about love, Grace. It always means pain eventually. It's worth the trade off. Life without the loving is an empty life. We pay for our joy with our pain. It's just the way it is."

"But Ben, it's going to happen." His future agony was a palpable figure in the hallway with us.

"Grace, you're talking months or years into the future. There is an époque between now and then. There are hours of compositions to create in the meantime. There are days and days of being happy together yet to savour. Yes, eventually there will be pain. That's a natural part of life. I am willing to pay the price."

"I don't think *I* am."

"Oh yes, you are." He chuckled, "You're already in deeper than I am, *Amata mia*."

"What?"

He shook his head with that secretive look he and my parents were so prone to after their irritatingly cryptic little remarks. "Never mind. The fact remains that I love you and you love me, and my love for you is fuelling some wonderful music. Let's just enjoy the process and the product. After school today, I'll play you the piece I'm sending to the national competition. You'll see then what you've created."

"What *you've* created."

He assented, "My fingers were involved, but the rest comes from you."

"Cut it out Ben." He smiled again, so tenderly that it made me angry. Why did he love me so much when I was doomed to let him down? "I can't come today; I have a dental appointment after school." It was hopeless.

Something passed across his eyes, but he shrugged dispassionately, "That's fine. I'll play it for you tomorrow."

I sighed. "Okay." I knew I wasn't showing the appropriate amount of enthusiasm for completion of his project. He was too accepting, too self-sacrificing.

He squeezed me again, nuzzling into the crook of my neck. "You make me happy Grace. Yesterday, today, and tomorrow."

Oh good grief. "You sound like a jewellery commercial."

He laughed as the jingle of keys announced Mr. Swan at the door.

"Hello, sir," Ben remarked pleasantly, glancing up at him.

"Hi Ben. Are you taking Socials 10 over again? Or are you just at my door enchanting my students?"

"Neither. I'm being entranced. I'm a helpless casualty of Grace's charm."

Mr. Swan smirked, "Yes, she *is* a charmer; I've noticed the looks she gets from the gentlemen in the class. You'd better keep an eye on her if you don't want her stolen away!"

"Mr. Swan!" I exclaimed, mortified.

He laughed as he unlocked the door and I stood up. "Ben, are you entering the National Youth Composition Contest?"

"Yes. I have my entry just about finished. I expect it'll be off sometime next week."

"I look forward to hearing it. Will you debut it at a concert this year?"

"Oh yeah, probably at the end of year band concert," Ben looked fondly down at me. "I think it's the best work I've ever done." Mr. Swan's students were beginning to file through the door as Ben spoke over them and added, "Excuse me. I have to go to class, sir."

"Yes, of course. Good luck in the contest Ben."

"Thank you, sir.

I walked up the aisle to my seat and Mr. Swan followed me, remarking casually, "Sounds like you're quite the muse, Miss Severin."

I gaped at him. Why was everyone saying that?

He chuckled as he reached the front of the room and called the class to order.

~~~

I was surrounded by blackness. I could hear a roaring of water. Was it a pounding of surf? Pouring rain? A rushing waterfall? The roar eliminated all other sound. In my mouth a strange taste: fear. It was an electric sensation on my tongue. With the logic of dreams, I knew exactly what it was. I was locked in a world of fear without sight or sound to guide me. Panic held me dumb and numb.

Then I was running through the blackness.

Something huge and terrifying was chasing a small glowing girl. She was running, careening down endless streets bounded with white stucco buildings set along dirt road ways. Then she was on cobblestone streets racing past stone houses. Then there were asphalt roads filled with cars alongside skyscrapers towering above the edges of sidewalks. She was running so fast that everything was a blur. She was running through places, running through time. Suddenly the streets became school hallways. She was running, running and the hallways didn't end.

Her pursuer was gaining on her inch by inch: a black silhouette in the dark, racing behind her, closer and closer. Not the triangular shape of a male, but the more curvaceous shape of a female, running like a marathon racer, relentlessly driving forward, echoing her every step.

The glowing girl stumbled and the pursuer was upon her. Her evil eyes were black; her hair was dark, almost purplish, and it glistened with long, thick dreadlocks. She came closer, smiling with an evil triumph. The girl felt death drawing nearer, searched within herself for a hidden reserve of energy, and realized she had nothing left. The evil one reached for her and then, suddenly, a golden warrior was throwing himself between them. He was taller by half that she was and much broader. His arms rippled with muscles; his chest gleamed, rock hard. He was an epic hero, glistening in moonlight like a marble statue come to life. The evil one howled in anguish at losing her prize, and then she split into the familiar faces the glowing girl knew as they leapt toward the golden warrior, snarling furiously like the two heads of a rabid beast.

He fought them viciously. A sword appeared in his hand and he was wielding it like a swashbuckling hero. He battled them up and down stairs, careening down hallways. The glowing girl was always behind him. The twin heads were fighting without weapons; he couldn't seem to strike them; they were trying to get between the warrior and the girl, but the warrior would not let them by. He was everywhere at once, but so were they. He lunged with his sword. Simultaneously the twin he was attacking pivoted out of the way, and the dreadlocks on their heads started to move with life of their own, shimmering in waves. The shapes became snakes that grew quickly in gleaming green, bronze, gold and black: one foot, two feet, three feet long. They slithered through the air, their eyes glowing red, their tongues flicking in and out, fangs glinting in half-light, hisses of "Orffffffffeeeussssss" filling the air. As the golden man passed by them in the follow through of his lunge, the snakes sprang after him; stretching four feet or more, they snapped their fangs toward him. As he fell, the warrior became Ben. Snakes engulfed him, as the twins roared with triumphant laughter.

The girl's heart collapsed as they turned toward her.

I began screaming.

I woke up with a start, my heart hammering, and my breathing fast and shallow. I could see myself in the mirror on the dresser across from the bed. My eyes were huge; my face was ghostly white in the moonlight leaking into the room between the blinds. My chest was heaving. I listened for any sound in the house that would indicate I'd screamed loudly enough to waken anyone else. It was eerily silent. I blinked in the shadows of my room, willing my body to relax. It was only a dream.

It was only a dream.

My cell phone rang and I jumped. I glanced at the clock. It was just after three o'clock. Who would be calling me at three o'clock in the morning?

I reached up and took the phone off the night table before it could ring again. Flipping it open, I glanced at the screen, but it shone too brightly in the darkness for my eyes to make out the number. "Hello?" I could hear that my voice was breathless, like I really had been running. I didn't sound sleepy.

"Grace?"

Ben. I hadn't realized that my body was still tense with fear for him, until hearing his voice flooded me with relief. I sucked in air to my toes.

"Grace, are you okay?" He sounded panicky at my silence.

"Yes Ben. I'm fine. Why?"

"I…" He paused. I felt his fear and panic through the phone while he wrestled with indecision. He gulped on the other end of the line and finally said, "I just saw you attacked." His breathing was loud again on the other end of the line.

I breathed in deeply, willing my voice to be calm so I could calm him. I had been dreaming. He had to have been dreaming, too. Gently I said, "Hush. It's just a dream, Ben"

He was silent for an interminable moment before he finally whispered, "No, I wasn't dreaming, I was *seeing*," he paused as if to emphasize his point, then added, "were you dreaming?"

"Yes." Obviously.

"About the twins?"

"Yes." How did he know that?

I could hear his breathing intensify again. His fear remained in the air between us.

"It was just a dream, Ben." I tried to make my voice soft and soothing, like I was comforting a child. "You were only dreaming. Everything is okay."

He was quiet again, but I sensed his disbelief. I watched the clock. Two minutes passed before he spoke very quietly and very certainly, "I *saw* it Grace."

It seemed very unlikely. Surely, our recent experiences with the evil twins had just triggered similar dreams in each of us. I smiled weakly as I calmly said, "Tell me what you saw."

He drew a shuddering breath and as he described the blackness, the racing streets, the hallways, my own breath grew ragged as fear began to pulse through me again. He *had* seen my dream. *How* had he seen my dream?

He described himself chasing the twins, the snakes growing out of their heads, and then his version changed.

"Say that again? *What* happened next?" I asked.

He choked out, "Then Enyo attacked you from behind, and you fell to the floor as the snakes bit you again and again until you lay bleeding and convulsing from the poisons, dying before my eyes..."

"Wow." I struggled to organize my thoughts. "That's interesting. I wonder what it means that they're different at the end?"

That appeared to take him aback. "What?" he demanded. "What did you say?"

"In *my* dream *you* were the one who died, although everything else was exactly as you described."

"I wasn't *dreaming* Grace." He sounded certain, though his voice was hushed.

"Whatever, Ben." His ridiculous assertion irritated me. What other explanation was there?

I heard footsteps in the hallway, and hesitation outside my door. I froze. My mother's voice called, just above a whisper, "Grace? Are you

154

awake?"

I sighed, and leaving the phone so Ben could hear the exchange, I tried to make my voice sound very sleepy, "Yeah Mom," I inserted a loud yawn, "I just woke up from a crazy dream." It seemed better not to mention the nightmare for some reason. I didn't want her worrying needlessly.

She opened the door a bit, and peeked inside, "Are you all right?" She studied me carefully, "you seem…disturbed."

"Yes, I'm fine, Mom." I smiled reassuringly at her. "See you in the morning." My smile was a little wobbly, spoiling the illusion somewhat.

She recognized the dismissal, but hesitated before she responded, "Grace, if you need me, just come get me."

"Okay Mom. I will."

She chuckled softly. "Say good night to Ben for me."

I smiled at her intuition. Moms were scary sometimes. "Okay."

"Good night."

"Good night." She shut the door softly behind her, but I didn't hear her footsteps leaving. She was going to be sure I ended the call and went back to sleep.

"Hey, Ben."

"Yeah. Your mom still there?"

"Yes."

"Are you *sure* everything is okay there?"

I smiled in spite of myself. "Yes, Ben, perfectly fine. It was only a dream." Despite my reassuring tone and words, my body remained tense. I knew that it was not going to be easy to fall asleep.

He sighed, as if he knew I was lying. "All right, then. You try to go asleep. I'll keep watch."

Keep watch? What on earth did he mean by that? I didn't have the brain function to analyse him tonight. "Fine, Ben. Thanks for the concern."

He laughed somewhat gloomily, "Okay. Good night."

"Yeah, you too. See you later."

I waited for the click as he hung up. He didn't. "Ben?"

Silence on the other end of the phone.

"Are you going to hang up?"

"I'm waiting for you." He sounded not in the least bit embarrassed with this confession.

Silly boy. "All right. I have to try to sleep. Later." I tried to sound both sad and sleepy, so he'd know I didn't *want* to hang up.

"Yup. G'night."

I felt a little traitorous actually pushing the button to disconnect the call. I did need to sleep, but I knew it was going to be an unlikely proposition at this point. I set the phone down on the night table, and pulled the quilt around my ears.

My mom's footsteps moved quietly down the hall.

I lay there waiting for sleep to find me. I was afraid to close my eyes in case the chase began again. I could hear a murmur of voices from my parents' room. Great, now Dad was awake too. I checked my clock. Four o'clock. I groaned, trying to breathe deeply, trying to lose myself in sleep, but I tossed fitfully for at least another twenty minutes wondering whether I should just give up and get out of bed, since I was having absolutely no success.

I thought I was still quite conscious when I felt an unexpected hush sneak stealthily into my brain. I could hear music. It was very distinct though it sounded far way. How odd. I focused on the sound and realized that I recognized the tune. It was as if Ben's voice was humming me a lullaby. That gave me an idea, and I rolled over and found my MP3 player by the phone. I clicked through the darkness to the section of quiet tunes, and setting the volume at a level just loud enough to block out thought, I hit play. The sounds of Ben's music filled my brain. Tunes he'd composed for me or with me engulfed me completely and I found myself drifting away on the notes of his music, warmly aware of his love for me. It felt like he was wrapped around me, protecting me from the evils of the world; there was no way bad dreams could find me in such a safe haven. Finally, dreamlessly, I slept.

The dream solidified us. Battling the forces of evil in our nightmares drew us together in peace. I stopped worrying about the inevitability of future pain. I allowed myself to accept the joy of the moment. I didn't go anywhere without feeling the glow of belonging with Ben.

At breaks between classes, at lunch, and during Leadership class we basked in each other. We did not have to be physically close. We weren't like those couples who had to be wrapped around each other all the time. Our eyes could meet across the length of the halls and the intimacy almost overwhelmed me. He was in the very air I was breathing, and I couldn't believe how, in a few short months, my world had so completely changed.

After school, I stayed if he was composing, or went home if he had band or choir practice. Today he was practising so I was walking home slowly, my head full of his smile.

"Hey there, Beautiful."

I wheeled at the familiar voice and exclaimed, "Josh!" I couldn't believe how delighted I was to see him, before my fears interjected themselves and I cut myself short and eyed him warily.

He returned my gaze frankly without a glimmer of guilt or regret.

Was I wrong? The flash of that face had been frozen on my brain, but such a steadfastly clear expression could surely not represent danger. Why would I superimpose Josh's face where there was evil?

"Why are you looking at me like I'm an anaconda?" he asked in amused curiosity.

"I thought, um…" No. I had been imagining things. "…never mind." I shivered in spite of myself, and I must have revealed something of my fear because he looked at me warmly and seemed to understand at least the tenor of my thoughts.

"Ah Grace," he said wrapping his arms around my shoulders and looking deeply into my eyes, "Why would I ever hurt you?"

My worries faded in light of his glowing expression. He was obviously happy to see me. He didn't really want to hurt me, did he?

I met his eyes and saw no guile in him. "I'm sorry." I said sincerely.

He grinned as he turned his body, leaving one arm over my shoulders in an affectionate gesture. "Glad to see you haven't forgotten me, at least."

It had been months since he'd been suspended and out of school, but the time off seemed to have been good to him. He looked healthy. He was dressed in a nice jacket, clean well cut jeans, and his hair was clean and styled. He looked casual, but polished. He didn't look like a teenage stoner loser. It was quite a contrast to the boy who'd made so much trouble at the back of the class.

"You're looking really great, Josh. Where have you been?"

He shrugged his shoulders nonchalantly, "Around."

"What have you been doing?"

He chortled, "Stuff."

"Wow. Informative, aren't you?'

He laughed then, but when I looked at him expectantly his face changed and he said sombrely, "Remember what I said, Grace, 'need to know.'"

"Ah. In that case, I'm just glad to see you're still alive."

"Thanks. I appreciate that." He grinned. "You're looking pretty good yourself. You look," he studied me for a moment, "you look *really* happy."

I nodded, "Yeah. I am happy. Really happy."

"I'm glad."

We walked along quietly for a few blocks with his arm still comfortably across my shoulders, each lost in our own thoughts until we reached Tims. I don't know what he was thinking, but I was trying to figure out how to ask him the question that had been irking me. He seemed so relaxed that I didn't really want to bring it up; I just wanted to enjoy him for a few minutes.

He stopped on the sidewalk out front, but did not look like he was planning to go inside. "So Grace," he remarked with a casual seductiveness, "I seem to recall that you owe me a date."

Oh. Oh dear. Hmm. What was I going to do about that now? I remained quiet, pondering my options.

"Grace?"

"Yeah?" I said innocently, knowing perfectly well he wasn't going to leave this alone and I'd have to face it eventually.

He stopped and turned to me. I didn't meet his eyes. He chuckled in amusement. "Oh no you don't, Grace. You promised me a date. You're not getting out of it. I've been waiting a long time."

"I know I promised, Josh, but things have changed since you've been gone."

"Oh?" He studied me curiously. "How have things changed? Has it recently become your habit to break promises made to your friends?" His look was challenging, but not angry.

I shook my head. "No, but before I wasn't in a relationship, and now…" my voice trailed off.

"Now you are?"

I nodded.

"I see. And who is the lucky guy? Is it that dark haired jokester from English? Isaac or whatever his name is? I know he's been crushing on you big time for awhile."

I blushed and stared off into the distance. "No."

"Don't play games, Grace. Who is it? If you're embarrassed to actually be dating him, I can get rid of him for you, and you can date me instead." He smirked, but there was an eerily ominous undercurrent in his tone.

I sighed. "Don't be ridiculous, Josh." I glanced at my poesy ring for courage before I looked up and met his eyes. "It's Ben Butler."

To my surprise, Josh tipped his head back and roared with laughter. "Ben Butler!"

I looked at him in confusion while he continued to guffaw.

"Why is that funny?"

He was laughing so hard he couldn't answer me. He shook his head and grabbed his side. People in passing cars were staring. I felt like every eye inside the restaurant had turned to watch him through the windows. I scowled at him.

"Josh! Stop it! Why is that so funny?"

He finally caught his breath and met my eyes. His were still gleaming with sardonic amusement. "You're dating Mr. Congeniality."

Yeah, okay. Ben *was* very congenial. "So?"

"Ah Grace. Come on. He's a little white bread, don't you think? Don't you want something a little more interesting to chew on?" He smirked again. "Don't you want someone like *me*?"

"Josh…"

"Seriously, Grace. Think about it."

I tilted my head and thought. Did I want someone like him? He was interesting, that was true, but although I found him intriguing, he also made me nervous. I didn't really trust him. I liked him well enough, but even if his wasn't really the face I'd seen through the windshield, the fact that I'd imagined his face suggested that my subconscious recognised danger in him. I was better off with white bread, even if it was boring. I looked back at him calmly and said firmly, "Nope."

Josh laughed again, but this time he was just amused. "Well, be that as it may, you still promised me a dinner date, and considering that I graciously took the rap for your violent attack on the aforementioned Mr. Congeniality, I think you owe it to me to keep your promise."

"Josh…" His vocabulary had certainly improved while he was gone.

"No excuses Grace. I'm serious when I say I've been looking forward to this date the whole time I've been gone. I have been planning a perfect evening, and I will not be thwarted by Ben Butler." He grinned again and his voice became seductively persuasive, "Come out for dinner with me this Saturday, Grace. I'm going away and it'll be months before I'm back in Calgary."

When I shook my head again, he smiled his goofy friend smile instead. "Come on Grace, just as friends. No strings. You *promised*." His eyes were all puppy dog sadness now. How was I supposed to resist that?

"All right. Fine. This Saturday, but *just* as friends. We're clear on that, right? No funny business this time."

His grin touched both ears it was so wide. "Awesome!" he beamed. "I will pick you up at 5:30, okay? Oh, and dress up, I'm taking you to a nice place."

"Oh Josh." I shook my head again, this time in exasperation.

He grinned again. "It'll be fun, Grace, and a perfect farewell to send me on my long, lonely journey. Oh look, there's your friend. I'll go now. See you Saturday!" He took off as I stood there feeling quite bowled over. How was it that I had just agreed to another date with Josh after the first one had gone so terribly awry, and while I was dating Ben? This was not good, not good at all. I was stupid.

Christie joined me. "Who was that?"

There was no way I was confessing this one to her. I knew it was impossible that she'd connect that polished person with scruffy stoner Josh Dagan, so I lied. "Oh, just a guy who wanted to know the directions to the next Tims since the person he was meeting wasn't at this one."

"Ah." That was common enough to avoid suspicion.

As we walked home, Christie talked animatedly about Lloyd's latest adventures with his new source of amusement: Random Acts of Trumpeting. I didn't have to do much more than listen enough to laugh at the right places, so most of my brain was free to debate the insanity of going out with Josh.

The next day, Lloyd came up beside us. "Hey, did you hear about Ben?"

"What?" Christie and I asked in unison.

"I overheard Mr. J saying that he'd just been listening to Ben's National Composition piece. It's going off this week."

"Oh," sighed Christie, "is that all? I was afraid he'd been hurt or something. She looked at me, "Have you heard the piece yet Grace?"

I shook my head. I had expected to be the first one to hear the completed piece. I found myself feeling irritated that I wasn't.

We went our separate ways to our classes.

I was grumbling to myself. You'd think that all the hours of sitting in that studio would be worth something. I was worried about hurting him; it hadn't occurred to me that he could hurt me by leaving me out of his life.

I was sitting in Socials class when Mrs. Nemeth came on the PA about five minutes before lunch. "Redman students! I know that you are all aware of what talented students we have in our Fine Arts department. I am so pleased to tell you that we have a candidate for the National Composition competition and we are going to play the composition our own Benjamin Butler is submitting. Enjoy!"

I fought down tears. I was no more special than anyone else in the school. We'd all share this moment.

As the music began to play, however, I decided Ben couldn't have had anything to do with this. He would never have tolerated the horrendous sound quality of the PA system butchering one of his compositions. I wondered where he was at this moment, gritting his teeth and grimacing in agony.

As it ended, Mrs. Nemeth announced, "Ben's lovely piece is entitled "Saved by Grace." Good luck Ben, we all wish you great success in the competition!" With that, she turned the mic over to the student who normally did the announcements.

Saved by Grace. Yeah. That was a subtle title choice.

I walked through the halls, very aware of the sneaky looks I was getting. I had just reached my locker when Ben materialized beside me. As expected, he looked rather pained. I smirked knowingly at him.

"That's not quite the debut I had anticipated," he growled.

I laughed.

"Would you come to the studio with me so I can play it for you the way I *meant* to have you hear your song the first time?"

I nodded. He was so cute when he was embarrassed. And it was definitely his turn to be embarrassed.

We walked to the band room, swinging our hands.

"'Saved by Grace,' huh?"

He grimaced again. "That was just the working title."

I giggled.

The band room was empty when we went in. "Okay. So I'm going to put this up on the main stereo. Sit here on Mr. J's conducting seat," he said as he fiddled with the controls on the amplifier. "All right then." He smiled. "Here is the tune that you inspired, my gracious one." His eyes were dark and sultry.

He was rather overwhelming at times, but before I could feel too put out, the song started, and there was nothing else.

The music rose like a living being. It swelled and rolled in waves of sound across the room. The melodies and harmonies danced through the air, weaving paths and crawling inside to squeeze my heart. I felt flooded by heat. I recognised the portion from the car and the tune from the park woven together. I was lost in the sound, pulled here and there, lifted up and wrung out. Tears began to pour from my eyes. I looked at Ben as it came to an end. I had no words. I simply opened up my arms and we embraced as tightly as one body, swaying gently back and forth until the warning bell broke into our reverie.

I leaned out of the embrace and wiping my eyes I whispered, "I have to go to class."

He nodded, leaning down to kiss me gently.

I could have stayed there forever, but suddenly there were voices on the other side of the door, and we broke apart as a group of students arrived for band class.

I smiled achingly at Ben, and almost staggered out of the room. I was too dazed to walk straight. I managed to get to my locker, find the right books and make it to class, but once I'd collapsed into my seat, I was locked in another world, still hearing the waves of the music reverberating through my soul.

What power that boy had.

Christie and I walked home together, but I still wasn't conscious of much going on around me. I wondered vaguely whether the piece would have the same impact on the judging committee. If so, he stood a very good chance of completely destroying his competition.

Competition made me think of Josh for some reason, though there was no competition between them. Josh. What was I going to do about *him*?

When I went to bed, my worries about Josh were accompanied by the soundtrack of Ben's composition. Such a dichotomy.

I was still lying in bed trying to sleep several hours later. What was I going to say to Ben about this 'date' with Josh? The clock said it was two in the morning when I decided to give up trying to sleep and go down for some crackers. I crept through the dark and was opening the cupboard when I heard the phone ring. All sensible people should have been asleep. I could hear a muffled conversation begin as mom picked up the phone upstairs.

Suddenly the murmurs came clearer. My mom said Ben's name. I strained to make out what she was saying. Why was she talking about us?

Ever so cautiously, I tucked the cracker box back in the cupboard. I crept into the office. While my mom was speaking, I gently lifted the receiver.

I listened with my hand across the mouthpiece, hoping desperately that they wouldn't notice the sound of my breathing.

"I think I should go look at the tapestry." Aunt Aglaea was saying.

My mother sounded concerned, "Why? Do you think something has changed?"

"Yes." Aglaea's affirmation was unequivocal. "I don't like what is happening there, Blythe. It feels wrong. Grace is being manipulated somehow. I don't understand it. Hopefully Clotho will be able to explain."

"But will you even be able to tell if the tapestry has changed?"

"She will be able to tell me."

"You think she keeps track of every thread?"

Aglaea's answer was typically business-like, "It's her job to, Blythe. She's The Weaver, after all. If for some reason Clotho doesn't know, then Kay may have some information."

My mom didn't say anything for a time, then she answered with a deep sigh. "That's what sisters are for. So long as Atropos doesn't get involved."

"Yes."

"All right then. Let me know what you find out."

"Tell Bright as well," Aglaea instructed.

"Bright?"

"Yes. She may be needed."

"She's trying to retire, Aglaea, that's why we're grooming Grace, remember?"

"Don't be sarcastic with me Blythe. She hasn't retired yet, or we wouldn't be having these problems. You call her and make sure she's up to speed on what's happening."

"Fine."

My mom didn't like taking orders any more that I did, but she was plainly taking orders from Aunt Aglaea. Orders about me.

I waited as they said their good byes and mom had hung up before I gently put down the receiver. A proverb says that eavesdroppers never hear good of themselves, but in my house, eavesdroppers just seemed destined for greater confusion. I was listening in to find answers, and I ended up with more questions. Why did Aunt Aglaea think that I was being manipulated? What did she know about my life? How could she possibly learn anything about me all the way over in Greece? Why was my mother taking orders from her sister about her own daughter?

My Aunt Aglaea was a high power executive. It was something of a family joke about her and her publishing empire, but no one disputed her brilliant abilities. She was always ferreting out new talents and propelling them to stardom. It's not usually the company president who does that, but she seemed to have an amazing knack of finding obscure works from up and coming talents and changing their lives. Her endorsement was like a magic ticket to fame. It just didn't seem to be an option that any venture that she was involved in was not thoroughly successful.

When we had visited her in Greece when I was a little girl she had been an object of awe to me. She was beautiful, intelligent, and incredibly confident. People were inclined to bow when they met with her because she had such a regal bearing. She looked like royalty. I would have looked up to her, but as I grew it was so daunting to imagine trying to live up to her expectations that I eventually gave up, and was thankful to have my far more approachable mother and my wacky Auntie Bright as role models. Their successes seemed far more attainable.

Aglaea's publishing empire consisted of three parts. The first was the huge prose division that she headed herself. It covered publication of both fiction and non-fiction works in over a dozen languages. Aglaea spoke most of the languages in which she published, and when I'd visited her office, as a girl the most astonishing thing was to watch her switch from language to language during a meeting or in the hallways. When I commented on it, she had just shrugged her shoulders and said, "This is the way it is in Europe, Grace." and then she'd thought a moment, and looked at me with her intense stare while she said, "I hope you're studying foreign languages in Canada?" in a way that informed me it was a demand, not a question.

Technically, my mom and Auntie Bright worked for her, each in a different division. The second division was concerned with music recording and sheet music publication. Bright had been in the music division for years until she'd moved to B.C. with Uncle Jim. I wasn't really sure if she was still involved in the company or not. I'd never heard her talk about it, although I knew she still had a passion for music. My mom still ran the poetry division, but it was the smallest division, and she was able to do most of her work from home in Calgary via the internet.

My mom's father had an airline. Her uncle ran a cruise line. The sisters just shrugged this off as normal, as if everyone had a family full of high-powered business folk around them. My father worked for his father-in-law arranging charter flights and tours to the Mediterranean. Apparently, he met with him on a regular basis whenever we were in Greece, but I had never met my grandfather. I thought that was odd, but my parents maintained that he was 'a busy man' and told me not to take it personally.

I crept back into bed and lay still. There was no way I'd be sleeping any time soon. Now there was more than Josh to worry about. What was this tapestry? Who were Clotho, Kay and Atropos?

I heard mom whisper to dad as they came out of their bedroom and walked down the hall. My bedroom door opened slowly. I tried to breathe deeply and evenly.

"Is she asleep?" Mom whispered.

"Yes." Dad sighed.

Their steps padded quietly down the hall. I heard him ask, "What are we going to do?"

Mom's voice was husky. "David, he failed before. We can't let him be involved again."

Dad's voice was sad. "He loved her, Blythe. It seems he still does."

"Of course he does. I know that. But you know as well as I do, David, that love is not necessarily the best trait in a guardian."

Their voices trailed off as they walked down the hall. I lay there, focusing on my breathing. In: one, two, three, four, five, six, seven, eight. Out: one, two, three, four, five, six, seven, eight. Guardian? What on earth were they talking about? It sounded like a video game or something.

The yoga breathing helped slow my heart rate, and I felt myself slowly drifting to sleep. I remember wishing that I would be free of dreams, as I faded off.

I didn't get my wish. It seemed I dreamt all night long, but they were beautiful dreams. Ben and I were strolling down a country lane, as horse and buggies passed us by. I was in pink silk and holding a parasol in my gloved hand. He was dapper in a navy suit, cut very differently from modern suits: it had tails. He carried a walking cane. A little dog ran along beside us. Ben was whistling. We didn't touch each other, but there was a lot of smiling. Very intimate smiling.

Another scene, this time it looked like Italy. It was Ben and I, but this time we looked like a scene from a Renaissance painting. We passed through the rich lush colours, ornate buildings and beautiful fountains of a town and settled in a country pasture. Next, we were sitting under a tree with a picnic lunch spread between us. Ben was playing something that looked like a mandolin. Again with the intimate smiles.

Another scene, now in Greece: the two of us draped in white. Ben was plucking a lyre; I was standing beside a mosaic wall with a fountain coming out of it. This one was different, domestic. A dark haired child was entwined between my legs; another was laughing and dancing to Ben's music. We were a happy family, so happy. So much, love in the room.

There were other dreams, too. There were different times and different places, but Ben and I were together in every one. There were different hairstyles and colours, different faces even, but I knew, as one does in dreams, that it was always us. The images became still, blurred, and then each one of them began to unravel, one after the other, as if the lives had been woven on a tapestry that was coming apart. Finally, there was a single picture of Ben and me embracing, with a thread running off at the bottom. A huge pair of scissors came close to the thread, but just as they were about to snip it, a hand covered them, and the scissors disappeared. Ben's music filled my memory.

I woke up gradually, feeling warm and contented. I felt richly bathed in love. I stretched luxuriously and smiled, slowly putting my feet out from the covers, not quite willing to leave my beautiful dreams of Ben.

I understood unequivocally that Ben and I were supposed to be together. All my fears about his strange stalker behaviours and his crazy declarations made perfect sense to me now. Of course, he should follow me until I talked to him. Of course, he should tell me of his love. We had to be together. Obviously.

We were sitting together in the lunchroom the beginning of June, staring deeply into each other's eyes. The dream pictures were passing before my eyes as I gazed into his and I remembered back to the day in September when he'd made me faint in the band room. It brought up a question.

"Hey Ben, why did you apologize to me the first time we met?"

"You don't remember?"

I shook my head. "I'd never met you before; why would you need to apologize to me?"

He smiled fondly, but there was an ache behind the smile. He shook his head, "I guess if you don't remember, I shouldn't say."

"No?"

"No. It'll come to you eventually."

I sighed. I saw another vision of us in old-fashioned clothes. I was crying. I shook my head. It was strange how I felt like I was on the edge of knowing exactly what was going on while being completely baffled. He picked up the novel he was reading in English with one hand, but held my hand with the other, our fingers woven together.

We sat there comfortably for a while until I got up the courage to ask, as nonchalantly as I could, "Do you ever dream about being with me in another time?"

His head shot up, but then he composed himself and asked just as casually, "What do you mean, 'another time'?" His stare was too intense for his feigned calm.

I shrugged, "Oh, I don't know. Say Ancient Greece perhaps? Or maybe Renaissance Italy?"

He just looked at me, his eyes growing larger, without replying.

I stared back. Aha. I knew it. "Well?"

"Oh, Grace."

"Ben?"

He shook his head. "No, Grace."

"No you don't have those dreams? Or no we're not talking about it?"

"You know."

"Do I?"

He looked at me cuttingly.

Yeah all right. I do know and he knows that I know. Except I don't know what I know. Wasn't anyone ever going to tell me what was going on around me? I sighed in exasperation.

"I am sorry, Grace. Again. Still." He sighed and shook his head again.

"*Why* are you sorry, Ben?"

He stood up determinedly. "I've got to go to class. At the end of the day I have to stay late after school for swing choir. Will you wait?"

I studied him for a moment before I decided. "No. I'll walk home. I want to call my Auntie Bright today." My parents weren't talking to me. Ben the Coward wasn't talking to me. Perhaps Bright would talk to me.

He watched me for a while, but I could tell I wasn't going to get any answers from him. He sighed and leaned over, "Give me a kiss."

I obliged, and we stayed locked together for a moment, our bodies bearing mute testimony to our unspoken thoughts.

We broke apart and he looked melancholy. "I love you, Grace."

"I know. I love you, too."

He took a deep breath as he stood up. "Okay. I'll see you later."

I watched him walking away thinking that my whole life was attached to him like a rope trailing from his ankles. I sighed again as I headed off to class.

At the end of the day, Ben only nodded at me from down the hall as I put my books in my locker and slipped my packsack onto my back. I knew he had choir practice, but I could tell he was purposefully keeping his distance so I couldn't question him again. If I strategized, *could* I pry information out of him?

I *would* have answers. If Auntie Bright wouldn't tell me what was going on, I'd use all my womanly charm on Ben until he crumbled like potato chips. I smiled a bit imagining the scene. With the right distraction, I bet I could make him do anything. I had to be ruthless about this.

I put on my earphones and stalked purposefully down the sidewalk with my head full of a pounding beat and wailing guitar licks. No soft piano right now. No love songs. I was plotting. I needed a hard edge.

Stomping along the sidewalk, I wasn't paying attention to the cars on the road. I wasn't paying attention to anything around me.

If I had been, perhaps I would have seen the car barrelling toward me.

Perhaps I would have had time to leap out of the way, or just to start screaming.

Perhaps I would not have suddenly found myself flying through the air being propelled through the windows of Tims and into an abyss of blackness.

When I came to, I was draped over a table inside the restaurant with the scream of a siren filling my ears. Amid tiny sparkling cubes of shattered window glass, I was a crucible of pain. There was room for nothing else in the entire universe but pain. The words of the people surrounding me were swallowed in pain. I was balanced with my torso across a double tabletop, my legs hung bulwarked by the chair. My arm was a broken pendulum of pain swinging limply. Pain dripped from a gash on my hand. Pain throbbed in my arms and crumpled my legs as I focused my entire world into paralysis. Any movement intensified agony. My very breath hurt.

The siren stopped screaming and moments later, I heard the slam of a door and the clatter of a gurney as the paramedics arrived. Calling my name, one touched me gently to check my vitals. In the resulting tiny movement, the pain exploded and I shattered into pieces as the world completely disappeared.

CHAPTER ELEVEN

START RUNNING!

Painfully Charis awakens and sees what has changed all around her
Orpheus grieves for his losses; Ares comes close and surrounds her.
All celebrate Saturnalia, Nemesis stirring and planning.
Life will be different for Charis now, lonely protection's expanding.

A voice was snarling out of the fog. "Girl! You! Come to me!"
She did not respond.
"Girl!"
"Me?" She whispered.
"Of course you! Do you see any other girl around here?"
"I can't see anything," she whispered.
"Open your eyes!" he commanded.
She looked at him, eyes wide open.
He shrieked again, "Open your eyes, girl!"
"They are *open," she muttered in frustration.*
He laughed. "Not your human eyes, foolish girl!" His laugh
became a taunt as she stared helplessly at him. "Lost your powers, eh?
Well I guess that is the death of him again. Pathetic boy. That's what he
gets for following a girl across time."
She took a deep breath and whispered, "How do I open other
eyes?"
Silence.
She raised her voice. "I said, how do I open other eyes?"
His fading, gleeful laughter caused a shiver to stutter up her spine.

Terror filled me until a very distant melody calmed my racing heart

169

and sent me back into oblivion.

There was a pull from the blackness and I felt myself rising. I couldn't see, but I could hear voices. Angry voices. One sounded like Ben's. He was screaming with a hysterical tone that shocked me. I couldn't make out what exactly he was saying. Recurring words were 'evil,' 'monster,' and 'destroy.'

When his tirade was over, an eerily calm voice replied. This time my mind formed a face to go with the voices. Black hair. Dark complexion.

No.

It couldn't be.

Could it?

"You see how easy it was, in the end?" the voice said. "One little automaton and she is in my power."

"You can't have her, Ares!"

"Oh yes. That's what you keep saying. But here she is, isn't she? On my altar. You cannot touch my offerings. She belongs to me."

I blinked into the light. Through a hazy filter, Christie and Lloyd were murmuring together beside the bed. I watched them, wondering if I had a voice. I was surrounded by pastel curtains and cards. Lloyd looked up and noticed my gaze.

'Well hello, Rip," he said quietly.

"Huh?"

"Rip Van Winkle."

"Ah."

"Yep. You're *totally* ripped…apart."

Ha ha. Leave it to Lloyd to make a joke at someone's hospital bed. I smiled shakily at him through the fog.

Christie pushed over to the edge of the bed. Her brows were crushed together in concern. "Oh Grace! How are you feeling?"

"Um. Sore. What happened?" I looked around. My legs were suspended from a rack at the end of the bed. I seemed to be encased in plaster. I couldn't move my arms.

"You were hit by a car," she said gently.

"I was? Oh…" My head was suddenly full of lights, noise and the memory of pain.

Christie's voice brought me back to the present, "What is it?"

"I remember flying toward the window of Tims," I whispered. I remembered the pain everywhere. It was an agony that was gone now, replaced with only a hazy shadow of itself.

Christie nodded solemnly. Lloyd piped up, "If you wanted quick service you should just have used the drive through like everyone else. It would have been *way* less painful."

Christie scowled at him, but I laughed weakly. It was good to know the world hadn't totally changed. I looked around my room. Things were becoming a little clearer. There were cards and balloons everywhere. The balloons were so old that they were beginning to look wilted. Huh. I looked at Christie, "How long have I been out?"

"Almost four weeks."

"*Four weeks?*"

She nodded. "You missed Grad."

"Oh, no! Who did Ben go with?"

She looked at me as if I was insane.

Lloyd asked very calmly, "So do you have *severe* brain damage, Grace?"

"Um. I don't know. Maybe. Why?"

He shook his head in disgust. "Who else would Ben even *consider* taking to Grad, Grace?"

I saw Meg's face pass behind my eyes. I could imagine her frustration and smirked to myself.

Christie shook her head. "Don't be an idiot." I couldn't tell if she was talking to Lloyd or me.

"Have you guys been here a lot?" I tried to shift position, but all the plaster kept me firmly anchored in the centre of the bed.

Christie nodded. "Yeah, we've all been taking shifts. Your mom does mornings, your dad does afternoons, we do dinner hour and Ben does evenings. Did you know your mother knits now?"

"My mother? No, my mother doesn't knit."

"See?" she looked over to Lloyd, "told ya."

"Why is my mother knitting?"

Lloyd smirked, "metaphorically stitching you back together, I guess."

"Huh. Weird."

Christie smiled at me. "I am so glad you're awake and talking and thinking and stuff."

"Yeah. Me, too I guess. So what happened? Why did the car hit me? Were they swerving away from hitting a squirrel or something? Was anyone else hurt in the accident?"

Christie and Lloyd exchanged an odd look.

"What?"

"Um. It wasn't an *accident*, Grace," said Christie in a voice barely above a whisper.

"Wasn't an accident?" I scoffed, "What do you mean it wasn't an accident? Of course it was an..." I froze then, suddenly remembering the car roaring toward me in Banff. I remembered the determined expression on the face of the driver. In a very small voice I asked, "Did they find the person who hit me?" I looked from one to the other looking for a lie.

They both shook their heads.

"Oh." The face from Banff filled my mind. It couldn't have been. Could it?

A nurse bustled in at that moment. "Grace! You're back! That's great!" She beamed happily at me, "We've been wondering when today those meds would finally take effect and you'd come out of that coma. We have a pool going in the nurses' station; I think you might just have won me a dollar fifty." She grinned, but I watched her a little foggily. "Let me get your blood pressure and pulse rate." When she had finished, she looked over to Christie. "Have you called her parents yet?"

Christie shook her head, "No, but they said they'd be here at five o'clock today, and it's almost that now, so I figured they were already on their way."

The nurse nodded. "You're probably right." She grinned back at me, "Won't they be delighted?" Still smiling, she swept out of the room.

For an hour, I dozed, waking to chat a little more with them, then fading back through the fog. I thought back to what I could remember since waking up in Tims. Basically, there was nothing except that evil voice and the occasional musical cloud break amid endless oblivion.

Eventually, Christie and Lloyd stood up. Christie said, "It's almost six, so Ben should be here any minute. I'll call and see what's keeping your parents. They're going to be so happy." She leaned over to give me a gentle hug, "Welcome back. I'll see you tomorrow."

Lloyd leaned over and kissed me on the cheek, grinning mischievously, then he followed her out of the room quipping, "Keep yourself together until then!"

I faded off again and the next time I awoke, Ben had appeared at my bedside. He was looking out the window and I stared at him, shocked. His eyes were red-rimmed, creased and puffy. He looked awful.

I sniffed a tear away, and he turned and looked at me.

I waited silently for him to speak, staring back at him.

Grief and guilt were written on his face. He looked more traumatized from pain than I was.

Finally, he leaned over my face and kissed me gently. I could feel his agony through his lips, tenderly pressing his distress onto me. He rested his cheek against mine and whispered, "I'm so sorry, Grace. I can never express to you just how sorry I am."

172

I scoffed with a huff of exasperated air, but he didn't let me speak. Why was he always apologizing to me?

"I was singing, Grace. You were in danger and I was singing a Celine Dion arrangement with the choir!"

"Get serious Ben. I was walking home. I walk home every day."

"I should have been with you."

"Then you would have been hit as well, wouldn't you? What good would that have done?"

"I should have been there."

"What could you have done? Could you have reached out with your superhuman strength and stopped the car?" I chortled. "You're being stupid, Ben. Stuff happens. This wasn't your fault."

"Did you see the driver this time?"

"What? How did you…?"

He interrupted with a shrug, "I could tell you'd seen more than you were letting on. It wasn't worth pushing you about at the time. I figured you'd say something later. Now it's important. Who was it?"

"I imagined it, Ben. It doesn't matter." He looked like he was going to argue, so I carried on. "I didn't see anything this time. I was hit from behind."

He pursed his lips in annoyance. "I'm so sorry."

"Stop it Ben, you're being ridiculous."

My mom and dad rushed in. Mom just squealed in joy and grabbed me in a hug. She turned to Dad and said, "See David! I told you we needed to hurry today!"

He smirked at me while I grimaced, "Ouch! Mom! Ouch! Gently please!"

She stood back, abashed, but almost bouncing in her relief. "I'm sorry, Grace. I'm just so glad you're okay!"

Dad stood quietly at her side, radiating satisfaction.

"Hi, Dad."

"Hi, Grace. Glad you're back." He leaned over and kissed me. As he straightened up, his smile reached to my heart.

"You guys been okay through all this?" I whispered to him.

He shrugged, looking meaningfully over to my mom before looking back to me, "It's over now."

Despite the obvious delight in my return to consciousness, there was an unmistakeable air of tension in the room. Ben was not meeting my parents' eyes, and they were completely ignoring him.

I studied him until he felt my eyes and looked back. I couldn't read the expression twisted into the guilt in his gaze.

173

We sat together, my mom and dad chatting about family news and rather obviously trying to divert my attention from Ben. After an hour or so, I found myself yawning helplessly.

My dad rose, leaning to give me another kiss as he looked at my mom. "Come on Blythe. Let's go so Grace can get some rest tonight. She's got to be exhausted dealing with everything all at once." He smiled at me gently and sympathetically. I felt another surge of affection for him.

Mom stood with a meaningful look at Ben, "Okay, we'll *all* clear out of here so you can rest." She kissed me and smiled. "I'm so glad you're back Sweetheart. You really scared us."

"I'm sorry Mom."

Again she glanced over at Ben, who was staring straight ahead, ignoring us all, "It's okay, Honey," she said adamantly to me, "it wasn't *your* fault."

"Mom, it wasn't…" She stopped me from defending Ben with a pat on my arm. "Bye, Sweetie. See you tomorrow."

"Yeah. Bye, Mom. Bye, Dad."

Dad reached a hand around her waist and pulled her out of the room. He waved to me with the other hand as they rounded the corner.

Ben was still staring.

"Ben…"

He stood up. "I'd better go as well, Grace."

"No. I love you. Don't go."

"Grace." His look was hard and determined for a moment, but as he looked at me he crumpled. The tears oozed down his cheeks. "I can't do it." He muttered. "They can't make me leave you."

"Good. I want you to stay."

There was a strange expression on his face that stopped me. "Wait, what do you mean by *leave*? Who's making you leave? You're not leaving. We're staying together. We belong together. Benedicta Gratia forever, remember?" I flexed my hands, longing to hold his and my poesy ring flashed in the light.

He understood. He reached out and he gripped my hands tightly. He squeezed them emphatically with each syllable as he said, "I love you, Grace; I'll always love you."

"I love you, Ben." I assured him nervously. He was scaring me.

He stood up and leaned over me, kissing me tenderly again. Then he put a hand on either side of my face and looked past my eyes into my soul. As I stared back at him, his face was a thousand familiar faces layered on one canvas. When he finally spoke, his voice was different: deep and cavernous somehow. "Grace, whatever happens. I'm not leaving you alone anymore. I will be with you whenever you need me.

174

I'm not letting you down again.'

"Ben…"

He silenced me with another kiss. I pushed against him, feverishly. I knew that if I let him go that my life was going to change again, and in response to his fears perhaps, I was suddenly very afraid.

Staring deeply into my eyes he said, "I love you, Grace."

I smiled, and tilted my head quizzically. His lips had not moved. How was his voice so loud and clear?

"Do you love me?" His lips hadn't so much as twitched.

I wrinkled my brows and studied him, "How are you doing that? Did you take ventriloquism lessons or something?"

He shook his head, and again without him speaking aloud I clearly heard him as he instructed, "It's not ventriloquism, Love. It's telepathy."

"What…" I began, but he shook his head and placed a finger across my lips.

Silently he commanded, "Don't speak. You just need to think."

I gaped at him. I couldn't do telepathy! He was a nut case.

He laughed, and as if in reassurance spoke aloud, "I'm not crazy and neither are you." Then he was back in my head, "We've been connected. This way, I can communicate more easily. You only have to call me, so long as we're in range of each other."

"How far is the range?"

"I'm not exactly sure, somewhere around a thousand kilometres, I think."

"Hmm." I paused to consider what telepathy would mean for us. "Is this why you saw my dream that time?"

He nodded.

Huh. "What was my head like while I was in the coma?"

He smiled sadly, "Very foggy."

I nodded slowly. That made sense. "Oh!" I remembered the peaceful accompaniment that sometimes floated on the fog. "At times I heard music. Was that *you*?"

He smiled gently as he squeezed my hand.

A surge of love flowed through me. I'd thought I had been imagining the music, but Ben had come to me even in the darkest clouds of my coma. I looked up at him with all the appreciation I could put into my eyes, "I *love* you," I thought to him.

He smiled and replied in my head, "As I love you, and have always loved you, and will always love you."

"Are they planning to keep us apart?"

"Technically they're still 'in discussion' about it, but it's not looking

175

good."

The nurse poked her head around the door and smiled apologetically, "Visiting hours are over, you two. Say good-bye to your Sleeping Beauty, Ben."

Of course, the nurses knew him by name.

"Yeah, thanks Judy," he said as she popped back into the hall.

He stood up, but I tried to grab him.

"Don't go." I'm not sure whether I said it aloud or not.

He shook his head gently and backed out of the room as the tears began to roll down my cheeks.

His voice echoed in my head, "Even when I'm not with you, I have never left you, Grace."

I opened my eyes hopefully to the empty room and sighed. It was weird to have him just show up in my head like that, but it was strangely comforting, too. I drifted off into an uneasy sleep filled with strange, horrible red dreams of flying and blackness punctuated with foggy moments of music.

"Welcome back, Grace."

I opened my eyes at the familiar, comforting voice of Dr. Kyle. Yawning, I uttered a muffled, "Hi."

"How are you doing?"

"I am stiff all over." I sighed. I ached from the depth of my bones. "It'd be nice to be able to move a bit."

He nodded. "Yes. I have kept you in a medically induced coma so that your body could heal without the pain overwhelming you."

I remembered the agony of regaining consciousness in Tims and said sincerely, "Thank you."

"You're welcome. Most of the broken bones are on the mend. We're going to change casts and check things out today. I'm hoping some have now mended almost completely, but your muscles need to be moving before you're going to feel a hundred percent, so we'll want to get you up soon. Once you're walking, you'll be feeling much better quite quickly."

"What all did you have to fix?"

He laughed grimly, "I lost track of the number of breaks. Four in one thigh, three in the other, two in one arm, three in the other, a crack in your skull, several ribs broken in at least one place, some in two or three, a compression fracture in your spine, your collarbone…" He sighed, shaking his head. "You were a mess, my girl."

That explained all the pain.

"My head feels so fuzzy—like I'm thinking through clouds."

"Yes, that's not unexpected. Your brain was definitely shaken up. We've been monitoring that carefully since brain injury is the greatest danger in these kinds of traumas. Early on there was a drain in your head to minimize the pressure of the swelling. We've taken some scans of your brain, and things are looking quite good now. I'm hoping you have escaped the worst-case scenario. It's going to be months of rehabilitation to get you feeling like you're used to. We'll set you up an outpatient physiotherapy program and work at getting you back to yourself."

"Sounds hard."

"Yes, but you may not realize yet Grace just how lucky you are. You can hear, see, and speak. Your limbs are all working. None of those things is guaranteed after a traumatic incident like the one you had. I have seen a lot of patients who became vegetables with far fewer injuries than you had."

I met his sincere gaze and decided to lighten things up. With a grin I remarked, "At least you didn't need the magic potion again."

He raised an eyebrow. "Actually, we did. You've been getting regular doses since the accident. No doubt it's the main reason you're doing as well as you are, to be honest."

Oh, no. Not again. He scribbled something on my chart while I studied him. He finally looked up and met my eyes. Neither of us spoke for a while, until finally I asked the question that I'd had simmering in my mind since last fall.

"What's in that elixir of yours, Dr. Kyle?"

He studied me for a moment before he answered. It looked like he was deciding whether he should tell me the truth or find something creative to divert me. I don't know which he chose, but finally he said, "It's a solution created with a mineral spring water from beneath the Parthenon in Athens, and a... an iron based mineral compound known as hematodexigorgonite. I keep the two ingredients and mix them when needed. Separately the components can be stored for decades, but once mixed, it doesn't store well." He smiled gently then laughingly added, "Don't try to buy it at a bargain internet pharmacy please, okay? There are a couple of similar formulations that can be toxic. You don't want to go looking for the sources to try to market it yourself."

"No, I didn't think I would." I laughed back at him quietly. Funny guy. "Do you have any other patients who use it, or am I the only one?"

"There are a few others. The use is very strictly controlled. I have to apply for permission on behalf of the patient. Not all who could benefit are granted use, unfortunately." He scowled. Obviously, this was a long-standing source of irritation.

"That must really bother you to know you have something that could help someone if you aren't allowed to use it."

"Oh, yes. But the penalties are too severe to mess with, so one just has to bear the irritation." The beeper in his pocket suddenly started to hum. He pulled it out, glanced down to read the message and stood up. "I'll see you later, Grace. Don't worry. We'll have you out of here soon."

When Dr. Kyle decided I was well enough to go home. I still had a walking cast on my right leg, but the rest of the plaster was gone. My arms were both shrivelled and grey, but Judy the nurse promised they'd be back to normal soon. While I waited for my parents I took down the cards and read through them. Bonnie. The staff at Redman. Christie and Lloyd. Josh. That gave me a jolt. I hadn't thought of him. He'd said he'd be going away. I wondered how he was, wherever he was. He'd written, *Kind of a drastic way to get out of our date, Beautiful. Be safe. See you at Christmas for a rain check. Love, Josh*

My parents arrived joyfully and gathered up all the cards and balloons to take home with us. As they opened the front door and helped me up the stairs to my room, it seemed like the house itself breathed a sigh of relief at my arrival.

I kept looking for Ben. I had been sure that he would be invited to join us on the festive journey home from the hospital. I know that my mom hadn't been thrilled with our relationship, but Dad had always been friendly to him. Why had Dad joined Mom's camp, and why had the two of them become so determined to push him out of my life? It felt like he'd become an imaginary friend, existing only in the voice in my head.

The next few months were full of physiotherapy appointments and struggling through school days, which seemed strangely empty since Ben had graduated. He was at University of Calgary, and though we talked often, either in our heads or on the phone, it was proving almost impossible to get together. Whenever we made plans, suddenly I'd have some specialist appointment or a relative arriving to visit, or Ben would call up to apologize, that he'd been unavoidably delayed and would have to re-schedule. Someone was very determined to keep us apart.

Christie and Lloyd were great; they did an awesome job of helping me with notes and organization since I was missing so many classes for all the rehab appointments and because it was sometimes difficult to stay focused for long in the classes I actually made it to. I wouldn't have been passing without their help. Lloyd's jokes and puns were a welcome respite from all the serious looks and whispered concern around me in the hallways. Everyone knew about the accident. I knew I wasn't quite the same girl I had been before I'd been sent sprawling through the window of

Tims, but I hoped that eventually I would be myself again, and perhaps then everyone would stop looking at me like car accidents were contagious.

There was a lot of whispering going on as the Thanksgiving long weekend approached. There'd been seven weeks of school so far, and I could not remember a time when weeks had been so paradoxically fast and slow.

Every day seemed to drag as I tried to keep my head clear enough to concentrate, and to force my body to obey me. I grew stronger every day, but it was through force of will. Every step on the treadmill at the physiotherapist office was another victory. I saw the horribly familiar face of the driver in Banff in my head at unexpected times. The vicious expression of those eyes haunted me, and I kept feeling them burning into my back, propelling the car that had succeeded in breaking me into pieces of pain.

On the other hand, the days were a blur as I raced from one appointment to another, one assignment to another, and basically just tried to keep the fracture lines from splitting me apart again.

When the weekend came, I arrived home feeling a little like I was walking through a hazy cloud again. This foggy state descended now and again, and was constantly threatening my academics. As I pushed the door open, I jumped from the shriek that erupted.

I crouched, prepared to defend myself from the attacker, when my mother's smiling face came into view. Christie and Lloyd were behind her, as were Bonnie, Taylor, and a crowd of other familiar faces from school, all grinning in delight.

They started singing and I realized with astonishment that this was a surprise birthday party. I was turning sixteen this weekend.

This was my Sweet Sixteen party and I was stranded on a foggy island.

I looked hopefully around for Ben, but there was no sign of him.

When the singing stopped, I met Mom's eyes and mouthed the syllable of his name. Her brows lowered and she shook her head. I pursed my lips and pushed past the confused crowd to go up the stairs to my bathroom.

I ran the water in the sink and just stood there shaking. All my friends were here, except the most important one. What was my mother playing at? I closed my eyes and called out to Ben with my mind. I sent all my longing and distress. I hoped I was as pitifully pathetic as possible so he would not be able to resist coming immediately.

Sure enough, he answered with a frantic, "Grace! What's wrong?"

I couldn't help the tears that filled my eyes. No one was watching. I didn't need to be strong right now.

"Grace?" he asked again with a twinge of fear. "*Amata*, what happened?"

I tried not to sound accusing when I finally was able to ask, "Why aren't you here?"

He was sincerely confused when he responded, "What for? Do you need me?"

"It's a birthday party. Everyone from school is here…"

"Ahhhh," he said, grasping the problem. "You think I didn't want to come?"

I nodded in my head.

"*Amata*, I wasn't invited to your birthday party. If I'd known about it, I'd be there."

I started to really cry then, and he continued softly, "Go down to your party. Have fun. We'll celebrate together tonight when everyone leaves."

"It won't be the same if you're not actually here."

"Well, that's true, but that doesn't mean it won't be special." He said it suggestively. I felt the hairs rising along my spine. He chortled, as if he could sense the effect he was having on me. "Be a gracious birthday girl and then come back to me when you've sent them all home. I'll be here." He started humming a tune that was strangely calming. I washed my face, used the toilet, and then, taking a deep breath, I turned on my smile and descended the stairs to laugh and enjoy myself.

I did, too. Of course, it started as an act, but my brain didn't seem to care that my smile was fake, and before long, the giggles were genuine. Mom had food all over the place and a huge ice cream cake. We watched movies, played games, and laughed until well after midnight. Finally, Lloyd stood up and announced in pun that Christie's mom had assured him that Christie needed to have beamed into her bedroom at precisely one minute past one, and so he had to get her home at warp speed, since he wasn't willing to risk The Wrath of Mom. When they headed to the door, everyone else seemed to follow, and in a few minutes, the room was empty, except for bottles, cans, and half-empty snack bowls.

Mom smiled contentedly as she surveyed the mess. "It was a great party, don't you think?"

"Missing someone, I thought."

She scowled, "Don't start, Grace."

"Let's be clear, Mother," I said, staring her down. "I love Ben and I'm going to be with him. You are not going to keep me away from him with stupid games. I was polite tonight because of the guests, but I'm done with your nonsense. You *will* invite him next time. Am I making this clear enough for you?"

"You are not the boss in this house, young lady…" she started, but then dad emerged from the basement, looked between us and casually asked,

"Have a fun party, Hon?"

"Yeah. Except for the missing boyfriend part."

He smirked and raised his eyebrows at Mom. "See, I told you she'd notice, Blythe."

Mom turned her scowl at him then and he laughed good-naturedly.

"Come on Blythe, let's get up to bed. You can clean in the morning." He wrapped an arm around her shoulder and started coaxing her to the stairs. He looked back at me and grinned, "Happy Birthday, Honey."

"Thanks, Dad."

"Next time we'll be sure to bring you a boyfriend."

"Good."

Mom huffed in irritation, but he gave her a squeeze and guided her through the doorway to their bedroom. "Good night, Grace."

I watched the door shut behind them, just standing for a while, thinking. My mom was becoming a real pain. I sighed, strolling into the kitchen for a drink of cold water. I sipped slowly before I went upstairs to go through the evening routine. I slipped on my pyjamas and shut my bedroom door. As soon as I folded onto the bed, Ben was there.

He started his seduction with a song that filled my brain and left me quivering. Then he filled my thoughts with poetry that had me weeping with joy. He may not have been there physically, but he was omnipresent in a way that I could not have imagined, and our intimacy intensified as thought was numbed by emotion and our love was woven together in an intricate pattern of adoration, commitment and desire.

It was an unforgettable night.

November was a hazy, intimate dream of him. My days were just a break before the evening's joy. I was tired of the looks at school, as I tried to both regain my strength and to focus on the boring, every day world around me instead of the paradise that exploded in my head every night.

If my mother had the slightest clue about this, she would have invited Ben to the party. If she hadn't forced us to find our own way to celebrate my very sweet sixteenth birthday, I would not have discovered this euphoria.

By the middle of December, I was thankful for the cold weather that allowed me to bury myself in sweaters and coats, and gave everyone else the same shuffling walk through the snow that I had indoors or out. It was a measure of camouflage at least. Finally, school was out for the holidays.

I could spend every moment with Ben, so I was determined to start immediately. I decided to surprise him by stopping off at his house on my way home as soon as the final bell released us for the holidays.

As I walked, my enthusiasm for this adventure began to wane. There was a tingling in my spine that made me twist uncomfortably.

"Hello, Grace," said a soft, sultry voice behind me.

I gasped and turned. "Josh!"

He smirked and grabbed my hand, swinging me to face him. "Hiya Beautiful."

"Wait. How did you find me here? Have you been stalking me?"

He shrugged. "Just from the school. You missed our date."

"Sorry. I was in a coma."

He laughed. "Yeah. I heard something about that. Still. Not a good enough excuse."

"Oh?" I fought a smirk.

"Definitely not. You should have crossed through the netherworld to come to me."

I thought of Ben's music calling from my foggy brain. "Sorry. I have to go, Josh."

"You're really serious about the white bread, eh?"

I nodded.

He studied me for a moment, reading my expression. "Don't go to him, Grace. I'm worried about you. Hell, I'm worried about me. I need you to give me something to live for."

"Josh." I sighed. "Don't say things like that. You're responsible for you. I can't..." I struggled to find the words and gave up. "I just can't. I have enough to worry about figuring out what is attacking me all the time and why everyone seems so determined to keep Ben and me apart. I like you, Josh. I really do, but I can't do this. I am with Ben. I can't play these games with you."

"This isn't a game, Grace. It's serious. Deadly serious. Turn around, Grace. Don't go there. It's not safe."

"Are you threatening me?"

"Ben isn't safe, Grace."

"Leave me alone, Josh."

"Grace."

"No. Go." I turned away from him and ignored the tingling sense of dread intensifying in my spine as I started walking away.

I heard him sigh behind me, but he didn't follow.

I approached the non-descript little beige house with some trepidation. Paradoxically, I'd stalked this house in the height of my avoidance of Ben, but even after we started dating, he had never invited me over. I knocked on the front door tentatively. Since I had never met his parents, I was more than a little anxious suddenly to appear on their doorstep unannounced, but I figured if they had a wonderful son like Ben, they had to be fantastic people.

After a couple of minutes with no response, I knocked harder, straining to hear a sign of reaction. No music, no dog barking, no footsteps, no voices. Nothing. After another couple of minutes of waiting casually, dancing a little on the steps, feigning that it was perfectly normal for me to be there, I got brave and tried the doorbell. The ring sounded like a tolling bell in a cavernous tower.

Weird.

Glancing around to be sure no one was watching me, I took a step off the entrance and went behind the bushes that were close enough to the house that they weren't covered in snow. Climbing up the shrubs a little in order to see in, I lifted my head to peek into their front window and was stunned by the vision inside. The living room was empty, except for two brown packing boxes. I craned my neck to look through to other rooms, but everything seemed bare. No paintings on the walls. No furniture to be seen.

I turned gradually trying to process this. What did it mean? Had Ben moved without telling me? We'd 'conversed' in our heads last night as usual. I strained my memory trying to recall any word that might give a clue to this move. I came up blank.

As I came fully around to face the door again, I jumped at the black form behind me and I screamed. It was a hearty full-throated scream that would surely have brought delight to any self-defence instructor. I would never have thought such an air-horn-like sound could have come from me, but there it was, a dramatic testimony to my lung capacity and vocal chords.

The man facing me on the steps winced and reached for his ears.

Something in his eyes looked familiar, and I managed to catch and squelch the scream. Was he a relative of Ben's, with that dark complexion and thick bushy beard?

The man took his hands off his ears, and stuck out his right as he said casually, "Jack Butler, and you, I presume, are Grace?"

What a way to meet the parents. My face began glowing scarlet.

"Um. Yeah. Grace Severin. Nice to meet you, sir." I said, shaking his hand and studying his rugged look, slightly ratty jeans and dark t-shirt. He wasn't quite what I was expecting from Ben's father.

He made me nervous. Not in a 'meet the dad' kind of way, but in a 'this guy wants to kill you' kind of way.

He laughed, "No 'sir' necessary; I'm not the future father-in-law: I'm just the wastrel uncle." He gave the door a shove. "Come on in. Are you here looking for Ben?"

"Yes."

"Why don't you text him and see where he is? He's probably on his way home right now. Step inside."

I hovered on the doorstep. This felt wrong.

"I don't have my cell phone at the moment." It was sitting on the charger at home. I wished it was in my pocket. Suddenly I really wanted 911 capability.

He looked at me in mock severity. "What? How can that be? I thought all youth of your generation came attached with cell phones in their placenta. You can't be real. You must be like one of those thirty year old actors that pretend to be teens on the TV shows."

Ha ha.

I decided to ignore his teasing and changed the subject. "Where are they moving to?"

He smirked and his eyes glinted with a secret, "Oh ho! You've never been to your darling Ben's abode before today, have you?" His laugh was a little demented. "Oh, this is much too fun! Well," he said, opening the front door behind him, "you'd better come in then, and explore."

I didn't like the glint of his eyes.

"Ah, no thanks." I said stepping back, "I have to be getting home now. I'll call him later."

He was suddenly behind me, blocking the way. "No Grace. I insist. Come inside." There was an ominous glow in his eyes. Inside the house, pain and death were waiting for me.

A paperboy came up the walk at that moment. It was a little kid hauling his stack of papers behind him on a toboggan. "Hey, mister. Here's your paper."

I sighed and took a step off the step.

"Mister, you owe me for the last bill. Could I collect it now?"

I wanted to run, but I forced myself to turn slowly and walk slowly down the steps.

He laughed that freaky laugh again and called after me, "Fine, scaredy cat. Another time…" I heard the jingle of change, but didn't turn back to see if he was paying the kid.

His voice made me shiver. I increased my pace, opened my mind and shouted, "Ben!" with all the power that I'd sent aloud when Uncle Jack had surprised me earlier.

He was there immediately. "What?"

I didn't know what to say. "Didn't you hear me screaming earlier?" I was getting breathless as I tried not to slip on the ice as I race-walked down the sidewalk.

There was silence.

"Ben?"

Very slowly, and so quietly that I could barely make out his thoughts, he whispered, "Why were you screaming?"

I could hear the fear.

"I went to surprise you at your house. I met your Uncle Jack."

I heard him gasp before he demanded, "Where are you now?"

I told him, and he said, "Near Lloyd's?"

"Yeah."

"Then get to his house as fast as you can and stay there."

'Why?"

"Are you running?"

"No."

"Start running, Grace.

"What…"

He shouted then, "START RUNNING!"

I was seized with his panic and I obeyed. I strained my hearing for any sounds, like a car screeching around the corner, or the rhythm of someone else's running feet.

I heard it just as I got to the end of Lloyd's road. A huge dog came bounding around the corner, snuffling as it sniffed a zigzag path that followed my steps.

Behind the dog was the steady pounding of powerful steps crunching on the squeaky snow. Someone far more used to running was definitely coming. A second set of steps echoed behind.

I was puffing from the exertion, and my lungs were burning from the cold, but the adrenaline was doing its job. I felt super-powered. Lloyd's house loomed ahead of me and I almost flew up the pathway. I glanced behind me as I arrived on his front step and began pushing his doorbell over and over.

A pair of shadows appeared at the end of the cul-de-sac and I started pounding desperately on the door with my other hand. Two tall men were silhouetted by the street light as the dog approached Lloyd's front yard. I almost punched Lloyd in the face as he opened the door. Low, menacing laughter cut through the cold air.

"Grace?" Lloyd exclaimed as I pushed past him into his house. "What's wrong?"

"Shut the door! Shut the door!" I screamed. He complied instantly, and threw the dead bolt for good measure. It made a reassuring clunk as it fell into position.

"I'm in," I thought to Ben. "I'm at Lloyd's."

I felt his wave of relief as I glanced out the front window to see a shadowy figure jog ever so slowly past the house.

"Are you going to tell me why I had to run?" I thought.

Ben sighed and my blood ran cold when he said, "I don't have an Uncle Jack, Grace."

I started to shake then, great rolling shakes like an ocean storm. I collapsed on the floor of Lloyd's living room, quivering and sweating. I was going into shock. This was becoming an irritating habit. Lloyd stood at the door, looking stunned.

There was a knock at the door and my heart leapt again, but Ben spoke in my head, "It's just me."

I sputtered out, "It's Ben, Lloyd. Let him in." Uncharacteristically, Lloyd had not said a thing since I arrived unannounced on his doorstep, and he looked uncertain about my mental state now. "Seriously, Lloyd. Let him in."

He shook his head, so I added. "You have a peep hole, right? Check."

He held his body as far from the door as possible while he looked out the peephole. He grunted, unlocked the bolts, and opened the door.

Ben sprang into the room and grabbed me demanding, "Are you okay? Say you're all right!" while the bolts all crunched into place again.

"Yes, yes," I insisted. "Except I may be going into shock." Maybe I was too lucid to be going into shock?

He started pulling off my winter coat, saying, "Let's regulate your temperature a little. Lloyd, can you get her a glass of water?"

Ben sat me in his lap and kept rocking me back and forth until my pounding heart settled and the shivering stopped. Lloyd just sat in a recliner opposite us, staring blankly at the TV, ignoring us. I wondered if he might be in greater shock than I was.

Finally, I looked up at Ben and asked, "Why are you moving?"

"Right. You were at the house."

I nodded.

"I don't know how to explain this, Grace."

My heart started to pound. I swallowed. "Truthfully."

"Of course. You need to know that I don't have parents"

"What? Yes you do. Everyone has parents."

He nodded once in assent, "I was born to parents, obviously, but I don't live with parents."

"Since when?"

He shrugged, but didn't reply.

"So you live in that house by yourself?"

"Yeah."

"Is that why you stayed at school so late? Because there was no one to go home to?"

He bobbed his head and gave me a little smile, "I hadn't really thought of it, but probably."

"You know, if you have an empty house, we could get a lot of privacy…"

He smirked and raised one eyebrow, "Indeed."

Lloyd stirred in the recliner. I glanced over at him. He was looking a little aggravated.

"We won't be going to my house, Grace."

"Why not?

"Because I'm not returning to that house anymore."

"So you *are* moving."

He flicked his eyebrows, "I wasn't, but I am now."

"What was with the boxes then?"

"Oh, I just never got around to unpacking those. Now I'll leave them behind or just have the movers take them on eventually—when the house is not so hot any longer."

"Hot." Like in a bad spy movie. "Just who is that guy?"

He shook his head, "No idea."

"Get serious."

He looked at me for a minute, clearly pondering whether to tell me the truth or not.

"Come on, Ben, someone has to tell me eventually."

Finally, he nodded, and said, "His name is Ares. I don't know if he was after me or after you, but it doesn't really matter."

True.

"Why is he after us?"

His mouth tightened, he looked over at Lloyd who watched us silently and then he shrugged his shoulders with a sigh. "That's the question, isn't it?" He glanced at his watch and remarked, "Grace, your folks will be worrying about you. Let's get you home."

187

"Lloyd, before we go, can I use your bathroom?"

He nodded at me and I headed down the hall.

I heard Lloyd say, "It's true, isn't it? They're *actually* trying to kill her."

Ben murmured.

"They're going to make sure you two are never together, aren't they? I don't know how you can take any of this."

Ben murmured again.

I stared at the wall and thought. No accidents. Someone wanted me dead. What had I ever done that this Ares guy thought I should die for it? I flushed the toilet and looked at myself in the mirror while I washed my hands. I was nothing special at all. I was nothing worth murdering. Was it all about keeping me away from Ben? It just didn't make any sense at all.

I joined Ben and Lloyd in the entrance. Ben gave me a shuddering smile. Usually he was better at faking cheerfulness.

He reached out and clapped a hand on Lloyd's shoulder. "Thanks man. I appreciate it."

"No problem," muttered Lloyd. "Any time."

I embraced Lloyd and he held on a little longer than was comfortable. I pulled out of the embrace with another blush starting. "Bye Lloyd. Thanks."

Ben drove me home. I watched him as he drove, pondering.

At my door, he held me for a long time.

"I love you, Ben."

He smiled softly. "I'm glad. I've loved you for so long. It is hard when you don't feel the same."

"I'm sorry."

He nodded. "I know." He kissed me softly to show his forgiveness. When he pulled back, he stared into my eyes with a longing that stole my breath. "It's going to become more difficult to be with you, Grace. But I want you to remember that my love for you is greater than anything else in my life. I want you to remember that I am always with you, even if I am not present with you."

My heart sank. "What does that mean?"

Ben lifted my chin with a finger and stared into my eyes. "We'll make it all right, *Amata*. We'll be together, if it kills me."

I'd have felt better if I wasn't afraid that he meant that literally.

EPILOGUE

"So he's revealed himself at last."

O looked intensely between Mars and Xandros. "He almost got her. We need to move now."

Mars shook his head. "He's just trying to bait you into action."

"It's working."

"Don't let it."

"If he'd been moving against her, she would already be dead. He's still playing with us," Xandros observed.

O shuddered. "He came too close."

"Not too close. Just close enough to let you know that he can get her if he wants to."

"Exactly! If he can get her whenever he wants, then he's too close!"

Mars rested a hand on O's shoulder. "Calm down. He only got that close because we let him. We want him to feel secure. We want him to get comfortable, because if he believes we're slacking, then he'll make mistakes."

"No."

"Yes. You know him. He's going to get sloppy. He always does. Trust me. I've been battling him a long time."

"If she gets hurt…"

"I'm with O. Let's just go now," muttered Xandros, rippling his muscles.

Mars sighed. "Xandros, your bravery is not in dispute, but you know very well that you also have had a tendency to race to a fight when preparations weren't as complete as they should have been."

"Hey!"

Mars shook his head. "Don't try to fight me Xandros. I am the tactician here, and you will obey my orders."

Xandros scowled, but remained silent.

O studied him thoughtfully before he looked back up to Mars. "You

189

have a plan?"

"I have a plan."

"Is it going to work?"

Mars raised an eyebrow. "Obviously I think so. No guarantees, though."

O's lips tightened.

Xandros flexed and then smirked, "I'll look after her O, one way or another."

O's nostrils flared and he took a step forward, clenching his fists.

Mars met his step with a glare at Xandros. "Enough, both of you. We will protect her to the best of our ability for the benefit of all."

BOOK TWO:

GRACE AWAKENING POWER

In a foggy forest, three men in ancient armour were gathered.

"There," the handsome blond declared, "Grace is moving to begin her training."

"Indeed. Did you hear that Thalia is called to Olympus? Her bliss has been wrapped in bitterness and anger for too long. Aphrodite is afraid." Mars observed.

Xandros smirked, "So you're saying motherhood stole her joy?"

O bit his lip to keep from smiling. This was serious.

Mars shook his head. "The stress of trying to nurture the hope for her sisters has been hard for her. She did not expect it. She must go regain her strength or she will be useless. Someone else has to look after the young one. It's time for me, O."

The blond nodded, resigned. "Yes. Are you prepared, Mars?"

"I'm ready."

O looked at the third warrior, who was leaning against a tree, looking bored. "Can you wait, Xandros?"

Xandros smirked, "Yeah. For a little *longer."*

Mars looked around. "I sense Ares' presence. He is feeling powerful after the success of his last attack."

O shuddered. "It was too close."

Mars nodded, "She's all right at the moment, but he will increase his pressure as she trains. I'll protect her, O."

"You'd better."

Xandros flexed his biceps. "I'm ready to take over if Mars can't handle it."

Mars gave a tense chuckle. "I know. O, you need to work here with Xandros to prepare for the next stage."

O nodded curtly at Xandros who smirked again.

"All right then. To the battle!"

CHAPTER ONE

THAT SOUNDED OMINOUS

Lakes are surrounded by mountains, Ida is watching above her.
Visions are clear to a new friend; Gorgon the monster will smother
Charis with fiery eyes glowing. Warrior grows with awareness,
Sensing that soon he'll be battling, questioning values and fairness.

As I walked into the house, Dad looked up from where he sat at the kitchen table. He had a serious expression as he stared at his coffee mug. "Grace, I don't want you to freak out, okay?"

I furrowed my brows. "About what?"

"Your mother wants what's best for you. I don't want you being angry with her."

I felt my ears beginning to burn. "This is about her irrational dislike of Ben, isn't it?" My mom seemed determined to hate my boyfriend.

"Just be calm, Grace. It's for the best."

His apologetic face was enough to tell me that I didn't want to hear whatever they were going to tell me. I stomped up the stairs to leave my school bag on the floor and flopped onto my bed, fuming in frustration. I was sick of this. Maybe Ben and I needed to go away, or perhaps I could stay at his house for a while.

The garage door opened. I sat up. Battle call.

Dad was talking to Mom as I came into the room. She whirled to look at me and then flashed an irritated look back to Dad. "Well Grace, I guess your father has told you that it's time for a family meeting?"

I scowled.

"Have a seat," she said.

I shook my head. "I'll stand."

193

She rolled her eyes. "Fine. Suit yourself." She pasted a fake smile on her face and perkily announced, "We have some great news! Your father has been called to do some work at head office for the next year or so." Dad gave her a quizzical look as she clarified, We're moving to Greece! Won't it be fantastic to stay with Aunt Aglaea?"

"No."

"Yes, Grace. You'll go to the International School. It'll be great."

"I'm not going, Mom."

"You love Greece!"

"I love Ben more."

"You can't rule your life by an adolescent crush, Grace. Don't be silly."

"It's not a *crush*, Mother."

She went to argue, but Dad cut her off. "Blythe, perhaps there's another solution?"

"No, David. She's too young to know better and she can't stay here in Calgary with all…" she glanced at me, "all *this* going on. Cars chasing her down. People attacking her on trains. No more of this. I want her out of Calgary. She's coming to Greece with us."

"I don't want to go anywhere. I want to stay right here with Ben."

She scowled at me.

I wanted to scream or burst into tears. I wasn't going to let her see that. Before she could say anything more, I stomped up to my room and slammed the door.

This could not be happening.

I'd just spent months recovering from a car accident. I realized that the pain of that nothing like the pain I was going to have to deal with next, because no one was going to put me into a medically induced coma to help me survive it.

"It'll be all right, *Amata*." Ben's voice came into my head. His gentle Italian endearment failed to sooth me. This strange telepathy between us was convenient at times.

"It won't," I thought back to him.

"We'll talk to each other every day. It will be fine."

His reassurances just made me sadder. I wanted him to come to my house and fight for me. Frustrated tears poured onto my pillow. He sent me calming waves and started humming one of his beautiful compositions. My body relaxed into his music and carried me into sleep on its strains, just as he had during my coma last summer.

I didn't let my parents off easily. They continued to pretend it was all about jobs and claimed that they were sorry they were tearing my life apart. They didn't fool me for one second.

At first, I'd thought it was about the hit and run that had put me into a coma last summer. It made sense that they were afraid of whoever was driving the car that had hit me. This didn't.

My mom had been mad at Ben, but now it seemed somehow that they were *afraid* of him. My family was moving me away from Ben, not because they were going to Greece, but because of fear. I didn't understand it, but I sensed the truth of it. It was a truth that would eviscerate me, and they acted like it was nothing more than a minor inconvenience.

All weekend I challenged them, ranting and screaming or just weeping and howling. They only looked at me with sad eyes and refused to respond. I guess they were hoping not to incriminate themselves, but it was too late for that.

"How can you pull me out of school, tear me away from my life just because you are worried about a teen romance?" I shouted at Mom. "If you are scared of Ben…"

Mother gave me a withering stare. "I am not scared of *Ben*."

"Fine. If you are scared of the way Ben feels for me, it seems like a huge over-reaction to send me half way around the world!"

"Grace, I know how you believe you feel about him. I know how he claims to feel about you."

"*Believe? Claim?*" Lights were flashing behind my eyes like fireworks, I was so furious. "You're completely *terrified* of the way I feel about him, aren't you? You can't stand the way he makes my knees weak with his music."

"That damn music again! Grace, you can't trust that kind of feeling!" Her eyes blazed.

"You are ripping my world to shreds, and leaving my heart in tatters because of *your* own stupid fears. I am a helpless victim!"

"Enough of the melodrama, Grace. You're not helping anything behaving like this. Trust us. It's for the best."

"He's at university now, anyway." I reminded her, my voice plaintive now. "It isn't like I can see him every day at school. If that wasn't been a problem in October or November, why is it a problem in January?"

Ben came into my head and tried to soothe me with loving whispers. It didn't work.

Sunday night I was watching TV with Dad when Mom came into the room.

Dad looked up at her with a thoughtful expression. "Blythe, what if we send Grace to your sister?"

She stared at him. "That's what we're doing."

"Not Aglaea, obviously. There are three of you, remember. We can send her to Bright in B.C. Bright is as capable as Aglaea."

Mom shook her head. "That's not exactly fair to Bright, is it? Saddling her with this kind of responsibility?"

"You're kidding, right?"

Bright would love an extended visit. I'd love to visit with her, but now I wanted Ben. "I want to stay here in Calgary!"

Mom gave an exasperated sigh. "That is not an option, Grace. Stop being ridiculous about this. David, help me out here."

"Look," said Dad, "she doesn't want to come to Greece, but we need to leave here. Things will be crowded in Aglaea's apartment with all of us there. Bright would love to have her, and you know that Grace was due to start working with her this summer anyway."

Huh? That was news to me.

"David."

"Think about it. You can go to Greece and focus on…something pleasant. Grace can go to B.C. where she'll have fun with Bright. You know this is the perfect solution."

She stared at him for a while, but then Mom sighed in defeat. "Fine. I'll call Bright."

Dad wrapped Mom in his arms and winked at me over her head, as if he had just achieved a victory for me.

I went back to my room. It did not feel like a win to me. Bright lived in the Shuswap, five hundred kilometres away from Calgary, all the way across the Rocky Mountains from Ben. I had felt safe and secure now. Life was good. No one had attacked me in over a month. I was happy.

Just when I thought the worst was over, they dropped this bomb. My life sucked.

I went to school on Monday with red, puffy eyes. I'd hoped no one would notice, but unfortunately, I did not attend a school for the blind. My best friend Christie came up to me at our locker and gasped when she saw me.

"Grace! What happened? Did somebody die?"

I swallowed. In a manner of speaking, *I'd* died, but she probably wouldn't believe me, considering I was still standing upright in front of her. I managed to croak out, "I have to move" before the tears overwhelmed me again and I crinkled to the floor. People were looking at me strangely. It didn't matter what anyone thought of me now, so I released myself again to my agony. I would stay for a week so I could write my exams. One lousy week. Who cared about self-control when my world was destroyed?

Christie settled on the floor beside me, eyes large with shared grief. "Why? What happened?"

I sniffled and explained. "My dad has apparently been called to the head office of his company in Greece. Mom is going with him. They're going to move in with my mom's sister Aglaea. I have to go live with my Auntie Bright in B.C. while they're gone." A fresh torrent of tears erupted as students passed me in the halls, sending curious looks in my direction. I tried to regain my composure.

"Is your aunt a shrew?" Christie asked.

I smiled in spite of myself. "No. In fact, Auntie Bright is wonderful, and I'd love to stay with her under normal circumstances. It's just that now there's..." Another wave of tears hit and I couldn't continue.

"Ben, right?" Christie guessed.

I nodded miserably. Ben. What would I do without the other half of my heart?

A week later, I walked down the ramp at the Kelowna Airport and looked for Auntie Bright. She wasn't usually very hard to miss, since she was always dressed very colourfully and had some trouble standing still. I looked for her bouncing cheerfully in the crowd, but she wasn't there. Instead, I spotted her husband, my Uncle Jim. He was tall with brown hair. Not exactly handsome in a conventional way, but with extremely kind eyes, which improved his looks considerably.

I threw my arms around him and he engulfed me in a fond bear hug, muttering brusquely, "Hiya Gracie!"

I giggled. He was the only person in the family who called me that. Mashed against his chest I returned the greeting and asked the obvious question. "Where's Auntie Bright?"

"She had a performance with her dance group tonight. She should be home by the time we get there."

At first, we filled the car with small talk about my parents. After an awkward moment, he carefully skirted around the 'boyfriend problems,' and we listened to music while talking about neutral things like the weather and the scenery. It was not uncomfortable; it was just safe. Jim wasn't stupid.

We pulled up to their house in Salmon Arm an hour later. I noticed Auntie Bright's empty parking spot. "No sign of Fatima." Fatima was Auntie Bright's rather colourful ancient VW Beetle.

He smiled. "Not yet. They'll be along shortly, though. I'll show you up to your room."

We walked up the stairs and he stopped at the first bedroom in the hallway. My parents usually used this room when we came in the summers. He smiled and waved his arm grandly at the doorway. "Your chamber, Milady!"

I stepped inside and then gasped. The walls had been red last visit, but they weren't now. I took another step as I gazed around dumbstruck. Auntie Bright had redecorated the room for me. Most of her rooms were decorated in vivid jewel tones: fuchsia, scarlet, emerald, purple and royal blue. This room was not her style at all. I recalled admiring a scheme like this in a decorating magazine with her last year. It was slightly reminiscent of my room at home in Calgary, but way more gorgeous. She'd painted the walls robin's egg blue. The doors, trim and furniture were white. There was a handmade quilt and piles of pillows in white, turquoise and teal. There was one of her hand knit rugs, similar to the one I had in Calgary, on the floor. The space was a dream room; it was beautiful.

I glanced back at Jim with my jaw down and managed to sputter out, "Wow."

"Bright said these were your favourite colours."

"Yes. Did she make the quilt herself?"

He nodded, "She wanted you to feel welcome. She knew you hadn't really wanted to come."

I grimaced a little. "It's not that I didn't want to come," I paused, thinking sadly of Ben, "It's more that I didn't want to leave."

He nodded, "I understand. We just want you to know that we are very happy to have you living with us, Grace, and we want you to feel completely at home here. You can't be more loved anywhere else."

I smiled. "Thanks, Uncle Jim. I know. I'm thankful you were willing to have me. It was always the highlight of my year when I could come to stay with you guys."

He grinned. "Bright will be delighted to hear that." He pointed to the pair of doors on the south wall. You have a walk in closet and your own en suite bathroom." He glanced meaningfully at my single suitcase and observed, "It should take Bright about twenty-four minutes to decide you need help filling up the space!" As we laughed together, he said, "I'll leave you to unpack. I have a couple of phone calls to make. Bright should be home any time. Are you hungry?"

"Not really."

"Come down when you are. We have some goodies in the fridge."

"Thanks."

He turned to leave, whistling quietly to himself as he headed down the stairs. I looked around my beautiful room. I felt very blessed. I stepped up to the window and looked out at Shuswap Lake sparkling in the distance, nestled amid the rolling hills of deep green and the purple tower of Bastion Mountain above. I thought back to the view out my window in Calgary: the siding of the house next door. Yes, I was very, very blessed.

I set my laptop on the little desk, glancing at the bookshelf above it. There were several books of assorted vintage and a few photo albums.

I hung my clothes in the spacious closet, which only made it look larger, since I'd used a scant eighteen inches of about eight feet of hanging space. I put my cosmetic case in the bathroom drawer, and I was unpacked. I stashed my empty suitcase in the closet and walked over to the desk. I contemplated sending an email to Ben, Christie, or even Mom, but the albums and books on the shelf above the desk distracted me again.

I pulled a white photo album off the shelf and studied it with interest. The cover was white lace over satin. On the front was a bridal couple in silhouette. It was Bright and Jim's wedding album. I opened it curiously.

There was Bright, breathtakingly beautiful in her white gown. It was quite different for a couple of reasons. First, I'd never seen Bright wearing anything as plain as white. Secondly, her gown was very different from the style of those I'd seen in the wedding albums of my friends' parents. Her dress seemed to have been made of a light silk; it flowed from her shoulders to the ground in a wave. A sheer train was attached at the shoulders, a diaphanous waterfall flowing down her back and then trailing out behind her like a river. Her hair was piled high on her head in an astonishingly complicated arrangement of braids and little curls that worked into a bun at the top of her head. Tiny flowers formed a crown at the top of her head. She looked ethereal. Timeless.

My mother and Aunt Aglaea had been her bridesmaids. Their dresses were the same style, though their trains only reached their ankles. The colour of the dresses was reminiscent of Auntie Bright's car and the Aegean Sea: a deeply intense Mediterranean blue.

In some photos, Jim stood beside her, looking incredibly handsome. He seemed to be glowing in her presence. I had the distinct sense that he felt he was the luckiest person on the planet and he was still reeling from the shock of successfully courting Bright. His bliss was emanating from his every pore.

One photo showed the three sisters on the dance floor, holding hands with their arms raised, circling together, faces beaming. Joy was evident in their glowing, youthful expressions. It was a pose I'd seen replicated in paintings and statues. Their joy, love and intimacy were captivating.

Something was odd, though. I looked from the photos of the sisters to one of Jim and back again.

I flipped through the album and studied all the photos again. I closed my eyes and visualized Uncle Jim waiting for me as I'd come into the reception area at the airport. Yes. There was no doubt about it.

In these photos, Jim was young. In fact, he was *astonishingly* young. He was clearly not much more than twenty. He had an innocent look about him. While Bright, Blythe and Aglaea looked young in these photos as well, they also looked knowing, as if they had seen the world. What's more, what was truly remarkable was that they also looked *exactly* the same as they did today. How was that possible? How could Jim age twenty years or more, while the sisters had not? I had never really thought about how young they looked. I'd just presumed they'd looked different in their youth and they were just healthy and active. Jim was healthy and active. I thought of his face as it was today. Though he was slender and athletic, his twenty years of marriage showed in the laugh lines around his eyes and the slight sag below his chin. In contrast, not one of the sisters had a line or a droop.

My stomach heaved a little. Why had I never noticed this before?

I pulled out a magazine and settled in to wait for Bright's return. I was trying to decide whether to ask her about whatever fitness and skin care regimes the three sisters had discovered that was keeping them so young. It was a bit creepy. I looked back at the wedding album and studied their laughing faces. I was an only child, and seeing their joy together gave me a twinge of longing. They were so close even though they lived far apart. I sighed and flipped through my magazine absently. Every once in awhile I looked around my room in awe at the effort that Bright had put into preparing a place for me in such a short time. Unless mom had been planning behind my back, she could only have given Bright a week's notice.

I heard the distinctive chug of Fatima the Bug as she came down the street. I didn't bother to suppress the grin as I visualized Auntie Bright emerging in all her eccentric belly dancing glory from the equally vivid and eccentric vehicle. I heard the thunk of the doors shutting and the beat of her feet as she came up the stairs. I opened my bedroom door with the grin still in place, but I didn't have a chance to say anything before I was enveloped in Auntie Bright's flowing sleeves and beaming smile.

"Welcome, Grace!"

I hugged her warmly and felt instantly at home.

She laughed again and pulled me in for another hug before she spun me away in a twirl, then pulled me back to arms' length away from her again. With her hands on my shoulders, she looked me over. "Well, you've certainly grown into a beautiful young lady." She met my eyes and added, "A young lady with a broken heart, eh?" I dropped my gaze, but she was all business now. "Will you show me the scars?" I met her eyes again, and she smiled gently as she added, "the scars on the outside, at least…"

There were never any secrets from Bright, and so I held my arms up for inspection. She studied the reminders of the gashes, tsking and asking questions about Ben, my physiotherapy, school, and friends. We sat together on my bed, and then wandered down the stairs to the kitchen while the tea brewed, and finally settled on the red couch in the living room. We talked for hours as she kindly and carefully pried everything from me, except the biggest secret. Ben had never said not to tell anyone, but I knew hearing voices in one's head was not something one talked about unless one wanted to enter a psychiatric hospital. Thinking back to the jealousy of last year, I wondered fleetingly if Rae-Ann's schizophrenic voices had sounded like Ben.

Finally, Bright stood up and announced, "Well, this has been lovely, but you need your sleep. Tomorrow will be a busy day. The school has a semester turn around day tomorrow, and then the new session starts on Monday. We'll deal with all your paperwork and then have some fun. Good night!" With a smacking kiss on my cheek, she disappeared. I wondered how long it would take me to get used to Bright's sudden flits of movement.

Bright took me to school the next morning to meet with the counsellor at my new school. As we walked from the parking lot toward the attractive, modern cement building, I saw the lake sparkling in the distance, and realized that rooms on the west side of the building would have wonderful views over the roofs of the subdivisions below to the lake and the rolling green hills around it. I shook my head, thinking back to the brick and cement of my formerly beloved Redman High. All the nature it could offer was the odd scraggly tree here and there and some unhealthy grass. This was so beautiful, so civilized. I wondered if perhaps life would be all right here, even without Ben.

"Not *without* me," he said in my head.

I smirked in spite of myself. I thought, "Fine, not without you. How is, 'without your physical presence'?"

I felt his melancholy agreement, "I'll give you that." I could hear a faint chuckle in my head. "Have a good day."

"Thanks Ben." I thought back to him.

We had reached the double doors and Auntie Bright looked back at me as she opened the door. She met my eyes and stopped mid-step, looking intensely into them. "Hmmm," she said cryptically.

"What?"

She shook her head. "I didn't realize…" she stopped herself. "Never mind. We'll talk later."

We stepped inside the school and my jaw dropped at the huge open space in front. Its high roof was glowing from the skylights above. Hallways ran in three directions, one ahead, and one to either side of where we were standing. The hub was the two storey open area that was filled with sunlight. "Wow." I said.

She smiled, "Yes, it's quite a lovely school, isn't it?" She walked over to the railing. Indicating the tables arranged below she said, "They call that area the atrium. You can buy your lunch there at the cafeteria. She pointed to an opening on the left. "They have quite a good chef's training program here. They're always winning awards in the trades competitions."

She turned back toward the entrance and now on our right I noticed the small counselling centre. We entered the round room which was edged in windows, some opening to the outside, some to the inside hallways. A few computers lined one wall; the rest of the space was filled with university and college displays, catalogues and posters. A couple of students were sitting at round tables with papers spread out in front of them. A hallway led to a series of offices. A middle-aged woman was sitting at a desk on the right side of the room. She smiled at us and asked, "Is this Grace?"

I smiled back and nodded, "Yes. Hello."

"Welcome to Shuswap Lake Secondary. Your appointment is with Mr. Stone. He'll get your classes all set up for you. I'll see if he's free."

She went to stand up, but before she could, a tall, friendly looking older man was standing in the doorway of the small office behind her, stepping forward with his hand outstretched in greeting. "Hello Grace," he said as he shook my hand. Then he nodded to Bright behind me, shaking her hand as well, and waved us into his office with a sweep of his arm. "Have a seat; this shouldn't take us long, since your aunt has already done the basic registration stuff. Everything has been approved for your transfer. Did you bring your report cards from Calgary?"

I nodded as I handed him my papers; he started typing right away. He was right. It wasn't even an hour later that all the paperwork had been dealt with, we'd had a tour of the school, and we were heading back across the parking lot to Fatima the Bug.

Like everything else about her, Auntie Bright's car was very distinctive. It was an ancient VW Beetle that she'd had painted a vivid Mediterranean blue, and then she'd hand painted it with a swirling variety of giant paisleys in purples, blues, yellows and reds. Here and there were dots of gemstones glued on as accents, just to add sparkle. At first glance, it seemed as if she'd upholstered the car with vivid cloth and sequins. People did double takes on the highway, and she generally had at least one person stop to admire and to ask her about it wherever she went. Children were drawn to it. People smiled as they saw her coming. Last summer she told me, "People are such cowards. They come and rave about how beautiful my car is, how they wish they could have a unique car, and yet they content themselves to drive around in boring mud coloured cookie cutters. I don't get it."

"That didn't take any time at all, did it?" observed Bright as we bounced over the first speed bump on the way out of the school parking lot.

"No, I expected to be there a lot longer."

She laughed, "You will be, I guess, just not today."

Ha ha.

"Let's go to Tims, Grace. There's one just up the road. We can have some lunch; there are a couple of things I want to discuss with you."

That sounded ominous.

Tims was only a few blocks up, so we were settled at a table with our soup, coffee and a doughnut in only a few minutes. Being her typical perky self, Bright had made our order, joking happily with the woman behind the counter, but as she set the tray on our table, her eyes grew serious.

She got right to the point: "You're connected to Ben." It was a statement, not a question.

I suspected what she was referring to, but thought I'd better be absolutely sure before I said something that would get me hauled off to an asylum. "What do you mean by 'connected' exactly?"

She studied me carefully. "You can hear each other now."

I glanced up at the ceiling, "No, not now."

She knew I was being evasive and she lowered her eyebrows in irritation as she clarified, "But you were communicating with him earlier, as we went into the school?"

I sighed and just nodded slowly.

She pursed her lips slightly. "Well *that's* going to be problematic."

"Why?"

Now it was her turn to sigh before she replied, "No one anticipated that." She looked up, leaning back in her chair and muttered to the ceiling, "All this planning and they make such an obvious oversight."

I wondered who 'they' were.

"We thought by bringing you here we could keep the dreams away. But now look what he's done. The dreams are walking."

"What does that mean?"

She shook her head. "For you, it means…" Her pause caught my breath. "For you it means *trouble*," she finally said. I was pretty sure that wasn't the word she'd stopped herself from saying. I met her eyes and saw the truth there. Walking dreams were going to bring death. Terrific.

"How long have you been connected?"

I thought for a moment, "A couple of months I guess. Maybe from the beginning. It's hard to say, really."

"You've undoubtedly been tuned into him from the beginning, but someone connected you. Who was it?"

"I don't know…" and then I remembered the strange musical murmuring and gasped, "Oh!"

Bright watched me calmly, waiting patiently for me to speak.

Finally, I breathed deeply and whispered, "He called her Connie."

Bright's eyes widened, and then she started to chuckle, shaking her head. "Concordia Iugo. Oh, that old fox!" she remarked in an amused tone, then she bobbed her head thoughtfully and clicked her tongue, but didn't say anything else.

We ate our soup. The conversation went along trivial matters for a while. As we were eating our doughnuts, I finally felt brave enough to ask, "Auntie Bright?"

She looked up somewhat hesitantly, hearing the seriousness of my coming question in the way I spoke her name. "Hmm?"

I met her eyes steadily. "Who are 'they'?"

She looked back just as steadily, holding my gaze as if searching for the answer in my eyes. Finally, she took a deep breath and said, "Need to know, Grace." She pursed her lips slightly, as if she was holding back something she wanted to say to me.

"Why? It's *my* life, isn't it?"

She smiled faintly as she said quietly, "In a manner of speaking."

What? My brows furrowed.

She grimaced, "Fine. It's your life."

Suddenly Ben broke into my thoughts, "Tell her that there isn't anything bad happening here. Tell her they're wrong. Tell her you should come back to Calgary."

This was a first. Now I was an instant messaging service. I sighed. He was insistent: "Tell her, Grace."

Bright was watching me, eyebrows raised. She knew he was talking to me. How could she tell? Was there an 'on' button blinking on my forehead somewhere?

"Grrraace…" Ben dragged my name out as a command.

"Fine." I muttered, half to him, half aloud.

With an irritated sigh I announced, "Ben says I should tell you that they are wrong; there isn't anything bad happening in Calgary, and I should be allowed to go back there." I felt like an idiot.

"Sorry Ben," she said, watching me carefully, "it's not in my power to make those decisions."

I felt his answering growl of frustration, and grimaced.

Bright gave me an apologetic smirk as she piled the dishes on the tray and stood up. "Let's go do some Back to School shopping, Grace," she said in an obvious attempt to distract me.

"It's February, Auntie Bright. That's August shopping."

She laughed, "Don't steal my joy, Grace. You're starting at a new school tomorrow and I saw that single, lonely suitcase you brought along. You obviously need a new wardrobe!"

Bright's laughter was contagious even when I was frustrated, so we climbed into Fatima, and headed off to Vernon and Kelowna to fill her dual needs to shop and to keep my brain occupied for several hours so I wouldn't ask her any more questions she didn't want to answer.

Monday was sunny and bright. There'd been a bit of snow overnight, and the world sparkled, looking clean and new again. My first day of school. Luckily, the new semester was beginning today, so I wasn't terribly out of place or too obviously the new girl. The school was big enough that I didn't stand out. I was thankful for that.

I glanced surreptitiously at the map Mr. Stone had given me, and managed to find my first class without difficulty. It was French with a teacher who looked like he'd gotten out of bed and headed straight to school without any stops in between. He was short and stout with a fat moustache and long curly hair that stuck out all over. He was bustling around his desk looking a trifle confused. My schedule said he was M. Lavoie. I looked at him and bit back a chuckle. The girl sitting in the next desk looked over curiously and smiled at me tentatively as she asked, "What's so funny?"

Glancing up to be sure Monsieur Lavoie wasn't paying attention, I whispered, "I'm just amazed at all that hair."

She smiled. "Oh I know. He can get it much wilder, too, just wait. Are you new? I'm Claire."

I looked at her more carefully, cracking a grin as I gasped happily, "Claire! Hi!"

She furrowed her brow and studied me for a moment, then I saw the recognition flash in her eyes, "Oh! It's Grace, isn't it?"

"Yes," I grinned. In all the distress over the move, I'd completely forgotten Claire and the crazy gang of kids from Salmon Arm that I'd met at the Leadership Conference in Banff last year.

"So you've moved here?" she asked. "Are you living with your aunt or did your whole family move?"

"Just me, and yeah, I'm staying with my aunt."

"Was it an unexpected move?"

I snickered a trifle grumpily. "You could say that. I'm not thrilled about it, but here I am."

"From Calgary, right?"

"Yeah." It was surprising how much she remembered.

"I'm sorry you're not happy to have had to move, but I'm glad to see you again." Her eyes were sympathetic and she smiled kindly, "Are you interested in joining our leadership group here?"

I smiled back; suddenly I felt so much less lonely. "I'd love to."

"Good." She looked genuinely happy to welcome me.

At that moment M. Lavoie seemed to have finally noticed that there were students in his room, and got up to teach us something.

Half way through class Claire looked over at me, "Grace? What's wrong?"

I shook my head, trying to shake up the cobwebs before they could settle over my thought processes again. "I'm okay. I'm just having a little difficulty concentrating. Can I copy your notes?"

"Yeah, sure," she said, passing over the pages she'd already done. Somehow, it was easier to absorb the information when it was sitting concretely in front of my eyes instead of floating through the air on waves of sound.

By the end of the class my head was so full of new verbs I was glad to be free.

"I'll watch for you at lunch," Claire promised as we walked out of class, "We usually sit around the stairs here." As we passed through the atrium, she indicated a curving central staircase leading to the second floor. "Your next class is just up there," she said as she pointed me to the smaller side stairwell that would lead me to my science class, "Have fun!" and then she wheeled around and disappeared in the other direction.

The wide science room with its rows of tables, black counters, and shelves full of dead creatures was typical. There were no outside facing windows in this room, but a row of windows looked out onto the hall. I sat at a table vaguely listening to the lecture while watching the students occasionally passing in the hall a few feet away.

A girl with Technicolor dreadlocks walked past, casually glancing into the room. Her eyes met mine and she smiled darkly. She slowed her walk and her head turned to continue staring until she was past the window and out of my sight.

I swallowed. My throat was suddenly parched. My eyes hurt. I could still see the look on her face as if it had been burnt onto my retinas. Creepy.

"Grace!" Ben. It was the first time he'd spoken to me since our nightly rendezvous. I could feel his mood: uncertain, worried.

In my head I tried to think soothing thoughts as I answered without speaking aloud, "Everything is okay, Ben."

"Who was that?"

"I don't know." I caught a glimmer of a question that sounded like "W*hat* is that?" but Ben blocked it. "What are you worried about, Ben?"

He tried to be nonchalant, but I could sense his growing stress, "Nothing. I'll talk to you later." Then he was gone. I wondered vaguely how he did that. He seemed to come and go from my head as if it was a swinging door, without me being able to do anything about it. It was as if he had a key to his own head, and could lock me out without any problem. It didn't seem fair somehow.

After science, I found Claire and a group of her friends already gathering to stake their claim to a lunch table under the main stairs. A couple of them went off to join the line at the café, but I'd brought lunch, so I just pulled the bag out of my pack. Claire had lunch from home as well. She sat down across from me and asked, "So how is the first day going so far? Are you relaxing yet?"

She meant it to be a comforting question, but remembering the disturbing stare from the girl with the crazy dreadlocks, I shivered a little before I attempted to smile in response. I guess the smile was too wobbly, because she suddenly looked concerned,

"Uh, oh. What happened?"

Did I want to confess to this? What had happened, really? Not much. A girl gave me a dirty look. It sounded stupid when put into words. I would sound like an idiot if I explained. There's no way I could express the bone chilling way the look had struck me. I shrugged. "There are some interesting students here."

I glanced up and noticed the dreadlock girl standing in the café line. She didn't look so dangerous laughing with her friends. I wondered if she'd just been messing with me because she thought I was staring at her when I glanced out the window.

Claire followed my eyes. "Are you looking at Sthenno?"

"I'm sorry?" It sounded like she had sneezed the name.

She laughed. "Sthenno Anistonopolis. The girl with the dreads."

"Yes." Yikes. What a name. "She's Greek?"

"Yeah. I guess so, eh? Her family is, anyway. I think they've lived around here for years though. She was in my class in grade three."

"The hair is rather crazy. What's she like?"

"She's actually...um...I guess you'd say she's *unpredictable* these days." She laughed. "She used to be very nice, but I hear she's getting into a lot of trouble lately, running with a crowd that is likely to get her a regular appointment with a Youth Probation Officer, if you know what I mean."

I nodded, chewing my sandwich thoughtfully. I swallowed and remarked as casually as I could, "She gave me a dirty look from the hallway while I was in Science. I wondered if she was into mind games or something."

"Maybe. She can be as sweet as anyone can, but I don't suggest you get her angry. I can remember some very dramatic, rolling on the floor tantrums in grade three!" She chuckled as she added, "I'm not convinced she's grown out of them," because as Claire was speaking Sthenno had slugged one of her friends in the arm with a curse, and he was now rubbing his bicep and looking more than a little irritated with her.

Just then, Claire's friends returned with their trays of food and joined us at the table. Claire introduced me to Susan, a short redhead with lots of freckles, then Dave, a gangly brown haired boy with an easy smile and long limbs, and finally she introduced Rafiq, a very nice looking, slightly built black haired guy who smiled quite entrancingly at us as he sat down. I recognized Susan and Dave from Banff.

Susan looked up at Claire as she sat down and exulted, "Guess who was behind me in line?"

Dave rolled his eyes. Claire grinned, obviously in on the secret romance.

Susan sighed dramatically. "He actually spoke to me today." She paused to sigh again before she added, "*And* he smiled at me."

Dave laughed derogatively. "Yeah, right. He said, 'It's okay' after you apologized for stepping on his foot, and he smiled because you looked like such an idiot about it." He looked at the rest of us. "You should have seen her, going all goo-goo eyed when she realized it was Marco she'd stepped on!"

Susan glared at him. "Don't rain on my parade Dave Matthews!"

Dave shook his head and laughed.

Rafiq spoke up, startling me with his sparkling smile and rather astonishing voice. It was very deep and sexy for a sixteen year old. "Where have you come from Grace? I'm sure I would have noticed you around here before now."

He made it sound like he thought I had materialized from heaven. His smile made my toes tingle and I felt a blush creeping up my throat. I endeavoured to answer in a calm voice, "Just moved last weekend from Calgary."

"Ah." He nodded as if this was fascinating news. "We are very lucky."

A tingle went down my back and at the same time, I felt Ben come into my head. "Hi Grace," he said quietly.

I ignored him.

Suddenly Susan gasped, her eyes widening and then fluttering down to stare into her lap. I glanced up to see what had caused the reaction, and saw immediately what had put her into a tizzy.

Dave groaned, "Get a grip Susan."

I glanced at Claire and muttered, "I can see her problem." He was about six feet tall and broad shouldered. You could say he looked more like a football player than a basketball player, but I suspected that he was one of those freakily unnatural athletes who joins every team and does well on all of them. He had brown curly hair, topped with a rather dapper fedora. He was cute. No. He was *gorgeous*.

Claire laughed, "Yes. I think I heard that a modeling firm spotted him in Vancouver this summer when he was on vacation, and tried to sign him. He's quite perfect, isn't he?"

I nodded. Perfect wasn't quite the word to capture how absolutely delectable he was.

The dazzling guy glanced over to our table, saw Susan, grinned at her, and then his glance swept over the rest of us. Was it my imagination or did his eyes linger on me? Wow. I was as bad as Susan was. I tried to keep a smirk off my face.

After he went past, Susan reached out with her arm to smack Dave lightly in the chest with the back of her hand while the other hand flew to her throat. "You guys saw that, right? You saw him grin at me just then? I didn't imagine that?" I could tell that Susan thought that she was having the best day of her life.

While Susan hyperventilated beside me, I pulled out my schedule to figure out where to go for my afternoon classes. Everyone else leaned in to study it with me. I was glad to discover Claire shared my English class as well as French, and that Dave was in my Theatre class. Rafiq looked crushed when he noted that we had no classes in common.

As we stood up to go to the theatre Dave remarked, "Ignore Rafiq, Grace. He's all charm and no follow through. His parents don't let him date." He smirked smugly over to Rafiq who was grimacing at him.

I smiled sympathetically as we headed off to class.

CHAPTER TWO

FANCY MEETING YOU HERE

Friendships are joyfully welcomed. Leaders bring sense of belonging.
Change offers new opportunities, though it does challenge old longings.
Gathering friends give a warning; danger draws steadily closer.
False friends are showing but disappear; warrior's ready to know her.

Claire and I were sitting at a picnic table outside the atrium with our books all around us, deceiving ourselves that we were studying. The grass was green on the playing fields already, and some kids were tossing a football around. As I sat there looking around at the green hills and the clouds reflected in the lake below, I wondered again at my luck to have been exiled to such a beautiful place.

"How did you end up moving here?" Claire asked curiously. "You seemed pretty settled and happy in Calgary when we were in Banff."

"Yeah, well, it was a combination of things." That was an understatement. I pondered a bit, deciding just what to tell her before I continued, "My dad got posted to Greece, and I didn't want to go with them."

"Why not?" she asked incredulously.

I shrugged. I debated for a moment about telling her about the accident. In Banff, she had pushed me out of the way of a speeding car, so I sucked in my breath. "I needed you around in Calgary."

"Huh?"

"I was hit by a car in June."

Claire gasped and put her hand over her mouth, her eyes huge. "Not again!"

"We don't know who it was, but I was deliberately run down and thrown through a window." I pulled up my sleeve and indicated the lacy pattern of scars down my arm. I was in a coma most of the summer. That's why I am having some trouble concentrating for a long time in class."

"Oh Grace, that's horrible."

"It was." I nodded, "On top of that, my parents thought there were some... well, I guess you'd say 'boy troubles'."

"In Calgary?"

I nodded grimly.

"They can't have been too seriously worried, or they'd have thought it better to haul you to the other side of the planet with them, rather than leaving you alone only five hours away from him," Claire observed.

Hmm. I hadn't considered that before. "I think they imagine Bright will ensure I'm well supervised. My Auntie Bright doesn't miss much. I don't think I would be able to sneak around her even if I wanted to."

"Who is the boy?"

"You saw him at the accident in Banff: Ben, the guy who was freaking out."

"Oh, yeah. I remember him. He was very protective of you."

"Apparently not protective enough for my parents," I sighed.

"It'd be pretty hard to protect anyone twenty-four hours a day."

"That's what I tell them. I thought they were being silly, that I didn't need any protection. I still don't know *why* I do, but obviously someone was out to get me, because I *was* deliberately hit."

"Is there anyone protecting you here?"

Now that was an interesting question. I hadn't thought about that. If Ben was supposed to be protecting me, had he had the responsibility before I had met him? I thought probably he did. *Was* there someone already installed here who was supposed to be guarding me here? I shrugged my shoulders. "I have no idea." The thought was uncomfortable. I glanced around the atrium wondering if anyone was spying on me. Maybe someone was watching me right now, in case Claire pulled a knife on me. I shivered then, as the errant thought swiftly brought the picture of a growing pool of red spreading onto blue into my mind.

"Well. The Shuswap is a beautiful place to be, Grace. It will be spring soon, and then it's even better. We all go camping and boating, and hang out at the beach. You'll like it here. I'm sure everything will be okay."

After school on Wednesday, I was unpacking my homework at a table in the atrium when Claire came up with her bag in her hands.

"So are you coming to Leadership class with me, Grace?" she looked expectant.

"Oh, yeah, I suppose I could. When is it?"

She looked guilty as she thwacked the palm of her hand onto her forehead. ."Sorry! I meant to mention it before. The class meets outside the timetable, after school or at lunch. There's a meeting right now. Are you free to join us?"

It was the end of the day. All I had to do was head home. If I didn't take the bus, I could walk. It would take half an hour, but it was a nice enough day.

"Sure," I said, gathering my stuff back up and following her down the hall.

Claire and I walked into the room and I recognized many faces from my classes. We arranged ourselves in a circle and chatted as people drifted in.

Beside me, Brittany was complaining about how irritating her little sister was, "and she thought Africa was a town in Alberta, not a continent!" to the laughter of the group. She shook her wavy, brown hair in frustration.

Susan, the redhead who was in love with Marco, laughed at her, "Oh Brit, quit picking on her. You know you love her."

Brittany sighed, "Yeah, I know, but it doesn't stop her from driving me crazy!"

Susan smiled and remarked, "If you didn't love her, she wouldn't drive you crazy."

I looked at Susan in surprise. Who'd have thought she was a philosopher?

Brittany sighed melodramatically and put her novel on the desktop.

Susan picked it up. "How many times have you read this series?"

"Careful Sue," Dave called walking over from across the room. "She'll have you quoting from the text and unable to date normal boys within days if you let her convince you to read that book!"

Sue dropped the book with an exaggerated look of fear, "Eek! Save me!" while at least half a dozen others in the group giggled in self-conscious amusement. It was plain they'd already been evangelized.

Dave grinned and as he walked by Claire, he chuckled quietly and winked at her. "Good, now I have a *chance* with her, at least"

Claire winked at me, "He's exaggerating. Don't be afraid if she offers to lend you a copy, just be prepared for addiction. "

I laughed. The series had already made the rounds of Redman before I'd moved. I leaned in and whispered back, "I know, I read the series last year!" We giggled conspiratorially as the teacher came in. He was quite different from Ms. Martindale. He was young and dressed in expensive looking athletic gear that suggested he taught Phys. Ed.

"All right everyone! We have a few activities coming up that need our attention. Brittany will tell you about Spirit Week, and then Skylar will give you a head's up about the Spring Dance. Brittany?"

Brittany stood up and described the various theme days and lunchtime games planned for the Spirit Week. School Colour Day, Twin Day, and Crazy Hat Day I'd heard of before. Crazy Walk Day and Athlete Day were new ideas. As we broke into teams and sorted out who would go around with tickets to check costumes, who would take photos and who would supervise the games, I noticed a face at the classroom window. I gasped, and did a double take. At first glance, it had looked so much like Josh, the boy who had haunted me in Calgary, that it had scared me. Those evil eyes didn't belong on my friend's face. The second glance suggested that it wasn't him, though. This guy was older, with stubble shadowing his chin. He didn't have Josh's mischievous grin or sparkling eyes. He smiled darkly at me. My heart started pounding, as if it wanted to escape my chest. "Claire!" I whispered insistently, "Claire, who's that in the window?"

She turned to look, but of course, he'd vanished.

"Damn. He's gone." I said, breathlessly.

Ben's voice echoed through my brain and I tried to look involved in the decision making of the class while I listened to him. "You're okay, Grace. It's okay." His voice was soothing. "Nothing is going to happen today. Just make sure you get a ride home. I don't want you walking."

"Grace?" Susan was asking me something, but I hadn't heard it.

"Oh, sorry. What did you say?"

"I said we need someone else to handle obstacle course equipment during lunch games on Athlete Day. Can you do that?"

"Oh, sure."

She nodded. "Good. Well that's everything we needed to figure out. Mr. Douglas!"

The teacher came up to our group then taking our paper and observing, "I see we have a new student with us."

Claire did the introductions, "Yes, this is Grace. She just moved here from Calgary, but we met her at the Banff Leadership conference last year. She was on our winning photo challenge team."

I saw a glimmer of recognition, as he nodded thoughtfully. "Ah, that's why your face is familiar then, of course." He nodded over to the

214

wall where I noticed a photo display for the first time. Sure enough as I tried to make them out from across the room, some of the landmarks and the poses looked familiar. "Welcome to S.L.S." He smiled and moved on to talk to another group.

I thought about how I was going to get home, if I wasn't supposed to walk. Just at that moment, Dave appeared at my side. "Hey Grace, don't you normally take the Raven bus?"

"Yeah."

"Do you have a ride home?"

"No, I figured I'd just walk."

"Nah, you don't want to walk. It'll take you half an hour to get home. I'll give you a ride." He turned to Susan before I could answer, "Hey Sue! Are you coming home with Grace and me?"

"Oh, yeah. Sure." She looked at me curiously, perhaps wondering why Dave had invited me first. I was wondering that myself, since obviously he was interested in her. Then she turned her confused expression to him, "Wait Dave, don't you still have your N?"

I looked at him in confusion while he beamed at her, "Nope! Passed the test yesterday!"

I whispered to Claire, "What's that?"

"We have graduated licensing for new drivers. If he still had his N, he would only be allowed one passenger."

"Ah." If he'd had to choose between the two of us, how would he have played his cards? It was clear he had some strategy.

He looked back at me with a grin. "Ready?"

I liked S.L.S. Even in a couple of weeks, I liked it far more than I ever had imagined that I would. Already knowing Claire and the rest of her friends from Leadership made it remarkably easy to slip into the stream of school life.

As far as my recovery went, although I found some difficulty concentrating in my classes after the first half hour or so, I had also noticed that most of the teachers mixed it up enough that my brain got a break in the middle of the long classes. With Claire in French to pass over the notes, I was able to keep up without much difficulty. Dr. Kyle had suggested that the headaches would go away over time, along with the soreness of the mending bones. I thought I perceived an improvement, but just the fact that I was alive and functioning was apparently a miracle, so I concentrated on being thankful for that.

Rafiq was always trying to charm me, and it wasn't long before I thought it was a good thing for the local female population that he wasn't allowed to date. He was allowed to hang around with us though, so he joined us for video game parties and movie nights, and occasionally tried to make a move on someone who laughed him off or flirted back, depending on their position on short-term romances.

I was walking down the hall with Susan on the way to Biology. Rafiq trailed behind, complaining that he had Biology across the hall, and it would have been so much more convenient if we were all together. We were ignoring him. Susan was bubbly and reminded me a lot of Bonnie, though with a lot less confidence than Bonnie had.

"So you have a boyfriend in Calgary?" she asked, conversationally. Rafiq took a couple of steps closer.

"Well, sort of."

"Just a friend then?"

"No, more than a friend." I probably shouldn't have bothered to add that.

"Ah. I see. So a lover then?" Rafiq made a choking noise behind us.

I sighed. No, but yes. It would not do to tell the truth on this one. They'd think I was crazy if I said, "Yes, I think in our past lives we were lovers, but not yet in this life." Ha. They'd be booking the straitjacket for me so quickly I wouldn't be able to blink before they would be fastening the buckles.

I glanced at Susan who was waiting for a response with an expectant look. I shook my head, wondering what the best neutral response would be. Finally, I said with a voice as dewy and gushy as I could make it, "Someone very special, with the potential to be even more special later." I already knew Susan was the romantic in the group. If anyone would fall for that, she would.

Sure enough, she nodded in understanding, so I guess it was appropriately lovesick.

For just a couple of weeks, I was feeling astonishingly settled into my new life. I missed everyone in Calgary, of course, but I had Ben and the internet, and really, I was only missing their physical presence. Despite the space between us, the friendships felt as strong as ever. Still, I was most glad to have Ben with me like an invisible friend. He was a constant source of encouragement. He seemed determined that even though we weren't together, I was going to be happy. I was even more grateful for his love.

All this contentment was why I was completely unprepared for what happened next.

I was sitting in the library waiting for Claire, gazing absently out the window toward the lake, thinking vaguely about how lucky we were to have such amazing views in school, and trying not to miss Ben, when Marco dropped into the chair next to me.

I looked up wondering why, with all the empty chairs in the library, he'd pick the one right next to me.

He beamed at me, "Hello there new girl called Grace. I'm Marco Diguerra." I looked at him with eyes widened by surprise, because while I knew who he was, of course, I never imagined any reason he'd have to talk to me. He should have had no reason to know my name. We had no classes together.

He was waiting expectantly, so I thought of something brilliant to say in reply: "Um. Hi."

Yup. Brilliant.

Marco was too gorgeous. Susan wasn't the only one crushing on him. In the short time I'd been here, I'd decided every girl in school knew who he was and more than a few of them sighed and dreamed about him. Considering that they were also not even vaguely subtle about their attraction to him, Marco was amazingly down to earth. He dressed like a prep school kid instead of the jock he was, but we couldn't hold that against him, because his shirts with the little alligators and the khaki chinos hugged him to perfection. The view was quite stupendous if you were walking down the hall a few feet behind him.

Now this same very handsome Marco was sitting beside me, with an annoyingly adorable smirk on his face.

"Grace, I have been watching you for a while, and it has come to my attention that you are not having enough fun in our little town."

"Pardon?" Why was he watching me? I couldn't think of a single reason that my fun would be of any interest to Marco Diguerra. I caught a whiff of the scent wafting up from the neck of his alligator shirt. Mmmm.

"Could I interest you in a rousing game or two of five pin bowling this evening? I think an evening out in the company of friendly people might be just the thing to release you from the bondage of your boredom."

I laughed in spite of myself. It wasn't as if I was actually bored here, but to go out, though? I hadn't considered that it might be possible to get Ben safely out of my head long enough to date anyone, even if I were inclined to. Marco was watching me with a benign curiosity. I wondered whether he would care one way or the other if I declined. Then again, why should I decline? Here was a very nice, very cute boy inviting me to spend time with him.

"Because he will never mean anything to you, that's why," Ben's voice came into my mind, deep and penetrating. "Because he's not me."

Well, obviously. *"But* you*'re not* here *Ben Butler!"* Was he trying to keep me from making friends? I thought I heard him chuckle in the recesses of my mind before I tuned back to Marco.

"So?" smiled Marco enticingly, "Will you come?"

I turned on my high beam smile and was pleased to see him blink at the intensity. "Sure Marco. Sounds like fun." I heard Ben growling in my head and I was amused by my power.

"I'll pick you up at seven, okay?"

"That's fine. Do you know where I live?"

I thought he smiled a little guiltily as he said, "Yeah. In Raven subdivision, right?"

I was shocked. "Yeah. How'd you know?"

"Spies. I keep a stable of them to do my bidding. To keep track of beautiful newcomers and all that."

"Ah. Of course. I should have expected that." I giggled. Marco was sweet. Charming too. I felt completely at ease around him. Beautiful newcomers. Sheesh.

I'd heard that he'd set a provincial record for track the previous year. He spent enough time in the gym that when his shirt was off, very few of the girls could keep their minds on what they were doing. He had sabotaged more than one young woman's team try out when she found herself distracted by his perfection and ended up tripping over her feet (notably Susan).

I'd heard someone say that his favourite sport was boxing and his goal was to box in the Olympics someday. He trained at a gym in Vernon and a few guys said he was lethal in the ring. That was a bit of a paradox for such a sweet gentle guy, but perhaps he got out his aggressive side in the ring and that was why he was so gentle outside of it.

Just then, the bell rang for next class. Marco stood up and smiled at me. "Well, see you at seven then. There will be four or five of us at least, so it should be fun."

"Great. See you at seven!"

"You might regret it," said Ben in my head.

"Shut up, Ben," I whispered back angrily. Again, I thought I heard him chuckling at my annoyance, which left me even more irritated.

At precisely seven o'clock there was a confident knock at the front door. Bright answered it, but I was right behind her, ready to go.

Marco stepped into the entry, sticking his hand out with a grin, "Hi there, I'm Marco; I'm here to pick up Grace?"

Bright stepped forward and took his hand, but instead of shaking it, she pulled him close to her and air kissed on either cheek exclaiming warmly, "Hello, Marco!"

I was horrified until I realized that Marco seemed completely comfortable with the greeting. Did he know her already? I stepped out behind her, awkwardly wondering whether I was supposed to hug him or what.

Marco smiled, "Ready, Grace?" and reached back to the door knob. I nodded.

He looked back at Bright. "There's a gang of us going bowling and then we'll probably go out for coffee. Is eleven okay?"

"Yes, that should be fine. Do you have your phone, Grace?"

I nodded.

"All right. Nice to meet you, Marco. See you two at eleven. Have fun!"

The door shut behind us and we went out to Marco's beaten up little blue car. Marco opened the passenger door and doffed his hat at me as he shut the door. I still hadn't said anything to him. It felt weird. I was going on a date with someone who was not the wonderful boy I loved. I was intentionally accepting romantic overtures from someone else. What was I doing? Suddenly I wanted, no, *needed*, to escape.

"Marco?"

"You know, Grace. I'm really glad you're expanding your horizons."

"Um. Yeah. I..."

"My friend Andrew is coming tonight, do you know him?"

"Ah. No. I mean, I don't *think* I know an Andrew. He's at S.L.S?"

"He is. He's bringing a girl along as well, but I'm not sure who. It's sort of a double date. I hope you're okay with that?"

"Well, actually, I...um...." I didn't know how to ask him to turn around. It was hard to breathe, because I could just catch the heavenly whiff of something musky and earthy about him that was short-circuiting my will. I wondered if it was a scent from a store, pheromones imported illegally, or just his natural scent. It was heady, whatever it was. I swear I saw the drama teacher swoon once. I'd thought it was funny at the time. It wasn't so funny now.

"Here we are." We had pulled into a dirt parking lot in front of a cement brick box of a building. A problem with living in a small town was that it didn't take longer than five minutes to get anywhere. I stayed in my seat, debating. Maybe I could just sit out here all night while Marco, Andrew and his girl went bowling. No one could call that a date, could they? All my earlier bravado was gone. There was no way to re-interpret this. I was cheating on Ben. What kind of tramp was I?

The passenger door opened and Marco stood there with a good natured grin. "Are you waiting for anything in particular?"

I opened my mouth to answer, but before I could speak my head was full of music.

"It's okay, Love. You need to have fun."

I closed my eyes, "Oh, Ben."

Ben laughed comfortably in my mind, "It's not cheating if your boyfriend knows about it and says it's all right, so have a good time."

"Ech hem?" I opened my eyes to see Marco standing outside the car door with a quizzical look on his face. "Are you feeling sick or something?"

"No, no I'm fine. Let's go in." I reached out my hand and Marco helped me out of the car. He kept my hand as we went through the door. At the counter he paid for three games and the rental on two pairs of very funky shoes. We were heading for a lane on the left side of the alley when I recognized the Technicolor hair of Sthenno as she let loose a ball and smashed the pins into the air.

"Yeah! Killed ya!" she hollered and whirled around to face her friends. She stopped dead when she spotted me.

I grabbed Marco's arm. "Wait. Can we just take this lane?" I said, indicating the one we were at, right in the middle of the alley. "I don't think that girl likes me."

He glanced down toward Sthenno and pursed his lips. "Ah. Sure, this will be fine." He turned to the cashier, "Hey, Bob! Can you activate this lane instead?" Bob nodded as the door opened. "Andrew, my man!" Marco called out as his friend came in. Andrew waved a greeting and went to pay and get shoes. Trailing behind him was Brittany from leadership class. When she saw me sitting beside Marco, she brightened.

"Oh hey, Grace! I didn't know you were coming!" She sat down beside me and whispered, "This is a first date, and I wasn't sure I was going to be able to stand it. So far, he's freaking me out." She grinned. "How's it going with Marco?"

I rolled my eyes as I finished tying my shoes, "First date, as well. 'Nuf said."

She laughed as Andrew flopped onto the bench beside her and dropped striped bowling shoes on her lap. "Here, gorgeous."

She blushed and hid her face by bending over to put on the shoes. I chuckled to myself, thinking traitorously how nice it was for someone else to be blushing for a change.

Meanwhile, Marco was busy entering our names into the scoring computer. He was snickering, so I was afraid to see what he'd labelled us. I was pretty sure it wasn't our real names.

Sure enough, he was WARMAN, Andrew was BUBBA, I was CHARM and Brittany was CUTIE. It could have been a lot worse, I suppose.

We were about four frames in when it happened. I was releasing my ball on the lane when Marco shouted and leapt up.

In my head, Ben's voice commanded, "Watch out!"

Instinctively I ducked. Marco was over top of me. There was a flash and then a resounding crack that echoed through the room. Pieces of a huge bowling ball showered to the ground around me.

Bob the cashier jumped out and stomped across the alley to the lane where Sthenno was playing. "YOU!" he shouted, pointing at her, "Out of here!"

She snarled and her dreadlocks seemed to squirm. She tried to argue but he wasn't budging, "I'm not having you risking the lives of my customers! You get out now and never come back!"

She grabbed a jacket and hopped as she pulled off her shoes. She threw them behind the counter with rather impressive force, muttering and cursing. Bob dropped her own runners on the counter in front of her and snarled, "Go!"

She stared venomously at Marco as she went by.

He didn't blink, but he doffed his hat at her. She scowled and looked away first.

I just sat on the foul line, staring at the chunks of bowling ball lying around me while I hyperventilated. Looks like I hadn't run far enough.

"You okay?" Marco asked quietly. Ben's voice echoed the question.

I nodded, "I'm fine. Thanks. That was quick action."

"Yeah."

I met his eyes and studied him.

He stared back frankly.

Huh. Guess I knew Ben's replacement guardian.

We finished the games. Andrew teased and flirted with Brittany. Brittany giggled, blushed, and rolled her eyes at me when he wasn't looking. Marco was as charming and easy going as usual. He took my hand. He had me rub the ball for luck, and then grabbed me for a happy hug when he got a strike. We pretended nothing had happened. I tried to ignore everything else and bowl. The sound of that crack above my head kept replaying in my ears. What had made it shatter? I tried to tune out the thought and to look happy.

The concentration paid off. I won all three games.

Afterwards we went to Tims, but I was home a good hour earlier than necessary. I guess each of us had our energy fade simultaneously. Marco escorted me to the front door. "I had fun tonight, Grace. Thanks for coming."

I smiled at him as I opened the door, "Yeah, me too. Thanks for protecting me from flying bowling balls."

He chuckled. "Any time. See you at school tomorrow."

I shut the door behind me. Bright peeked out from the kitchen. "Have fun?"

"Yeah, it was okay. I sure wish I could go somewhere without needing someone to protect me from weird attacks, though."

My mother would have freaked out if I'd made a comment like that, but Bright just nodded serenely. "Yes. Hopefully we'll get there eventually," and turned back into the kitchen.

"She's harder to protect than you'd think, isn't she?" O said pointedly to Mars.

Mars inhaled deeply. "I thought the Gorgon was tamed. I should have been more attentive."

Xandros laughed. "Tamed? Gorgons are barely able to be contained. I'm surprised she hasn't turned the entire school into stone."

"That would hardly fail to escape the notice of the humans. She's been playing it so low key that I hadn't considered her a danger. I won't make the same mistake again."

O nodded, accepting the apology. "Please don't."

"I'm ready to step in if you're not up to the job, Mars."

"Thanks, Xandros. I'll call you, if I need you."

"You'll need me soon enough. When there are creatures like Gorgons entering the fray, you can be sure other creatures will be coming. Ares isn't shy about recruiting dangerous beings."

O nodded. "Xandros is right. You need to be watchful."

Mars nodded. "It's under control. Aphrodite has a spy in his camp. We're getting good intelligence."

"Are more creatures coming?" Xandros asked.

"Possibly. He's approached the Cyclopes."

O's eyes tightened in concern. "Are they joining him?"

"Nothing seems to have been confirmed yet."

Xandros smirked, "I'd love a good fight with a Cyclops. It's been ages since I took out an eye."

O sighed.

Mars shook his head, "Xandros, don't go looking for stupid fights. O, it'll be fine. I'm protecting her."

"I hope so."

"Grace!" Jim called as I walked in the door. "Your dad's on the phone!"

My heart gave a little jolt. I knew Mom called Bright, but so far I hadn't spoken to her. They both knew I was still too irritated to be polite on the phone.

"Hi, Dad," I said warily.

"Hey, Hon! I miss you! How are you doing?" and that was as much as it took to pour out how my days had filled with school, homework, hanging out with Claire, Dave, Susan, Rafiq and the gang from leadership, or with Marco and his gang of friends.

"Is there anyone special in that group?"

I sighed. "I still love Ben, Dad. Tell Mother I'm not going to change my mind."

"You are still young, Grace. Take advantage of the opportunity to know lots of people. You don't need the distraction of a boyfriend right now, anyway."

"Distraction from what?"

"Um." He gulped as he struggled for an answer, and I smirked, imagining his expression. "School!" he shouted triumphantly, then coughed and said in a normal voice, "We don't want you distracted from your studies."

"Uh huh. Fine Dad." I chuckled. The groupings of my friends at S.L.S. were fluid and that was comfortable. Most of the kids seemed to know each other from years of small town life. I liked it.

Dad didn't ask about anyone in Calgary, so I didn't have to tell him that I was glad for the internet and messaging, because I never felt far from Christie, Lloyd, Bonnie, and my friends at Redman. In some ways, I felt just as involved in their lives as before. I watched Bonnie's status change with almost every daily activity, read positive affirmations on Christie's status line and groaned over the goofy puns on Lloyd's.

"How are you and Mom doing?"

"We're enjoying the opportunity to explore lots of historical places."

"So I'd be bored out of my head, if I were there?"

"Well I hope not. I think you'd find it fascinating. You used to like exploring ruins."

"True." That was before I discovered some of them were places I'd lived. That made it all a whole lot freakier.

"I'm glad to hear you're doing so well. Blythe will be relieved. Say hello to Ben from us."

"Ri-i-ight." I said sarcastically before we hung up. Like my mother wanted to greet Ben. Unless perhaps it was to gloat about how she'd separated us.

Ben and I did not bother to use technology to communicate. I lay in bed every night while he asked me about my day and told me about his university classes. That evening ritual was the best part of my day. I looked forward to the moment when I could pull the lovely quilt around my shoulders and feel him in not only my head, but also curiously all around me. He had been right, if I'd known this was what he wanted Connie to give us, I *would* have wanted it. I still was irked he hadn't given me the option to decide for myself, but I didn't bring it up. It seemed kind of petty, all things considered.

Sometimes he already seemed to know stuff I'd done during the day, and that bugged me a little, because behind the part of *his* head that filled my thoughts when we 'talked' together, there was just a big black hole. He seemed to be able to see into me as if my head were a glass house, but I couldn't see into his. He didn't think this was unfair. When I brought it up his thoughts were blasé: "Perhaps you'll get better with practice." Huh. Practising every day didn't seem to be making any difference at all, so I was pretty sure he had some way of blocking me from thoughts he didn't want to share, and he wasn't telling me how to block his thoughts from intruding wherever he wanted to go within *my* head.

He would pop into my head during the day if something strange was going on. His protector side was still working, even if my mom had fired him. It was pretty obvious that if some demon possessed car was going to come after me, Ben wasn't going to be much help from all the way over in Calgary, but perhaps a well-timed "MOVE!" would be effective in escaping some dangers.

Ben seemed to approve all of my new friends, but despite his casual attitude, I wondered if he was more jealous of Marco's attachment to me than he was acknowledging. He was always more 'present' when I was with Marco than at any other time, but he would only rarely interrupt until our prearranged nightly rendezvous when he'd express his delight that I'd had a good day. What was wrong with him? His unselfish manner over

Marco made me irritated, and I found myself, contrarily, flirting more with Marco than I ever would have if Ben could just admit he was jealous that Marco was with me while he wasn't. How perverse I was.

Bright and I were hanging around in the living room with our teacups after dinner one evening. The TV was on, but neither of us was paying much attention to it. She was flipping through a magazine, and I was lounging on the couch pondering the events that had landed me in Salmon Arm.

"Auntie Bright, why is my mother so adamantly against musicians?"

Bright laughed quietly, "Thinking about Ben again, eh?"

I nodded. "She doesn't like him. I think she believes he's unhealthily obsessed with me."

She shrugged with a soft smile. "Ben would doubtless walk into Hell to rescue you, but I think that's more about adoration than obsession, myself."

"Tell that to her," I grumbled before I looked back at her. "She always said musicians were more trouble than they're worth. Why does she feel that way? Do you know?"

"Well, your mother is rather partial to poets to the exclusion of all others."

"Poets?"

She grinned, "Oh yes. Didn't you know that your father is a rather brilliant poet?"

"*My* dad?" I sputtered.

She laughed again, taking a sip of her tea.

"Oh yes. You should see some of the love poetry he wrote to woo her. It's pretty steamy stuff!" She was chuckling, enjoying my shock. "She was his agent at first, that's how they met."

"I thought they met in Greece when he was there on vacation!"

"Half right. They did meet in Greece, but he was there to finalize publication of a book of poetry. In the end he finalized a wedding instead." She giggled at my gaping mouth.

"They lied to me!"

"Oh I don't think so; I think they just neglected to give you all the details. After all, any day visiting in Greece is a day that seems like a vacation right?"

I was still choking on the idea of my father as some kind of Lord Byron or Robert Browning. "Does he *still* write poetry?"

She looked at me fondly, enjoying my astonishment. "He published two volumes last year. He also has a really great spoken word piece making the rounds on the internet."

I shook my head incredulously. "I can't believe it. Why don't they talk about this with me?"

"Hon, do you remember all those bedtime stories your dad used to tell you?"

I nodded.

"Well, some kids had Dr. Seuss or A. A. Milne, but the books you begged for the most often were your dad's books."

"Sev Davidson is my dad?"

"I'm surprised you didn't make the connection, Grace: Sev Davidson, David Severin. It's not such a stretch." She smirked at me while I struggled with this concept.

"It doesn't make any sense that they haven't told me. I just thought he was a travel agent. All those basement projects were poetry? Why didn't they say anything?"

"Oh I don't know, Grace. I guess he and your mom thought they'd keep that part of their life private. He is a travel agent, too. No one can make a living on poetry. Don't stress about it."

A thought came to me. "She looks after the poetry division and she's married to a poet."

"Yes." She smiled.

"Aglaea married a writer?"

"Non-fiction, of course," she said matter of factly.

"So," I said, looking her in the eye, "is Uncle Jim a professional musician?"

"No." She smirked at my raised eyebrows.

"No? You're in charge of the music division, but you didn't marry a musician?"

She smiled again, more softly this time. "I'm rather partial to musicians, but I didn't marry a professional musician, no."

"Because?"

"Long story." Her smile was melancholic. "You know that Uncle Jim plays the piano."

"Yeah." I'd heard his playing floating up from the basement now and then.

"So he's a musician. He just doesn't make a living playing music."

"Ah. That makes a difference?"

She just smiled back at me.

I looked at her face and read something there. "So is *that* the reason my mom doesn't trust musicians?"

"What?" she was taken aback with the question.

"Whatever is making you sad. Is she mad at all musicians because one hurt you?"

She looked at me for a moment and then shook her head slowly. "You are amazingly intuitive, Grace. I guess I shouldn't be surprised, but that's pretty impressive."

"I'm right?"

"Hmm. I suppose so." She was lost in thought for a moment, cradling her teacup as she stared into the distance. She didn't elaborate.

I loved spring in the Shuswap. It didn't get any better than new green and apple blossoms. The sun made me blissful. Watching the sparkling lake below the house made me wonder again at the incredible luck that brought me here. If I couldn't be in Calgary, this was a pretty amazing second option. Tied to that feeling was the joy of being in Bright's company. She exuded a lightness that made it impossible to be sad or dreary. Even if I had wanted to keep mourning, it would have been impossible.

Saturday afternoon Claire phoned. A gang were going to meet at Tims and then go off bowling. Who could resist? Bright dropped me off on her way to get groceries. Claire was already at a table when I arrived. I ordered my drink and we sat happily looking out at the sunshine.

I told her about Lloyd's latest thing. He'd signed me up for an email "Pun of Day," on the premise that I would not be able to forget him if I got a daily bad joke, I guess. Today's pun was so awful I was having trouble articulating it.

Claire giggled at my hysteria and took a sip of her iced coffee.

"Well, fancy meeting you here," said a familiar voice.

My head shot up and I locked into the eyes that had haunted me. "Josh!"

Josh had been a troublemaker at the back of my English class, and he'd insisted on a date that hadn't gone very well. His dark hair and eyes seemed to show up in my nightmares.

"Hello, Grace." He was still wearing his brown leather jacket, but it and his jeans were clean. He wasn't as highly polished as I'd seen him when we'd gone out for dinner, but he wasn't rough like he'd been at school either. He had cultivated a broodingly casual, sexy look. It suited him, but I missed the warm smile he used to have for me.

A girl in a black mini-dress with shiny red knee boots sauntered up beside him, draping an arm possessively across his shoulders. Her lips tilted up slightly, but you couldn't really call it a smile. At first, I thought she could be a hooker, but then I gasped as I recognized her.

Josh's dark smile stretched a little; the mischievous grin I remembered had been replaced by something darker and more menacing. "I think you know Eris?" Under a sleek pixie cut instead of gelled spikes was the familiar face of one-half of Bonnie's Scary Twins. They'd been behind a few of my bad experiences at school last year.

She smiled maliciously at me while I stared back at her, stunned. What was *she* doing with Josh?

"Of course. Hi, Eris." I fought to keep my voice calm. I could feel the adrenaline coursing through my system. I wanted to run. Or fight.

I looked at Claire's confused face and pondered the best way to get out of this situation. Then Ben's voice echoed in my head, "Stay there, Grace. Keep Claire with you. You're both safe so long as you stay in the building." His thoughts brooked no argument, but I was still engulfed in panic. I could taste it in the metallic tinge on my tongue. I reached out and took a sip of my hot chocolate.

Josh glanced down and smiled again; this time I saw a glimpse of the boy I'd known in Calgary, "Still hot chocolate and topping, huh?"

"With sprinkles today."

"Ah. Good to know you're branching out a bit."

"I try." I attempted to say it lightly, but my laugh was forced. This was painful.

Claire was still looking from me to Josh in confusion. Josh flicked his chin at her and said, "Since Grace isn't introducing us, I'll do the honours. I'm Josh, and this is my girlfriend Eris. We went to school with Grace in Calgary."

Huh. Not 'friends' anymore apparently, just someone he 'went to school with.' I wondered about the verbal distance. Was that for my benefit or Eris'?

"Claire," she said quietly, nodding at each of them in a vague sort of way. She could feel my tension. She didn't smile a greeting.

Josh nodded and acknowledged, "Claire." He looked at her appraisingly.

She met his eyes without any sign of fear or trepidation.

Taking another sip, I forced myself to ask casually, "So what are you doing in Salmon Arm, Josh?"

He pulled out a chair beside Claire for Eris and then sat down next to me. "Eris and I were in Vancouver for a concert. We're just driving home. What about you? You living here now? Or just passing through?"

Ben interrupted with a whispered instruction: "Lie."

I glanced at Claire and smiled weakly at her, hoping she wouldn't give me up. "Neither. I'm living down in Penticton these days, but I came up to see my friend here." I hoped two hundred kilometres was far enough away to distract him if he came looking for me.

"Really?" he said calmly, but I read the doubt on his face. He suspected I was lying. Terrific.

"I wondered where you'd disappeared to. I stopped by your house, but new people were there. They said you were in Greece." He clearly thought they'd been lying to him, too.

"Yeah. Some of the family is in Greece. Some of the family is in BC." I shrugged my shoulders, "You know how it goes. Families change."

"Hmm." He bobbed his head thoughtfully, watching my face.

Feeling perhaps braver than was warranted, I returned Eris' black look and asked casually, "So how are Enyo and Meg, Eris?"

She just stared at me for a moment, and then glanced at Josh, who gave just the slightest hint of a nod. "They're fine. Meg is at U of C," she paused before adding, "in the music department." She smirked and raised an eyebrow meaningfully at me. In the music department. Like Ben. My heart skipped a beat, but Ben started humming soothingly in the back of my head and I heard his chuckle. Nothing to worry about. I'd fallen for it once, but I wasn't that stupid anymore.

"How nice for her. And Enyo?"

She shrugged. "Oh. She's around. Doing this and that."

That was informative. I nodded as if I understood more than she said. "Ah. I *see*." I looked over at Josh, wondering how long this torture was going to go on. "So how was the concert?"

"Good." He smiled a little seductively, leaning closer as he said, "I still can't hear anything properly yet." His words didn't match his posture.

Eris glared at us as I leaned back as far away from him as I could without moving my chair.

At that moment there was a loud slamming of car doors and an almost simultaneous hammering on the window beside us. I jumped, and then beamed when Marco waved enthusiastically at us through the glass. In a moment, he and his car full of friends were gathered around us, smiling happily. They pulled chairs from neighbouring tables and made a circle two deep around us.

It was as if they brought sunshine in with them to shine into the dark corners. I felt lighter.

"Hey Grace! Claire! Who are your friends?" Marco said it in the same friendly tone he always used, but I could hear a hint of wariness behind it. He could sense the tension, too.

Josh sized him up, leaning back coolly into his chair. "Josh Dagen. And you are…?"

"Marco Diguerra." He swept his fedora off his head with a dramatic bow, smiled winningly at Eris and asked, "Who's this glamorous creature?"

In the back of my head, I heard Ben mutter, "Creature is right!" and my mouth twitched.

Eris glared at me, then at Marco. He put his arms out in mock fear and said, "Sorry! Sorry! No offence meant!"

She turned her glare to Josh and narrowed her eyes.

Josh stood up. "Well, I'm sorry to have to cut this happy reunion short, but Eris and I need to get re-fuelled and back on the road. It's been a joy and a delight seeing you again, Grace." Under Eris' glower, he leaned down and rested his hand suggestively on my shoulder, giving it a squeeze before he trailed a finger languidly over my cheek murmuring, "I've missed our…*talks*, Grace."

I was trembling a bit and completely at a loss about how to reply. I could still feel his hand on my shoulder and my cheek burnt like tracks of flame had singed it. I swallowed hard and looked up at him blankly.

He laughed then, reaching his hand back to grab Eris' he said, "Come on Eris, time to leave Graceland." They walked out the door without a backward glance while the table followed them with our eyes. As Josh started the engine, he looked up and gave me a sardonic wave. Eris stared at us sulphurously.

I realized that I hadn't been breathing, and I exhaled a quivering breath as they pulled away.

Claire sighed and glancing at Marco, she remarked with studied casualness, "Hmm. Do you think that girl is just a *little* jealous of Grace?"

Marco leaned over my shoulder and planted a kiss where Josh's hand had squeezed and then trailed his lips along the path of my cheek. Amazingly, it seemed to erase the lingering burn. I smiled up at him appreciatively and he dropped with a grin into the seat Josh had vacated. As confidently as usual he asked, "So where did you find that one, Grace? Was *he* the source of the boy troubles back home?"

"No, believe it or not my parents actually *liked* him."

Claire shook her head, "Hard to believe. He looks very dangerous."

I nodded. "He is." I looked from face to curious face around the table and then I confessed aloud for the first time, "I think he's the one who ran me down last June."

Eight pairs of wide eyes stared at me as I drained the last of the hot chocolate from my cup.

CHAPTER THREE

SHE'S THE INSPIRATION FOR EVERY SONG

Hope for a time of reunion, dashed by the rules of her parents.
Charis is grieving for Orpheus; loneliness fills, that's apparent.
Music is dancing around her; joyfully she hears his voice call,
Strains of his music bring hope to her; melodies excite and enthral.

Spring Break loomed and for a few weeks, I wondered what I was expected to do with the time off. Susan was heading off to Disneyland with her family. Claire was visiting relatives in Northern BC. Even Rafiq's family was going to Mexico together. I was feeling like the only loser who had no vacation plans. I didn't have any exotic dreams for the time. All I wanted to do was go to Calgary to spend it with Christie and Ben, but I was almost certain that that wasn't going to be something my mother would endorse.

Bright broke the news just as I heading off to the bus on Friday. "When you get home tonight Grace, you'll need to pack. We're spending the week in Vancouver. I'll leave a list of things you'll need on your bed."

"Oh." My disappointment was obvious.

She smiled sympathetically. "I'm sorry Grace. You knew that your mother wouldn't let you go to Calgary."

I nodded and quietly left the house, walking up the hill to the bus stop. I ached as if each muscle was grieving. I had only dared to dream with a tiny, tiny part of my heart, and yet that was enough to leave me feeling like a mourner at hope's funeral.

Melancholy overwhelmed me, but Ben took pity on me. "It's all right, Grace. They're not going to keep us separated forever."

"It's been two months, and if feels like two years."

"Two years ago you didn't even know me; it couldn't be that much of a loss."

"Don't be a pain, Ben. I want you near me."

"I'm always with you, *Amata*. I'm in your mind, remember? I couldn't get much closer."

"Yeah, yeah."

"Come on *Amata*, it's okay. It'll be over soon."

Now he had my attention. "What do you mean? What will be over soon?"

Silence. Very obviously an "Oops" silence.

"Ben! Don't ignore me! What will be over?"

I sensed his sigh more than heard it.

"So you're going to Vancouver for vacation," he commented in an obvious bid to change the subject. "It'll be beautiful this time of year. All the cherry and plum trees will be in bloom."

"Why do you know where I'm going? I didn't tell you."

He paused again with an exasperated sigh, "Look, I know what you think Grace. You know that."

"I hate that you go poking inside my head where I don't invite you."

"Sorry, *Amata*. I can't do anything about it. That's just the way it is."

"The way it is sucks."

"Would you prefer if I left you alone?" he asked wistfully.

I couldn't believe he'd even imagine that's what I meant. "Ben, I don't want you gone." I sighed, thinking carefully how to put it. "I love you, Ben, but everyone needs a little privacy now and then. You can keep me out of private places in *your* head; I'd like the same option. That's all."

"I'm sorry, Grace. I can't explain how it's done."

Can't or won't? I wondered to myself. "I'll talk to you tomorrow, Ben."

"Good night, Grace."

He shut the blinds on his brain then, like a switch snapped him shut. I sighed again and walked through the front door of the school.

We drove to Vancouver. I had expected that we'd drive Fatima, so I was surprised when I stepped outside with my bags, and there was a gorgeous silver BMW sedan parked in the driveway. It was long and lean with chiselled sides. It looked more like sculpture than transportation.

"Whose car?" I asked curiously.

"Oh. Jim thought he'd buy us some new wheels for Spring Break. What do you think?" She glanced at Jim with a fondly reproving expression. He ducked his head, hiding a grin.

"It's nice." I remarked, handing over my suitcase, which Jim loaded into the ample trunk.

We all settled into the roomy interior, luxuriating in the classic new car smell and the comfort of the leather seats.

I had never been to Vancouver, so I was surprised that it was such a fast trip. We set off toward the desert city of Kamloops at nine o'clock and we were heading down the Coquihalla Highway by just after ten. There was snow in drifts along the sides of the high mountain road, but the highway itself was bare and dry all the way. Trees stretched in all directions, with the occasional white forest cut block, like a square of mown velvet to break the pattern.

I kept thinking, "This is the wrong direction. I should be travelling closer to Ben, not farther from him!" I was a little sullen, thinking about my conversation with Ben the day before. An additional five hundred kilometres was a thousand kilometres from Calgary. How would Ben feel if, when he stretched out his mind to me tonight at ten o'clock, I wasn't there? The thought brought a wave of panic.

Bright turned around with a smile, "How are you doing back there, Grace? Do you need a juice box or some crackers?"

I shook my head, noting with vague amusement as Jim shot Bright a very alarmed expression at the very idea of crackers in his new car.

At eleven o'clock we were descending into a valley.

"We might as well stop here in Hope for lunch, don't you think?" interrupted Auntie Bright in a voice that Jim knew from experience wasn't really a question at all. He pulled off the highway and headed up the main street.

We found a cute café across from the cinderblock city hall and a park full of kids. I had a wrap. Uncle Jim ordered a quiche ("What? I *like* quiche!") and Auntie Bright had a creamy soup that wafted the warm exotic scent of curry. "Mmm. I just love Mulligatawny," she sighed. "It's my absolute favourite."

"Is that a chunk of potato?" I asked, thinking the potato didn't seem particularly exotic.

"No," she savouring another mouthful, "it's apple."

"Apple?" That was weird.

"This soup has a real history. It is from India during the time of the British Raj; the soldiers serving there got a taste for curry and brought this recipe back to England." She smiled, "It brings back a lot of memories. I

234

love it." She was already scraping her bowl and leaned back in her seat to watch Jim and I finish our lunches.

We sampled some sweet treats, and strolled down the main street looking at the wooden carvings, peeking into shop windows, and enjoying the small town atmosphere. The hum of the highways was ever present, however, as almost all the traffic going between the Coast and the Interior passed through this corridor. After a pleasant hour-long break, we climbed back into the BMW and headed west again.

Before too much longer, the air was filled with the earthy scent of cows as we traveled through the rich farmlands of the Fraser Valley and through Chilliwack. I studied the canals with fascination as we drove on. Traffic was picking up.

The highway wound through mountains, rocks, moss covered trees, and then the scenery changed. The pace picked up with a palpable energy that bore us forward through urban municipalities, one flowing seamlessly into another, until we were surrounded by the towers of downtown Vancouver. Uncle Jim pulled under a hotel awning and announced, "Here we are!"

We unfolded ourselves from the car and stretched. With a smile and a nod to the doorman, we followed Jim into the spacious and bright lobby.

The hotel was modern and gleaming. Bright and Jim had rented a two-room suite so we all had privacy. I squirmed a little when I looked on the back of the door and read that the room rate was nine hundred dollars a night. I hoped that they had coupons or something. We laid low for the rest of the day, just exploring the area around the hotel a bit. I was impressed to see rows of flowering plum trees and beds of pansies blossoming around a light rail transit station. What a lovely way to incorporate green into the urban landscape. The faint floral scent stirred in the breeze off the water. It smelled like spring.

That night, worn out from racing Jim in the hotel pool, I lay in bed and waited for Ben's voice. He didn't come.

By ten thirty, I was hyperventilating in panic. What had happened? There was a soft knock at the door and Bright whispered my name.

"I'm awake, Bright. Come in."

She came and sat on my bed. "What's up?"

"Ben."

"Oh. Not answering tonight?"

I nodded. She smiled and rubbed my shoulder. "I'm sorry, Hon. I guess you are just a little out of range, eh?"

"I suppose."

"Go to sleep, Grace. We can always phone him tomorrow." Her smile was wistful as she leaned over and kissed my forehead. "Love surmounts distance, Grace. It'll be fine."

It didn't feel fine now, though. I fell asleep several hours later, but it was a turbulent night. I woke on Sunday morning feeling like I'd been pummelled in an upright washing machine.

The day was brilliantly sunny and at breakfast, Bright announced that Jim was going to do his own thing, while the two of us went to Stanley Park and the Aquarium. She ordered me into comfortable walking shoes. I wondered what we would find to do for an entire day, but it wasn't a problem. We began with a long stroll to Stanley Park, and a walk along the sea wall. We sat on the rocks watching ships come in and out of False Creek, chatting companionably. We walked along the wooded paths and were amazed at the blow down that had destroyed a whole section of forest in a storm a few years earlier. It was exhilarating to be out in the woods while in the middle of the city.

We had a picnic lunch at a cement table and giggled as we watched the squirrels and gulls chasing after tidbits. Families played and children climbed on anything they could: tables, play structures or each other.

After lunch, we went into the Aquarium. I loved watching the faces of the little kids as they played with the interactive components of the exhibit: their faces hugely magnified in a dome within a marsh habitat or squirming in squeamish delight as they reached into a pool to touch an anemone.

We went outside and joined the crowds to watch the belugas and dolphins cavort. We stayed safely out of the splash zone. As we watched, a shiver ran up my spine despite the sun shining on me.

Bright glanced over, "Grace?"

I shook my head, "It's nothing."

She studied me for a minute, and then she began scanning the crowd. "Let's go, Grace."

"But I want to watch…"

"Now." Her tone did not allow any argument. She looked at me with aggravation as she stood, "Grace, you really need to learn to listen to your intuition. When you get a signal, you need to obey!"

"Signal?"

"It's an alert. Your body is warning you to pay attention."

It irritated me that my weird little sensation bothered her more than it did me. Why did she trust my instincts when I didn't? How did she know about it anyway?

She started through the crowd, offering gentle, "Oh, excuse me…I'm sorry…Pardon me," all along the row as we worked our way out.

I followed with a frustrated look, rolling my eyes when anyone looked at me. Other teens smirked in sympathy; parents scowled. At least the generations were consistent.

Once we were out of the crowd, she sauntered casually over to where the otters were entertaining a couple of families with their antics. She stopped far enough away that no one would be able to over-hear and whispered adamantly in my ear.

"Grace, you have instincts for a reason." She was eye to eye with me as if she was trying to push the understanding in through my vision. "When you get a feeling like that, it is absolutely crucial that you don't ignore it. It could be your life in danger, or you could be putting other people at risk. Listen to your body, please."

I breathed deeply. She was so melodramatic.

She narrowed her eyes, "Alayna Grace Severin don't you dare look at me like I'm insane. One of us knows what's going on here, and one of us doesn't. Guess which one is *you*?"

"Fine. Are you planning to *tell* me what is going on?" Using my full name was a mother trick. She was playing foul.

Her sour face crumbled then and she grinned mischievously, "Maybe later." It was impossible for her to stay angry, especially when we both knew she wasn't going to tell me anything.

I felt a vague shimmer between my shoulder blades and looked around warily, her lecture in my mind.

Bright smiled and nodded, "There you go. *That's* better. Keep looking. What do you see?"

I spun around in slow motion, surprised to realize that as I tuned in to the feeling I saw everything. It was as if I could see three hundred and sixty degrees simultaneously, as if I had spider eyes. It was more than vision: it was spherical *perception.* I could sense everything around me. This awareness was an attack of sensation from every direction; it was overwhelming. I backed against a wall and closed my eyes, feeling for the danger with my mind. I caught the sense in the northwest. It was as if a dagger of malevolence was hovering there. I angled my body toward it and opened my eyes.

I could see him as if he was the only person in the park. Past crowds of children and walking families, there he was. Tall and bearded, he stared back at me. "There," I whispered to Bright, "under the tree."

She followed my gaze, nodding with satisfaction. "Yes. Very good."

"Who is he?"

"A watcher, I'd say."

"Then is he going to hurt me?"

She shrugged, "Hard to say. Probably not while I'm here." She stared at him with an intensity that dared him to come closer.

"Why is he watching me?"

She turned to me. "Curiosity, I expect. Maybe orders. It's hard to say."

I met her eyes briefly, and then glanced back to the watcher. I gasped. "Hey! He's gone!"

She nodded. "Yes, I doubt we'll see him again this trip, but stay tuned in. I may be wrong, or there may be others."

I didn't get the feeling again, and I was able to relax. Ben didn't show up to talk to me, and I was getting more and more worried about it. I asked Bright and she nodded sympathetically. "It's probably just distance, Grace. I wouldn't worry about it. He knows that you're here in Vancouver. He could always phone you."

It didn't feel right, but there didn't seem to be anything that I could do about it. I tried to relax and enjoy the city. It was hard. I kept thinking of things I would talk to Ben about when he finally showed up again. I tried calling his phone, but he didn't pick up or answer my messages.

We spent the next few days hitting all the tourist sites. We admired the view from Grouse Mountain, spent a day exploring at Science World, drove to Whistler to explore. On Thursday, Bright announced we were on a hunt for 'the perfect dress' for an evening at the theatre. We were apparently going to a concert tomorrow. She marched me down Robson Street with a purposeful gleam in her eye. She had me try on about forty dresses before I stepped out of the dressing room and her eyes lit up.

"*That* one. No doubts. It's perfect!"

I pivoted in front of the three-way mirror, astonished by the vision. It was like a stranger was in front of me. My hair was shining in waves down my back, and my eyes were sparkling. The dress was doing something amazing to my figure: my waist looked tiny and the fabric clung to the curve of my breasts in a way that caught my breath. The colour was dark red with an iridescence that made it look like a living thing. It rippled as I moved, playing in the light. Yes. It was definitely *the dress*. Of course, the next stop was the shoe store. Bright decided that I was getting yellow stilettos that made my legs look another foot longer. I thought the yellow was a weird choice with a red dress, but she assured me it would give the dress 'pop.' I knew better than to bother to disagree.

Bright decided that we would really make it an evening and booked hair and nail appointments for us. I thought that was a bit of over-kill, but if we were going to have a spa day of pampering, I was just going to enjoy it. I'd never had the experience.

The next day, by the time we'd been buffed, polished, washed, styled and gowned we looked ready for a photo shoot. Bright was glorious in a dress that looked sometimes blue and sometimes purple like a midnight sky. Her hair was piled on top of her head with wispy tendrils playing around the edges. Jim beamed as us, looking handsome and distinguished in his classic black tuxedo. He pulled out his camera and took a few photos of us around the hotel garden doing our best imitations of high fashion models, and then we were off. They said they had decided to avoid parking issues by taking a taxi, but it was a limo that showed up. I felt like a movie star.

As we pulled into the Orpheum, a crowd of people turned to watch us emerge from the limo. I wondered if they thought we were famous. Bright smiled and nodded like she was, and Jim glowed like he was basking in her glory. I decided to take advantage of the audience and I nodded and glowed in my best starlet style. I was surprised and amused when more than a few flash bulbs snapped. Wouldn't they be surprised when they got home and found out their photos were of a little nobody? Bright caught my eye and grinned.

"Come this way," Jim indicated, as I we entered the ornate theatre. The high ceilings glowed with golden light. The red carpet beneath our feet reflected opulence. People around us were well dressed, but we still seemed to be attracting everyone's attention. Bright smiled and nodded like she was at the Oscars. Cameras flashed at us as we moved through the lobby toward the doors. Every once in awhile she'd pause to pose, smiling up at Jim, or out to a camera. She was in her element. "We're seated in the Dress Circle," said Uncle Jim, his hand on the small of Bright's back. "All the way to the front." An usher looked at our tickets, beamed at us, and began escorting us to our seats.

As we made our way down the aisle, people turned and murmured as we went by. I ended up mimicking Bright's smile and nod technique, feeling simultaneously foolish and glamorous while the cameras inexplicably continued to snap around us.

When we got to the front of the balcony the usher raised his hand and directed us into the red velvet seats, "Here we are. Seats 141 to 143. Enjoy the show." We murmured our thanks as he headed back up the aisle looking a little star struck. Bright sat between Jim and me. I thought Jim would want the aisle so he could stretch out his long legs, but he took the interior seat, as if to protect her from the rest of the crowd. I could feel the eyes of the people behind us, but I didn't sense any malevolence here.

Contrarily, I could feel waves of affection, happiness and pleasure, as if the theatre was a hive of joyful expectation.

The concert hall itself was a thing of beauty. The subtle use of lighting intensified the ornate Art Nouveau angles and patterns of the ceiling and walls. A magnificent glass chandelier drew the eye to a stunning fresco of a conductor and a sky full of cavorting bodies. The edge of the ceiling had a golden glow. The towering walls were crowned with a series of arches like a medieval cathedral. I sat in awe, wondering if this was what it was like to be in the middle of *Phantom of the Opera*.

As we waited, looking around and murmuring to one another, the symphony musicians were slowly filling the stage, arranging their chairs, tuning instruments and preparing their music. Before long, the stage was full and a definite air of expectation hovered in the room. The concertmaster entered to spattered applause. He raised the baton for the oboe to give the pitch. With howls and moans, the other instruments matched it. The concertmaster then took his seat beside the other violinists, and set down his instrument. Coughs and crinkles echoed through the space.

The house lights dimmed and the crowd hushed expectantly. A man walked onto the stage and raised the microphone. "Welcome ladies and gentlemen to a very special evening for our symphony. This evening we are delighted to present the compositions of some very talented Canadian youth. In the first half, we will hear a seven to eight minute piece from each of the five finalists of the National Youth Composition Competition." My eyes grew huge and I snapped my head around to look at Bright, one question in my eyes. Her eyes twinkled as she smiled and nodded. I inhaled joy and it felt as if I was inflating, floating over everyone. I started panning the seats, searching for a familiar head. The announcer was still speaking, "This evening is the final judging and at the end of the performances we will be awarding the prizes." Then with a flourish, he announced Wesford Kraft as the conductor for the evening, and the crowd applauded as the young conductor came on stage. He looked like he was in his late twenties. His hair was tied in a ponytail. It contrasted with the tails of his formal jacket. Kraft bowed and took the mic. He added his own greetings, made a general comment on the many talented composers who had submitted work, and then announced, "Now without further ado, let me welcome to the stage our first finalist, Suzanne Lee of Vancouver!" The crowd went wild at the name of their hometown girl, and a tiny, black-haired girl came onto the stage. As she nervously waved to the crowd, the announcer gave her biography. The conductor asked her a couple of questions about the inspiration for her composition, and then Suzanne sat down in the front row while the conductor raised his baton and the piece began.

I couldn't concentrate on her song at all. I stared at the back of her head where she sat in the front row watching the symphony perform her piece and I gazed longingly at the four empty seats beside her. I could feel Ben waiting behind the curtains. I closed my eyes and called out to him with my thoughts. "Ben? Ben, are you there?" I felt an awareness touch my mind, but he didn't answer with words. He just sent me love, and it filled me so fully that it brought tears to my eyes.

I glanced over at Bright. She was listening, her head and body swaying slightly with the music, but she felt my gaze and smiled knowingly at me.

Suzanne's piece lasted about seven minutes. It seemed to me to be clinically beautiful: all structure and rules, but no emotion. Lovely, but shallow. As the last notes died away, the conductor turned to face us, and swept his arm to Suzanne. She stood bowing to the audience and they clapped appreciatively, but like her composition, they were without much passion.

The second piece was by a boy called Matthew from Newfoundland. His piece was jaunty and rollicking and definitely conjured the feeling of family and friends. Although it was an orchestral piece, it gave one the sense of a raucous Celtic kitchen party. I glanced around at the audience and saw a sea of smiling faces rippling and waving with the notes. Matthew, sitting down front beside Suzanne from Vancouver, was a metaphorical boat tossed by an enthusiastic tide. When his piece ended the audience roared appreciatively, and hoots were shouted from proud Maritimers as he took his bow. Someone in the balcony behind us shouted, "Go Buddy!" and everyone laughed.

The third piece was by a girl called Jilly Tomm from Saskatchewan. Her name is not one I'll forget because her supporters stopped the concert with their thundering chant of "Jilly Tomm SaSKATCHewan!" They stomped their feet to the rhythm of their chant and with the acoustics of the theatre the few became a mob of sound. When they finally settled down, after a bemused shrug from thrilled and embarrassed Jilly and a scowl from Wesford Kraft, her piece began with a crash that jolted us all in our seats. I don't know what I'd expected, but this wasn't it. Her composition had the beat and dissonance of heavy metal. It throbbed like a pulsing headache, like some computerized anthill, all parts moving to the same agonized rhythm. It sped up and slowed down, but the hammering beat bore into the brain with a powerful consistency. When it was over, the audience sat as if Caged and stared dully for a moment, before they began

241

their applause. It was hard to read how it would fare in the voting, because while it was obvious the composition was very powerful and mesmerizing, it wasn't exactly pleasant.

When Philip from Ontario was announced, he strolled onto the stage with a guitar around his neck. He grinned and waved while his biography was read, and made jokes out of all the inspiration questions. The audience was ready to love him. Instead of joining the other competitors in the front row, he perched himself on the edge of a stool on the stage to the right of the conductor with a guitar on his lap and when the baton was raised Philip began to play. He was a master of classical guitar: that was plain. As his fingers raced up and down the frets, the audience all seemed to lean forward as one. We almost seemed to be breathing in time with each other. With rapt attention every eye was on his hands, every ear tilted to catch each note. His piece was captivating. After a minute (or was in an hour?) of his guitar solo, the rest of the orchestra joined in, first the other strings harmonized with him, and then his hands dropped and the orchestra took over, enlarging his motifs and exploring with depth and breadth. In a rousing explosion of sound, the brass and woodwinds joined. We jumped in our seats, but we were captivated. One by one, the instruments dropped out, and Philip's hands positioned on the guitar again. Finally, it was just guitar and cello, and then the cello faded off, and Philip took two or three more bars and then the sound trickled away. The audience erupted with pleasure. I was enthralled. There was one composer left. Could Ben possibly beat that?

My heart was thundering in my chest when the announcer introduced, "Benjamin Butler of Calgary" but when he stepped out onto the stage it almost stopped. Ben was breathtaking. His cheekbones were chiselled, his pale brown hair was golden again, and his tuxedo was cut like something James Bond would wear. He looked completely comfortable on the stage. When he was asked about the inspiration for his piece, he looked up to the balcony and straight into my eyes as he replied, "I wrote this piece as a celebration of the kind of love that can not be stopped by time, the kind of love that makes the universe worth inhabiting." Tears were already pouring down my face. Like Philip, Ben did not go sit in the audience next to Suzanne and Matthew; instead, he walked to the gleaming black Bösendorfer grand piano and sat down, nodded to the conductor who raised the baton, and then with a nod to the violins, the piece began.

The violins began the work; when the other strings joined in, they chased each other as if searching for something—loneliness wept from their strings. Then the flutes entered, dancing along the edges, twitters of hope flitting here and there. Ben's hands rose and the piano came in. As he struck the keys, the audience seemed to inhale. At first the piano played a gentle game, an introduction, laughter, then the passion grew, brass and percussion joined in to call out the joy and the power of the love. Murmurs travelled throughout the auditorium, the odd person laughed with the sheer joy of the happiness dancing through the air. I recognized this section: it was the piece that Ben had played for me in the car the day I'd fainted on the sidewalk. It seemed so long ago, and here was an entire concert hall held mesmerized just as I had been. When the piano dropped out, the other instruments carried on and the audience let out their collective breath. The drums signalled trouble and the tune grew mournful again; deep sighs were drawn around me, then the piano came back singing hope and expectation before the orchestra and piano sounded a chord that had me reverberating and there was silence. Ben dropped his head to his chest, frozen.

The audience was absolutely still, as if they were still entranced. Ben stood slowly up, kissed his fingertips, pointed to me in the balcony, and bowed. I leaned over the rail in front of me and stretched out my arm. Tears traced a path down my cheeks and I realized Ben was crying too. Suddenly the audience seemed to awaken from a stupor; they erupted in a thunderous applause and rose in unison. They did not roar, hoot or scream; they just kept applauding. For one minute, two, three, four it did not lessen or waver; it was as steady as a rainstorm on a roof.

The announcer came on the stage and escorted Ben to the side to join the other contestants in the audience. The crowd gradually quietened, and the conductor announced that after intermission we'd hear a twenty-minute composition from the previous year's winner, and then they'd reveal the results of the competition.

I knew already what the result would be.

As the lights came up I looked at Bright and she grinned, "Go ahead." I tried to be contained, but I almost flew up the aisle. Ben obviously was feeling the same way because we met in the lobby and embraced as if there were no one else in the world. His mouth found mine and it seemed as if it was several minutes before I realized that I needed to breathe. Ben filled my head with such a surge of joy at our reunion that I thought I would explode from the happiness. When we finally broke apart and whispered "I love you" into each other's eyes, the lobby was full and we were the centre of a circle that broke into smiles and applause as we finally noticed them.

Of course, I couldn't let go of him, or perhaps it was he that wouldn't let go of me. When the lobby lights flicked to send us back in, he grasped my hand and I trailed behind him to the front of the auditorium.

243

There he wrapped an arm around me and I nestled in, feeling like I was finally home. The other contestants just grinned as if they weren't surprised by this development.

We listened to the previous winner's composition, and what I heard of it was lovely, but of course, I wasn't paying very close attention. I was basking in the glory of Ben's arms. When the judges announced the winner, it was anti-climatic. Of course, Ben had won. Philip from Ontario was second, and Matt from Newfoundland took third. When Ben was called onto the stage the announcer glanced down to me and asked, "So is that lady in red your inspiration for tonight's song?"

Ben smiled and affirmed, "She is the inspiration of this song, and for every song there ever will be."

The audience gushed with an "Ahhhhhh…" that made me smile as the announcer said, "I guess she should be up here with you, then." The audience began to applaud and Ben smiled at me, hopping off the stage, taking my hand, and leading me up the stairs through the proscenium. The applause grew as the audience rose to their feet. When Ben leaned down to kiss me gently, the audience went wild. I snuggled into his embrace as the announcer, conductor and judges laughed, handing over a cheque and plaque. Ben received them, and passed them for me to hold while he waved to the crowd before we were escorted backstage.

Several hours and a hundred smiling photographs later we joined Bright and Jim, who'd been standing off to the side watching everything with amused grins. We went out for a midnight dinner, and then Ben came back to our suite. Bright and Jim headed off to bed, but Ben and I nestled together on the couch all night. We didn't need to speak much; all we wanted to do right now was to bask in each other's presence. I had kicked off my shoes, and he'd taken off his tie and jacket, which he arranged over us. I'm not sure we were speaking aloud as we laughed about the surrealism of the evening and the joy of being together at this moment.

When the dawn came, the end of our time together came rushing toward me. Fifteen short hours total, and only five left. Ben's flight left at noon and neither of us planned to spend a moment away from each other before his departure.

When Jim came into the room in the morning he made me go change and have a shower. I didn't want to leave Ben's side, but decided it was probably better if I didn't stink during his last hours.

When I came back into the main area of the suite, room service had brought breakfast. I joined Bright and Jim at the table while Ben went to have his own shower and change out of his tux. Jim tossed me the morning paper with a smile, "You're famous, Gracie."

There I was on the front page of the Entertainment section with Ben's arm draped across my shoulder, both of us obviously glowing. The caption read, "National Youth Composition grand prize winner Benjamin Butler and his muse, Grace Severin, stole the hearts of the audience." Huh. There were several other photos from the evening in a montage, including a stunning shot of a beaming Bright captioned, "Music impresario Bright Nicholas dazzles the crowd."

I looked up in shock. "Bright?" I choked a bit as I asked, "You're an *impresario*?" I didn't even know what that was, but it was obviously a big deal.

She shrugged as she took a bite of her croissant, then to my still astonished face she clarified, "It's just a fancy title, Grace. Don't get excited."

"I thought the photographers were just impressed with how beautiful you were. I didn't realize you were *actually famous*." I couldn't believe my aunt was famous and I hadn't known. What planet had I been on?

She laughed, "What's famous? I'm just well known, Hon, because I'm involved in the industry. You know that I handle the music division."

"Yeah, but..."

"You look positively star-struck, Grace," she chuckled. "Really, I'm the same person I was yesterday, though admittedly considerably less glamorous out of the gown..."

Ben interrupted then, towelling his damp hair as he looked over my shoulder, "It's a beautiful photo of you, Grace. We should see if they'll send us an original."

I looked back at him and he took away my breath. His naked muscular torso was very distracting. How did he manage to look that good? He draped the towel across his shoulders and I noticed his hair again. "Ben, did you bleach your hair blond? I'm sure it was darker when I first met you."

He laughed at me and ruffled my hair fondly.

Four more hours. We talked and laughed until the phone rang. I answered and was told, "A taxi has arrived for Mr. Butler."

At those words, I was broken again and the tears returned. As Ben and I went down to the cab, my tear-streaked face brought a few sympathetically curious looks as we walked through the lobby.

"Don't cry Grace," Ben said, tilting my chin up with a finger, "I'll talk to you tonight."

"I already miss you," I sniffled into his shoulder.

He said softly. "It won't be much longer."

"What?" I looked up surprised. "What do you mean?"

He glanced up to see if anyone was around then whispered in my ear, "I choose to believe that we *are* going to be allowed to be together, Grace. I won't tolerate the possibility that we won't." He bent his head and his kiss silenced any questions beginning to churn in my brain, then he stepped back and the doorman loaded his luggage into the trunk.

I was about to ask how he knew about our future, when he smirked and kissed me again in a way that left me tongue-tied. He dropped into the back seat of the taxi with an amused chuckle at my glazed expression. The doorman closed the car door as Ben blew me a kiss off the tips of his fingers while the taxi pulled out of the hotel lot and onto the street.

CHAPTER FOUR

YOU'RE THE COMMON DENOMINATOR

Ares comes flying from far above, aiming for Charis' downfall.
Cyclops awaits in the forest, every visit's a closer call.
Sparkling waters for summer fun, change in a moment of terror,
Stirred by Limnades in jealousy, tossed into water by error.

Claire, Rafiq and I were sitting at a table in the atrium working on dance posters for leadership. There had been another group of kids working on the other side of the space, but they'd just left. The low spring light was shining in through the windows high above our heads, hitting the mirrored ball mounted above and filling the entire atrium with polka dots of light. It imparted a cheerful atmosphere.

"You know," Claire said, studying her poster, "I never have been able to draw before. This actually looks like a person."

Rafiq leaned over, "It does. It looks like me. Are you trying to tell me something?"

She blushed and looked over at his paper. Then she blushed even more and hid her eyes behind a swath of falling hair.

I glanced at Rafiq's poster. He had drawn her. "Oh." I said.

He looked from Claire to his poster and wrinkled his brows. "I have never been able to draw, either. This is weird."

I coughed and grabbed at the first thing I could think of. "How was your Spring Break?"

Claire seized on the topic, explaining that she had had a frigid spring break up north, but she giggled about the crazy sing-a-long her family had during the nine hour drives to and from. Her cousin had gotten married, and Claire had caught the bouquet. Rafiq offered to marry her immediately, which made us laugh.

While in Mexico, Rafiq's little sister Nimaat had fallen into a hole as they were exploring an Incan pyramid, and a rescue unit had to be called in to pull her out. He laughed grimly as he observed that he doubted his parents would ever take them on vacation again.

I recounted my adventures in Vancouver at the concert hall, and while I deleted the part about the paparazzi experience, I knew I was glowing with the memory of the evening and the night that followed. Rafiq looked rather disconsolate. "So that is your boyfriend who won this big prize?"

I nodded. A distinct tingle rose up my spine and I wondered if it was from thinking about Ben.

Rafiq looked sadly into my eyes remarking, "He is very lucky." He managed to convey quite clearly that he wasn't talking about the music prize.

I blushed, noting that the sensation running down my back was stronger, "Thanks Rafiq," I said, avoiding his eyes by staring resolutely at the poster.

At that moment, there was a noise on the second floor above our heads and suddenly I recognized the feeling travelling though me.

"MOVE!" I shouted and all of us leapt to our feet and shot away from the table, at the very moment that a body landed with a crash upon it, then the crasher rolled over his shoulder and onto the floor. It was like a scene from a movie.

"YEAH!" he shouted exultantly, punching the air. The poster I was working on had torn under his feet, and he'd knocked all our felts onto the floor.

He whirled and glared at me as he took a purposeful step toward me.

I felt the anger rise like a tide with my adrenaline. Without a thought for personal safety or the fact that I didn't know who this scruffy guy was, or why he was jumping from life risking heights, I flew right into his face shouting, "What the *hell* are you thinking jumping down two storeys! Are you an *idiot*?" The question was rhetorical; the answer was obvious. I poked a finger at him and smacked his chest with it as punctuation to my rant. Each poke sent a static charge through my finger that sparked as it touched him. "That (poke) is the stupidest (poke) thing I've ever seen! (poke). You could have killed us! (poke) You could have killed yourself!" (poke) I was steaming mad at such stupidly reckless behaviour that had put my friends in danger.

Claire and Rafiq stared at me with their mouths agape.

The guy just stood there with cold eyes, staring as if he was trying to make a decision.

A vice-principal came running down the stairs then, sputtering with anger, "Get over here, young man!"

The jumper took one look at him, glanced back with a malevolent shrug at me, and then he ran straight for the principal. With a laughing deke to the left as the V.P. lunged futilely for him, he took off through the back doors, heading for the playing fields.

The V.P. came up to us then, "Who was that?" he said to me, plainly presuming my rant suggested I had a history with the guy.

I shook my head and snapped, "I'm new here. I have no idea who he is." I was still shaking from the adrenaline rush.

He seemed doubtful, but then looked at Claire and Rafiq in turn as each of them shook their heads as well. "Sorry Mr. Grey, I have never seen him before." Claire remarked in her calmly authoritative voice, which hopefully cancelled any suspicious surliness in mine, "If you have photos of all the students, we can look through them, but I don't think he's a student here."

Mr. Grey nodded, "Yes, come up to the office and you can look at the photo book."

As we turned to follow him, Rafiq asked him, "Did you see what happened from above? The first thing we saw was him landing on our table."

"Yes. He came in the main doors, walked right to the railing and was over it in a moment. It looked like he'd planned it."

"Huh," responded Rafiq. "I wonder if it was a dare or something?"

Mr. Grey shook his head in irritation, "That's quite possible. He's lucky he didn't break his neck or take someone out when he landed."

He took us into his office at the back of the main office area, and pulled out a black binder. "These are this year's school photos of every student at S.L.S. If you find him, let me know." He stepped out of the room, I presumed to go back on his prowl.

As we flipped through the book at the rows of tiny smiling faces, Rafiq asked edgily, "How did you know to move, Grace? You were looking down at the poster when you shouted and jumped away from the table."

My heart started to pound, but I shrugged my shoulders, trying to be blasé about it. "Just instinct I guess. I've had so many nasty experiences lately I seem to be developing a sixth sense for danger."

"Ah," he said with a forced laugh. From the corner of my eye, I noticed that he glanced at me like I might be growing another head.

I pretended not to notice and focused on a student Claire was pointing at, wondering if Rafiq thinking I was a freak would be enough to stop his flirting.

We flipped through the book twice looking for the dark hair, scruffy half-grown beard and unfeeling eyes of the jumper. We found a couple of boys who looked vaguely similar to the jumper, but we decided neither of them was actually the guy who'd landed on our table. I had the feeling that he was familiar somehow, but I couldn't place it. None of the student photos matched. Where could I know him from?

We came out of Mr. Grey's inner office and told the secretary that we were sure the student wasn't in the book. She nodded and we headed back down to the atrium to clean up our poster making supplies and salvage whichever posters we could. Thankfully, we'd been tossing the finished ones onto a pile on the floor, so they were all okay. The table looked a little splay legged, but I was surprised that it hadn't been destroyed. It was a twenty-five-foot drop from the railing of the level above, so he must have landed with force.

Claire drove me to the end of my street on her way home to the lakeshore suburb of Canoe, saving me twenty minutes of my walk. As I waved her off down the road, Ben came to me.

"Hello, Love," he said in my head.

"Hi," I replied, remembering our Friday night and feeling warmth surge through me.

"Very quick action today. I was impressed."

"It was nothing." I didn't bother to wonder how he'd known about it. Unlike everyone else around me, I didn't get to keep secrets these days.

"Oh, it *was* something. You are getting much better at perceiving the danger. He was planning to take you out, but you avoided it masterfully, and then you disarmed him. *That* was the best part." His laughter echoed in my head.

"What do you mean? He didn't have a weapon

"He did, actually; it was in a chest pocket. He didn't get to use it though, before you had de-sensitized it. He was in big trouble over it. I am so proud of you!"

"I didn't realize…"

"It doesn't matter, you responded instinctively and it was exactly what you were supposed to do. You're getting amazing." I could feel his smile. "You are awesome, my girl."

As usual, he was talking in riddles, but I knew from bitter experience that it was pointless to ask any questions. I sighed as I approached my house. "I miss you."

His response echoed my melancholy. "I miss you too…"

"…but it won't be long, right?"

He laughed, "Exactly."

"I'm home now; I'll talk to you later."

With a casual, "See you," he faded out.

I was walking through the door when it occurred to me to wonder what Ben had meant about the jumper getting into trouble.

"He's convinced one to join him." Mars dropped casually.

Xandros looked up curiously, "One what?"

"A Cyclops."

O groaned. "That's all we need!"

"Calm down. We can manage this. We just need to ensure it doesn't get a hold of any natural god fire."

"One abandoned camp fire and we're doomed!" O was slightly hysterical.

"No. It's more complicated than that. It can only use a fire that originates from Olympus. You know, from Vespa's hearth or Zeus' arrows."

Xandros laughed. "Who's going to give god fire to a Cyclops?"

Mars nodded, "It's a small danger, true enough. Ares might, but he's not likely to risk the wrath of Zeus. I think the greater danger would be someone accidentally providing fire."

Xandros scoffed. "Accidentally? Like who?"

O sighed. "Grace."

Mars nodded. "Exactly. She has growing power. You saw what happened at her school. Her own spark in a fight, for example, could start a fire."

"So. No fires." Xandros muttered.

A rumbling on the horizon drew their eyes to darkening clouds. There was a flash.

Mars looked over to O. "They're summoning you."

"I know." His lips tightened.

"What will you do?"

O shrugged. "I will try to convince them that we should be together, of course."

Xandros looked serious for once. "You know, if you don't seem so desperate for it to happen, perhaps you can assume a stronger negotiating position. You give them too much power when you care that much about the results. Loosen up. She's just a girl."

251

O's sudden fury surprised all three of them. He turned scarlet and stepped forward with his fists balled.

Xandros stepped back, hands out. "I'm just saying! Relax a bit. Perhaps you'll get what you want if you use a different tactic." He looked over at Mars. "Tell him it's good advice."

Mars nodded. "It's true, O. See if you can be creative. Maybe get Aphrodite to help. She generally will support love causes."

"I'll try. You protect Grace while I'm gone."

"We will."

The following evening I was sitting doing my homework in the living room when Uncle Jim shook his newspaper and called, "Bright, did you see this headline in *The Shuswap View*? They say there's been a Sasquatch sighting."

"Sasquatch?" I asked, curiously looking up from my books, "What's that?"

"Do you know the legends of Bigfoot?"

"Yes, big hairy thing that walks on two legs?"

"Yes, exactly. The British Columbian First Peoples call the same creature a Sasquatch. We haven't had any reported sightings in something like twenty years, though."

Auntie Bright came into the room and perched on the edge of Uncle Jim's chair, reading over his shoulder, "Where was the sighting?"

"Not too far away, out by Magna Bay. Some house boaters were picnicking on the shore and caught a glimpse of it."

"It was probably just a bear or something, right?" I asked. "It's just a myth, right? No such thing really?"

Bright laughed. "Grace, Grace, Grace. All myths have their origins in truth, you know. Bears don't run on their hind legs." Then she grinned at me, "but if it will help you sleep better, you can pretend there is no such thing as a Sasquatch or any other mythical creature." She chuckled and muttered something under her breath that made Jim laugh. He leaned over and kissed her softly on the cheek, smiling so lovingly at her that I looked away. Her smile echoed his affection and she nuzzled next to him, looking up at me contentedly. "Mythical creatures can be quite nice, actually."

Jim gave her a squeeze.

Crazily, having seen Ben made it worse being without him. I was feeling particularly thankful for Marco today, because I was missing Ben so desperately after our short time together in Vancouver. It was as if the short time with him had opened the wound of loneliness and made the pain sharper. Having him tell me that the jumper was supposed to have been attacking me just intensified my sense of isolation.

Marco was an oasis in the midst of insanity.

I was profoundly grateful that at least with him life did not take on the surrealism that seemed to touch everything associated with Ben. Marco was a calm breeze to my anxiety.

The wonderful thing about Marco was just how easy he was to be with. It was simply impossible to be stressed out or lonely around him. He was always relaxed and cheerful. He had a quiet, open nature, and it was comfortable to be around him. He was always making funny remarks, but it was a gentle humour that didn't put down anyone.

Ben was never out of my mind, of course, because he was quite literally there all the time, popping in to ask a question or make an observation. I knew I was not ever in danger of forgetting him or how I felt about him, but he wasn't here, and his thoughts were not always adequate consolation for the lack of his warm arms around me.

Since I was just going to have to suffer the loneliness and desperation of physical separation from Ben, Marco was exactly what I needed. His charm, goofiness and easy-going nature made me feel safe and content. He wasn't Ben, but I didn't want or need him to be. He seemed to know that I was not completely present all the time, and it seemed quite okay with him. I liked being with him. He was a good friend—a kind hearted, easy place to keep my head when my heart was already occupied. Since Ben also occupied much of my brain these days, I needed whatever peace I could get.

The fun of the bowling night had led to many similar outings. He had a very nice gang of friends. I always felt safe with him. Sometimes Claire and I went along together. Once the ice was off the lake, we took out boats. In May, we went swimming in the still frigid spring water. We climbed the Enderby Cliffs. We camped. We had shopping days in Vernon or Kelowna. We drove go-carts. We even tried to learn golf. Mostly, whatever we were doing was just an excuse to be together and spend a lot of time laughing. One comfortable month passed, and then two. I realized that Marco and I were generally seen as a couple. I worried that this made me look like a cheap two-timer, because my friends knew about Ben. But Marco didn't seem concerned, and in his strange, easy-going way Ben was utterly relaxed about it, so I just let it go, bemused as I was, and just concentrated on enjoying our times together. Ben was still in my head, humming his tunes and occasionally acting as a

Greek chorus to my social plans, nauseatingly supportive and encouraging whenever I was out with my friends, as if he were right there with us.

"Huh," Jim exhaled the exclamation.

I looked up from my homework as Jim shook the newspaper. "What is it, Uncle Jim?"

"It's another Sasquatch sighting, at Cinnemousun Narrows this time. The people saw it from the lake after they'd left their picnic site. This time someone had a cell phone with a camera, so there was a photo of the creature. Look…" he folded the paper back and handed it to me, "not a bad shot, eh?"

It was a very clear shot, though grainy, taken from a boat. The water was sparkling in the foreground and standing on the rocky shoreline, clearly outlined in front of the trees, was a large two-legged creature. It was taller than a man, by the looks of the trees, and much wider than one, too. It was facing the trees, so you couldn't see its face. "Wow. Someone is perpetrating a pretty impressive hoax."

Jim smiled. "Could be."

I interpreted the lightness of his response and cocked my head, "You don't think so?"

He shook his head noncommittally, "Until someone sees it up close, no one will know for sure, but I'm inclined to think there's something out there."

"Maybe just some high school kids on drywall stilts."

He laughed, "Maybe."

The next weekend Marco, his friend Andrew, Brittany from Leadership, Dave, Claire and I were all out on Dave's family's boat. Claire had not lied when she'd said there were benefits to living here. That weekend there was a snowstorm in Calgary and I had teased Lloyd and Christie about living in an ice cube. They were not amused. Here in Salmon Arm it was feeling like summer already.

The sky was the kind of blue you see in paintings and can't believe actually exists in nature; the hills snuggled around us like a hug and I thought with a giggle how boating on Shuswap Lake beat shopping in a mega-mall by a long shot.

Dave was driving. His boat was about fifteen feet long, and a pretty turquoise blue. We were enjoying the wind across our faces when Andrew called, "Hey Marco! Since when do you play an instrument?" He waved a hand toward the upper pocket of Marco's jacket where a little rectangular bump was evident.

Marco grinned in response and pulled out a shiny new harmonica. "I just bought it! I thought I'd see if I can play some heavy metal on it."

Andrew laughed, "Marco, I remember recorder class in grade four. You couldn't find two notes in a row. How are you ever going to play something as complex as a harmonica?"

Marco shrugged. Still grinning he winked over at me and said. "I don't know, but I feel inspired lately, so who knows?"

We laughed at him as Dave opened the throttle and we grabbed the edges of the boat as the bow rose into the air.

Today we weren't doing anything particularly exciting on the lake. We only had a couple of hours so we were sticking within the lake's Salmon Arm (for which the town was named), driving between Sicamous and Sunnybrae and back again.

We stopped near the inlet to Sicamous to chat and float for a bit while we watched a little tugboat chugging by, hauling a boom full of logs to the mill in Canoe. Marco pulled out his harmonica and managed some reasonably melodious music that a couple of them recognized, much to their astonishment. He smiled proudly. "It's like all of a sudden I have to make music!" He looked at me meaningfully while the others laughed.

When it was finally time to get the boat back, we waved to the tug pilot as we passed. Once we were out of his way, we played in the water carving patterns and bouncing over our own wake with squeals and shouts. Suddenly, a huge white cruiser came flying out of nowhere. Aside from the tug, which was well behind us now, there weren't any other boats around, so it was impossible that they hadn't noticed us, yet still they almost clipped our starboard side.

Dave was at the wheel and let out a curse as he swerved to port.

The white boat came flying back, this time intercepting us on the port side. We were caught against the wake and tipped shockingly. I didn't have time to realize what was happening before I went flying right out of the boat. Everyone had been focused on the white boat, and Dave kept going, trying to avoid the vessel, which had turned and was coming for him again.

I bounced in the water, buoyant in my yellow life jacket, heart pounding, wondering how I was going to draw attention to myself. Before I had decided what to do, I realized that the white boat had turned and it was coming right at me

I couldn't tell whether it was trying to run me down, or whether it just didn't realize I was there. It didn't really matter: one way or another I was in trouble. I had only a second to decide what to do. I couldn't go to either side quickly enough, so I unbuckled my life jacket, flipped my butt into the air and kicked, diving straight down as I slipped out of the jacket that trailed out behind me.

I rolled over onto my back to watch as the boat went over me and then kicked back up behind it. I popped up with a gasp, glancing around for my life jacket. I spotted it about three metres away and swam over to it. It looked a little worse for wear after a trip under the boat. A sharp slit through the cover and into the foam and a missing tie suggested the jacket had gotten up close and personal with the propeller. I slipped my arms back through, and clipped the one buckle that remained while I watched the boat heading away.

I couldn't believe I was stuck floating here in the middle of the lake. Surely, by now someone would have noticed that I wasn't on board any more? Were they just going to leave me out here? I called in my head for Ben, but uncharacteristically, he was quiet. I wondered why he was better at showing up when I was fine, and why he was missing big things like near death by drowning? This was the very behaviour that got him fired, I thought bitterly.

The little tug was chugging off in the distance. I was sure that the pilot wouldn't hear me over the noise of his engine if I shouted, but perhaps he'd notice if I waved? I tried, but the tug kept right on moving. That's when I realized I was still in trouble, because while the tug was a fair distance off, the boom he was hauling was wide, and it was about to mow me down.

The revving of an engine drew my notice and there was the white boat coming for another pass. This was insane! I decided not to bring attention to myself, instead I swam to the edge of the boom and tried to camouflage with the logs. If they got close to the boom they'd wreck their boat, it was a safer place to be than out in the middle of the water waiting for them, or the boom, to run me over.

I didn't consider how slippery wet logs are when I made that plan, or how the logs inside the boom are moving all the time, turning and bumping into one another with a force that would crush my head like a peanut. There was no way I could be inside the boom without risking being flattened between logs or drawn beneath them, but there was no other option, so hooking my elbows over the chain connecting the outside boom logs, I clung rather desperately to it and slipped inside the boom as the white boat came by. There were some long strips of cedar bark caught around the logs and I pulled some around me to try to hide the brilliant yellow of the life jacket.

Two people were in the boat. They were looking for something with grim expressions. I gasped as I recognized them. There was the bearded young man I'd seen in the window of the school. He was the same guy who'd jumped into the atrium, and he was leaning over the back and port side of the boat. The girl with the dreadlocks, Sthenno, was driving it, looking mostly ahead. They gave only a cursory glance to the tug passing on their starboard side.

As I floated with the boom, there was no way I was calling out to *them*. I was very sure now that the attack on our boat was intentional, and that they were looking for me. I concentrated on looking as much like a log as possible, hoping that my life jacket was less conspicuous with its bark coating. I wasn't about to take it off again, I was too cold and tired to risk it now.

After two or three passes, they seemed to give up, and their engine revved as they roared off to toward Salmon Arm. I bobbed along, feeling about as in control of my life as the logs I was floating with.

I floated, shivering, growing really irritated with Dave. Why hadn't he come looking for me? I was pretty certain that when one goes boating, one would usually want to return with all the passengers with whom one had embarked. It seemed to me he was being very irresponsible. Even if the others hadn't noticed my absence, I'd have thought Marco liked me enough to realize I wasn't on board anymore. I was pouting like a petulant toddler.

The little tug wasn't travelling very quickly, and it was cold in the water. My eyelids were drooping sleepily, so it was all I could do to keep a hold of the chain with my shuddering arms and to avoid the pinch of slimy logs. A still conscious part of my brain wondered whether I was going to succumb from hypothermia before the boom arrived at the mill when I heard another boat coming closer. The engine wasn't the powerful one of the white boat Sthenno had been driving. I squinted through the evening glare on the water and with relief, I recognized Marco straining over the side. Dave's boat. Everyone was leaning over in one direction or another scanning the water.

At last, I thought grumpily.

I gave as much of a shout as I could, fearful that they wouldn't see me, but I heard Brittany shout, "There she is!"

The engine cut to a slow chug and the boat pulled up along side the boom.

"About time!" I said aloud through vibrating lips.

257

Marco tossed the ladder off the back, but I didn't have the strength to climb it. Andrew grabbed one side of me and pulled, Marco grabbed the back of the life jacket and between them, they heaved me aboard.

I lay on the floor of the boat shivering. Brittany said calmly, "Where's the blanket? She needs to get warm."

Claire handed it to her, remarking, "We need to get under it with her and give her some body heat. She'll never warm it up by herself."

"I'll do that," said Marco, squeezing in beside me. "She should get out of her wet clothes as well." Claire gave him a dirty look before he continued, "Does anyone have anything she can change into?" He was rubbing my arms and back forcefully, in time with the clatter of my teeth.

Claire had brought jeans in case it got too cold for her shorts, and Andrew had a hooded sweatshirt. Marco held the blanket up discreetly while Claire and Brittany helped me out of the wet clothes and into the dry stuff. My skin was pasty white and covered with goose bumps.

As we travelled back to the dock, I could feel Marco's heat warming my body. Wherever our bodies touched, I burned. He rubbed my arms or my back while he leaned tightly against me, humming softly to himself, but he didn't say anything. Claire dug into her pack and pulled out a thermos of coffee. I don't normally drink coffee, but I took it gratefully, welcoming the warmth that I could feel travelling all the way down to my stomach.

We landed at the wharf in Canoe, which was confusing since we'd left our cars across the lake from here. How were we going to get home? I tried to get out of the boat, but my legs wouldn't work properly. They were seized up from cold. Andrew took my shoulders while Dave took my legs and they hauled me off the boat onto the boards of the dock like a sack of vegetables.

I lay there stretched out on the dock, still shivering, and watched them unload my stuff from the boat. Just as they finished, there were footsteps on the dock and I cranked my head to see Jim and Bright jogging toward me.

As Bright caught up to us, she squatted beside me, her eyes reflecting her concern. "Hi there," she said softly. I heard a hint of a chuckle in her voice and scowled a bit.

Brittany and Claire nodded hello, and Jim said, "I've left the car unlocked, go load her stuff in." Andrew and Marco followed the girls, while Dave was busy with the boat.

Looking up at her with my head on the dock, I tried to keep my tone light and quiet enough not to be overheard, "Got any of Dr. Kyle's elixir in your pocket, by any chance?"

258

After my near death experiences last year, at every hospital visit Dr. Kyle had saved me with his special mixture.

Bright smirked, pulling a pair of vials out of her pocket. She poured one into the other and shook it in front of my face. "One dose left from my own personal stash. Can't leave home without it if Grace is around..."

I cringed at this sad but true fact. She helped support a shoulder to raise me to a sitting position, "Here, have a sip."

I chugged it back observing, "This is getting to be a much too common habit."

She laughed as I lay back again and let the ice and fire burn through me. I breathed in slowly and tried to relax while the elixir did its work. The wind coming off the water was cold. I was going to be very glad to get into a hot bath tonight. I felt the bounce of the wharf as the gang returned. Claire spoke, "We'll head back to the cars in Sunnybrae; Marco is going home with you. We'll come by your place later, okay?"

"Yeah, sure." I nodded, as Marco and Jim each grabbed a shoulder and eased me up to a standing position. I weaved a little as I watched Dave pull away from the dock. Then with Marco's arm firmly around my waist, we turned and walked in a procession to the car.

I flopped into the back seat as Marco climbed in beside me, pulling me close and wrapping an arm around me again. "Feeling any better?" he whispered.

I nodded, and then scowled at him as I remembered my earlier irritation. "So what happened? Why did it take so long for you to realize that I wasn't in the boat?"

He shook his head in irritation. "Oh it was ridiculous. We were minutes away in Salmon Arm Bay when we realized you were gone, but as we were pulling around to come get you, the police boat came up to us because they'd had a complaint about kids driving recklessly." He almost growled. "We explained that *we'd* had a boat attack *us* and described it to them. Apparently, the boat we were describing had reported that a little blue boat had been buzzing *them*. It took about half an hour before they decided to let us off with a warning. We came right back to get you. I was freaking out a bit, I can tell you!"

"You didn't tell the police you had a man overboard?" Presumably the authorities wouldn't want to risk a death in cold water, wouldn't they have let them go find me then?

Before he could answer, Bright turned around. "They couldn't tell the police, Grace. There is no Dr. Kyle at the hospital here." Then Jim turned the car into the driveway and before I could ask her for more details she announced, "There, we're home."

Marco helped me out of the back seat and stood looking worried, Bright smiled at him, "Thanks for your help, Marco; I'll get her inside and Jim will take you home."

"I'd like…" he started, but Bright had an arm around my shoulder and turned me toward the house.

I glanced back shrugging helplessly at him, "Thanks, Marco."

He nodded grimly and climbed into the passenger seat next to Jim.

As Bright shut the door behind me, I wanted to scream in frustration. Why did all this stuff keep happening to me? Stupid stuff was going all around. What would happen next? This was *not* fair. I collapsed onto to couch with an irritated exhalation.

"You know, Grace," Auntie Bright said quietly behind me, "the one common denominator in all your life experiences is you."

I thought about it for a moment. "Yeah? So?"

"You're more extra-ordinary than you know, Grace. Consider that perhaps no one else is the cause of the trouble, but you."

"Are you saying I bring the trouble on myself?"

She studied me before she replied. "Yes. You're drawing trouble to yourself. You need to sort out why and figure out what you can do about it."

"I'm not doing it intentionally."

"Oh, I know. No one would ask for this." Her eyes softened. "I'm sorry about all of this, Grace, but no matter the cause, you still bear the responsibility for how you react to the things that happen to you and you need to be self-aware enough to recognize that. Once you understand that, then you'll be free from the angst and free to take your place."

Angst? What kind of insult was that? Bright was usually kindness itself, so this was an uncharacteristically sharp comment. I considered that as a sense of anger brewed. Bright had also been honest and direct with me when no one else in my family was. I sighed. She could handle my annoyance if I was forthright about it, rather than bottling it up and having it ferment. "I find being told I'm showing *juvenile angst* a little insulting, Bright."

She smiled. "Sorry. In a couple of years, you will see that angst is the correct label. It's not juvenile, because angst isn't limited to teens, Grace. It's about immaturity in dealing with your emotional response to situations. I know more that a few forty year olds who are under the illusion that they've been used and abused by everyone they ever met, and don't seem to make the connection that they themselves are the one, single commonality in every event of their lives. If crap is always happening to you, you need to look long and hard at yourself and decide what you're going to do to stop it!"

I reflected for a moment on her words. She had a point. But it was kind of unfair. Was any of the stuff happening my fault?

She read my irritation. "What's wrong?"

"I don't *deserve* this."

"I know. But it's not about fairness. It's about understanding and accepting your own power. It's about knowing and moving on with... well," she grinned, "with grace."

I grimaced, and she smiled affectionately back. "No one said it's easy, Hon."

I reflected on her earlier words. '...you'll be free from angst and free to take your place.' Take your place. Hmm. "Bright?"

"Mm?"

"What do you mean 'free to take your place'?"

She smiled gently. "That's the most important part of this. We all have a role to play. Once we reach the understanding of what our role is, we tend to be far more content with all aspects of our lives."

"What's my role, Bright?" I met her eyes boldly. If she was going to lecture me, she could provide some straightforward answers. I knew that she had them.

"In your case, Hon, it is important for you to first figure it out and then accept it yourself. If you feel your task is imposed on you, it's going to be a lot harder than it needs to be."

"Bright." I tried to sound insistent and assertive, but I think that maybe I just sounded like I was begging pathetically. It was as if she had a fish and was refusing it to the starving person because it was better if he learned to fish himself. How irritating. "Please, Auntie Bright? How can I know if you don't tell me?"

"Sorry, Grace. I'll help you sort through things, but you really do have to work it all out yourself. I can assure you that it's not coincidence what's happening. Pay attention to people around you. They will be reflecting your power. Listen."

I sighed. It would be so nice if someone would just tell what was going on so I could get on with whatever it was that they thought I was supposed to do. I was so tired of feeling clueless and beset. A little expediency would be so nice in my life right now. I wanted peace. I wanted comfort. With a sigh, I realized that I wanted Ben. "I'm going up to take a bath, Bright."

She nodded. "A good a place as any to contemplate the world," she commented with a grin. "I have some nice spa products in the cupboard; feel free to help yourself."

"Thanks."

"Say hello to Ben," she added with a chuckle as I trudged up the stairs.

I didn't bother to respond.

Ben was sympathetic. "I know you're frustrated, Grace, but I'm so proud of you. You were brilliant today."

"Brilliant? That seems excessive."

"Nope. You did so well today, I feel a bit better about leaving." He paused to let the words sink in.

"What do you mean, leave?"

"I need to go away for a bit."

"Go away?"

"I'll be out of range, I'm afraid."

"Where are you going?" I asked, feeling lonely already.

He paused before he replied, "I have to go to Europe. It's...uh...something for school."

"Oh?" I didn't disguise my doubt.

"I'll be back in three weeks."

I gulped. "A lot can happen in three weeks."

"Yes, and with you, I'm sure a lot will."

"Knowing that, you're still going to still going to go away?"

He chuckled again, but there was ill-disguised frustration in his tone, "I can't do anything about this, Grace. If I had any say in anything we wouldn't be apart right now, would we?"

"Would we?"

I felt his irritation as he responded. "I'm not even going to answer that. It's unfortunate that I have to go, but you'll be all right Grace. You're doing fabulously."

"Right, and of course I have *Marco* watching me."

He was silent for a long time before he said quietly, "Nothing is going to hurt you, Grace."

I sighed. "Can you guarantee that?"

His responding chuckle sounded slightly weary. "Good night, Grace."

CHAPTER FIVE

WHAT A FASCINATING DANGER

Forests shield unwelcome visitor; fear grows as battles draw closer.
Warrior Mars sets a challenge; Charis longs for her composer.
Powerless she's drawn to the battle; Warriors great in the fight ring.
Victory's won without trying; Erato knows it's the right thing.

Notwithstanding my frigid adventure hiding in the log boom, the best thing about living in the Shuswap was being at the lake with friends, I thought, as we laughingly pulled up Dave's boat onto a lovely little patch of shoreline. It was May Long Weekend so there were boats everywhere for the official start of the houseboat season. We had found a tiny bay to spend the day in; it was too small to provide houseboat anchorage, but perfect for our little cruiser.

As we stepped onto the beach Dave called, "You guys go find some wood. I'll put together a fire pit here."

"We don't need a fire, do we?" Marco looked worried.

I laughed, "A fire is great on the beach! Of course, we need one. Were you planning to eat raw wieners in your hotdogs?"

He grimaced, adjusted his fedora, and went into the woods.

I followed behind him stealthily, feeling a sudden urge for some entertainment. Let's see if I could surprise him, then I could tease him around the campfire.

He was bent over a bush when I jumped out and shouted, "Mrrraw!" I expected him to squeal and collapse onto the ground. He didn't do either.

In one smooth move his body had twisted around and he had me by the neck, bent over backwards, gasping for air. His face was cold and ruthless as he raised his other arm.

"Marco!" I wheezed.

He froze. "Oh gods! Grace! I'm sorry!" He eased me to the ground.

I sat rubbing my neck, watching him warily. "I thought you were going to break my neck."

He gulped. "I was." He inhaled deeply and shook his head. "I have warrior instincts. We react, but I shouldn't have reacted against *you*."

"Because you're supposed to be protecting me?"

We studied each other for a while before he finally nodded. "Yes."

"From?"

He didn't reply.

"Come on, Marco. Sooner or later someone has got to tell me what's going on."

He nodded. "Someone will. Eventually."

I batted my eyelashes, "Take pity on the sweet, confused girl. Make her happy. Tell her the truth."

"Oh, Baby," he sighed, "The truth isn't going to make you happy. Why do you think we're all so hesitant to tell you?"

"What?"

He shook his head. "Look. I agree that you need to know. Maybe I can tell you later, but I can't say anything without authorization. Horrible things tend to happen when we do things without authorization."

"Who's *we*?"

"You. Me. The family. All of us. Grace! I can't tell you now; quit looking at me like that. I promise to tell you, if I'm allowed."

"You'll ask?"

He scowled at me. "Hold this log," he said, thrusting it at me and turning away.

He refused to say any more, no matter how much I pleaded.

A few minutes later we'd returned with a good sized haul of wood, which we piled around Dave's circle of rocks. Marco piled it into the circle and stuffed some leaves at one corner. "These will start perfectly," he said confidently.

Claire and I looked at each other and smirked. "Um, Marco? Can I help? I don't think you'll get that lit."

"I'm fine," he grumbled. He'd lit three matches so far. The leaves caught, but then burnt out without catching the logs on fire.

Dave joined Marco and started adding more matches to the pile. Ten minutes later they started talking about how they could get gasoline from inside the boat's gas tank. At that point Claire and I looked at each other and grimaced.

"Guys! Seriously! I can have that fire going in two minutes, would you let me try?" This was stupid.

They didn't want to let me in, but they had to admit they weren't having success. Dave muttered, "I think the wood is too wet," as he backed up.

"The wood isn't too wet. You just don't know what you're doing." I looked at Claire, who had some dry moss and tiny sticks in her hand and smiled. "Marco—if I get this lit in two minutes, I'm wearing your hat for the rest of the night."

"You won't."

I built a log cabin structure, laying two-inch diameter logs in a square. Claire came over and dropped in her moss, and then carefully layered the small sticks above it. "Watch and learn boys," I said as I lit my match and set it to the moss. The match had bloomed in my fingers like a flower. The moss caught immediately, within ten seconds the smaller sticks had caught, and within my prophesied two minutes the logs had caught.

The boys looked at each other in shock, and then Marco presented me his fedora with a solemn bow.

Claire and I laughed.

Dave, noticeably chagrined asked, "How did you do that?"

"Girl Guides, Dave. 'Be Prepared' and all that. One-match fires. Knots to secure a tent in any weather. You should have gone to Boy Scouts, Dave, THEN you *might* be able to give me a run for your money!"

Dave groaned, and then looked over at Claire, who was grinning in agreement. "Not you, too?" She laughed and nodded.

"I can make an oven out of a cardboard box and cook a cake in it. Do you need a toaster from a coffee can? I'm your girl! Very valuable life skills." We laughed at the boys' faces.

The fire was crackling merrily as the sun dropped behind the hills.

Claire and I were driving the guys crazy re-living Girl Guide camping trip adventures and singing crazy camp songs at the tops of our lungs. I hadn't laughed so much in years. It was beautiful there by the lake. Ben seemed a lifetime away, but I had good people with me, and at the moment, I was happier than I'd been in a long time.

"Don't Girl Guides do anything competitive?" Dave asked.

Claire giggled. "Sure! Have you ever had a marshmallow-roasting contest?"

The guys perked up. Competition: the key to a man's soul.

Dave and Marco lined up 10 paces from the marshmallow bag. Claire stood solemnly by the fire and made the official announcement, "You each get one stick and one marshmallow. Your goal is a perfectly roasted marshmallow: golden brown all the way around. You lose points for any ashes or any white spots. Any flames and your marshmallow is disqualified. Go!"

The guys raced to the sticks then reached for the bag. Dave hip checked Marco, who almost went over, but he'd managed to get a marshmallow first, so he just rolled toward the fire. The game suddenly seemed deadly. Guys. The two of them had stabbed their marshmallows almost simultaneously and then taken their positions on either side of the fire. Within two minutes, Marco shouted victoriously as Dave pulled a flaming marshmallow stick out of the fire pit.

"Damn!" groaned Dave. "I was sure I was going to win!"

Marco answered him in a Yoda voice, "Defeat me you cannot, when using the Force I am, young one. No need, there is to try! King I am of the Perfectly Roasted Marshmallow!"

I laughed and was reaching for the marshmallow bag to attempt to challenge him when a twig broke very loudly right behind us in the forest. I automatically looked around the circle to ensure that everyone was present. All accounted for. Who was in the woods?

Or *what* was in the woods?

Four flashlights were pulled out of pockets at almost the same instant, and just as quickly all four were trained into the same spot in the forest. As the lights illuminated the area, we gasped collectively, and then Claire began to scream.

It was the Sasquatch. It had to be. It must have been at least nine feet tall, and it stood just inside the trees. It must have been injured at some point, because the flashlights had caught in their beams just one, large glowing eye.

As the screams began, the creature turned, and with a crunch of twigs disappeared from the light.

Dave shouted, "Get in the boat!" Claire and I didn't have to be told twice. We were touching the bow within seconds.

"Wait!" shouted Marco. "We have to put out the fire first. Douse the flames!"

I couldn't believe we were in imminent danger of death from Sasquatch, and Marco was worried about our campfire. "Marco! Come on!"

He glared up from the beach, while the remains of our fire sputtered and steam rose dramatically. "It's gone. You saw it leave, didn't you?

266

I'm not risking burning down the entire forest just because we might have seen a giant thing in the trees!"

Dave was mad and cursed his opinion of Marco's intelligence at this moment, as he pushed the boat off the shore and we leapt aboard.

Marco shouted back, "Come on guys! My dad's a firefighter! Do you want me to risk his life later when I can prevent a fire now?"

Marco the hero.

Marco the idiot.

We sat bobbing in the boat and scanning the edge of the woods with the flashlights while he worked, bringing buckets of water up from the lake, dousing the fire, and then spreading the blackened remains of the fire with his boot. He pushed the bigger logs right into the lake.

"Marco!" Dave shouted.

Marco looked up and smiled, "Okay. I'm coming."

Just as he approached the water, a flashlight beam on the far right caught a gleam. I shouted in horror, "Marco! NOW! It's back!"

With a fearful look over his shoulder toward the trees, Marco splashed toward the boat. Dave twisted the key desperately. My flashlight beam caught the creature stepping out of the trees at the same moment that Marco reached the boat and the engine caught. Claire and I each grabbed him under an arm and heaved him aboard as Dave turned the boat and set it full throttle toward the middle of the lake.

As we raced away, we saw the creature looking from us to the remains of our fire. It looked to me like it was poking into the pit with a stick. It seemed far more interested in the fire pit than it was upset about its disappearing dinner. After the first initial look, it hadn't look after us at all. How weird was that? I was about to make a comment when I saw Claire had her eyes closed, leaning against Dave as he drove.

I started to shake. Shock. Dave was cursing a litany of creative epithets as he steered. Claire began to laugh slightly hysterically. Marco, lying soaking wet in the bottom of the boat calmly asked, "Did anyone get a picture?"

We all joined Claire in her hysterical laughter.

"Tell me again, Grace," Bright asked, staring intently into my eyes. "What exactly did it look like?

"It was about eight or nine feet tall and we think it was injured because it had only one eye. It was hairy, but not furry, if you know what I mean."

267

She nodded, and I had the eerie sensation that she did know exactly what I meant. She glanced meaningfully over at Jim, who got up and left the room. "So, what did it do, precisely? What did you all do?"

Dave explained, "When we shone the lights on it and Claire started screaming, it took off back into the woods. We all raced to the boat, but Marco here," he punched him in the arm, " insisted on putting out the fire, even though we told him he was being an idiot and risking all our lives."

Bright looked over at Marco and nodded her head ever so slightly. He smiled a bit in return, but straightened his expression when he caught me looking at him.

Dave continued, "Then Marco got to the boat as the thing came back, and we managed to escape with our lives."

Marco popped in, "But these idiots were all so freaked out no one thought to pull out a camera and get a photo of it. Can you believe it?"

Bright laughed.

Jim coughed, "Hey guys, I have a movie on the projection screen if anyone wants to watch. Bright, can you make popcorn and get them something to drink?"

"Sure!" she remarked as Claire, Dave and I started filing into the living room.

Dave was already leaning into the stack to check whether he approved of the movie.

Marco lingered behind, "I'll help you, Bright."

Under the increasing volume of Jim's home theatre system, I heard Bright's urgent whisper to Marco, "Did you get the fire completely out?" but I didn't hear Marco's low reply. I knew the answer anyway, but why was the question so important to her? I thought I caught just a word of another whisper as she replied to something he'd said, "Ben." Ben? She didn't really say that, did she? I shook my head. I was imagining him again. Wishful thinking.

Just then, Uncle Jim called my name and forced my consciousness back to the living room. "Hey, Grace?"

"I'm sorry, what?"

He laughed, "I was just wondering if you noticed the footprints the drywall stilts made on the shore?"

"Ha, ha. Very funny." I threw a piece of popcorn at him, but he caught it in his mouth with a grin.

The movie was a light comedy, very good for distracting us from the trauma of the afternoon. As the screen shot to a scene in a boxing gym,

Marco glanced over at me. "You know Grace, you should come see me box sometime."

I shuddered and he laughed.

"Seriously, Dave's come before; it's fun to watch."

Dave grinned, "It is really wonderful to see Marco punching the crap out of some big mouth when he'd get expelled from school if he touched the guy outside of the gym."

Marco grinned, "This is true. It's my favourite fringe benefit."

I shook my head. "It doesn't sound like fun to me. I don't like violence. I can't even watch fake violence like TV wrestling. No, thanks."

"Ah come on, Grace, I'll even dedicate the fight to you."

I'm sure that was supposed to be an honour, but it seemed more than a little perverse to me. 'I'll pummel some anonymous stranger for you, darling.' Right. Very chivalrous of him. "Thanks for the invitation, Marco, but I really don't think I have the stomach for it."

He laughed and plopped down beside me on the sofa.

The doorbell rang then, and Dave looked up hopefully as Bright answered it and said, "They're in the living room."

"Hi!" announced Susan as she followed Bright into the room.

Dave slid over on the loveseat to make room for her, and she flopped down obligingly beside him with just the faintest melancholy glance over to Marco and me on the sofa. I felt a twinge of guilt, because I didn't have a romantic interest in Marco like Susan did, but he seemed determined to hang out with me without any hope of a romantic relationship developing and what was I supposed to do about that?

Dave remarked casually, "Feel sorry for Marco, Sue. He keeps trying to get Grace to come watch him box and she's been remarkably insensitive to his desire to impress her with his pugilistic talents."

Susan looked over at me. As I considered her expression I blurted, "Why don't you invite Susan, Marco? I bet she'd love to watch you."

Susan's eyes got huge and she flushed scarlet as he considered that option. I bit my cheek, realising my mistake too late to retract my words.

Marco studied her emotionlessly while she changed colour and looked around wildly, avoiding his eyes. "It looks like the very idea terrifies her," he finally observed matter of factly.

Susan blushed even redder and Dave smirked before he distracted her with a completely off-hand, "So Susan, have *you* ever seen a Sasquatch?" She looked at him with her eyebrows up as he continued, "Because we saw one up close today and we're all feeling a little freaked out tonight."

Of course, she didn't believe him, so then we had to tell her the entire story. She looked at Marco with a mixture of awe and shock at the idea that he had worried about a fire instead of running for safety. As she shivered, Dave leaned in melodramatically and gushed, "Hold me, Susan! Make the bad dreams go away," as he wrapped his arms around her.

She looked at him with her lip curled in amusement, but she wrapped her arms around him and patted his back absently. He lifted his head from her shoulder and winked at me.

I chuckled and shook my head as Marco caught my eye and whispered, "Now *that* boy is a real master. I should take lessons from him. Maybe then I'd be able to get you to come see me box…" His voice trailed off sadly.

"Oh, come on. Why on earth do you want me to watch you fight?"

"Because it's something I love, and I'd like to share it with you, that's why." He shrugged his shoulders, "It's not very complicated."

He looked like a sad puppy dog. Damn.

I sighed. "Fine."

"Fine?"

"Fine, I'll come watch you box some time." Hopefully 'some time' would be a long time away.

His face broke into a grin of unabashed delight, quite out of proportion to a rather vague agreement in principle. "Really? You'll come?" He squeezed my shoulders tightly.

I sighed again. "I said I would. Don't make me regret it." Actually, I already did. I was a complete sucker for those puppy dog eyes.

"Perfect, I have a major bout next weekend. You can come to that one."

So soon. "*Next* weekend?" I searched vainly for some excuse not to be free. He looked so hopeful I caved without fighting. I had no backbone at all. "Yeah, okay."

He beamed at me, "All right!"

O was lying on the grass, lyre on his chest, staring up at the sky while he strummed. Mars and Xandros sparred a few meters away, their swords flashing in the sunlight.

As Mars jabbed, he said, "You know, you can't win, Xandros. You're only a made-up god. You don't have real power."

"My people said otherwise. When people declare you a god, you become one. You know how it works."

"There are gods and there are gods, Xandros. Ask anyone who the God of War is and they'll say it's me."

Xandros laughed, "Not in Macedonia." He parried a particularly well-aimed slash and stepped back. "Of course, Ancient Greece had other ideas, as well."

"Ares isn't a god of war. He's a god of blood-thirsty battle. It's not the same thing."

"Of course not."

"Rome taught the world about well-waged war."

"Indeed, and I was undefeated in battle. So who deserves the title more?"

"And you died of food poisoning, which is pretty pathetic if you ask me." The sweet, feminine voice froze them and they looked up in astonishment as a glowing apparition melted out of the air and materialized in front of them. "Boys, you need to talk about something more enlightened

O scrabbled to his feet. "Euphrosyne! What are you...?"

"We need to talk."

O's eyes betrayed his fear. "What's wrong? What's happened?"

Euphrosyne looked at him sympathetically. "I'm sorry, O, but it's getting too dangerous. Even Mars can't manage this alone."

Xandros flexed and stepped forward. He was all business, but still cast a lewd grin at O as he walked, "She needs me?"

Euphrosyne nodded. "We need you. You're ready?"

"Of course." Xandros strode into the forest and disappeared in a flash.

O set the lyre against the tree and turned his back to them. His chest heaved.

Mars sighed and spoke quietly to her, "I've waited too long. I was too conscientious of O's concern about their attraction."

She whispered back, "Yes. I know. O doesn't like it, but it may save her life. That's why it exists." She raised her voice, "The battle is coming closer."

O turned. "How close?"

"I don't know," Euphrosyne sighed, "but I feel the evil drawing in. Be prepared."

Mars nodded, and rested his hand on O's shoulder. "We are."

I was running a bit late as I ran into the gym a week later. Bright had dropped me off with enough time for me to get here punctually, but I had dawdled. Truth is, I didn't really want to see Marco fight, and I'd been hoping that if I was late, I would miss it. I didn't want to see his perfect body pummelled, beaten, bleeding. I didn't want to see the sweet, kind boy I was so fond of deliberately hurting anyone *else* either. I didn't much care that they were doing it completely rationally—if fighting could ever be rational.

Of course, I hadn't missed the fight; I didn't have luck like that. I was just in time. Marco and his opponent were standing in the centre ring while the introductions were read: "In the blue trunks, Marco Diguerra. In the green trunks, Davie Ryan."

Davie Ryan stared at Marco. His wiry red hair was flaming above his headgear. He was huge. I thought boxers had to be evenly matched, but Davie looked about twenty pounds heavier and was easily a head taller than Marco was.

Marco smirked up at him. "Good luck, Davie Boy. You're going to need it."

Davie's ears turned red. He looked a bit like a smoking fire.

They thumped their white striped gloves together, shook their padded heads and started bouncing around each other. Marco looked confident and calculating. Davie looked wary and mean.

Davie swung with his right, Marco shifted his weight and the punch passed him, as he brought his own left and nailed Davie in the ribs under the outstretched right arm. Davie huffed and pulled in his elbow, Marco's right smashed into Davie's head and Davie dropped to the mat like a boulder.

The ref's whistle blew and Marco bounced back into his corner. He looked down with a grin warped into a cartoon by his mouth guard. Davie stood up, glaring over at Marco and went to his own corner.

A man sat down beside me, with a coffee in his hand. He noticed Marco watching me and glanced over, "Friend of yours?"

I nodded.

"He's good. One of the best around. Knows how to find his opponents' weaknesses and exploit them." He flicked his chin toward Davie's corner, "Went for Davie's temper, didn't he?"

I nodded again.

The man sighed. "Davie's my son. He's good, but he won't win this bout. I wish it were otherwise, but he won't win against Diguerra any time soon."

"Have they fought before?"

He shook his head. "No. His trainer wanted him to wait. Now perhaps he understands why. When you find a brilliant tactician like Diguerra, you can't let your emotions get the better of you. You have to have few surprises up your sleeves. Diguerra hasn't lost since he started boxing with this club."

The minute was up and the boxers started dancing around each other again. This time Marco didn't wait for Davie to make the first move. He fired off a left right combo so quickly that his arms were a blur. Davie only managed a weak flailed smack as he staggered backwards, but it just brushed Marco's arm. The white strip didn't even make contact.

Davie's Dad shook his head with a sigh.

Marco took a step forward, feigned with his left and curled his right in an uppercut with so much power behind it that it lifted Davie right off his feet.

The ref blew his whistle.

"What's happening?" I asked Davie's dad.

"The ref's stopping the fight because Davie is out-classed. He doesn't want him to get hurt." He shook his head again. "His pride will have taken a beating with this one. He's two weight classes above Diguerra, he has a couple years on him, and he has been fighting for several years longer. He had to get special permission to fight someone so much smaller." He sighed. "Diguerra is a power house. No doubt about it. Never turns down a fight from any fighter, no matter his weight class."

In the centre of the ring, the ref was raising Marco's arm. Davie was standing sullen on the other side of him.

His dad shook his head and muttered under his breath, "It will be interesting to see who defeats that kid." He looked up at me as he stood, "Got to see to my boy. Bye now."

Marco was hanging over the ropes. He had hardly broken a sweat, but he was glistening under the lights. "Hey! What did you think?"

"Impressive." I didn't want to hurt his feelings.

He grinned. "I have another bout in a couple of hours. Will you stay?"

I didn't want to sit in a sweaty gym for two hours, watching boys pounding each other, but he looked so hopeful I couldn't turn him down. I glanced at my watch, "I'll go over to the mall for awhile, but I'll come back at three o'clock, okay?"

"See you then!" he grinned as his trainer came over to hand him a towel.

I made it back just in time. The ref was calling out the introductions, "In the red trunks, Alex Megas." Marco caught my eye and grinned down, but I didn't really see him this time. All I could see was his opponent, a sculpted statue of masculine perfection, bronzed and dazzling.

Alex.

273

He stood imposingly, his head rising above everyone else's, ready to do battle. His brows were down, stance tense. The muscles on his shoulders and arms rippled as he manoeuvred into position. I stared at him. He was beautiful. He was dangerous. He was terrifying. I had never wanted anything as badly as I wanted him. The shock of this sudden awareness jolted me back to reality.

My very handsome, very likeable friend was about to fight this otherworldly creature: this mythic god. Any moment now, the bell to start the match would sound and the fists would fly. I knew that Marco was a good boxer, but I knew somehow that Alex would be better and Marco would soon be lying on the mat. When the match was over, I would not longer be dating Marco, I would belong to Alex, the spoils in a battle held between ropes. What an astonishing thought.

Alex looked down from the ring and met my eyes. His eyes swept up and down my body, lingering along the way. When he came up to my face, he smiled. Not an appreciative, 'hiya cutie' kind of smile, but a hard, determined smile. A menacing smile. A seductive smile. I returned a quivering, astonished look, feeling primal passions rise in me that I had never felt before. I monitored the heady rush of adrenaline and endorphins with amazement. I felt flush with power. Perhaps a second had passed, and yet everything had changed.

Marco was watching Alex, too. He had noted his stare and turned to see the object of his focus. As he found my eyes still staring primally at Alex, his grew large. I'm not sure what exactly he was able to read in my eyes, but he turned and glared at Alex with an aggression I would never have expected from him. The bell rang, and they started toward one another.

A boxing match is a parody of a dance. The fighters bob and weave around each other, bowing and dipping. Right hook. Jab. Left hook. Undercut. Bouncing around and around each other. Heads flying back with the impact of the gloves. Sweat glistening and running down their faces and torsos. It was a macabre dance: terrible and fascinating. They were beautiful as their muscles rippled and they glistened with perspiration, but it was a horrible beauty.

Marco's tousled dark hair seemed out of place with the lips that bulged around his mouth guard. His marble fairness contrasted with the bronze of his opponent. He fought with focus and determination; I could almost see him calculating, first this, then this, next that… Alex fought instinctively; his arms were up blocking, seemingly unconsciously, his punches shot out with uncanny precision whenever Marco left the slightest opening.

Then a rhythm began as Alex started hammering: right, right, right, over, and over. I could see Marco begin to stagger. Instead of reaching in with his own right hand, he dropped it, just a bit, and Alex's left hand flew in with an undercut to Marco's jaw that lifted him right off his feet and sent him flying. He crashed onto his butt, his back on the ropes, and looked up, vague and stunned, shaking himself to try to get his brain back into focus. It didn't work. He just sat there dumbly as if he couldn't make his body move. The referee counted up, "…eight, nine, ten!" and the bout was over.

Marco and Alex stood on either side of the referee in the centre ring. Marco's head was bowed. As the ref raised Alex's arm and announced his victory, Marco looked up at me and smiled a tiny, self-conscious smile as he shrugged his shoulders sadly, and looked away. His farewell gesture, I presumed.

Alex found my eyes and smiled triumphantly at me. The planets all seemed to re-align. He was now the centre of my universe. I smiled back slowly, feeling again the rush of his presence, of a fascinating power drawing me inextricably toward him.

I walked out of the gym feeling a strange disconnect. Although it seemed to me that I had just given my body and soul to Alex, so far I hadn't said a word to him. The idea of being face to face with him was oddly disconcerting, and there was, of course, the small matter of the other men in my life. Marco. Ben. What would I say to them? Obviously, the relationship with Marco had changed in a heartbeat. How was I going to explain it to him? Or did he really understand what had happened to me in that look that passed between Alex and me? What could I say to him if he hadn't? It was so shallow to say, "He beat you, so I'm breaking up with you?" I mean, we weren't even going out. Besides, the fight was only incidental. Just looking at Alex I'd known my world had changed. What about Alex? What would he say? Did he already have a girlfriend? Or perhaps a stable of them? Did that look mean anything to him? Such perfection was unlikely to be without female admirers. Was I going to have to fight for him?

What about Ben?

Nothing had changed in the depth of my love for him, yet all I wanted at this moment was Alex. My body was traitor to my heart.

Somehow, Marco knew his fate. He drove me home without a word. I was torn by guilt. I couldn't get away from him fast enough. Alex overwhelmed my thoughts, and it was actually a physical irritation that I was stuck sitting beside Marco. That feeling made me cringe in powerless disgust with myself. What unkindness to the guy who'd made my life without Ben bearable these last few months!

He walked me to the front door in silence. I turned with my hand on the doorknob and just looked at him. I didn't know what to say. We just stared at one another, until he gave a curt nod, sighed, and whispered, "See you around, Grace."

I nodded as I went in. "Yeah. Bye."

When Dad called that week, I could help whine to him about my irritation with Marco. He just kept showing up, and hanging out with me.

"Grace, don't push him away. You need your friends."

"I thought you said I shouldn't have a boyfriend."

"It's not the same thing and you know it. Besides, I'll bet he loves being around you. Everyone does."

So, Marco stayed around. He kept smiling and laughing, but I caught his reflection looking at me in windows when he thought I didn't see, and the smile would die on his face when he wasn't facing me, to be replaced with a grim determination I couldn't read.

I wished he would get mad at me, challenge me—just do *something*. I didn't have the heart to hurt him by discussing my feelings, and apparently, he didn't have the heart to change anything on the surface, even though we both knew everything had changed underneath. We just kept hanging out at school, going out for lunch, and walking home together, but instead of our easy friendliness, now there was a lot more quiet. I was with him in body, but not in spirit.

There was another body I was yearning for. Nothing felt easy any more.

Marco wouldn't leave and Ben didn't come. I needed Ben desperately, because this attraction to Alex scared me. I wanted the security of Ben's love to make some sense of it.

It wasn't helped by Alex. If he'd just come out and declared himself there might have been some ease to the tension, but he did not. He kept appearing around town. I started to see him everywhere. He met my eyes and smiled his surly smile as if to say, "The time will come..." I'd blush and turn in the opposite direction for a moment or two, before I'd be drawn back within his sights again.

He seemed to find me amusing. I felt like a meteor being drawn slowly and inevitably toward him. The tension mounted, but still we had not actually even met. We were still just looking at each other, and not even surreptitiously. Who was going to give in and be the first to speak? I wanted it to be him, because it seemed like weakness to be pulled in so powerlessly, but who wanted to fight such a strong draw? It was as inevitable as breathing that I was going to end at his side. The only question was *when*?

It was a shock to me when Marco pulled up at my house Friday after school and announced we were going out.

"I thought the gang didn't have any plans tonight?" I asked in confusion.

"The gang doesn't," he replied, "but we do."

"We do?"

"Yeah. We're going hiking."

I hated hiking here, because around here, hiking always meant uphill. Hard slogging all the way. It was exhausting just thinking about it. "Where?" Maybe it'd just be a nice leisurely stroll along the lake.

"Enderby Cliffs."

Yuck. Worst case scenario. Two hours straight up.

"Will we be able to get back before dark leaving at this hour?"

"We don't have to go all the way up. We'll stop for dinner if we don't get all the way up, then we can start down after we eat. We should have plenty of time. We need to talk."

I sighed. He was determined. "Wait. What do you mean talk?"

"You know."

I gasped. "Really?" I was finally going to learn something! I grabbed some water, an extra jacket and socks, and stuffing them into my daypack, I climbed into the passenger seat of his little blue Mazda.

As we drove, he kept glancing over to me like he had something to say. Ah. So this would be it. We were going to have it out on the trail. I hoped he didn't get so angry that he left me there. I was a wuss in the woods at the best of times, and it was scary to imagine being left there. He would easily beat me down the hill to the car, and I'd be stranded. I tried to shake the picture that came to my head. This was *Marco* I was thinking about! The most decent guy I knew would not be leaving me abandoned on a trail no matter how ticked off he was with me.

I hoped.

<u>CHAPTER SIX</u>

TERRIFIC. I WAS ABNORMAL

Mars decides Charis needs answers. High on the cliffs far from danger,
Visions are clear in the distance. Lightning from Zeus betrays anger.
Silence is quickly a blanket, stifling desire for such knowledge.
Eros is laughing as passion's flinging her closer to the edge.

We parked the car on the side of the road and stepped onto the trail along the farmer's field that was the trailhead. I looked up at the cliffs towering about me and groaned inwardly. "Did you get permission to access the trail?"

He nodded.

I sighed. He was torturing me.

He reached over to take my hand and smiled with a gleam in the eye that told me he had deliberately chosen this route for exactly that reason. Thanks. I sighed, as we came out of the field and started upward.

"Grace, things have changed."

I nodded, "Yeah." That was an understatement. "Did you get permission to tell me?"

He shook his head. "Never mind that. I wanted to tell you that I'm sorry."

"For what?"

"That I didn't beat Alex. And that it was necessary for them to call him in at all."

Huh? We walked along without comment for a while. He still held my hand and pulled me along after him. I wished desperately that Ben were around to offer me some advice. Suddenly I had a lot of questions. "Alex was called Alex? Who called him? What do you mean?"

Marco glanced up at the sky, which suddenly seemed to be darkening. His brows lowered.

"What's wrong?"

"I don't like the look of the clouds rolling in so quickly." We were passing a little hunter's cabin in a meadow and he nodded to it. "We'll keep going, but if we can't get back before the worst hits, we can take shelter here."

The idea of stopping there now seemed pretty good to me, but apparently that wasn't an option. He kept walking, and I obediently trudged along after him, wondering what the heck the point of all this was.

He was silent again as we hiked up the cliffs. My legs and chest burned. We seemed to be creating a lot of comment in the animal world as we passed; there was quite a bit of chirping, chittering and twittering along the path. I hoped we didn't run into any bears by being so quiet. I knew that making a lot of noise helped keep them away, but somehow a surprised bear seemed less ominous than what might be coming with Marco, so I remained silent. As we reached a plateau, he stopped and turned, looking out at the vista below us. "Beautiful, isn't it?"

I sensed this was the moment. I hoped he wasn't going to push me over or anything crazy like that.

He stared down the valley at the patchwork of greens below us. The wide winding blue veins of the Shuswap River and the green trees tracing alongside it intersected here and there with the thin grey arteries of roads. The darkened sky contrasted a golden light that illuminated the scene like an Old Master's painting. I suppose it was beautiful, but I was too stressed and too tired from the hike to really appreciate it. I sat down on a boulder and pulled out my water bottle to take a long draft while I waited for Marco to start talking.

When he finally spoke his voice was low and business-like, "I don't like these changes, Grace."

I just looked at him without commenting. What could I say? It wasn't like any part of this was rational. Every stinking aspect of the situation was surreal. I just sighed again hopelessly, shrugging my shoulders in helpless understanding.

He studied me, waiting for more response. When it became apparent that I wasn't going to say anything he shrugged and continued, "I know our friendship has changed Grace. I'm not happy about it, but I do understand. I'm sorry you came to watch that fight." He shook his head regretfully, "You were right. It was a *really* bad idea."

I couldn't help but smirk at that as he caught my eyes and smiled ruefully.

"I'll always be your friend, Grace. You can depend on me whatever happens. If Alex hurts you, I will kill him, in the ring or out of it. If this mythical Ben of yours abandons you permanently, I'll be here to pick up the pieces. But, there is more going on here Grace, and I think you should know the truth. Whether they think you should know or not, you need to know."

What was I supposed to say to that? *Finally* someone was going to tell me something!

The thunder rumbled through the sky and Marco looked up with alarm. "Come on," he said, reaching out his hand, "let's head back down."

At that moment, the weather seemed to echo his passionate concern. I could see the black clouds tumbling in the sky toward us. Suddenly my hair started to rise, as if I'd been rubbing it with a balloon.

"Get down!" Ben's voice shrieked inside my head; Marco tackled me and we hit the hard ground between the rocks at the same time that a bolt of lightning illuminated everything in a blinding flash, exploding the rock beside us with a sound like the crack of an exploding bomb.

Marco rolled off me and mouthed something. His eyes were full of concern, as he looked me up and down searching for injuries. The rock beside us was split and partially melted; I checked to see if Marco was bleeding or burnt. I could see no damage on him, nor feel any damage in myself. It seemed inconceivable that we could be so close to that much power and escape unscathed.

Well, not entirely unscathed. Marco was still trying to talk to me, and I still couldn't hear a thing. I swallowed, and tried to speak. I didn't know for sure that the words came out, or at what volume; I could only feel the sensation of speech without hearing it from outside through my ears. "I can't hear anything, Marco."

I could read the question in his lips, "Nothing?" So I could speak, at any rate.

I shook my head.

Marco pantomimed that we needed to gather our things and head down the mountain. I nodded, muttering "Okay," though I wasn't sure he heard me.

I looked up from arranging my pack to see him standing on a neighbouring rock, shaking his fist at the sky and getting red faced with shouting. The sky was growing even darker. The vivid blue that had been above our meadow was turning into navy blue now.

I felt the telltale tingle in my scalp from the electricity in the air again, and I didn't need to hear Marco to know I had to hit the ground. From the corner of my eye, I saw Marco drop while almost simultaneously another lightning bolt slashed to the earth. This time it struck a pine tree only metres from where we stood, cleaving it in half, and leaving it blackened and smoking. My eyes were red with the after image of the slash through the sky. The air around me smelled singed. I had heard nothing, though I had felt the ground moving from the force of the sound waves.

The rain started falling then. The blue sky that had been above us was now a lid of blackness, and a sheet of water was being poured out of some giant bucket. We were drenched before we had a chance to even consider getting under cover. I hadn't even had a chance to get my hat on before I was sopping wet.

Marco grabbed my hand, and we worked our way down the trail as quickly as we could. The dirt was soon a slippery slide, so we were gliding on our butts more than on our feet.

With a slightly hysterical giggle, I remembered my last walk in the rain with Ben, so long ago. Marco glanced back quizzically.

We reached the meadow in about half an hour; soaked to the skin and shivering, we ran hand in hand across the grass to the little hut, throwing open the door and shutting it behind us with relief.

My teeth were chattering as he spun me around into an embrace. We stood there behind the door for ages, his face buried in my damp hair, until finally he stepped back, loosening his hold and rubbing my upper arms, trying fruitlessly to warm me up.

He spoke to me again, brows furrowed in a question that I could not hear. I shook my head, putting my hands around my ears, and waving them to show him I still couldn't hear anything. He tried to smile soothingly in response, obviously attempting to console us both. He leaned down and gently kissed one ear and then the other. He indicated that I should sit down, and then stepped outside, returning shortly with some logs and kindling. He set the fire up in the little stove in the middle of the room and soon it was crackling happily. The rain was still pouring outside, but our little haven was growing warm and cozy. I found a blanket folded neatly in the tiny cupboard next to the bed, and we sat down on the bed with the blanket wrapped around our shoulders.

A million questions raced around in my head, but although I could ask them, I wouldn't be able to hear his replies, so I just sat absorbing the imposed quiet in my world. I remembered the biology class when we'd been told about how too much noise, like music played too loudly through earphones or a bomb blast, could cause acoustic trauma. We'd been warned that the damage was progressive and that it was permanent. I was cautious not to play my music too loudly in my ear buds, but that care was irrelevant now. Permanent hearing loss.

I was thankful that Marco was with me. Outside the world was wild and uncontrollable, but inside the cabin was comfort and security. I considered the strange fog of my hearing. I pondered whether it would come back, or whether I was really going to be deaf from now on. I wondered where I would have to go to learn sign language, and I wondered how I'd heard Ben's voice calling the warning. That vague thought of Ben instantly shattered any hope for peaceful contentment. If I remained deaf, I would never hear Ben's music again. A wave of profound sadness swept through me and sucked out all my oxygen. I was gasping from the fear that struck me. I felt a drip on my hand, and glanced up to the ceiling to check the roof for the source of the leak. At my movement, Marco looked down solemnly. As he gently brushed my face with a finger, I realized with surprise that he was tracing the path of a tear down my cheek.

I looked up into his face feeling the crushing weight of loss and my eyes were immediately overflowing with tears. Marco reached across my shoulders, pulled me onto his lap and held me against his chest. He gently rubbed my back as he murmured something into my hair. I heard nothing, but I felt his lips moving and his warm breath stirring in the strands of my hair as he rocked me slowly back and forth.

I felt like such a traitor crying for Ben in his arms. I hoped he was only thinking that it was the loss of my hearing or the shock of nearly being hit by lightning that was freaking me out. Hearing loss was enough, I suppose, but it was nothing. If the rest of the world was silent, I could cope. Not hearing Ben again was something different. That was the end of my universe. My shoulders heaved as the tears streamed.

"It's okay Grace." Ben's sudden arrival in my consciousness was loud after hearing nothing for so long that I startled with a jolt in Marco's arms.

Marco leaned me back with concern. I couldn't give away the voice in my head, so I just smiled at him weakly and pushed against his arms, burrowing faithlessly back into his chest. Traitorous me. Wonderful, kind, sweet him.

I focused on Ben's placating words. I knew he had to be lying to me. "No, Ben, it's *not* okay," I sighed deeply before I added, "This is the end of the world."

His soundless voice was calm and warm in my head. I could practically hear his fond smile as he replied surely, "It'll be fine. I'm sure it's just a temporary thing, Love. You'll hear again."

As I thought, "What if I don't? What if I never hear your music again?" a wave of devastation caused a choking gasp and the tears started rolling again. I was getting hysterical. It was probably the shock from the lightning strikes. I wondered faintly if I had a granola bar or something in my bag.

Ben's soothing thoughts calmed me as he whispered, "At the very least I will hum to you. If you hear me now, you'll hear that. I will not leave you, Amata. I've been here forever and I'll be here forever. You know that."

"I've missed you."

"Me too. I'm back for now."

Marco tenderly caressed my hair with his hands. Cupping my head affectionately, he brushed his lips on the top of my head. Ben whispered words of love inside my head. I was being comforted within and without and it all seemed so remarkably perverse. What a crazy life I had. How lucky I was to be loved like this. How astonishing it was to be loved like this.

Marco drove me home. My silent world oppressed me, and I was more than thankful for Ben popping in and out of my head to encourage me. As we pulled into the driveway, Bright and Jim came out of the door to meet us, oozing with concern. I wondered if Ben had called them. With arms around me, they brought me into the house. As I sat on the red couch Bright spoke to Marco for a while, I watched their lips move and drowsed. It was hard to focus on anything.

"Hey," Ben whispered in my mind.

"Hmm," I thought back sleepily.

"I've been speaking to Dr. Kyle. He thinks the elixir will help on this as well."

"It's an acoustic trauma, Ben. Even I know that acoustic traumas don't get better." I couldn't help a little sob as I added, "just worse."

"No so. There are some very good results with rodents in re-growing the acoustic hairs which would indicate a future cure."

"I'm not a rat."

"No, but you're not exactly like everyone else either. You have a physical reality that doesn't apply to others." He was very solemn.

"Physical reality?"

"Grace, I am not at liberty to explain who you are—what we are—just yet, but trust me that what is true for the normal population isn't necessarily true for you. Dr. Kyle's medicine will cure this hearing loss. Just be patient. He's put it on the plane, and it'll be at the Kelowna Airport within the hour. Jim has already left to pick it up."

283

I looked up and glanced around the room in surprise. Sure enough, Jim wasn't there. Bright caught my eyes and smiled warm encouragement.

I didn't want to sit in a room watching them watching me. I sighed. The best thing to do would be to try to rest. I could almost hear Dr. Kyle's words as I thought it. I tried to speak at a reasonable volume, but I have no idea if I was loud or normal or what. I looked between Marco and Bright and said, "I am going up to try to have a sleep, come get me when Jim gets back."

Bright nodded.

Half way up the stairs, I turned back to Marco, "Oh—and thanks for the help up there."

He smiled and came over to wrap me in his arms. He was so sweet. It was at odds with his competitive excellence, since his kindness and decency might be seen as weakness in a fight, but to my mind they were his greatest strengths. I clung to him, thinking that if I didn't have Ben in my life, Marco would be the perfect boyfriend. Then I sighed, because everything was just too complicated. I knew that he hoped for more from our relationship, but I didn't have it to give. My very soul belonged to Ben. It didn't lessen the warmth of his embrace or my fondness for Marco. My affection for the two of them didn't override the intensity of the attraction I felt for Alex. It was perverse.

Marco grinned and mouthed, "Good night." I don't know, maybe he said it aloud.

I tried to smile and dragged myself up the stairs. I dropped onto my bed fully clothed, staring at the ceiling. Ben had said I wasn't part of the normal population. Terrific. I was abnormal. Was I even human? If I *wasn't* human, what was I?

I lay there for a long time. I was exhausted with every fibre of my being, but my dull brain refused to shut off and let me fall into the nothingness of sleep. I wanted to erase time, but it stretched and lengthened instead.

Then, far in the back of my brain came the low humming of song. It was Ben's competition tune, with the 'graceful' piano part. Ben was humming me a lullaby. My bones loosened and I felt my tension leaking through the mattress to the floor. I filled my head with thankfulness for him as I drifted out of time.

When I awoke, it was black inside the room. I pulled myself off the bed and paced over to the window. The night was moonless, but the stars pricked the blackness and their glow echoed in flickering squiggles on the water. I stared out at the lake, wondering about normality. I didn't feel abnormal, but I guess if I'd always been that way, I'd think that was normal.

I jumped as the lights of my room flashed on and off. I spun around to see Bright standing at the door with a cup. She was stirring it, and then lifted it to me in invitation.

Aloud I asked, "Elixir?"

She nodded, handing it to me.

I lifted it without enthusiasm to my lips, and swallowed it down, focusing on the odd freeze and burn sensation as it went down. Then I took a deep, shuddering breath.

Bright touched my shoulder and pointed to the bed, and then she opened a dresser drawer and pulled out my best satin pyjamas. She smiled, wiggling her index finger to beckon me into the bathroom. She set the pyjamas on the counter, and started a bath for me. Fine. I'll have a bath.

She stepped out into my room, and then returned with my book, setting it on top of the pyjamas. She gave me a hug, and then glided out of the room, pulling the door shut behind her. I had just slipped out of my clothes when a note came under the door. "Dr. Kyle says you should regain some hearing within eight hours. I'm to bring you another dose every four hours. He thinks six doses will be ample. No school for you today." I smirked at that, and climbed gratefully into the warm bath, opening my book to lose my troubles in someone else's world for a while.

I crawled out of the bath about three hours later with my feet shrivelled up as if I was ninety. Wrapped in my fluffiest towel, I stepped into my room and stopped cold. I looked around trying to locate the source of the odd buzzing before I realized that Bright had left my radio on. I couldn't make out any words yet, but there was sound. For the first time I actually believed that I *was* going to be able to hear again. Even though it was still dark outside, my world suddenly seemed to radiate once more.

It took a couple of days before I felt like myself again. I still heard odd echoes and strange bells ringing in my ears now and then, but it was definitely improving almost by the hour. I was thankful beyond words for Dr. Kyle's magic potion and for whatever mysterious genetics I was blessed with that allowed me to make it through another life-changing trauma without permanent damage.

I won't lie. I was also thoroughly enjoying the break from school. It was the end of the semester. I should have been focused on finishing strongly, but the idea of seeing Marco's crestfallen face in the halls or even Claire's silent curiosity was just too irritating to contemplate. As a result, I was glad to be stretched out on the couch in the empty house reading my novel as I endeavoured to forget all that was waiting for me in the real world.

The doorbell rang. I set down my book with a bit of irritation. The hero and heroine were about to get together and the sexual tension was at its peak. I muttered a bit to myself as I went to the door. I peeped out the little window and gasped.

Alex.

How did he know where I lived? What was he doing here?

With a deep breath, I opened the door, attempting to look nonchalant. "Hi there. Can I help you?"

"Hello, Grace." He purred it.

My knees started to tremble. I tried to settle my breathing and managed to ask, "What would you like?" but I heard the quaver in my voice.

So did he. He smiled seductively as he answered, "You." He stepped across the threshold, shutting the door behind him, and in the same move, he reached for my shoulder, pulled me toward him with an enigmatic smile, and then his mouth found mine. This was no gentle, tentative first time kiss. This kiss was lush with desire. His arm reached around and pulled me closer and I felt the desire pulsing through his body. I felt the answering quivers of my own treacherous body as tingles raced up my back and warmth began to spread through me. My brain completely disconnected. He was all that existed in the universe. Him and the sensation of being in his arms.

He loosened his embrace and stepped back. He grinned, studying me appreciatively, his eyes travelling down my body and back up again. I felt naked. What on earth was happening here? I stumbled back a bit. He grabbed my shoulders until I regained my balance. Just looking at me. Not speaking. Then so casually that it might not have been planned, he started walking down the hall to my bedroom, undoing the buttons on his shirt. I stood watching him and my mouth grew round as reality gushed into my brain like a tidal wave.

A small gasp of "Oh!" brought his head up and he glanced back at me, still smiling seductively, while he peeled the shirt off. I backed slowly into the bathroom, as I fought hyperventilation, then shut and locked the door.

I put the lid of the toilet down and sat, concentrating very, very hard to breathe slowly and deeply. It had always worked when Ben was overwhelming me. It didn't seem to be working very well right now, until a thought hit me.

Ben.

Ben!

Where *was* Ben? He was always in my head for minor stuff, why wasn't he in my head now? This was HUGE! Where was he? I sent out the call, straining with my mind. *Ben!*

Nothing.

Well, what was I going to say to him even if he answered? *Oh hey, Ben? There's a stunning piece of manhood undressing himself in my bedroom at the moment, and I think the plan is that I'll be next. Do you have any comments or suggestions?* Good grief.

Another wave of panic rolled over me when I imagined Alex, down another article of clothing or two, in my bedroom. I was not ready for this. I had no intention of having sex until I was sure I could deal with the consequences of having sex. I didn't have any birth control. I didn't feel an emotional attachment to Alex. I was definitely attracted to him, but it was purely, profoundly physical. I didn't know him at all. Did I want to have sex with someone before I knew his favourite food or colour? This whole scenario seemed so shallow, like some desperate loser chick cruising bars imagining she would find her one true love. As if you could. How many words had he spoken to me? Four? Five? Who would sleep with someone without even a little conversation? Didn't prostitutes get even more communication than that? Suddenly I felt nauseous, not dizzy like I'd felt at the beginning around Ben, but bile rising in the throat, thoroughly, painfully nauseous. Plainly, I needed something more than purely physical attraction.

This was insane. Would a purely physical encounter with another man be enough to erase Ben? To sever whatever chords tied us together? He'd always been in my head whenever I was with Marco, but I'd never had these overpowering feelings for Marco. How was I driving Ben away now? Was this crazy, brain dazzling passion erasing our bond?

The passions burnt through me again and I whacked myself in the forehead with the heel of my hand. *Why* was I thinking about Ben when that absolutely gorgeous god was, by now, naked in my bedroom waiting for me? Ben was safe and wonderful. Alex was dangerous but oh so beautiful. Marco was, at this moment, nothing. A pleasant diversion. A brother. I was one of those girls who stepped on boys' hearts without any feeling. Who knew? I had always thought I was nice. Crazy how one's body just takes over and leaves the brain in the dust.

My heart thudded and skipped a beat. What was I going to do? In my mind, I saw his confident smirk and finger wiggle. He was so sure of my responses.

With a rush of awareness like being pushed off a deck into the lake, my sense returned to me. I remembered the arrogant look in his eye: so confident that he knew what I would do. Deep breath.

There was no way I was going to have sex with Alex. Well, at least not today. My desire had completely cooled with the memory of the casual way he presumed that I would follow him down the hall to my bed. That was sick. And Ben, of course. My safe, wonderful Ben. Such pure love there. Nothing like this insanity. Funny, silly, healthy Marco flitted briefly through my brain as well. Ah Marco. My safe, goofy brother.

I sat on the toilet seat, trying to figure out my next move. If I went in there, would Alex be angry? Would he take me anyway? Honestly, if he kissed me like that again, all my resistance would probably melt completely away. Would he be reasonable? He was a boxer. Would he get violent? I sat very still, pondering for a very long time, before I took a deep breath and walked to the sink.

I splashed cold water on my face and patted it dry. About ten minutes had passed. I had never felt braver or more cowardly. I opened the door slowly, and looked up and down the hall. No sign of anyone. Another deep breath and I walked down the hall into my bedroom.

He stood, back to the door, looking at something on my desk. He was completely clothed. Thank heaven.

"Um, Alex?"

He turned slowly around to face me, still smiling, but this time the smile was easier to read. There was a little embarrassment there. That was a surprise. I hadn't considered how he'd be feeling in this situation. Did he feel rejected? Had I given his self-esteem a direct hit to the gut? Did he normally walk into girls' houses and have them rip off all their clothes and race him to the bedroom? The thought made me giggle a bit in my tension. At least he didn't look upset or angry. Embarrassed was easy enough to relate to.

"Alex, I'm…"

He put up a hand to stop my words, shaking his head. "No, I'm sorry Grace." He sat down on the chair at my desk, "I didn't think that through."

The meaning of his words was briefly lost in the sonic wonderland that was his voice. He sounded like a professional actor; each word was enunciated clearly, but with the most seductive purring. I felt my body stirring again.

I objected automatically. "No, I mean...considering...well... It is not unreasonable that you would think..."

He shook his head again. "No, this was a really stupid thing to even contemplate, Grace. I should have realized that you are not *that* kind of girl."

I couldn't help it: I giggled. It was such a cliché.

He looked up at me with surprise. "What's so funny?"

I smiled crookedly, "You're right. At least, I never have been that kind of girl before." We stared at each other for a while before I said, "Alex. I think I would like to get to know you a little better before I seriously consider... well... you know."

He nodded blandly, "Of course. That is perfectly sensible." He stood up and stepped over to me on his way to the door. I presume it was the pheromones that made me want to grab him as he went by. My heart began to thud again and I felt myself battling very elemental urges. I would not be a slave to my body! "I have your number. I'll call you," he said.

"Ah. Sure. Great. Thanks for understanding." I followed down the hall to the front door. How did he get my number? Obviously, he had my address though, so I suppose it shouldn't be a surprise.

He waved away the thanks as he opened the door, "No problem. See you around, Grace."

The door shut behind him, and as I exhaled in relief, I heard the chuckle at the back of my brain.

"Ben!"

He laughed out loud and said cryptically, "Miss me?"

Arrrrrrrrrrrrrrrrrrrggggg! If he'd been close enough I would have hit him.

Mars shook his head at Xandros. "You're going to make poor O crazy with all that sexual posturing, you know."

Xandros grinned. "I know. It's too easy to be sport, but it's entertaining to watch him squirm."

"You're mean." Mars smiled as he said it. O was pretty funny. "You should be concentrating on the team work necessary to make this mission a success, not torturing your team mates."

"Yeah, yeah. There's no fun in that, is there?"

In a flash of light, O strode from out of the forest. He looked from Mars to Xandros. "You two talking about me?"

Mars shrugged, but Xandros smirked. "I nearly got her into the sack, O. She wanted me. She was aching for me."

O shook his head. "I saw it, Xandros. She kept her pants on, and she sent you packing. I told you. She's mine."

Xandros rolled his eyes. "It's just a matter of time. Look at this body!" He flexed his arms and kissed his bicep. "If you were watching, you saw her looking at me. She has never looked at you that lustfully, O, and you know it."

O sighed. "Give it up. She's not yours, Xandros."

"I don't necessarily want her permanently. I'm happy with conjugal visits."

O's brows lowered.

Mars stepped forward. "Well, as entertaining as all this is, we have a girl to protect, so she can save the world. Let's get on with it, shall we? Xandros. Leave us."

Xandros shrugged again and sauntered off, disappearing in a flash.

Mars turned to O. "Don't let him get to you."

"It's not him."

"Right. The music is fading, and it has nothing to do with Xandros stealing your girl?"

"It's not about him. She can't help the physical connection they share, and I am not letting it tear me to pieces, but I need her. She's too far away. The mental connection isn't strong enough when we can't get close enough to re-charge it now and then. I don't want to tell her, in case it scares her. It's killing me."

"Killing?"

"Not literally. It just...hurts." He looked up at Mars, standing in battle gear, his breastplate catching the light, dazzling. "You must think I'm ridiculous."

Mars shrugged, "Well. Wars aren't your thing, O. I know that. I'm doing my best to compensate. You've done very well, all things considered."

"Not well enough."

"Don't beat yourself up. Xandros and I will protect her. You focus on the music, and convincing the family to let you stay with her."

"They're afraid we'll be too powerful a block, if we're together."

"Yeah. I know. I heard it. Convince them you're a wimpy little musician and perhaps they'll fall for it."

"Right. So far that seems pretty obvious."

Mars laughed.

CHAPTER SEVEN

FOREVER WAS PASSING ME BY

Orpheus struggles for music, lost in his world without Charis.
Presence is needed to inspire him; sadness can't hide the unfairness.
Longing for what isn't there for him, Charis is guilty and lonely,
Needs explanation available from wise Euphrosyne only.

I peeked around the corner and saw Auntie Bright sitting on her purple loveseat, needle in hand, a vividly crimson bundle of cloth on her lap, a box of sparkling beads on the table in front of her. She was working on a dance costume, concentrating on her tiny even stitches as she sewed on the sparkling beads. Some Middle Eastern song was playing loudly on the stereo. She was bobbing her head and swaying her shoulders to the uneven rhythm that was shaking the floor even as she stitched. She was dancing while sitting still. "Hi Auntie Bright."

She glanced up and smiled beatifically, as usual. "Hello Grace! I didn't hear you!" She indicated her stereo, where the insistent beat of the tabla was quite mesmerizing. "You'd better turn that down, if you want to visit."

I nodded turning the dial until there was only a faint, complex hammering of rhythm in the background. "What are you working on?" I asked as I turned around and sat on the floor in front of her, so as not to disturb her work.

"I was asked to belly dance at Wednesday on the Wharf, so I thought it was time for a new costume. You know how it is." She giggled, as she held up a much-embellished bra, dripping with beads and dangly fringe. "We can't perform in old costumes!" She glanced across to the couch where Uncle Jim was sitting reading. "Isn't that right, Jim?"

He glanced up and shook his head with an air of benign resignation. "You've never been able to do it before, so I'm sure it'd be impossible to start now."

Bright laughed while she smiled at him fondly. They were so different and yet so contented. He was tall and quiet. She was short and loud. He walked into a room like a cat. She bounded into a room like a boisterous puppy. He was the epitome of responsible adult. She was child-like. They were opposites in every way, and yet they were also like matched puzzle pieces. She studied him for a moment, then after carefully setting her sparkly bra and needle on the loveseat beside her, she popped out of her seat, flew over to him and planted a kiss with a grin while he laughingly fought her off, pretending to try to read his book amid the tangle of limbs. She attacked him with tickles, looking for another place to land a kiss. She succeeded with a puckering smack, to kiss him on the top of his forehead, leaving a vivid, sparkly fuchsia pink lip print emblazoned there, and backed off smiling triumphantly, to drop back onto the loveseat. From calm to flurry to calm, *like Calgary weather*, I giggled to myself.

They were just so comfortable with each other. The warmth of their affection made the room toasty, and I felt secure in their presence as their comfort spread to me as well. There was no tension in this room, just contentment, and I needed to absorb that feeling to still my brain's turmoil. All afternoon I'd been trying to sort out the perplexing mix of emotions that competed for my attention. Alex. Marco. Ben. It was all so mystifying. I felt a unique passion for each one of them, but what was I to do about it?

Jim's mild voice followed Bright back to the loveseat, "Can I read now? Or are you planning to attack me again?" There was nothing but fondness in his voice.

Bright looked at him as if she had no clue what he was getting at, and remarked, "Of course you can read, dear. No one is stopping you." His slightly melodramatic sigh was followed by her quiet chuckle as she picked up the costume piece again and glanced over to me. Jim was already reading again. I wondered if he knew that he had lips imprinted on his forehead, and whether he'd care if he did.

Looking away from him, Bright asked, "So Grace, how are you today?"

I sighed out, "Okaaaay." I drew it out, and a sigh escaped. I sounded so morose.

She could read my tone without any difficulty, apparently, because replied with a knowing, "Ahhh. I see." She studied my face, needle paused mid-stitch. "Not Marco, eh?" Hmmm. I glanced down at my lap, twisting my hands a little. Bright's intuition was sometimes a little creepy. "Hmm. So Alex is creating complications already…"

I looked up at her. That was a LOT creepy. I had never mentioned Alex to her. How did she know Alex? I felt the colour rising in my cheeks as my heart started to pound in panic. I wasn't sure *why* I was panicking, but I suddenly the world seemed to spinning more quickly.

Bright smiled gently as she looked down and pulled the thread through the fabric. I knew she was assessing my discomfort. "You know Grace, there is always an Alex." She continued stitching while she spoke, and though I had the distinct impression she didn't need to ask, she queried, "How do you feel about him?"

Feel? Upside down. Caught in a windmill. Like I'm drowning. Inside out. I feel too overwhelmed to know how I feel and too confused to do anything about it. I feel inexplicably drawn to Alex, in a scary way, like I have no control over myself. Like my body is betraying me as it finds him in any crowd like he is a lightning rod. Like my stomach will never stop heaving after a thought of him crosses my mind. Like I am in a perpetual motion machine and I am never going to relax again. Just to illustrate, my stomach gave a churning lurch as his face flashed across my mind. I swallowed nausea as I looked up at Auntie Bright, stitching calmly, and then over to Uncle Jim immersed in his book. My shoulders drooped and I muttered, "I don't know how I feel."

Bright nodded thoughtfully without looking up. "Physical attraction can be overwhelming. It's like someone suddenly turned on the electro-magnet and things that were just standing minding their own business a second before are now irresistibly pulling together."

I gasped, "Yes!" staring at her with wide eyes. How did she interpret 'I don't know how I feel' into that? How did she know exactly what I was thinking? I pondered for a moment before I asked her the more important question in a tense whisper, "Does anything ever turn *off* the magnet?"

She smiled at me sympathetically. "Sometimes." She glanced over at Jim and sighed to herself before she added slowly, "Not always."

The ringing of the phone jangled my nerves. I was in my room lying on my bed pretending that I was doing homework. I strained my ears to hear who was talking.

Bright opened the door and handed me the phone with a smile. "A call for you, Grace." Something in her tone told me that it was long distance. Ben came to mind immediately, though we had not bothered with phone conversations for a very long time.

"Thanks," I said to her, then held the hand piece to my head and said, "Grace here."

"Hey, Hon!" called a familiar voice.

"Christie! Oh, how great to hear from you!" Just the sound of her voice made me glad as a rush of happy memories flowed over me. "How is everyone?"

She regaled me with Bonnie's latest schemes, and had me laughing with a couple of stories of pranks Lloyd had pulled in Mr. Moore's class.

"And you? How are you?" I probed.

"I'm fine. Lloyd and I are officially going out now."

"That's awesome!"

She laughed, "It is most of the time. Sometimes it just drives me crazy as he's working out his jokes. Did you know he actually works out hundreds of puns so that he can casually drop one into conversation and sound witty? I figured it was a natural talent. He made a very big deal out of letting me 'behind the scenes' with this knowledge." She chuckled and added, "Oh, come to think of it, now that I've told you, I might have to kill you."

I responded with a mirthless chuckle of my own. "You'll have to take a number."

"What?" She was immediately serious. "What do you mean?"

"Oh, same ol' same ol'" I said wearily. "Most recently I've had a near drowning, a lightning strike and an attempted crushing. My life, you know, can't have a single month go by without a little drama…" I trailed off. I was being melodramatic. It was silly of me, but it was so nice to be able to talk to someone who knew me well.

"I'm sorry to hear that, but Marco is there, right?"

I sighed without answering her. Interesting that she knew that Marco was watching me.

Her voice grew concerned. "Grace? What happened to Marco?"

"He's okay, Christie.

"But?"

"But we're not hanging out as often any more."

"Because?"

I didn't want to say. The whole Alex thing was too embarrassing and too unbelievable to explain. I sought for some other explanation that would do. I came up blank.

"Grace."

"Ah. Well. Um."

"Graaace." She held the vowel in a way that brooked no continued avoidance.

I wondered if she was going to say my full name next. That errant thought brought me the perfect way to distract her.

"It's no big deal *Crystal Visions of Rainbows*."

She sucked in an irritated breath. Score. Heh, heh. She hated being called by the legal name her hippy mom had cursed her with.

"Enough playing games Grace, what happened?" She was mad now.

I sighed. "Fine. We broke up. It was painful. I don't want to talk about it." Let's see what she made of that.

"You and Marco were *going out*?"

"More or less." I so did not want to get into the details of this.

"What about Ben?"

"He lives in Calgary, remember?"

"So?"

"So I *don't* live in Calgary." I paused. I could feel her disapproval leaking through the phone and it made me defensive. "Ben knew about Marco, Christie. I wasn't cheating on him or anything."

"He *knew*, did he?" She sounded slightly sarcastic.

"Yes. He *did*. That's neither here nor there, though." I tried to sound dismissive.

"Hmmm." Christie murmured thoughtfully at the other end of the line. "Maybe *that* explains it?"

"Explains what?"

"Well," she said, clearly still thinking aloud, "this is actually why I called tonight." She paused for a moment before she went on. "I ran into Ben at the mall the other day and we got talking. Did you know he'd been away?"

"Of course. I talk to him every day."

Her voice softened to a whisper, "Grace, he doesn't look well."

"What?" My heart started to pound. "What do you mean?"

"I mean he looks *awful*. He's got full-time classes at university, and he has to have a competition piece ready for the international round of competition in a couple of months. It's not going well. I don't think he's sleeping for one thing, but I don't think the composing is going very well either. He seemed…" she paused thoughtfully. "…I don't know how to explain it, kind of like a balloon that's had all the air let out. He is just a skin of his former self. It's sad Grace. No, it's worse than that. It's pathetic."

Ben was pathetic? I thought back to how great he'd been at the Nationals in Vancouver a couple months ago. I remembered how I'd felt after we'd had to leave each other. I'd felt empty too. I wondered if he'd been actually ill.

"Grace?" Christie called then she added more loudly, "Are you still there?"

"Sorry, yes. I'm still here. I just can't believe it. He looked so great the last time I saw him. I wonder if there's anything I can do?"

"I don't know, but I hope you can do something. I'm worried about him; I really am." There was a slam and a lot of barking on her end of the phone. "Sorry Grace, I've got to go. Take care of yourself, eh?"

"Yeah. Thanks for calling Christie. I appreciate it a lot. Say hi to Lloyd."

"I will. Bye."

I went down to the kitchen to put the phone back on the cradle. Bright was sitting at the kitchen table reading a cookbook as if it was a novel. She glanced up at me mildly, "Everything good in Calgary?"

I shook my head and sat down at my seat resting my elbows on the table and cupping my chin in my hands. "No."

She closed the cookbook and tilted her head curiously, "No? What's up?"

"Apparently something is going on with Ben. Christie says he's sick and she thinks he's having trouble with his music." I sighed. "I'm worried."

Her brows furrowed, "Really?"

"I wonder if he caught some bug on his trip abroad."

Auntie Bright was looking at me, but her eyes were distant; she tipped her head to the side as if she was listening to something.

"Bright? What do you think?"

"Mmm? Maybe," she said, but I got the impression that she hadn't really heard my question. Her eyes became all unfocused then, like she was concentrating on something far away. Her head bobbed a bit and tilted one way and another like it did when she was talking to someone and her lips even twitched a bit like she was talking, but she wasn't saying anything out loud.

I watched her curiously, wondering what was going on. I pondered calling Jim to come and see whether she was okay as I grew more and more nervous.

"Auntie Bright?" I whispered. "Bright? Are you okay?"

Then as suddenly as she'd left, she was back. Her eyes focused on me and she smiled.

"Auntie Bright? What happened?"

She looked at me with a bewildered expression, "Nothing happened, Grace. I'm just worrying about Ben."

"You looked like you slipped into a coma or something..." I said, my voice trailing off as she scowled at me.

"Don't be silly, Grace," she remarked with a scoff, but she left the table, got the water pitcher from the fridge and filled a glass with her back to me. She stood looking out the window at the lake while she sipped, and I had the distinct impression she was avoiding my eyes. Fine then.

I stood up. "I'm going up to my room to see if I can talk to Ben." I announced.

"Good idea," she said, still not turning around.

Sometimes my Auntie Bright freaked me out.

Often my Auntie Bright freaked me out, actually.

Ben didn't respond to my calls, so I lay on the bed with a book for a while. He tuned in for our regular ten o'clock visits as usual. He seemed just the same as always. I could detect no sign of illness or melancholy, but I didn't ask him straight out. To be honest, I was a little embarrassed. I figured if he was having a hard time, and he wanted me to know about it, then he would tell me. If he wasn't telling me, I guess he had his own reasons for maintaining that façade.

I worried. I worried about Ben. I worried about myself. Before long I was worrying about Marco, and Bright as well. Everyone was linked somehow. So far the only person who had actually let anything slip was Jim. He was the weak link. Maybe if I knew what Bright was, I'd know what I was. I waited for a night when Auntie Bright was out of the house, and he was quietly reading.

"Uncle Jim?"

"Yes, Gracie?" he pushed away his book and looked over the top of his reading glasses.

"I'm wondering if I can talk to you about Auntie Bright."

He looked at me quizzically. "Sure. What about her?"

I didn't know where to begin. Is my aunt an alien? Did you marry a supernatural being? No. Those were probably not the best ways to start. Hmm. I looked over him, sitting in his usual chair, waiting expectantly.

"Well, I guess I'm just wondering if, um, if you've ever noticed anything weird about her." There. That was safe and general.

He laughed out loud. A booming burst of laughter. "Weird? Bright? Surely, you haven't noticed anything slightly *odd* about Bright? HA!" He guffawed. He almost fell off his chair he was laughing so hard.

This was irritating. "Uncle Jim! I'm not talking about obvious eccentricities! I don't mean her crazy clothes or her hobbies. I mean… um… I mean the way she seems to know what you're thinking and stuff." I harrumphed and flopped down on the couch. He had made me grumpy with his laughing fit and I hadn't asked the question nearly as intelligently as I'd planned to.

He was serious at once. "Ah." He looked at me knowingly. "I see. *Mind reading*, and stuff, eh?"

"I'm *serious* Uncle Jim. I used to think she just had really good intuition, or that she was talking about me with my mom or something, but I don't think that any more. She knows stuff I haven't told anyone; stuff I wasn't even sure I'd told myself. It's not normal."

Jim studied me carefully before he replied. He seemed to be weighing out several options. Finally, he spoke very slowly. "Bright does seem to be very… ah... intuitive, as you say. Yes. I know what you mean."

He was playing it safe, but I wanted more from him. He lived with her. He had to know the truth about her. "Jim, a while ago something really strange happened, and I can't get it out of my brain."

He looked at me with vague curiosity, wondering what had tipped me over the edge, I guess.

"She seemed to lock on someone, and have a conversation like I wasn't even there. Then after she snapped out of it, she looked at me like I was crazy when I asked her what was going on."

"What do *you* think it is?" he asked casually.

"Well, I think she's crazy and she's hearing voices…" Oh damn, that probably meant I was crazy, too. Damn Ben. "…or she is reading minds." Am I reading minds, too? Does hearing *Ben* count as reading minds?

Jim nodded, "I don't know Grace. I can't answer your question."

"Can't?"

"Can't. Won't. Whatever. I try very hard not to think about these things Grace, because it's safer for all of us if we don't try to figure out too much. Why not leave some mystery in the relationship?"

"You're scared!"

He smiled. "Probably. But I don't want to push her either. We've been together a long time. I just want to enjoy her. Can you understand that?"

"Well yes, of course." Who wouldn't want to just enjoy her? It was too scary considering other options! "Have you seen what I'm talking about though? Did I imagine it? Do you know what I mean?"

Jim smiled softly at me. He nodded gently. "I've seen it a few times. The time it freaked me out the most was when we were at a wedding." He shivered and went silent.

I could tell he'd rather not talk about it, but I couldn't help breathing out the question, "What happened?"

He looked like he was re-living something horrible. He sighed, lost in the memory for a moment. I had never seen Jim look quite so intense about anything. He was always so… unruffled. "You really don't want to know, do you?"

When I nodded, somewhat apologetically, "I do, Jim. Please tell me." Ha. Wedding. I do.

He studied the floor for a while.

I waited patiently for a minute, two minutes, three. The only sound was the ticking of the little antique mantel clock. Then he took a deep breath and looked up at me with resolution. "Well, as I said, it was at a wedding. One of Bright's old family friends had gotten married. We had only been married ourselves for just over a year. We'd just come from the ceremony and had gone into the hotel for the reception. It was a huge banquet room, chandeliers glowing, filled with two hundred people, maybe more. The atmosphere was buoyant; we were laughing and celebrating the joy of the new bride and groom. Typical wedding, right? Bright and I were just sitting there visiting with the people at our table; the priest had sat down with us and I had asked him something, when I saw a shiver run up her back. It was almost a convulsion, rippling very obviously up her spine and when it reached the top, she gasped and whipped her head around as if someone had screamed her name from across the room. No one had, of course, there was just the hum of two hundred chattering voices, but there she was staring across to the opposite side of the room with these huge eyes. Scary intense eyes." He shivered again, "I was alarmed, because it was—well you know how she can be—it was creepy."

I nodded. I knew exactly how creepy it could be.

"She just stared, and all the blood drained out of her face. She wasn't breathing. I was afraid for her and asked, 'Bright, what is it? Who is it?' but she just kept staring into the distance, her eyes glued on some distance point without breathing. I turned to follow her sight line, but there were so many people in the room I couldn't tell exactly where she was looking. I asked her again, and she just whispered, 'Xander.' I didn't know a Xander. I didn't know what she meant, so I repeated the name as a question and she whispered again without being aware, I think, that she was even speaking, 'waiter.' Then I saw him of course, because he had felt her eyes, too. He was staring back at her. It was a huge room, Grace, there a football field width between them, but they were staring at each other like they were right next to each other—as if none of the rest of us existed." He shook his head like he was trying to get the image out of his head. "He stared and she stared, until it seemed like forever was passing me by. I glanced at my watch as they just kept looking at each other. I kept thinking, who is this guy? Why is my wife responding like that to him? But I couldn't ask her, could I? I mean, that's part of being married. You just have to trust each other, and so I just asked if she was all right, and waited for her to say something.

"Finally after I'd said, 'Bright, are you okay?' for about the tenth time, I looked at the waiter and he had moved, picking up a tray loaded with meals. She was shaking her head as if she was clearing it out, and she started to breathe again. I swear she hadn't taken a breath the whole time she was glued to him. Then she smiled at me and said, 'Pardon honey? Oh, I'm sorry. It's nothing.'

"Nothing!" Jim grimaced painfully, "She had been frozen for five minutes staring at that waiter and she honestly seemed to think it'd been a momentary kind of thing. The other people at the table looked at her a bit strangely, but they hadn't seen the expression in her eyes, so they went on with their chatter. She joined in with them soon enough, but she wasn't there, you know? The rest of the evening, I could actually feel her tuned in to him wherever he was. Her eyes would find him unconsciously, I thought. If he was out of the room, she visibly relaxed, but the moment he came in, whether she was facing him or not, her body seemed to know it and her shoulders would tighten."

He looked at me as if he was re-telling a nightmare. I wanted to tell him not to continue, but I was glued to my seat, wide-eyed, waiting for more. I could imagine the scene from Bright's perspective all too well. "Did she talk to him? Or was it just staring all night?"

He breathed deeply again. "Toward the end of the evening he came to our table to clear off the dishes. He smiled at her and said, 'Hello Brigit. How's wedded bliss?' She smiled at him with what was clearly a false calm and replied, 'Blissful, Alexander.' He'd nodded at that and wished her luck; she'd thanked him. She still didn't relax that night. She didn't speak to him again even though he passed our table a few times."

"Wow."

He nodded. "Yeah. That's one way to sum it up." He grimaced at me. "I'm not sure why I'm telling you this. I've never mentioned it to a soul before now." He sighed and looked toward his book.

A thought hit me, "Did you say his name was Alexander?" That was a strange coincidence. I remembered what she'd said, 'There's always an Alex.' An Alex. As if, she knew the feeling. As if she'd felt the draw herself.

"Yes. That was the name. It burned into my brain."

"Did you ever ask her about it? Ask her who he was?"

He shook his head. "Nope."

"Why not?"

"I figured it was her business. You know that old adage, 'If she wanted me know she'd tell me.'"

"But Jim, you're married. Aren't you supposed to talk about everything? Why wouldn't you ask her about something if it was that disturbing?"

He shook his head, "Grace, there are some things it's probably better not knowing about. Part of being married is protecting one another, and sometimes it's better not to know things that would be too painful for the other person to bear. We hadn't been married very long at that time. It just wasn't worth bringing it up."

"Isn't it worse *not* knowing? What could be worse than what you would be imagining?" I was imagining a passionate affair... a teen pregnancy... Weird. Auntie Bright was always so *present* that I'd never really thought about her having a past, but she had always been an enigma; who knew what history she had lurking behind her?

He exhaled deeply. "I know exactly what you mean, Grace, but we're talking about Bright here. With her, whatever it is *could* be a lot worse than I imagine." He met my eyes, and I knew he'd thought of all the explanations that had occurred to me, and more. I knew from the pain behind his eyes that he also knew more than he was telling me, but I could also feel that he was telling the most he could. "I just concentrate on the fact that she married me, that we enjoy being together, and that we'll be together for the rest of my life. Whoever this Alex was, he's not in her life now, and so I have let it go."

"You're brave."

He shrugged his shoulders. "I love her. I trust her." He shrugged.

I understood what he meant. I could see that you'd have to trust her. She was imminently trustworthy, my Auntie Bright. This was so weird, though. She had never seemed like the kind of person who kept secrets. Then a thought struck me and I looked up, "Wait a minute." I paused, thinking this through. "Uncle Jim?"

"Yes?"

"Did you say that he called her Brigit?"

"Yes."

"Who calls her Brigit?"

"Almost no one."

I narrowed my eyes, tilting my head, trying to figure out what this could mean. A slow smile grew on his face, as he watched me thinking. He chuckled. "Have you never heard her called Brigit?"

I was searching my memories of Auntie Bright. I'd known Bright wasn't her real name for a decade at least, but no, I'd never heard of a single person who ever called her anything but Bright. She wasn't Brigit. She was Bright. I shook my head. "Never. It means he wasn't close to her, right?"

Jim chuckled again at the hopeful glimmer in my eyes, but shook his head, "No, I don't think we can presume that at all. I think it just means he was from long ago and far away."

That was a strange thing to say. "Like a fairy tale, huh? 'Once upon a time' and all that?"

He nodded quite seriously. "Yes. I think so."

Huh?

"I think we should probably end this conversation here, Gracie. It's been good talking to you. I hope it's been helpful for you. Don't worry about the weirdness, all right? Bright doesn't worry about anything, so it'd be silly of us to worry on her behalf."

"Um... Okay." Case dismissed. Obviously, I was getting too close to something I was not supposed to know about. I wasn't going to push it now, but I *was* going to find answers eventually.

So we turned on the TV and I flipped to some sit-com. I tried not to worry or to wonder. I really did. It was impossible. It was all so confusing. I felt like there was something I was missing that was going to make all these pieces fit together, but I couldn't quite see the missing link. Jim had a book in his hand, as usual. While I stared unseeingly at the TV, he stared at the book. I'm not sure either of us was really succeeding at our attempt to distract ourselves, because I didn't see him turn a page. The silence was companionable, as usual at their house, and so we sat while rain pounded the roof and bounced off the windows.

Waiting.

Probably an hour or so later Fatima puttered into the driveway. The car door slammed, and moments later Bright appeared in the doorway, beaming at us as usual, her hair glistening with rain droplets that had covered her in the trip from the car to the door. "Whew! Wet out there!" she exclaimed as she shut the door behind her and shook her hair in a mini-rainstorm. Her Victorian style wool coat was wrapped around a royal blue belly dance costume: harem pants and a short crushed velvet choli top. Not a fancy outfit, just a regular dance class ensemble. She looked awesome in it, rather than goofy like I would have. There was a strange gypsy vibe about Bright that suited all her crazy bohemian outfits. She shook out of her coat, hanging it on a hook in the hall, and then she dropped the velvet patchwork bag she'd made for her dance gear and looked at us curiously. Her pause was palpable. She looked from Uncle Jim to me with a look of growing concern. "Hmmm. What have you two been up to?" she asked suspiciously.

I looked over at Jim, wondering if we looked guilty or something, but his face was its usual mask of calm. I wondered if I was the one giving away my frantic thoughts.

He raised his book slightly, "Just reading. How was dance class?"

"It was fine." Her eyes narrowed thoughtfully as she looked over at me, "Grace?"

"Oh, I've just been waiting for you Auntie Bright, watching TV. Can't say that it was anything worth watching, though!" I giggled uncomfortably, hoping she'd believe me.

She stood there for a moment, just looking at me, and then she said quietly, "Ah. I see."

I knew again that she really did see. She saw that I had not really watched anything on TV at all. She saw that Jim and I had been speaking about her. She saw my uncharacteristic discomfort in her presence. Auntie Bright was not normal, and she saw things the rest of the world didn't see. Who was she? *What* was she?

I watched her back, wondering what she was going to do. She seemed to be pondering that herself. She strolled gracefully into the room and settled beside Uncle Jim. She leaned over to kiss him gently on the cheekbone and whispered something into his ear. He nodded, meeting her eyes with typical affection. She kissed him again, and as she stood up, added, "Love you." He smiled and whispered affectionately back.

Then she glanced over to me. "Come on Grace. Come with me while I change. You can find something to wear in my closet, too. We're going out for dinner."

CHAPTER EIGHT

BETTER SMILING THAN FROWNING

Answers come vaguely and cryptically; what is the truth that is reaching?
Trying to push through her consciousness, what is the lesson it's teaching?
Warriors guarding her safety, filling her heart with their caring;
Love is the fuel for protection. Value is strength, and it's daring.

Dressing up at Auntie Bright's had been a favourite activity when I was little. Aside from her absolutely amazing costume collection, her regular clothes were something that many people would consider Tickle Trunk material. Vivid colours—crimson, violet, royal blue, emerald green. Large gypsy skirts, bright vests and jackets, blouses with flowing sleeves. Sequins and sparkles. It was a veritable treasure trove of dress up. And her shoes! Shoes in all colours and styles: besides the bright colours of her clothes, there were metallic silver, gold and bronze in flats, pumps, clogs and mules. It was an insane variety. She had once told me she was leading a campaign against boring black shoes. It was obvious. Mind you, she did have some black shoes as well, but not a single pair of them was boring. Auntie Bright has a colourful personality and her clothes reflect it. It had been fun to dress with her when I was a kid, but I wasn't a kid any more. I was vaguely uneasy about my chances at finding something appropriate for myself that wasn't going to look like I was playing dress up. I assumed 'going out for dinner' involved being out in public.

I needn't have worried. As we walked into her dressing room, where the closet wrapped the entire room, she reached into the pants section and pulled out a perfectly neutral, beautifully cut pair of grey pants. "I can see your panic Grace. Trust me: I know what will suit your shape and colouring. Here, I think these will fit you." She dragged her fingers along the hangers in the blouse closet and pulled out three tailored blouses in a variety of colours and cuts. "Each of these will suit you, see which one you prefer." I tried each one, and each was stunning in a different way. I chose a silk blouse in baby blue that flowed while it hugged my body: gorgeous, tailored and feminine at the same time. Of course, this wasn't an outfit I would have put together myself, nor one that anyone in the halls at school would be wearing, but I would have had to be blind to see how astonishing I looked in it. I appeared about five years older, several inches taller, and quite a bit thinner.

"How is this possible that I look so different in this, Auntie Bright?"

She laughed. "You know what they say, Grace, 'The clothes make the man' or in this case, the woman." She looked me up and down, "Yup. Definitely a good look for you. I can tell you like it, because you're standing taller. It's amazing what a great outfit does for the face and the figure, isn't it? I wish young girls didn't feel obliged to wear the same old sweats and hoodie look that the magazines push. So few girls look good in those slobby clothes or in the trashy music video outfits either." She sighed. "I could reform teen fashion and make you all look beautiful, but you are all so stubborn I bet you wouldn't let me in the door!" She laughed.

Bright changed into a fuchsia blouse with flaring bell-like sleeves and a grey pencil skirt that was made of some amazing fabric that looked alive when she moved. "So Grace, how about Greek?"

"Greek?" I asked, my mind still trying to get over how unlike myself, how much better than myself, my borrowed clothes made me look.

She giggled then winked her big stage wink at me—the one that involved scrunching up her cheek and raising her shoulder very dramatically, and in a funny accent said enthusiastically, "Yes! A Greek boy would be perfect for you! How about a cute one like Dimetrios or Kosmo perhaps?"

"Huh- wha...?" I gasped. Bright was fixing me up?

She laughed loudly and punched me gently in the shoulder. "Just joking Grace. Greek *food*. You have enough boys after you."

"Oh, duh." I was an idiot. "Yes, Greek food would be great." I loved Greek food. Mmm. Just thinking about the pita bread and tzatziki had my mouth watering. Souvlaki, Lamb. Greek potatoes. Baklava. Mmm. Greek was a great idea. I hadn't realized I was starving.

At the door, still chuckling to herself on the success of her joke, Bright grabbed her coat off the hook and called to Jim, who was still reading on the couch, "Jim, do you want us to bring you something back, or will you fend for yourself?"

He muttered something indistinct, but plainly Bright could translate because she said, "Okay!" as she opened the door for me to follow her out to the car.

I loved Auntie Bright's car, Fatima. She was as much a member of the family as I was. I settled into her turquoise seats, embroidered in a paisley pattern down each side that coordinated with the bejewelled paisley exterior of the car, for the short drive to the restaurant. Comfortable in each other's presence, Bright and I didn't speak. I could almost feel her mind turning repeatedly, pondering. There was an air of expectancy in the car with us. Fatima seemed to know the secret too.

The restaurant was in what had been an old house. The hostess seated us over in a corner hidden behind the fireplace. It was a good place for the kind of private conversation that I suspected we were going to be having.

"Auntie Bright?"

"Hmm?" she glanced up from the menu

"When did you get your nose pierced?"

She laughed and sighed nostalgically, "A very, very long time ago."

"Oh? Was that a fashionable thing to do then? I thought it was a recent fad?"

She grinned at me with crinkled eyes. "Well, at the time I was living in India and head over heels in love for a quite astonishing young Indian man…" Her voice stopped, but I could almost see the memories continuing as her eyes stared unseeingly toward the ceiling, smiling fondly to nothingness.

"And?" I prompted.

"Oh, it's not complicated, just that as I result of my adoration I got carried away with all things South Asian. That's around the time I took up belly dancing, as well. Wonderful fabrics in India. You can feel so absolutely beautiful and feminine in a sari and jewels…" She grunted then, with a mutter under her breath that sounded like, "But purdah! BAH!"

"Purdah?"

She chuckled, "Indian curse word, Grace." She grinned and sighed dramatically, as if she was on the stage. "But to the good stuff — Ahhhhhhhh—Umed! He was *quite* something." She laughed, "I think you would have liked him."

"Oh? Why?"

She smiled fondly, "Your Ben reminds me quite a bit of him. Very sweet. Funny. He was a talented musician as well, though his family would not let him pursue that, of course."

"Really? Why not?"

"Wrong class. Very inappropriate. Like me, unfortunately." She clucked her tongue and then said, with a distinctly melancholy tone, "Ah well, the world went on."

"Musicians were the wrong class?"

"Indeed."

"*You* were the wrong class?"

"Most definitely."

"And therefore inappropriate..."

"Oh yes. Absolutely and completely inappropriate. We tried to.... well... his parents were absolutely firm that he meet his family expectations and marry the woman they'd chosen for him."

"An arranged marriage?" I hadn't imagined such things still actually happened.

"Yes. Beautiful girl, Brahman class like him. It'd been planned for years. He liked her quite a bit actually. They'd played together as children. She was a good choice for him."

"But he was never able to play his music?"

"No, not after I left." She sighed. "His father destroyed his harmonium in front of our eyes. That was how he forced me from the house actually." She sighed again, staring off into the past. "I'll never forget the agony in Umed's face as he bowed before his father. He handed me a broken key from the harmonium and told me to leave him forever." Her hand moved involuntarily to her neck and I saw the creamy white rectangular pendant with the black carved design that she often wore. Suddenly it seemed more significant. Could the abstract the design actually be writing?

She seemed quite calm, though her eyes were lost, and I whispered, "Was it horrible?"

She looked at me, then slowly down to the menu, then back at me, breathing very deeply before she remarked, "Oh yes. Beyond horrible. I thought I would die, actually, from the pain of it. I cried for days, or perhaps it was years..." She sighed again and stared blankly at the menu. "I was *quite* inconsolable..." Her voice drifted off into the past again.

I waited somewhat hesitantly for what might come next. Bright had never shared such intensely personal information with me before. The waiter came over and stood expectantly beside the table. "Are you ready to order now?"

Smiling at him without any shadow of the sadness she'd shown me only moments before, Bright ordered her favourite chicken Souvlaki. I chose mousaka.

"Are you up for ouzo, Grace, or would your mother disown me if we had some?"

"I think that would cause them to lose their liquor licence, Auntie Bright. Under-aged minor, remember? I'd better stick to pop."

"Yes, I suppose you're right. Always so practical. I forget you're a teen. You have such an old soul, Grace." She dazzled the waiter with her smile and he walked off with our orders looking somewhat shell shocked.

"You shouldn't do that you know, Auntie Bright. These poor normal people can't handle your intensity."

She laughed. "Well, better smiling than frowning, right? Who needs more negativity in their life?" She gave me a determined look and stated firmly, "I had enough of negativity after Umed's family destroyed us, and I vowed to keep it *out* of my life. No one needs to have a depressing life. Every look is a decision. We can choose to be happy."

"Is that why you changed your name from Brigit to Bright?"

She giggled and leaned in confidentially, "Actually, at *that* time, I was usually called Sabiha." She carried on chuckling under her breath

She was baffling me, and I was feeling a little uncomfortable being out of the loop of her inside joke. "Auntie Bright?"

She looked back and I saw her suck in her cheeks to attempt a straight face. Sometimes Bright was like a five year old. "Sorry Grace." Her attempt at contriteness was unsuccessful, but I ploughed on nonetheless.

"So it was very bad after Umed, and then…?"

She sighed and smiled fondly, silent for a while, clearly back in her Indian memories, then she exhaled purposefully and looked up at me. "Yes. It was hell for a very long time, but I knew that Umed really had no choice. He had to do what was expected of him. He'd been raised to be a certain person. I did not fit into his life, and moreover, I would have taken him away from all that was most important to his family's future. There was no one who knew that better than I did. We'd loved each other beyond reason, but love just wasn't enough. For a while, we thought that we could defy the conventions, but eventually we had to make rational decisions. He chose the life his family had ordained for him, with a very suitable girl who truly could make him successful. I chose to leave and not to fight it. We could have stayed…close… but it was better for everyone if there was no hypocrisy. I can't bear hypocrisy, Grace. But hypocrisy is very close to irony, and I almost did." She sighed, "It was the darkest period of my life, but then…" she shrugged, "I recovered."

"That's it? You just left and recovered?"

She smiled again but sadly, "Well, not *quite*. There was a very long, very lonely time, with a few false starts along the way, but eventually, I found someone who could really truly love me, and I chose to be happy, and *that* is when I changed my name to Bright."

"You chose?"

"Yes. I found Jim. We chose to be happy. That has been a wonderful thing."

"Chose?" I asked again.

"Chose, Grace."

I shook my head in confusion. "No lightning bolts? No violins? No debilitating pheromone flash?"

She threw her head back and laughed. Her dark curls caught the light and twinkled almost as brightly as her usual sequins. People at the neighbouring tables looked over first with alarm and then smiled at her joy before turning back to their own meals, sending only the odd curious glance in her direction. As she continued to laugh for longer than I thought was necessary, the colour rose in my cheeks at the humour she found in my serious question.

She wiped her eyes with her napkin and attempted to catch her breath. "Ah Grace, you're priceless." She smiled at me fondly.

"Well?" I was serious.

"Well okay—there *were* some violins involved. The Calgary symphony is quite good and we attended concerts while we dated. Obviously there were enough pheromones to have lasted us through years of marriage, but so far, you're the only one who's been struck by lightning." She chuckled again at me. "You should see your face Grace, you look quite depressed. Did I break a bubble?"

"I expected more."

"More?" She chuckled softly and remarked, "Actually, Jim might know something about metaphorical lightning bolts." She smiled at me fondly, willing me to understand, "Not everyone has the same experience even in the same relationship, you know."

The waiter suddenly appeared with our food. Good smells wafted up and I turned my attention to the meal.

"Bright?"

"Yes?"

"I'm still waiting."

She laughed. "Tenacious little thing, aren't you?" She kept slicing and chewing, ignoring my question.

I pondered whether this was the moment, and then suggested, as nonchalantly as I could muster, "Maybe it would be easier if you told me about Alexander."

She raised her head and studied me pensively while she chewed.

I gazed back, fighting to remain calm, though my heart began to thunder in my chest. Minutes passed.

Finally, Bright set down her fork, and picking up her glass of ice water she casually proposed, "Why don't *you* tell me about Alex, Grace?"

Damn. Outmanoeuvred.

I grimaced and looked down at the table.

Bright waited, eating quietly. I could feel her eyes watching me.

I peeked up at her and took a deep breath. "Why does he make me feel so…uh…?" A blush stole into my cheek and Bright smiled.

"Because you're meant to be together."

How could I be meant to be with Alex if I was meant to be with Ben? I blushed more deeply, picturing Alex and I rolling around on my bed.

Bright giggled. "The loves in your life each serve a purpose. Ben will always be there, don't doubt that bond, Grace. Marco is nice guy. It won't hurt to keep him around, too." Something in her tone made it clear that Marco wasn't just going to be hanging around because he wanted to be with me.

"You're suggesting that I can't fire him, eh?"

She smirked, "Exactly."

"And Alex? Can I fire Alex?"

She chuckled a little bawdily, "Do you really *want* to?"

I was shocked. "Auntie Bright!"

She grinned mischievously, "Everyone has a role to play, Grace. You can't make all the decisions. Don't worry about it. Everything is under control."

Except me. I didn't feel at all under control, particularly when Alex was around. She obviously wasn't going to be any help with that.

"What everything? What jobs? Bright, this is so frustrating! I thought you were going to actually tell me something worthwhile."

She looked sympathetic. "I've told you as much as I can tell you now. You have to put the pieces together yourself. Remember: you're the common denominator."

I grimaced and she smiled again. "I promise that if you pay attention, you'll be properly prepared. As soon as you're ready you *will* understand everything." She caught the waiter's eye and nodded. A cheque arrived silently on the table.

Shawn L. Bird

CHAPTER NINE

ENTHUSIASM IS ALWAYS INFECTIOUS

Memories emerge from their past lives, happiness looks from above them.
Time is a circle entwining, laughter and tears in their heaven.
Even for Orpheus, truthfully music requires inspiration;
Charis provides what he's needing. Orpheus gives her elation.

I pondered. I waited for enlightenment. Life went on. I talked to Ben in the evening. I dreamed of Alex at night. I spent my days with Marco. I enjoyed my friends, but I didn't gain the understanding I'd been hoping for. Life was fine. I had fun, but I was missing some link to connect everything, and in the back of my mind, I still worried about Ben.

He didn't let on that he was having a hard time, and I just kept hoping, fervently, that Christie was either wrong, or that his trouble had passed. Not knowing hung above me like a malevolent cloud. Bright watched me with a serious expression.

Then leadership class was handed a project guaranteed to provide ample distraction. I didn't know how we could possibly pull it off, but everyone had embraced the idea with such enthusiasm that here I was, ready to take on the most difficult part of it.

It was a strange request, but I knew that Auntie Bright would be able to deal with it better than anyone else in town could. I don't know whose idea it had been, and I still wasn't sure it wasn't all a hoax, but Bright's reputation was well know, and it'd been unanimous that she was to be brought on side.

I peeped around the corner of the living room and saw her sitting quietly reading. That was unusual. Uncle Jim always had a book around, but I had to stretch my memory back a long time to remember Bright

312

sitting still long enough to read. She looked up at me, and set her book down.

"Hello, Grace." She studied my expression and added, "You look worried."

I sat down beside her on the couch. "Not worried exactly, but slightly irritated. I need your help."

"It's yours. What do you need?"

"The leadership class is doing a community fundraiser with the Senior Centre, and it's a costume ball."

Bright's eyes twinkled in delight at the word. Costumes were her favourite thing.

I continued, "The Senior Centre people have chosen the period of the First World War years. It's a strange time and I'm having trouble figuring out what to wear. Can you help?"

Bright glowed. "Of course. That was a wonderful time for clothes, very transitional. Are you going to be a socialite or a working class person?"

"Why? Does it make much difference?"

"Definitely." She nodded exuberantly. "There were some very distinct movements in dress styles around that period. The opulence and volume of the Victorian era was disappearing, as the huge Victorian skirts came in and hems came up a bit." She rambled on about French heels, Oriental style, Art Nouveau and hobble skirts. Finally, she sighed happily and said, "So—pick your position in society and I'll fashion something stunning for you. We will have you stepping from the pages of history within the week."

I grinned. I wasn't particularly keen on costumed events, but it was nice to be able to make Auntie Bright so happy, and Bright's enthusiasm was always infectious.

By the time the dance came around, Bright had created a glorious costume for me. On the day, we gathered at my house to get dressed. I had chosen to go with an Art Nouveau look, so I had an azure blue dress with fitted straps over the bust, a wide tight waist and then a gold skirt that belled out like a lampshade above the knees. There was an underskirt in the same azure as the bodice that went to mid-calf level, with a slit in the hem for mobility. The dress itself was amazing. There was also a huge silk over-jacket that Bright had handed painted with a smiling woman standing on a shell while a dove flew over her head. "She's Aphrodite, goddess of love," she simply remarked. "It's a good idea for you to honour

313

her as often as possible." To top off the ensemble was a fabulous hat with an ostrich feather. The whole effect was stunning. I felt like a silent movie star. Bright had helped Claire as well, but she had chosen to be a military nurse, so Bright had created her a very authentic looking uniform. We looked like two women from different worlds, and I guess that's what we were representing.

Dave had a military uniform, with puffy hipped jodhpurs and puttees wrapping his shins. Susan was in a dressier outfit with a long fitted cream skirt and a black trimmed cream tunic that almost reached her knees. She had cream and black shoes as well and a huge black hat with giant cream roses and black ostrich feathers. It looked fabulous with her red hair. We looked like time travellers when Bright had finished with us, and we headed off to the Central Senior Centre for their dance. Those in leadership who were also involved in musical theatre were going to be performing some numbers and the rest of us were helping to serve snacks, mingling with the guests and cleaning up.

Dave picked us all up. When we pulled up there were a few antique cars like Model Ts and those of similar vintage. We joined the other guests and workers, draping ourselves over them dramatically or posing primly beside them for photos.

My heart felt as if it was making swoops through my chest as the strains of ragtime music flowed out from the hall. A strange elation filled me and I flowed inside on the bouncing melody. We entered the hall laughing. I immediately felt overcome with a joy that filled me. The man playing the piano was in a black suit with a green trim. His bowler hat added to the ambiance. From the costume books I'd studied with Bright, I recognized he was wearing a minstrel suit such as a vaudeville performer would wear. He had an impressively huge handlebar moustache. Buoyed on his music, I moved into my food station checking that all the drinks and snacks were there and organized for later. My head bobbed and my feet moved to the catchy tunes ringing out from the piano. It flooded me with longing for Ben.

A tiny, white haired lady grinned up at me and asked me to spin in my hobble skirt and vivid butterfly jacket. I extended my arms and turned slowly, noticing that the piano music had changed. It kept the same ragtime bass, but something in the melody seemed familiar. As I pivoted, it became something completely different: it transformed into a romantic melody that it was impossible for me not to recognize. I glanced up to the stage in shock, my mouth agape.

Looking down at me in the minstrel costume, his eyes twinkling above the crazy moustache, was Ben.

"Hello there," he whispered into my head.

314

"Hello," I echoed back silently, stunned.

"Grace?" said Claire, looking at my glossy eyed expression with concern. "Are you okay?"

I smiled, "Yes, I'm wonderful. Do you see the piano player?"

She looked up, and he nodded to her. She looked back at me. "Yeah?"

I sighed happily as I beamed, "It's Ben."

Claire's mouth dropped, and she did a double take to the stage, struggling to find the boy she'd seen in Banff with the person beating on the piano in a handlebar moustache. "No!"

Ben smiled and nodded again at her from the stage while she stared in shock. She looked over to me and asked, "What's he doing *here*?"

I shrugged, "No idea and I don't care. I'm just glad he is." With that, I gave up standing there staring at him and flew onto the stage. I suspected many eyes were following me, but I didn't care. I wrapped my arms around his shoulders. He shrugged my arms over to the side of the piano away from the audience, and removing his left hand from the keys to wrap around me. I bent over, my huge hat blocking us from the audience, and without missing a beat in the music with his right hand, he kissed me warmly. His moustache tickled.

"Very cool fake moustache," I giggled happily.

"Fake?" he remarked in feigned astonishment, "What do you mean, 'fake?' This is one hundred percent real! I take my jobs seriously; I've been working on this baby for a ages!" At the shocked look on my face he laughed. It was amazing me how he could play and talk at the same time.

"It's not real."

He raised his eyebrows, "Oh? Give it a tug."

He couldn't be serious, so I did and he grimaced as he cried, "Hey! Ouch! Careful!"

"It's real?" I gasped.

"Yeah. Like I said." He wiggled his upper lip.

"Why?"

He laughed, "Realism, Hon. Play the part with gusto. Commit to the role. Don't you think it suits the character?"

"Yes, but…" I couldn't think of anything to say, so I just shook my head in bafflement. "Where'd you get the costume?"

"Bright, of course, where else? She's the one who arranged my job here."

Ben gave a nod with his chin to the floor, "Looks like you'd better get back to work; the white hair brigade appears to be a little irritated with you for distracting their piano player."

I looked down to see a few sour expressions brewing, "Yeah. All right." I smiled at him and added, "I'm glad you're here."

"Me, too. Talk to you later."

I took up my snack station again and dutifully served and smiled at the dancers. There was a good mix of the community: seniors, middle aged, and even some teen couples who weren't from leadership. By their amazing dance moves, I presumed that most of them were from the performing group of one of the dance schools. Everyone was sparkling tonight.

Whatever I was doing, my gaze kept being drawn to the stage. I couldn't help devouring Ben with my eyes. Being in his presence was as paradoxical as always, simultaneously calming me and making me hypersensitive.

The musical theatre kids went up on stage to perform a few song and dance numbers, including a very impressive Charleston. They used recorded music, so Ben was free for a while. He came and stood beside me, helping himself to punch and smiling in seductive amusement while I served others and quivered from his proximity. My hands shook as I poured. It was embarrassing.

The Charleston dancers passed us and a girl said, "We've never done that so well! We should dance here more often!"

Her friend had nodded and added, "My sprained ankle doesn't hurt at all."

Ben watched them pass and then turned to me. "That was you, you know."

"Me? Doing what?"

"Making them so good tonight."

I snorted my disbelief. "Yeah, right. And how did I do it? All my hours of choreography work with them?"

He laughed. "I'll take a little of the credit. Your joy is infectious. Look around. Have you ever seen old people dancing with this kind of vigour? You're shining, and you're making everyone else here shine, too."

"You mean you're making them shine."

"No." He shook his head brusquely. "I make you happy, because you love me, but I'm not making them happy. You're doing that. You're radiating joy."

Right. I shook my head. "You're crazy, Ben."

He headed back to the stage, and I watched the seniors. He was right: they were awfully energetic for old people, but I hadn't been to any other seniors' dances, so I had no way of knowing whether that was normal.

I pushed away the thought. I wondered instead how many calories I had burned with my heart pounding and my body shaking for three hours. I felt a little as if I'd been running a marathon. Finally, it was time to clean up, as slowly the dancers filtered away. Ben was helping me carry out bags of garbage to the bin when an old guy who was in a suit that didn't even vaguely match the vintage of the evening waved, "Thanks for your help this evening, kids!"

We grinned and waved back. A Model T was still in the parking lot and Dave called, "Hey Grace, you should pose with Ben! You didn't get any pictures with him!" We positioned ourselves in a variety of poses, telling a romantic story with a flower from Susan's hat and the car as props. It felt strangely familiar in a surreal way. When we had a dozen shots or so, I flicked through Dave's digital camera at the photos and felt the oddest sensation of déjà vu.

Ben was watching over my shoulder and squeezed my shoulder fondly. "They're good. Thanks Dave."

Dave nodded, "I'll email them to you Grace." Then he looked meaningfully at his car, "So are you both coming with me?" He was clearly pondering seat belts. "We'll have to squish."

Ben shook his head, "No, thanks, I've got a car here, so I can take Grace home."

Ben had a car here? We said our good-byes to the gang who looked very anachronistic in their vintage clothes climbing into Dave's Subaru wagon. Ben took my hand and led me behind the building where I saw Jim's BMW tucked away behind the building. "Jim let you drive his million dollar car?" I whispered in surprise.

He chuckled, "Bright made him. You should have seen his face."

I could imagine. I didn't know exactly what the car was worth, but it was Jim's baby. I couldn't believe he'd let it out of his sight.

Ben added, "She said that Fatima would stand out too much, and it was logical that I take his car." He laughed as he opened the passenger door for me. "Bright can charm a meow out of a Rottweiler. Like you, actually." He grinned at me. "Poor Jim had no chance against her."

Being sparkly turquoise and studded with jewels did make anything much harder to camouflage. A staid silver grey tended to blend. I chuckled, imagining Jim's chagrin over Bright lending his baby, as Ben walked around to climb into the driver seat.

"So," he said, as he started the engine, "what are we going to do for the rest of the evening?"

"Go home to change first of all. Where are you staying?"

317

He grinned and waggled an eyebrow with obvious meaning as he said, "At your place."

My breath stopped. I know my eyes got huge as I stared over at him, imagining how that was going to work. Would we be chaperoned within an inch of our lives, or would we be able take advantage of the situation? I really wanted to take advantage all of a sudden.

Ben grinned, and I knew he'd been spying in my thoughts. I blushed. He glanced over and patted my knee sympathetically. "Sorry love. I try to give you some privacy, but I completely relate to that particular thought." My blush deepened and he laughed aloud as we pulled into the driveway. "You'd better clear those impure thoughts from your head or Bright will drive me to a hotel in Kamloops."

As he came around to open my door, I wondered if he realized that he'd just made a huge slip. Bright *could* read minds. I knew it. I set my lips grimly and concentrated on happy thoughts. Grimly happy. I was an oxymoron.

Before we'd even reached the door, Bright had it open and was giving me an enthusiastic hug. "Well?" She said, pushing me out to arms' length with her hands on my shoulders, "Was it a good surprise?"

I laughed, "Yes. Definitely. Thanks for arranging it, Auntie Bright."

She beamed as she gave Ben a warm hug, too. "I guess you two plan to change out of your stunning clothes into something boring and then to go out for the rest of the evening?" she asked.

I nodded before heading up the stairs to my room. Half way up I paused to ask, "Auntie Bright, where is Ben sleeping?"

She paused for a moment before she said firmly, "Not where you're imagining him, my girl!" I blushed again and turned around rapidly.

"Hey! I didn't say…"

She looked abashed and just said, "Be sure to put everything on hangers, please," as she turned and headed toward the kitchen.

I looked down on Ben, by now my face was glowing scarlet. He was just standing there grinning in amusement. "Don't blame her. The time will come. Can you imagine how many rules she's breaking letting me come here? Do you know what your mom will do when she finds out?"

I shivered a little, imagining *that* conversation. I would probably be able to hear my mother screaming from Greece. "Yeah. I guess. Are jeans okay? You didn't want to go out to dinner or anything?"

"No, that'll be fine. We'll see who's faster. On your mark, get set, go!" We sprinted in opposite directions. I raced almost against my will. It was childish, but it was as if those words were pre-programmed to force the competitive nature to erupt.

Miraculously, I beat him. So much for girls taking too long to get ready. I had pulled off the hat, jacket, dress, nylons and shoes and then slipped on a tank, hoodie, pulled up my jeans, and slipped into clogs. It had taken me under two minutes. My hair was still in finger waves, just to keep a little anachronism. I wasn't exactly a fashion plate, but I would be warm and comfortable at whatever we ended up doing.

Ben emerged a full five minutes after me dressed in jeans, a t-shirt and a tan suede jacket. His hair was damp from his shower and his moustache was gone. His lip looked paler than the rest of his face that had gotten a bit more sun in the last few weeks. My eyes could not leave him as he sauntered toward me like a model. He had gotten so gorgeous in the last year; it was hard to believe he was the same boy I'd met in the band room a year and a half ago. His hair had gone from a nondescript light brown to a dazzling golden. His shoulders had broadened, and his jaw line had become more defined. How was it possible?

He returned my admiring gaze with a sultry smile, wrapped his arm around my shoulder and kissed me gently. "Let's go get some privacy," he whispered, and a tingle travelled slowly down my back and lodged at the base of my spine, burning.

Bright coughed in the kitchen. I wondered whether she had heard.

We took Jim's BMW again and drove to the wharf. We parked in the circle above the low water and strolled the length of the long wooden structure, holding hands, nodding to other walkers, and looking at the reflection of the city lights twinkling in the lake.

"How long are you here for?" I whispered, breaking the silence.

"Not long enough," he sighed.

I searched in his mind for the specifics he wasn't uttering aloud. I felt his reticence, but gave the barrier a push. Ah. There it was. Just two days. I echoed his sigh, slightly smug for pushing through to get a thought he'd been hesitant to share. Maybe I was getting better at this whole mind-reading thing.

Ben pulled me close and wrapped an arm around my waist. While we stood together watching the water, I wondered idly whether it really was better to have a few moments of Ben's glorious presence and to suffer so greatly when the inevitable separation came, or whether I was better off just holding him at a distance until we could really be together. He squeezed me again, and I knew he understood the dilemma. We listened to the lapping of the water on the posts below us and the squawk of gulls.

Suddenly I felt electricity in the air. It wasn't the power of a lightning strike, but it was powerful in its own way. I stiffened instinctively.

"What?" Ben said, stepping back and looking at me in confusion, "What is it?"

"Can't you tell?" I was flooding with heat and I could sense the pull toward the park. It took all my concentration to focus on staying calm beside Ben.

He shook his head with curious concern. "Is it okay? What's going on?"

I shrugged. "It's Alex. He's here somewhere."

"Alex." His lips tightened.

"You okay?" I asked quietly.

He tightened his hold around my waist. "Where is he?"

Weird that Ben couldn't sense Alex when my whole body was straining toward him. I tilted my head to the parking area. "He's back there."

"Does he know you're here?"

"I don't know. Probably, I guess."

"Huh." He pondered that for a while before he added, "Does he know I'm here?"

"I don't know that. I don't know anything he thinks." I looked up to meet his sorrowful eyes and reminded him, "I'm not connected to him like I'm connected to you."

He leaned down and kissed me softly on the forehead. Apparently, lack of telepathy was a consolation for having his girlfriend lust after someone else. I wasn't connected to Alex with my mind or heart, but my body was a different matter.

We turned together and started strolling back up the wharf. My body was burning and yearning toward the park where I could sense Alex waiting for me. Paradoxically, while I ached to burst out running, the thought was also repellent. My body was a curse. I fought against the sensation of physical desire drawing me to Alex as I walked slowly with Ben, my thumb hooked into a belt loop on his jeans, breathing slowly, willing my blood to pulse slowly.

We reached the end of the wharf and stepped onto the cement sidewalk. I allowed myself to look up and find Alex. He was sitting on the steps of the bandstand gazebo, watching us.

The pull was even stronger and I took a deep quivering breath as I steeled myself against it. Ben tightened his grip around my waist again, and looked around at the people in the park until he spotted Alex's focused stare. He nodded to him and my heart started to pound. I wondered if they would fight.

Alex continued to stare but he dropped his chin ever so slightly to Ben's acknowledgement.

"Let's go." I wasn't sure whether Ben spoke aloud or in my head, but I allowed him to lead me to the car, and slipped in silently as he opened my door. I could feel Alex's eyes still burrowing into the back of my head. I wanted to go to him even while I was sitting beside my dearest love. It was so perverse.

As we pulled out of the roadway and headed back home, I suddenly felt overwhelmingly exhausted. The long school day, the dressing up, the dance, Ben's arrival and now this incident with Alex: it was too much. I was shaking. Ben looked over and rested his right hand on my thigh. "I'm sorry, Grace."

"What are *you* sorry for?" I was the one craving someone else's body while I was with the one I loved most. I was the one who should be apologizing.

Too late, I realized that thinking that thought gave it to him. I glanced down in disgust with myself. We pulled into the driveway and just sat there for a moment, before he reached over and raised my chin so he could look into my eyes. They were mournful eyes. My thoughts were hurting him. My self-loathing intensified and he pulled me closer. "It's not your fault, Grace. I know that." His understanding was more than I could bear and the tears began then, raining into puddles down his back.

I was the common denominator in all my life experiences.

I don't know how long we'd been sitting there absolutely still, while I wept on him, before he pulled back, tenderly kissed each eyelid, and then stretched back onto the driver's seat. When I looked up at him, he whispered fondly, "You have the reddest nose I've ever seen. It's absolutely adorable." He leaned over and kissed the tip of my nose before he pushed back and opened his door. "Come on kiddo, enough of this. Time to enjoy being together. We don't have enough time to waste any of it on sadness."

He stepped around and opened my door for me. He was the only boy I'd ever known who was that chivalrous. Well, almost the only boy. A vision of Josh's grin flashed into my head. Dear Josh. He'd been so sweet in Calgary. Had Eris made him so menacing? Was it my fault for rejecting his affection? Where was he now? Was he safe?

Ben glanced over to me kindly and squeezed my hand. "I'm sure he's okay, Grace."

I still wasn't used to that. Someday I was going to have to learn to block him from my every thought. It'd be kinder if he didn't know everything I was thinking.

He squeezed my hand again and smiled gently.

Torturing him wasn't fair. If I got thinking about... No. I imagined a wall in my mind and stepped behind it. I imagined Ben in a soundproof booth, surrounded by water. I needed a safe test. Hmm. I looked over at him as I thought, 'Kiss me, Ben. Right now. Turn around and kiss me!' If he heard me think that I'd know.

He didn't react at all.

I *was* getting better at this mind-reading thing.

We walked through the front door to see Bright and Jim sitting in the living room, each reading. We joined them, hand in hand, and settled on the floor in front of the red chesterfield so we didn't have to separate. Bright studied us carefully and her lips tightened. She looked over at Jim and casually suggested, "Jim, why don't you take Ben down to your recording studio?"

I looked up in surprise. Jim had a recording studio?

Uncle Jim stood up with a smile and raised his hand to indicate Ben should follow him down the stairs. "Come to the Man Cave, Ben. Join the fraternity of music making men."

Ben laughed and allowed himself to be coaxed away with only the smallest apologetic grin to me. He couldn't resist the lure of a studio.

I looked over to where Bright was sitting, pretending to read.

"Since when has there been a recording studio in the Man Cave?" I asked with studied casualness. I'd been living in the house for four months, and coming here summers for years, and I'd never heard an inkling of the existence of a recording studio in the house.

She shrugged, "It's a Man Cave thing. You don't get invited unless you have a Y chromosome. Don't worry about it."

Huh.

She stood up suddenly and glanced over her shoulder. "I think I'll make a pot of tea. You want to come?"

Again, an invitation that was really a request. I followed behind her and sat down at the kitchen table. While she puttered around getting the tea ready, I looked out at the spectacular view of the lake glistening with the city lights. She set the teacups on the table, and then returned with the teapot. She sat down at the end of the table and looked at me for a minute before she picked up the pot. "I've already put the stevia in the pot."

"Good, thanks."

I sipped. The tea was a fruity herbal concoction; likely, from dried bits and pieces she'd harvested herself. "What is it?" I asked quizzically.

"Rose hip, orange and peach. Do you like it? The peaches and rose hips are from our garden."

I smiled to myself as I stared out at the lake again waiting for whatever she was going to say. Was it going to be a lecture on safe sex? Some lesson on the need to be kind, because boys are really just as fragile and confused as girls in the matters of romance?

She surprised me again.

She set her teacup down with a determined clunk and faced me. "You were right the other day at the restaurant."

"Pardon?"

"You were right. It is time to talk about Alex."

"Oh."

She leaned back in the chair and looked out over the lake view, shades of black and midnight blue sprinkled with glimmering pinpricks of light. Finally, she took a deep breath and said, "You did well tonight to resist the draw." I didn't bother to wonder how she'd known.

"Ben was crushed."

"Yes, of course he would be, because he's the reason Alex is here. He'll be feeling inadequate."

"Why? What did Ben ever do wrong?"

She shook her head, and thought for a moment before she said, "An Alex is a necessary evil, because sometimes a guardian with additional strengths is needed."

"*An* Alex?"

She smiled. "Alexanders are special protectors, Grace. They receive special training and they are probably the most important members of the family."

"Are they always so..." I paused, searching for the right word, "well, are they always quite so *magnetic*?" I flushed with embarrassment, remembering his over the shoulder look as he had tried to entice me toward my bedroom.

She laughed, "Yes. Usually they have to be. It serves an important purpose to have the guardian and his charge linked. It is rather elemental, isn't it?" She shook her head chuckling softly. "It's hard to be aware of much else when an Alex is in the room, no matter how big the space is. You'd know where he was every moment even in a football stadium."

"Bright?"

She looked up. "Yes?"

"Why is he guarding me?" I was confused.

"Can you think of nothing you need guarding against?"

"I don't know the black haired guy."

"Aside from him. You've read the papers. Think."

"I have no idea," but as I muttered it, an idea hit me, "Oh!"

Bright looked at me with her eyebrows raised expectantly.

"Not the Sasquatch?"

She nodded, "For one, yes."

My eyes widened in shock as the thought formulated in my brain. "Why is a Sasquatch after me?"

"Well, it's not *exactly* a Sasquatch." She continued watching me carefully.

"Not a Sasquatch?"

"Grace, I'm not sure you're ready to hear everything. I don't want to freak you out."

"Bright, you've just told me a giant Sasquatch-like creature that is not actually a Sasquatch is after me. Me. Grace. A little nobody who's spent her whole life in Calgary or Salmon Arm. Boring little me apparently has a special protector guarding me from Sasquatch attack, and no doubt also from men with knives, sadistic drivers, and boaters. You think I'm not already freaking out?"

She laughed, and draped an arm around me. "You have a point. This is not easy stuff, Grace. If you are actually freaking out, you're holding yourself together amazingly well. That suggests you will be able to bear it all." She sighed then, placing her hands on my shoulders and turning me to face her. "There's a whole world out there that you've always belonged to, but you don't know it.

"It's a lot easier not to know about it. I don't relish being the one to tell you about everything. I am not sure you'll be happier knowing. A little confusion can be eminently easier to live with than overwhelming certainty." She studied my eyes carefully, obviously trying to decide whether she was going to enlighten me. She shook her head suddenly. "You need to know, Grace, but I just don't think it's my place to be the one to tell you. I think perhaps it's time for us to see your mother."

"My mom?"

She nodded. "Yes. I'll email Blythe and she'll probably be here within forty-eight hours. Can you wait until then?"

I nodded, "Yeah, I suppose so, but can you answer one question?"

"I'll try."

"You said that Alexanders are 'the most important of the family,' right?"

"Yes."

"Whose family?"

"Our family."

I cringed. "So does that mean I'm *related* to Alex?"

She smiled in understanding. "Ah, I see. Yes you are, but distantly, not incestuously."

I cringed again. Bright smiled fondly at me.

"Grace, you really need to wait for your mother. She's the responsible one. She'll be able to explain it better than I can. Maybe she'll bring your Aunt Aglaea along, and that will be even better. You just have to be patient for a little long. It's okay. You'll be fine." She gave me a hug. "I promise, Grace."

I looked at her doubtfully.

"You should be glad. It's finally the time when you *need to know*, Grace."

I didn't laugh at her joke.

CHAPTER TEN

CRAZY WORLD WE LIVE IN, EH?

No matter how sadly they've ended, past loves are precious forever.
Hearts travel round us eternally. Charites three come together,
Working out peaceful transitions; Thalia, trusting Euphrosyne,
Knows with Aglaea they'll strengthen her: sisters in labour and destiny.

There was a danger in summoning my mother with Ben in the house, and that didn't escape me. I didn't want to rush him away, so Auntie Bright agreed to hold off her call until after he'd gone. We agreed to keep his visit quiet. I suspected that my mom was going to figure it out soon enough, but I was counting on the Alex thing to distract her.

While I tried not to think about that coming disaster, I focused on keeping Ben in my sight. It proved interesting, because now that he knew there was a recording studio in the house he seemed to want to spend a lot of time down in the Man Cave, and Uncle Jim seemed only too willing to let him.

Bright smiled at me, "Go down with them, Grace. He needs you."

"What can I do?"

"Just being there will help, but why don't you see what happens if you try to be inspiring?"

"How am I supposed to do that?"

She laughed, and the melody of it instantly made me feel happier. Her eyes twinkled as she watched my growing awareness of the correlation. "Exactly. Let him feel the love. Watch what happens."

So I went into the room and watched discreetly from the corner for a while. Once they seemed settled, I let my mind wander. I remembered all the times I'd been in his arms. I thought about every kiss he'd given me. I let my mind release the present and reach for the visions that came in my dreams. If those people through history had been us, then I would bring them, too.

Jim looked over at Ben, adjusting his headphones and reaching for a knob. "That's amazing! How are you doing that?"

Ben glanced over to me and tilted his head.

I shrugged non-committally. Then I put him in my mind's soundproof booth, bricked in my metaphorical wall and stood behind it jumping in the joy of my achievement.

Ben's brows went down as he looked over to me. "Grace? Are you okay?"

I grinned. I dropped the wall and sent him love. "I'm going to help Bright with dinner."

As I came into the kitchen Bright grinned at me, "Well?"

"I'm good." I said.

She laughed. "Yes, you are. Keep it up. You're going to see magic happen around you."

So Bright had known that I was the answer to Ben's writer's block. I was pretty sure that she had deliberately brought him here, set him up in the recording studio and freed me up to sit around and be his inspiration again. It was rather contrived, but for the rest of the week Ben seemed to be composing like a mad fiend, so how was I supposed to be upset with that? I was able to be with him. I hoped Christie would see a difference if she ran into him next week. Next week. Next week he'd be in Calgary. Next week we'd be apart again. The thought compressed my heart. I tried not to think about it.

For the next two days, he played music and I watched, pouring love out to him. Knowing that I was making a different made me feel powerful. I felt like my life couldn't be more perfect, but all too soon we were piling into the BMW and Jim was driving me to see Ben off at the Kelowna Airport.

I snuggled up under Ben's arm as he worked through the check in line. "Can I come in your suitcase?"

He laughed softly and pulled me closer, "I think the airport security might have some issue with that, though it's okay with me if you want to try."

I watched glumly as he went through security and then Jim and I sat on the grass by the parking lot watching the sky and waving until the plane disappeared from sight. I felt like my heart had been taken on board and was unravelling along the white vapour trail.

"It's so weird," I muttered. "He seems to get more handsome every time I see him."

Jim nodded. "Of course. He is."

"What?"

"People always grow more beautiful as we love them."

I pondered that as I watched the plane, listening to Ben humming his farewell to me.

"Ready?" Jim finally whispered, as the dot of the plane disappeared.

I nodded and climbed silently into the car, heavy with melancholy.

As we drove home to Salmon Arm Jim turned on his favourite recording of Goldberg Variations and hummed along, his fingers twitching on the steering wheel. I kept hearing snatches of Ben's music in my head between the Bach, and tried not to weep at the emptiness creeping through my consciousness.

When we pulled up to the house an hour later, Jim said, "Gracie, I'm just going to drop you off; I have to go run some errands. Tell Bright I'll be back by eight, all right?"

"Yeah, sure," I said with a little wave as I grabbed my purse. I watched the car drive away and then patted Fatima on my way inside.

When I walked into the house, I heard a strange, otherworldly music. It was scratchy, ancient, strange, and distant. It was haunting, like listening to a ghost. I shut the door behind me and looked into the living room to see Bright sitting cross-legged on the floor, tears streaming down her face. The sight froze me. This was beyond sad, this was mourning. I didn't want to intrude on her grief, so I went to creep past the doorway to sneak up the stairs, but she heard my footfall, and opened her eyes.

She smiled weakly at me, and closed her eyes again.

I felt an overwhelming urge to comfort her. I stood hesitated a moment at the doorway, before I crept quietly into the room, and lowered myself into the same position, to be her companion in grief.

We sat for a long time, neither moving, until the scratchy music faded away, and she opened her eyes slowly. Still immersed in her sadness, she smiled fondly at me, reaching out to rest a hand on mine.

"Thank you, Grace."

"Are you all right?"

She nodded. "Yes, I'm just indulging in some memories of my Umed. Today is an anniversary…" Her voice trailed off.

"Oh." So long after. I paused, considering whether it was fair to ask her the question, but feeling oddly compelled to know the answer. "Auntie Bright?"

"Hmm?" she raised her eyes to mine.

I whispered, painfully, "Still? Even after all this time with Uncle Jim?"

She understood more than I said. She smiled faintly as she nodded. "I love Jim deeply, but love has many guises. He is everything I need and I'm better in all ways because of him, but sometimes we leave little bits of ourselves in our past, no matter what joys our present gives us." She shrugged feebly.

"Grace, in our job we're supposed to be impartial, egalitarian. We are usually quite successful, but there always the danger that some can sneak through our defences. So many just need a little of us to reach their potential: just a little more inspiration, just a little extra confidence in themselves and they are able to do amazing things. Others need us so much more or perhaps relish us so much more, that in pouring ourselves into their dreams and rejoicing with their successes we can become too attached, like nurses falling in love with the patients who worship them as the saviours who rescued them when they were at their weakest. Sometimes love works out. Sometimes it doesn't. When that kind of attachment happens to us, we risk losing our calling, amid our personal joy. We walk a tightrope all the time.

"I made the mistake of falling in love with him." She sighed and shook her head sadly. "In all those millennia, he was the only one I ever let slip through." She paused and looked into the past. "I was warned to guard my heart, but I was so sure of his devotion." She tightened her lips sadly and shrugged, staring for a moment. "I didn't realize adoration isn't the only important component for a successful relationship."

She glanced over at me. "Have you heard how the archaeologists have excavated three thousand year old honey from within the pyramids?"

I nodded and whispered, "Yes, they discovered it was still perfect, because bacteria don't grow on honey."

"Exactly. Like ancient honey, a first love remains ever incorruptible despite the passage of time. Though the boy may no longer exist, the memory of him is always pure and sweet." She gazed at me thoughtfully for a moment, and then closed her eyes again.

"Umed was to me like your Ben is to you, but I did not get to stay with him through time. He chose to take a different path and he was lost to me. The decision was right. At times I looked in on him after we parted, though he never knew." She glanced up at me sheepishly. "At times I saw that he wasn't happy, and I knew that, even though his wife loved him wholly for a time, he would have been completely fulfilled in my devotion for all time. His joy would have flown on the wings of the music he would have made. Instead, he toiled miserably and shrank into a broken egg. She was only briefly his wife, and then she was the mother of his children. They had so many children—I lost track of how many—and they became her only joy. She loved each of them equally, and him less and less. They encompassed her world; he became a tool for them to succeed as his family had ordained. He played his role at cost to himself. He sacrificed happiness for family duty. He was faithful to his vows, but while he appreciated his wife for her devotion to their children, he needed that kind of adoration himself. I don't think she was capable of adoring him." She sighed deeply again and sniffed back a tear. "He had made his choice. I grieved knowing what he would have been with me—the joy we would have had. He loved her; he stayed with her, but he never knew the joy or the music he'd have known with me. That's my greatest grief: that the world lost what he could have achieved...." Her voice trailed off and she sighed. "In my head, I *know* it was the decision he had to make. I had wondered if perhaps we might have another lifetime to try again, but it was not ordained. Perhaps someday he'll return as a nightingale and then he'll live for music as he should have." Her melancholy smile at this thought twisted my heart. "I know he didn't regret leaving me, even at his unhappiest, but I have found over the years," her voice dropped to a whisper of sadness, "that the heart never forgets its first awakening."

I was surprised to hear her talk so matter-of-factly about ideas like reincarnation, but then Bright never did what was expected. I considered her sad heart and the parallels she saw in my relationship with Ben until I realised what it probably meant. She was sorry for me. She wanted to protect me from her pain. "So that's why you let Ben come?"

She smiled softly. "Partly. Also, because he really does need you right now. Your mother should have understood that you have a role to play in his success. She forgot our professional priorities in her personal concern for your safety."

"Your professional priorities?"

"Mine. Yours. We're inspirational, Grace. People need us."

"But Mom doesn't think I'm safe with Ben?"

She sighed very deeply and thought for a moment before she replied carefully, "Ben himself is not a physical danger to you."

"But?"

She nodded, "But... Oh, Grace. Our hearts can be such fragile things, and eternity is a long time to mourn." She reached over and gave me a hug. "Just enjoy him while he's around, okay?"

I stared at her earnest face. I wondered if I would ever feel the depth of loss that she imagined would last eternally. *Ben was not a physical danger* she'd said. What other kind of danger was there? "I will cherish every moment of his visit, I promise, but I need to know," my tone became serious, "*what* is the danger, Bright?"

She shook her head. "Cherish the moment, Grace. Cherish every moment you can." She reached over to the c.d. player and hit play. The scratchy music filled the room again. It was as if heard from a distance, with a staticky wave rolling around and around, louder than the music below it. I was dismissed.

"Bright?"

"Mm?" She already sounded distant herself.

"Why is this music so scratchy and ancient sounding?"

She closed her eyes again, "Because it's a recording from a series of early Edison wax cylinders." I could feel her wishing me away.

"A wax cylinder?"

Her voice was even softer. "Yes. The first phonographs played cylinders rather than disks."

"Oh?" An eerie thought occurred to me. I asked quietly, almost fearfully, "Umm. When were cylinder recordings made?"

She smiled faintly and replied in a whisper, "These were made in 1889." Her face took on a lost quality. She had entered the music completely.

I waited while the ghostly music continued, afraid to ask the question that churned in my brain. That was a ghost playing over a century ago. It couldn't be possible, could it? Bright was silent and still. I watched her melancholy face and I had to know. When the last song finally faded away again, I whispered in a shaky voice, "Is that *Umed* playing, Auntie Bright?"

She didn't say anything, but as her eyes filled with tears again, I understood. She hadn't been metaphorical when she'd said that in all those *millennia* he'd been the only one to slip through her defences.

My life was far more complicated than I had ever imagined.

When I got back from school on Tuesday, I heard a familiar ring of laughter and realized that my mom and Aunt Aglaea had arrived. I took a deep breath before I walked into the kitchen.

"Hi, Honey!" Mom smiled and came over to give me a hug. "How are you doing?" She looked a little travel worn from her journey from Greece, but she looked happier than I had seen her in a long time.

"I'm okay." I shrugged. She looked at me dubiously.

Aunt Aglaea walked over to me and kissed me on both cheeks in her formal European way. She did not look travel worn. She looked like she

331

was stepping out of the pages of a French fashion magazine. As usual. Without a word, she studied me appraisingly for a moment before she glanced over her shoulder at Bright and in her crisp voice said, "Yes. You were right to call us. It's time."

My heart started thumping in my breast and my breathing got all quivery.

Aunt Aglaea spun on her heels and started to walk into the living room, turning her head to me and demanding, "Come." No preamble. Straight to the point. Aglaea was all business, as usual.

I glanced rather fearfully over to my mom who'd gone back to the table and was standing behind Bright's chair. Bright looked sympathetic. My mom looked... hmm... hesitant, maybe? Or perhaps worried. This was not reassuring. "Are you guys coming?" I asked them quietly.

Mom shook her head with a wistful expression, but Bright pursed her lips and snarled quietly, "Aglaea doesn't think it's a good idea."

Mom smacked her in the arm, "Bright! Shhh."

I smiled at Bright, appreciating her support.

"Grace. I am waiting," Aglaea called from the living room.

I glanced over my shoulder in her general direction and then looked plaintively back at Mom and Bright. Bright gave me a little nod of encouragement as I turned, straightened up my shoulders, took a deep breath, and stepped into the living room.

Aglaea was sitting primly on the edge of the loveseat looking perfect. She nodded imperiously toward the couch.

I sat.

"What do you know about Ben?" she asked without preamble.

"Ben?"

"Don't be obtuse, Grace. Don't repeat after me. Answer my questions."

I blushed angrily, but didn't respond.

"What do you know about him?" she repeated insistently.

I glared at her, and she raised her eyebrows at me. She was being condescending and it was irritating, but no one argued with Aglaea. Ever. I took a breath and said, "I know that I love him. I know that he loves me."

"Yes." She nodded. "Why do you think that is?"

What a stupid question. I shrugged my shoulders and wrinkled my brow. "How do I know?"

"Think please." Her tone had gentled somewhat.

"Well, the first thing I remember was being amazed by his music."

She nodded, "Yes, and then?"

"Then he was… I don't know… I guess he was attentive and adoring, and it was hard to ignore him."

"Right.

"Can you describe the feeling you get around him?"

I sighed. There were so many feelings. I thought for a while, and she waited patiently, knowing, I suppose, that I wasn't ignoring her this time, but that I was actually trying to answer. "It's a bit of a mix." I said quietly. "At first it was confusion; I couldn't figure out anything and being around him turned me inside out." I glanced up at her and she was nodding in understanding. She looked a little softer. "Now I guess the main feeling is comfort. I feel secure with him. Safe. Loved."

She nodded. "Very good."

I wondered what was so important about me being able to analyze my feelings for Ben. Was she going to make me analyze my confusing attraction to Alex next? I studied my fingernails for a moment, thinking that it was time for a nail file. I glanced automatically to Aglaea's impeccable manicure. I sighed; I would never be as perfect as she is in anything I did.

Bright came into the room then and sat down beside me. She took my hand and squeezed it. She gave Aglaea a look that was part challenge, part irritation, and then she looked at me, staring deeply into my eyes.

I lost myself in the warm brown of her gaze as she squeezed my hand again and spoke to me in a soothing voice, "Grace, first love is monolithic. It's all encompassing. It fills every part of you until it seems like you're made of love."

I nodded, understanding the sensation very well.

"In your case, it's even more profound than that, because what you feel for Ben is not only first love, but old love."

"Huh?" This was just what I needed, more paradox in my life.

She laughed fondly, "You and Ben have grown old together many, many times, so even though you're feeling overwhelmed right now with the newness of the love in this place and in this time, you're confused because it's *not* new. This has all happened for you and Ben many times before. That means you are also like an old married couple, comfortable and at ease with one another. Haven't you sensed that?"

I thought about that and I nodded slowly. That explained the strange sense that I knew him better than I knew myself, that I'd known him forever. Whenever I had been able to get over the freaking out parts of Ben's odd pronouncements of his adoration, it had always been beyond comfortable. I looked up at Bright in astonished awe, "It was weird for me, because I never understood what was happening when I was around him, but I always felt like he did. He always treated me like he knew me so well, even when I didn't know who he was."

She nodded in agreement. "Of course. He did know you."

My mom came in then and sat beside Aglaea who scowled at her as she was bounced on the loveseat. She re-adjusted her position until she looked impeccable again.

I remembered all Ben's cryptic comments and suddenly they all made sense. Sense. Ha. As if *any* of his made *sense*. I was in someone's fantasy novel. I looked into Bright's sincere eyes and asked the next inevitable question in a whisper, "Why did he seem to remember so well, when I didn't remember at all?"

Bright looked over at Aglaea.

Aglaea gave a curt nod. Apparently Bright was finally allowed to give me information.

Bright looked thoughtful for a moment as she figured out what to say. I held my breath. Finally, she said, "Ben has already been... well, I guess the best word would be 'activated.'"

"Huh?" I glanced between Bright beside me and my mom and Aglaea across the room. Aglaea was scowling again. Strange how she managed to look like she was on the cover of an haute couture magazine when she did that.

Bright laughed. "You know in the movies how countries send sleeper cell spies who just live normal lives, building connections and just fitting in until such a time as they are called upon to start actively spying or fighting?"

I giggled somewhat incredulously. "Yeah?"

"Well, until recently you were both like sleepers. Ben was basically oblivious like you to what he was until the time he was activated as a protector. As soon as he was called upon, he went to Olympus, and during the ceremonies there, he received all the memories back. Usually they just give the memories that would help to do the job well, but Ben's feelings for you are so intense, they couldn't be minimized."

I tried to absorb this information. I'm a *sleeper spy*? This was insane. For whom was I going to be spying? I felt no other national loyalties. What tools would be used to wake me and set me on the path for which I'd been ordained? It was too much to consider. I had more pressing curiosities. I asked the question that came instantly to mind, "So if I am going to be activated, will I get all my memories of Ben back?"

She looked at me sadly, biting her lip as she pondered. "Actually, there is some discussion about that."

"Discussion? With whom?"

"Ah…" She seemed at a loss for a moment, until she grinned and said, "Head office." Her eyes twinkled in amusement.

"Bright," Aglaea warned in a sharp tone, but we ignored her.

"Some head office is discussing me…" I prompted.

"Yes. They are wondering whether you *should* be given your memories back." She looked over to Aglaea.

"Why wouldn't I?"

"You only get the memories if they help you do the job you need to do." Aglaea answered. "There was some concern that your memories will impede your success at your task…" her voice trailed off.

"What?"

She sighed, and my mom interjected, "I think it's too late. Just being with Ben has started you remembering, hasn't it? I think you've been dreaming about him, haven't you?"

I gazed down, flashing through all the dreams and visions I'd had about him. I had had so many dreams about Ben. I nodded, but then my eyes grew large as I realized what she meant. "Those were actual *memories*?"

She nodded.

"I'd thought I was just imagining things." I was suddenly overwhelmed by the sheer volume of times and places I'd seen. "Wow."

Bright smiled softly at me, studying me carefully for any sign that I wasn't coping with all of this insanity.

While she watched me, I felt like my brain unlocked. With a click, visions flashed before me: Ben and I wearing different faces in many times and places. They went back farther and farther in time until I began to have trouble breathing. I had begun to hyperventilate when Bright put her arm gently on my shoulder.

She smiled gently, and eyes glowing with concern she asked, "Are you okay?"

I gasped, shaking my head, fighting for breath. I put my head between my knees, concentrating hard on breathing deeply. I sounded choppy as my breath rasped in and out and I fought not to throw up or pass out.

She continued rubbing my back while she waited for me to recover myself. "Okay yet?"

My voice came out cracked. I was overwhelmed with the visions, "How *old* am I?" I looked between the three of them with wide eyes.

"How old do you think you are?" asked my mom.

"Old."

"Yes." She nodded.

"*Really* old?"

She smiled, but didn't add any comment.

I thought of the images I'd seen in my head and calculated backwards. "One thousand?"

She shook her head with a bemused expression that I understood, incredibly, to mean one thousand was too young. One *thousand* years old was too *young* for me!

My voice shook as I suggested, "Two?"

She kept smiling, tilting her head to the side as an encouragement to continue counting.

I gulped. "Three?" looking over at Bright this time.

"Close enough." Her smile was gentle.

I collapsed into the chair, my head swimming. Three thousand years old? Oh my. I looked up at Bright and asked, "How long have I known Ben?"

She grinned in amusement and chuckled, "Oh, say, since you were two thousand ninety or so…" She laughed outright at the look of shock on my face. She rubbed my shoulders briskly. "It's okay Grace. It's a wonderful thing."

It says a lot about the insanity of my experiences lately that it didn't even occur to me not to believe what she was saying. As absolutely crazy as it was to even imagine any of it, it also made complete and absolute sense to me. I sat there letting the million thoughts brewing in my brain settle into some order before I asked, "Does this mean that I am being activated now?" I shook my head to try to clear a bit of room for thoughts of the present. The past was pressing all around me. "Didn't you say that I would need to be activated in order to remember? I seem to be recalling an awful lot at the moment."

Her look was tender as she smiled at me. "Ben kind of bypassed the regular rules. I think he knew what was being planned this time, and he didn't want to miss life with you. He started the process of opening up your memories, which is how he got in trouble." She added mischievously, "Now I've helped things along as well, which could be problematic." She didn't look like she was too worried about it. "Since you've come to your memories on your own, I hope they'll just let you be."

I smiled. "Really? So I'll get to be with Ben after all?"

"We can hope so. I think it would be the most logical thing, but then," she grimaced and a vague look of concern furrowed her eyebrows as she glanced at Aglaea, "Head office isn't always known for being the most logical place. It all depends on the boss's state of mind when it's time for the decision to be made." Her voice lowered to a confidential whisper as she added, "He tends to be governed by passions rather than common sense."

I thought about that. Some crazy head office manager with a temper. Weird. Then I remembered something else she'd said, "So, you said Ben was activated on Olympus, right?"

She nodded. I glanced over to Aglaea and mom watching from the loveseat.

"Mount Olympus? Like in Greece?"

"Yes, usually Greece," said Aglaea.

Mom grinned and added, "But thankfully a couple hundred years ago they decided to set up what I guess you could call a branch office in North America, and we have a Mount Olympus here as well."

"We do?"

"Well, it's not here in Canada; it's just over the border from us in Washington State. It works very well for our purposes. It's much easier to get away for a weekend there than to travel to Greece, at least in the warmer seasons. In January one tends to feel the trip to Greece is the better choice!" She laughed.

"That's why we had to go to Seattle at Christmas." Ah. I looked at Bright who nodded in affirmation.

"This is crazy." I shook my head.

She laughed. "Oh yes. It definitely is. Wait until you start meeting the rest of your relatives!" Her laughter rang around the room.

Aglaea scowled again and stood up elegantly. "That's quite enough Bright."

Bright looked down into her lap as if she was contrite, but I saw the corners of her lips twitch. I glanced over at my mom who was watching Aglaea warily.

Aglaea came and stood in front of me, "Grace, as you come to know what you are, it will be time for you to make a choice about whether to accept the responsibilities you have been groomed for."

"What if I'm not interested in what you're grooming me for?" I asked querulously.

Aglaea shook her head, "Grace, we all have to choose eventually, whether we will maintain our Olympian responsibilities and live in this world but apart from it, or whether we will embrace mortal life and give up our responsibilities. There are consequences either way, and they are *monumental* consequences." She glanced pointedly at Bright who gazed down and, unbelievably, actually seemed ashamed of herself. How weird. Aglaea continued, "You exist as a consequence of such a decision, and like

337

a child born to royalty, you will assume your duties at the appropriate time. "

"Couldn't I abdicate?"

I was being frivolous, I guess, but she paused and thought for a moment, watching me carefully before she added, "I suppose it is possible, but I don't think you will. There are even greater consequences then. I don't think you would be able to live with the guilt," she looked at me with narrowed eyes as she added, "not to mention what that would mean for Ben."

"I'm sorry?"

"Don't worry about it for now Grace.   Right now you need to concentrate on learning as much as you can." She reached into her gorgeous leather satchel and dropped a huge volume on my lap: *Tales and Myths of Ancient Greece*.

"Huh?"

"Start reading. We'll talk again when you're done."

I flipped through the book in shock. "Aunt Aglaea! It's 1500 pages long! It'll take me forever."

She laughed. "Good thing you have that long…" Her voice trailed off as she sauntered out of the room as if she was walking a runway. "I'll see you in the morning, everyone."

Only a few moments later we heard a door slam in the driveway. Jim was home.

Mom, Bright, and I stared at the door. He stepped over the threshold and looked up to see us all watching him. He smiled quizzically as he felt the tension in the room. "Hello, ladies," he said gently.

Bright beamed adoringly at him, "Hello, Honey. Welcome home."

His own smile became warmer as he stepped into his slippers and came into the room. "Hi, Blythe," he said grasping my mom in a warm hug. "How was your trip?"

"Long."

He nodded and glanced back the designer shoes in the hall. "And you brought Aglaea with you, I see?"

She nodded, rolling her eyes a bit. It was amusing to see how the younger sisters chafed under Aglaea's authority as if they were all teenagers instead of wise immortals. I wondered how much more Jim knew about all of this than he'd let on to me.

Mom stood up and looked over at me, "I think I'm going to head off to bed as well. The jet lag is catching up with me."

"Sleep well," I said.

"Good night," she called as she headed down the hall to the guest suite.

I looked over at Jim who was standing with his arm wrapped around Bright. She stretched up to kiss him and whispered something in his ear. He nodded and smiled at me as he said, "If you'll excuse me Grace, I'm going downstairs to do some work. Good night."

I nodded to him while Bright watched him go, smiling fondly. When the door shut behind him, she looked over to me. "How are you doing, Grace? You've had a crazy day."

I took a deep breath and bit my lip, "I don't know. Fine I guess. I should probably head up to bed myself."

She nodded, "If you think that's the best." She studied me as I started to move toward the stairs and added, "Have a good sleep."

"Yeah. Thanks."

I went up to bed, but sleep didn't come. I called for Ben and though he sent me soothing music, he didn't speak to me. I hated it when he did that. I had so much I wanted to ask him and he was playing coy. Finally, around two o'clock I gave up and slipped out of bed. I thought I'd go get something to eat, or watch TV for a bit. When I opened my bedroom door, I was surprised to see light glowing from the kitchen. When I walked around the corner, Bright was sitting at the kitchen table, staring into the black silhouettes of the mountains, her hands cupped around a mug of tea.

She looked up at me, "Couldn't sleep either?"

I shook my head, and she pushed over an empty mug, "Help yourself." I poured myself some tea and sat down opposite her.

"Crazy world we live in, isn't it?"

I nodded, "You can say that again."

"Do you feel any better knowing?"

I shrugged. "I don't know. I think I'm too busy being confused and overwhelmed at the moment to feel *better*."

She nodded slowly. Finally, she looked up at me and I saw that her eyes were sad. "You know, Grace," she said quietly, "I can't tell you how sorry I am about all of this."

"What do you have to be sorry about?"

"If I wasn't retiring, you wouldn't have to worry about any of it." She sighed, taking another sip of tea, watching me with sorrowful eyes.

I didn't see the connection. "So what exactly does it mean that you're retiring? I don't get how you quitting your music job means that my life changes."

Her smile was faint and melancholy. "It's not about my production duties, sweetie. This is about passing a torch and leaving the world."

"What?"

She stared into my eyes intensely as she explained, "'Retiring' means I will live out a mortal life with Jim."

I looked at her in confusion for a moment trying to read the message in her eyes before I got it. I gasped and asked, "Live out and then *die*?"

"Yes."

"And not come back?"

She sighed, "No. At least I don't expect to."

I blinked back tears and whispered, "Why?"

She shrugged her shoulders apologetically. "I feel *done* Grace. I've been in the cycle celebrating the artists for so many millennia I've lost track. I'm tired of it. I was ready to choose my final love and with him, I chose my fate. He's mortal. I chose mortality." She smiled gently.

"But you're still not aging?"

"Not yet."

"You will?"

She nodded. "Once my successor takes over my role, then my mortality is sealed, and I will age like everyone else."

"Successor?" I asked quietly.

She nodded, watching me carefully.

Her eyes were speaking to me again, and suddenly I knew. "Me?"

She nodded.

"I don't understand. I'm already immortal, right?"

"When you're a part of our world, the rules are a little different, Hon. I know you're going to feel that some of this is insane." She shrugged sympathetically. "I wish we could make this easier, but we've run out of time." She paused for a moment, sipping and studying me before she took a deep breath and began, "There are plain mortals, who are born, who live a brief life, and then die. Their essence, their soul you might say, follows the path ordained by the faith they espoused, which could be a type of immortality or not. Then there are the mortals who've been touched by the gods. They can die, but they revisit life repetitively. Usually they have no memory of their past existences and just cycle through again and again." She stood up and added more boiling water and a fresh teabag into the pot, then brought it back over to the table before she continued. "It's interesting to watch actually, because even in a new time or place, sometimes their personalities are so fixed that they replay the same stories over and over again, making the same kinds of mistakes with new relationships as they did in their last lives. Others are constantly evolving, growing and improving. Ben is like that. His initial talent was blessed by the original Muses so he has a desire to create song, the fortitude to practice until his skills are prodigious, and the memory to remember and build upon them life after life. He has almost always been a musician of some sort, but he has done very well as a poet too. I think you have seen that?"

I thought of the sonnet he'd shared in Fish Creek Park when he gave me my poesy ring and nodded.

"The one thing that has never changed for Ben is that he has always loved you."

I nodded. He'd made that pretty clear. "But who was I?"

She shrugged, "You've been many women, in many places. You've been in waiting, as you know now, for a role that was prepared for you. You are as yet without a position, but you are still of Olympian royal birth. While Blythe, Aglaea and I have kept our role, form and age, you have been cycling through like a blessed mortal in waiting, in case you were needed." She smiled, "Usually Ben has been pretty close to you. He has an uncanny knack of finding you, but then," she smiled fondly at me, "he has always felt you were his own particular muse. In some lives, he could not reach you before you'd been married to someone else, or your ages were too out of synch for propriety. When that happened, he'd watch you, keep you safe if he could, and he'd mourn for a lifetime until he got a new start."

Wow. That was a lot of loving. I thought of the story of Laure and Petrarch and it suddenly had greater poignancy. No wonder he had trouble with preambles.

I sat sipping my tea and gazing out at the blackness of the lake like Bright. Finally, I asked, "If I'm already three thousand, why would I just be starting something new now?"

She grinned. "You've been promoted."

I looked at her blankly. "Seriously, Bright."

"*Seriously*, Grace." Her eyes were unequivocal. This was no joke.

"So, what? All these people have been attacking me because they want to take out some minor muse?" I asked incredulously.

"No muse is minor," she stated matter-of-factly. I stared at her, and she stared back. "Besides," she added, "you're not technically a Muse. You're a Grace."

"Ha ha."

"I don't mean your name. Did your academic studies ever inform you about The Three Graces?"

She was serious. I whispered, "Not really." I was suddenly fearful of the destiny she was about to reveal. I remembered paintings I seen of

341

The Three Graces, always three sisters circling in a dance. My brain flashed back to the photo from Bright's wedding.

She smiled fondly, "To be a Grace is to bring joy, radiance and beauty to life. We bring all that is the best of human existence. It's an important job. Without us, the world would be a very dull place. Without us, life would be dark, full of foreboding and horribly lonely. If we didn't exist, evil would reign; everything would be horror and chaos. Without us, there is nothing for muses to inspire, because with only oppression feeding the artists, their art, whether music, story, poetry or whatever it may be, is only an agonized cry into oblivion."

I shivered, feeling the cold of the world she described. Memories came flashing down upon me like bolts of lightning. I looked at her feeling besieged. It all made sense. "So that's why I've been under attack for the last couple of years?"

She nodded. "Once you were beginning to get glimmers of your role, your threat became clear to some of the darker elements of our world."

"Have I always had a guardian?" I asked, thinking of Ben, Marco and Alex. I wondered whether they were just one end of a long line of mysterious protectors, I hadn't known about.

She nodded. "Your parents are your main guardians, but when you started going to school, various others watched you."

"I feel like some kind of china doll everyone is afraid to drop."

"You shouldn't," she replied to my astonishment. "They aren't watching you because you're fragile, you know."

"Huh?"

"Grace, they're watching you because you're the most powerful of us all."

"That's not possible." I shook my head in irritation. "I don't want to take on this role, Bright. I have no powers."

"You have power. Love, happiness and beauty are the most powerful things in the universe. You can defeat anything if you accept that you own that power."

"But I *don't* own that power, Bright."

She smiled softly, "We'll see."

I scowled and snorted my disbelief.

She laughed. "Think for a moment about what happened to all those who tried to attack you. How did it go for them?"

I thought and the realisation of what she meant was a surprise. I whispered, "Not well."

"Exactly." She nodded.

"Except the car."

"Yes. An automaton does have some advantages, especially when, as in your case, you didn't see it coming. That one was, I'm sorry to say, your own fault."

I pondered my mother's anger with Ben over the accident. "What do you mean?"

"If you'd been paying even the slightest attention to your surroundings, it wouldn't have been able to hit you. Having recognized and absorbed the damage an automaton could do in Banff, you'd have been able to guard against it."

I considered how distracted I'd been by Ben that day, before I reflected on her actual words and looked up at her. Automaton? "Don't you mean automobile?"

"Whatever."

"It's not polite to blame the victim, Auntie Bright."

"There is no blame here, Grace; there is only fact. You were not attentive, and it was able to sneak up on you. You're the common denominator, remember. Still, it is unlikely that such a mistake will happen in the future. Your memory is good. Next time you should sense a vehicle attacking from the rear."

It seemed absurd, and yet as she said it, I realized she was right. I hadn't consciously noticed a heightened awareness of the vehicles around me, but it was true. Even now, inside and away from any windows, I knew that at this moment there were three cars approaching our road from the north, and one turning from the south. None were a danger to me. Whoa. This was very freaky. It was like a radar system humming in the background monitoring everything. Presumably, when there was peril it would move into red alert and I would become aware of the danger like the mysterious man in Stanley Park. It was kind of creepy, actually. I shivered and asked, "So how does it work? I mean, if I'm a Grace what do I actually have to do?"

She smiled, "It's actually a pretty simple job. You just have to *be* what you are. You have to be the epitome of grace, in time, you'll take over from me, and you'll be the epitome of radiance. Your joy and beauty and charm will radiate in the world, and the sculptors, painters, musicians and poets will feed off it." She grinned and added, "Whoever their muse is."

"I'm to replace you? I thought the Graces were sisters?"

"They are."

"I'm going to mess that up aren't I? I'm a daughter and a niece."

"You're a sister," Bright said evenly, her eyes unblinkingly focused on mine.

343

"How is that…?"

"Just trust me."

So my mom is actually…"

"Your sister."

"And I am actually your…"

"Sister, yes. My much younger sister." She giggled.

"I'm not so young you know. I'm three thousand!" I huffed dramatically. I was beginning to believe, but I couldn't help the feeling I was going to wake up in someone's dream before much longer.

"Hon, I'd probably lived two millennia before you came along. Trust me, you're young."

"Who are our parents?"

She groaned, "Do I really have to go into it? Just read that big genealogy book Aglaea gave you."

"She gave me a book about Greek myths."

She smirked, "Indeed."

"This is ridiculous."

She didn't reply; she just wrapped her arms around me and held me close for a long time. "I'm sorry that you have to take on this role. If I had been able to be content enough, you could have just continued cycling through lives without waking up to all the complications of knowledge of the other world. It's been hidden in myth for millennia; I know that I found it very freeing when we faded from general consciousness. Our task was still just as important, but we didn't have to be on public display all the time. Going about one's day incognito is something to rejoice at."

"This from the woman who drives an art car…"

She laughed, caught, "Well, a *little* celebrity can be fun.'

CHAPTER ELEVEN

NOTHING WILL EVER BE WORTH THAT

Finally, battle lines glistening, fortifications Cyclops built
Ares is ready for fighting, doom rolling over the green hills.
Monster descends to join Ares; danger comes silently stalking her
Carried away into undergrowth, Charon is laughing and mocking her.

What was I supposed to make of all this? Thanks to Bright's revelations, I didn't feel even slightly more relaxed or sleepy after the three cups of chamomile tea. I glanced at the clock on the microwave and was surprised to see it was almost three in the morning. I groaned. "Bright, look at the time!"

She smiled and snickered quietly, "Oh come on, like you'd actually be sleeping if you weren't here in the kitchen with me."

"I *need* to sleep. I have school tomorrow!" She was a bad influence.

She shook her head with a gentle grin. "I think we'll excuse you. Even Aglaea wouldn't be heartless enough to send you to school after all this."

"Wanna bet?" I muttered.

She laughed. "Well, if they call you tomorrow morning, just refuse to get up. I'll cover for you."

I stood up and set my mug in the dishwasher. Auntie Bright was awesome. With a sigh I announced, "I'm going to try to go to sleep."

She smiled. "Good luck with that."

I shook my head and padded up the stairs. I heard her rummaging around in the kitchen for a bit, but eventually her soft steps were on the stairs. She paused at my door, perhaps debating whether to come in, or perhaps listening to see if I was still awake; finally she headed off to her own room and shut the door quietly behind her.

I waited fruitlessly for sleep to come, staring up at the ceiling, willing the turmoil in my brain to shut off and let me drift into oblivion. I wanted to escape everything. I was beyond overwhelmed. I couldn't absorb what they had told me.

The birds were beginning to twitter outside and I groaned in aggravation, rolling this way and that. I put my hands over my ears and burrowed my head into my pillow.

Finally, I gave up. This was ridiculous. It was only four o'clock. Perhaps some fresh air would help.

I left a note on my bed: "Walking along the foreshore," and slipped quietly out of the house. There was a slight breeze flickering the leaves in the trees overhead and the early morning birdsong tickled my ears. I headed south along the silent street toward the path that followed the marshy shoreline of the lake into downtown. It was peaceful enough there even when the path was busy with commuters walking or jogging along it. It would be perfect in the dawn stillness. The streetlights were still on, but the sky was blushing in the east; it was easy enough to make out the route.

I worked my way down the packed earth onto the gravel path lined with grass and trees. Something small scampered into the underbrush. A family of ducks launched into the reeds along the lake in a precise series of small splashes. I chuckled to myself as the little ones raced to catch up with their parents in a regimented line. A little farther along the path I glanced up in time to see a fish jump, marking the spot with a bull's eye of concentric rings. The air was clean and crisp.

I breathed in deeply, strolling slowly, absorbing the peacefulness of the water lapping in the reeds and the rustle of leaves overhead. I was glad I'd decided to do this. Watching the water soothed my thoughts. A few metres from the path the CN Rail line was raised above on its own hill of gravel, beyond that was a steep hill covered in brush and long grass leading to the road and the residential areas up the hill on the other side of it. There was a loud grating squawk on the other side of the tracks. I jumped, but at the second squawk, I recognized the familiar call of a pheasant, and I exhaled deeply, releasing the fear that had filled me. I tried to regain a sense of peace by listening for the more melodious clicks and whistles of the Red-winged Blackbirds calling in the rushes.

It was calming to stroll along breathing in the fresh morning air. Nothing was stirring at this hour except the small creatures and me.

And one not so small creature.

Up ahead, emerging from the trees between the path and the rail line, was a large, brown shape that I recognized from our terrifying boat trip. Standing half again as tall as me and filling the path with its massive bulk was the unmistakable figure of the Sasquatch. Or what Bright said was not a Sasquatch. It seemed unhappily surprised to see a human intercepting its way. It froze. One eye stared out at me malevolently. It was definitely hairy, but more like a giant with a lot of body hair than a big furry animal. Its hands (or should I say paws?) looked brown and leathery with thick, black nails. Its feet were black platters. The birds and other creatures had sensed this interloper, and even they were completely silent now, so that the creature's low rumbling growl carried easily to me where I stood, motionless, ten metres away, certain that I was about to meet my death.

It stared back and we stood watching each other as the sun started to climb higher above the mountains. I wondered what it was waiting for. I took a step back and it took one toward me. I stopped and it stopped. Hmm. Stalemate. I planted my feet and stared back at it, our positions apparently fixed.

Something crackled in the bush behind me and I focused my energy as Bright had taught me, seeking the sensation that would indicate the danger. The feeling was different now; it was an overarching aura of evil all around me. I wondered how I had missed this sign with my supposed radar for trouble. You'd think something as obvious as a giant mythical beast should have triggered *some* sort of warning. Had I been so distracted with all the crazy myth talk last night that I had lost my focus? That seemed strangely ironic.

There was a crunch of gravel behind me and I dared to take my eyes off the one-eyed Sasquatch to look behind me. I was growing more aware of the evil in the air; I focused my senses to reach for awareness. It came clearly. I knew exactly where the newcomer was standing. Hopefully, one quick glance to get a look of his face should be all I'd need to identify him.

I turned and gasped in shocked recognition.

"Isn't this going to be fun," drawled the dark haired guy I'd seen in the boat; the same one who'd jumped into the atrium. He'd shaved off the beard, but the eyes were unmistakeable. They were evil eyes, but they appeared in a face so like that of Josh. He strode forward and I let out my breath. No. It wasn't the face of my friend, but it was clear why I'd thought at first he *was* Josh. Standing like this, he had Josh's hair and build. They were almost the same height. But those were not my friend

347

Josh's warm eyes. These eyes belonged to someone else. These were eyes simmering with dark intent.

My crazy, imperfect radar was telling me that the Sasquatch still hadn't moved, so I kept my eyes on the human. "You were the one driving the car in Banff…." I whispered, realizing with joyful relief that my fears about Josh were groundless.

He laughed and the grim evil behind it made my spine spasm. "I was. Not one of my prouder moments, that." He shook his head in remembered frustration, "You have been remarkably slippery, considering the Keystone Cops watching over you." The grim laugh sawed through the air again and he added, "No matter. You're on your own this time, and I have got a brilliant ally to make sure you don't sneak away from me again." He flicked his chin behind me at the Sasquatch and I sensed it take a step toward me, but I didn't bother to take a step away. There was unlikely to be a lesser between these two evils. I was dead either way.

The irony of the situation was not lost on me. Here I had all these protectors to watch over me, but what good were they when I was left alone to face monsters and assassins on my morning walk? *Thanks guys,* I sighed to myself, *you're doing a great job!*

At that moment, I noticed a familiar hum off in the distance, as the rails beside us began to vibrate. A freight train was on its way.

In my head, I felt something like a light switch come on. I realized that Ben had just awoken and opened his thoughts to me. "Hey," he thought, "you're awake early. You won't believe the crazy dream I just had about you."

"Did it have a Sasquatch and a murderer in it by any chance?" I thought back to him, with more than a little sarcasm.

His hesitation would have been funny in less dire circumstances. "Um. Yeah. As a matter of fact…"

"*Not* a dream, Ben…"

He cursed then, and the explosion of his anger in my head made me jump. "Crap! I'll get help!" he shrieked, and then he was silent.

My would-be-assassin grinned and took a step forward. "Allow me to introduce myself," he said silkily. "My name is Ares. I believe you met my younger sisters at school in Calgary."

I knew at once whom he meant. I saw their eyes in his. The scary man had equally scary twin sisters. I wondered what their parents were like to have produced children like these. All the incidents in Calgary flashed through my mind: the trip on the stairs, the poisoning, the bomb in the hall.

Well. They were going to be successful with their assassination after all. Lucky me. Joy and beauty were about to be sucked out of the world because I had to take an early morning stroll and figure out the meaning of my life. What an idiot I was. Why hadn't I just accepted what my aunts had told me and stayed at home? My sisters, I amended.

My panic was building as Ares stood there with his mocking eyes daring me to make a move. I had no idea what to do.

I sensed the magnetism before I saw him. I was drawing him toward me. I breathed a sigh of relief as the irresistible gravity was finally doing the job it existed to do. There was a rustle in the bushes and then there he was behind Ares: my Alex. Bronzed and muscular, a grin of pure delight on his face, he laughed blissfully to be facing a fight. The sound of his exultation echoed around us.

Ares turned in surprise at the noise and the raised an eyebrow as he commented in cold disgust, "Ah, Alexandros." He paused, studying Alex with a scowl. "I see you've come to join our party."

"No," Alex contradicted with his sultry, self-satisfied grin, "I've come to break it up." He smirked wider and asked, "Who do you want me to break first? You or the fur ball?" Alex looked between them as if trying to decide, "Okay then! You," he announced and strode confidently forward until he and Ares were arms' reach apart.

Ares dropped into a crouch and snarled at Alex's confident leer. They began to circle as if they were in a ring.

While Alex kept Ares distracted, I turned back to look at the Sasquatch. It was watching events carefully, as if trying to assess its options. I could almost see the wheels turning in its head. I suspected it wasn't used to long-range planning or formulating contingencies.

If it moved to attack me while Alex was busy with Ares, I was in trouble, so I concentrated on remaining silent and still, hoping that meant I was inconspicuous.

The rhythmic hum of the rails had grown loud now, and the earth was shaking.

Ares reached out with his right hand in a sudden, powerful punch that I guess was meant to surprise Alex. It didn't. Alex ducked his head out of the way as if Ares had hit out in slow motion, and shot off his own powerful right with an uppercut that sent Ares' head snapping back like a slammed gate.

Ares staggered backwards as the train came into sight. Alex came forward to attack him, but Ares had regained his footing and returned the blows at an impossible rate. They were pummelling each other with rapid-fire precision. My eyes were glued on them as the train roared past us, obliterating all sound, so that the fight seemed to be a silent movie played in fast forward. I was thankful now for Alex's skills.

Too late, I became aware that the Sasquatch had moved. A huge hairy arm reached down, grabbed me around the waist and hauled me into the air. My scream of horror was lost in the noise of the train, so Alex didn't even turn around as the creature leapt with me onto the narrow platform between a pair of coal cars and we roared down the rails toward downtown.

I leaned my torso as far as I could away from the beast and felt the magnet between Alex and me first clinging, then stretching and finally snapping. Alex seemed to feel the loss at last and he looked up as the train pulled me and my captor around the bend. Before they disappeared from sight, I saw Ares seize advantage of Alex's momentary distraction and land a hard left hook that dropped Alex to his knees. I cried out, but my cries were lost in the sound of the rails.

The train wasn't travelling very quickly, but I didn't relish the pain of leaping into gravel or asphalt. Mind you, it was a moot point, considering that I was pinioned against a filthy coal car by a huge monster that seemed to find me about as powerful as a gnat. I wiggled a little to test the theory, but my hips didn't move. The Sasquatch flexed his hand and his grip tightened. Yeah. Great. Now I didn't even have wiggle room. Any moment now, he was going to crush me or toss me off our precarious ledge or eat me or worse. There was no way that this was a scenic tour to Kamloops. I sighed, wondering why my brain was so calm. I should rightfully be screaming in terror.

Ben joined me in my head then. "You're doing great, Grace."

"Yeah, right," I thought back sarcastically, "I am being carried off by a monster, Ben."

I could sense him fighting to show a calm demeanour amid his rising panic. "I'm doing all I can from this end."

"You're a little far away from the action, guy."

Ben snarled back, "Oh, trust me, I *know*!"

The train clattered through the silent town. It wasn't five o'clock yet. There was only the occasional light glowing from houses in the distance. I wondered how Alex was doing in his battle with Ares. Did he get up after that last ferocious blow?

The train headed out of town and rounded another bend, following the shore of the lake. Suddenly the grip around me tightened, and with a bound, we had left the train and were on the ground, running through forest following the lake. I tried to scream and a giant hand immediately covered my mouth as the creature growled menacingly. Impossibly, through the growl I thought I made out the word "SILENCE!" I obeyed in shock. Could the creature speak? Through a blur of trees, I recognized the beach at Sunnybrae Provincial Park, so we were now on the opposite side of the bay from where he'd grabbed me. He was holding me so tightly that my legs were growing numb. I was being lashed by brush and bumped against rocks as we travelled impossibly quickly along the edge of the trees. I knew that I was going to be covered in cuts, abrasions and bruises by the time we got to wherever it was taking me. Not that it would really matter. It was probably just tenderizing me before his feast. I sighed hopelessly.

I could see glimpses of the lake as we flew through the trees. Looking across I noticed the distinctive line of houses on either side of the wharf at Canoe and the sawmill beyond just as the Sasquatch left the lakeshore and started heading up hill.

We emerged from the thick fir trees onto a logging road, and suddenly we were not alone. I stared at the black haired man standing in front of us. His face was a mask of determination, as he raised the huge gun in his hand. I choked in surprise: he was the last person I would have expected to see on a remote logging road in the middle of the woods.

The creature growled and dropped me. My knees scraped the gravel and blood rushed back into my legs with the sensation of a thousand stabbing needles.

"Step back, Grace," my saviour demanded in a low, authoritative tone, as he levelled his shotgun on the Sasquatch.

I dragged myself off the road, and slid awkwardly into the ditch. Gripping tightly to a bit of bush, I pulled myself up, shaking in shock at the scene before me.

The creature snarled and lunged. The gun exploded. The Sasquatch was blown back a couple of steps, but didn't fall. It shook its head and stepped forward.

The double click of the gun being pumped seemed to echo in the still of the morning. The creature charged again, and again the gun exploded, sending the beast recoiling back a couple of steps.

Like a rewinding movie, it happened again and again: cla-click, boom, cla-click, boom. The creature just kept taking a few steps forward, then a couple of staggering steps backwards as it was hit. Its torso was a pulpy purple mass.

A steady hand reached into a pocket and reloaded the gun without his eyes leaving the advancing monster. Before he could raise the gun again, with a snarling roar, the creature slashed out with its arm and four vivid red gouges appeared across my greatest protector's face.

He stepped back and fired once more, point blank, as he collapsed onto the ground, and the Sasquatch teetered, and then crashed forward like a falling tree on top of him.

A primal howl burst from me and I raced forward shouting, "Josh! Josh!"

I ran to him sobbing and knelt in the gravel beside him. "Oh, Josh! You were so brave!"

I certainly didn't feel very brave as I tried to find the man amid the mound of flesh above him. The Sasquatch bulk completely covered his body. I picked up a stick and poked gingerly into the bloody mass, but there was no response. It had taken five shotgun shells, and perhaps the life of my friend, but the Sasquatch was dead.

"Josh!" I howled, "Be okay!" I tugged on the beast with as much power as I had. "Oh get off him, you brute!" I kicked it angrily and began chanting, "Josh, be okay. Be okay. Be okay." I circled the mound frantically pulling, prodding, and pushing while repeating the mantra: *Be okay*. It was hopeless. I didn't have the strength. If Josh was alive under there, he wasn't going to last much longer. He was going to suffocate because I was a wimp.

Suddenly I was flooded with fury. The aunts had told me I was *going* to be powerful, but I needed to be powerful *now*. I threw my head back and bellowed all my frustration and anger into the firmament: "NOOOOOOOO!" As the sound of my agony reverberated around the mountains, I felt an answer given back, not from the air, but from the earth. A rush of energy entered my feet like an electric shock. It spread in a wave up my body, down my arms and blasted its way into my head. Another surge detonated in my chest and blew through me. My body suddenly expanded like I'd become a giant. I had to look at myself carefully to ascertain that I was actually still the same size, because I felt twenty feet tall and strong enough to move the mountain towering over my head. I raised my hands like a triumphant boxer and spun in a slow circle, savouring the sensation of omnipotence for a moment before I returned to Josh and grabbed the Sasquatch's legs. I gave them a tug and they pulled completely away from the torso, dripping purple blood onto the ground at my feet.

Feeling a little disgusted, I tossed the legs off to side of the road. More gently, I took hold of the torso and lifted, concentrating on keeping it all together. It rose as effortlessly as if I was lifting a loaf of bread. With a gentle lob, the torso rejoined its legs.

"Josh?" I whispered. "Josh? Are you alive?" There was no way he was okay, so I saved him the trite question everyone was always levelling at me.

He looked…flat. I supposed this was the logical result of being stuck beneath a couple hundred kilos of monster. His ribs were compressed to about half the width they'd had normally. I suspected most of them were broken. He was bound to be riddled with internal injuries. Had the ribs punctured his lungs?

Nausea flooded through me. He had to be dead. I tilted forward to rest my head on his chest and heard a sputtering inhalation.

He was breathing. Incredibly. Unbelievably. He was alive.

"Josh? Oh Josh, please wake up!"

His eyelashes fluttered.

"Josh, it's me, Grace. Come back!" I was going to become hysterical any moment. Omnipotent hysteria was probably not a good thing to unleash on the world.

His lips moved and I leaned in close. "What is it, Josh? I'm here. Please speak to me!"

With a gurgling whisper he murmured, "Ouch."

"Oh Josh, it's going to be okay. We'll get help. Stay with me Josh."

Then I shouted in my head, "Ben! I need some help here NOW!"

I heard a distant murmur from the back of my brain, "Yup, on it."

I returned my focus to Josh. I smiled tenderly at him. "Thanks so much Josh. You saved my life."

He nodded weakly with his eyes closed. "Yeah."

I had a hundred questions for him, but obviously, this was not the time for them. I took a deep breath and wished I had him at my house where there was elixir that would return him to health no matter how badly he'd been crushed.

I heard a vehicle coming up the narrow winding road. It could be Ares, or it could be help. I contemplated moving Josh off the road just in case it was a maniacal logging truck barrelling down on us, but I didn't want to risk shifting him. Besides, with my newfound power I was equal to anything Ares might want to do to me. I suspected I could stop a run-away semi truck, too. The thought brought another surge of electricity through me; who knew an adrenaline rush was this powerful?

A vehicle rounded the corner. It was a logging camp ambulance: just an old pick-up truck with a beaten up white camper on the bed and a large red cross painted across the back. It stopped a couple metres from us. A middle-aged man in coveralls stepped out of the driver's seat and flipped the seat back to haul out a pack. "Are you Grace?"

I nodded, "Yeah."

"We got a call that there'd been an accident on our road." He had reached us and was studying Josh with concern, "What happened to him?"

"He was crushed."

He nodded, leaving his bag but heading to the back of his truck, "That much I can see." He pulled out a backboard out of the camper. "How?"

I shrugged my shoulders. The Sasquatch was out of sight in the ditch beside the road; I determinedly kept my eyes from wandering over to the corpse. I should have thrown some branches over it or something. Too late now. "I don't what caused it. Some kind of animal was attacking him. He shot at it, but it's gone."

He picked a clump of fur out of the blood coagulating on Josh's shirt and nodded at the physical corroboration. He had a stethoscope out and spread the fabric to get to Josh's bare chest. "Where were you?"

"I was hiding." I flicked my hands off in the opposite direction from the corpse, "over there."

He nodded again, but he wasn't paying much attention to me. His face was grave as he arranged a brace around Josh's neck.

"Is he hurt badly?" I whispered.

He nodded again, "Yes. Um. Can you please help me slide this backboard under him?" Together we gingerly arranged Josh on the board with as little movement as possible. "Do you think you can lift him?" he asked, realising suddenly that his partner today was just a petite girl.

I wondered if the power rush of adrenaline that I'd had when I'd pulled off the Sasquatch was still functioning. I still felt strong, so I assured him, "Yeah. I think I will be fine." I hoped I wasn't lying.

He took the head and I took the feet. We slid Josh into the trailer. The driver looked over at me. "You'll ride in back with him?"

"Yeah." It was good he didn't ask what we were doing on the side of a mountain without transportation. I didn't know what excuse I would have come up with to cover that one.

He took a magnetic emergency light out of the cab and set it on the roof, switching it on so it spun red and white. "If he seems worse, whack on the front of the trailer and I'll pull over, okay?"

I nodded. "Of course." He slammed the trailer door closed and then the driver's door opened and shut.

The engine roared to life and we jerked down the road. Josh groaned.

I leaned over him, "It's okay Josh; we're in an ambulance. We're going to the hospital."

"Uh." He said noncommittally.

The ride was rather fast. The driver was plainly well used to windy logging roads. Not much more than ten minutes later, we were in the hospital emergency department. A crush of doctors and nurses surged out to reach the truck, transferred Josh to a gurney and had him in the hospital before I could catch my breath. Oh, Josh. *You just need elixir.*

Bright rushed in with Alex at her side while I was standing helplessly at the admission desk. I had no information for them. I felt completely useless. All I knew was his name; I couldn't give them his address, his phone number, or his family contacts. I realized I didn't know much about him at all, and yet it didn't matter. He was my friend. He'd been my friend from the first day he took me to Tims. He had to be okay. He had to be.

"Bright!" I gasped, grabbing her shoulders and collapsing against her as I turned from the desk. "You have to help him! Get him some elixir!"

Bright's eyes were sad. She held me without responding, rocking me gently back and forth. "Shhh, Hon. Shhh."

"Bright? Come on, let's go get it."

She pursed her lips and shook her head sorrowfully, "We can't, Grace."

"What do you mean we can't? Of course, we can. It's right inside the medicine cabinet. It'll take fifteen minutes to get there and back, and then he can start healing! Let's go!"

She tightened her grip around my shoulders and pulled me closer, speaking so that no one else in the waiting area could hear, "Grace, the medicine isn't for everyone. I know Dr. Kyle told you that. It's not for Josh. It would probably do more harm than good."

My eyes flashed, "He's going to die, Bright. There is no worse *harm* than that."

She gave me a gentle smile and shook her head. "A death saving the world is a pretty good death, Grace. He succeeded in protecting you."

"That means I killed him, Bright," I sobbed.

She nodded in understanding, "I know it feels like that way right now, but Josh chose his role, and he knew this was the likely end. He was willing to sacrifice himself for you, Grace. Celebrate his gift. Make your life worth his death."

Tears poured down my face as I sputtered, "Nothing will ever be worth that."

She patted my back, "I know, Hon. I know. Someday you'll be thankful, though."

A doctor stepped out the door and nodded to me, "You're Grace?"
"Yes."

"He's asking for you. Come this way."

I wiped my eyes with the backs of my hands as I followed him into a curtained room. Josh had been cleaned up a little, but the pallor of death was evident upon his cheeks. They hadn't bothered to stitch up the gashes where the Sasquatch had ripped into his face, though I think they were cleaner. His eyes were closed. His breath was raspy. I leaned over his head and fought to keep my voice light, "Hey Josh. I'm here."

His eyes fluttered open. He swallowed feebly. There was blood in the corners of his mouth. I focused on his beautiful flecked eyes. "I love you, Grace," he sputtered weakly.

I nodded, "Yes, Josh. I know."

"But you're sticking with white bread, eh?"

He was so quiet.

I smiled weakly at his joke. "I love you, too, Josh."

His voice was faint. "You gave me hope, Grace. You gave me beauty. It was all worth it," he whispered, "everything."

I couldn't help it then. My eyes filled with tears that blinded me. "Oh Josh."

His hand flexed, and I reached down to hold it. He gave a shuddering gasp and more bloody bubbles appeared at his lips. I waited in silence for the next breath. This couldn't be happening. I lowered my head across his chest, careful not to touch him as he rasped again. His mouth was against my ear as he whispered, "Be, Grace. Be," on his weak exhalation. He didn't inhale again.

I watched the light fade out of his eyes. As the golden flecks disappeared, the grief settled across my shoulders like a cold, wet blanket.

I sat beside him, counting my own breaths and feeling like my world had just ended. My chest was a cavernous ache that threatened to swallow my being. I gave myself over to the pain. Beyond the tears now, just empty. I was a hollow room for a long time, but then oh so softly music began filling the void as Ben gave me the comfort only he could give. The only way to make sense of the paradox. Death and life. Horror and beauty. Music was reforming connections to life.

I sat a long time holding Josh's hand and wishing that somehow I could go back and change time so that none of this had happened. I could have just stayed at home in bed and he'd still be alive.

Oh, to have just stayed at home in bed.

I heard faint footsteps behind me. There was a hand on my shoulder and I glanced back to Bright. "Come on Grace," she said gently. "Time to go home."

I nodded, and leaned down to kiss Josh's undamaged cheek. I followed Bright out of the room, turning back from the doorway to look at the shell of my friend lying still on the bed. "Bye Josh," I whispered, "Thank you."

As we went through the waiting area, Alex stood up and followed us out to the car. The sun was blindingly bright as we stepped into the afternoon. The sky was a vivid blue with only the lightest of white wisps. The Redwing Blackbirds were calling from McGuire Lake. I squinted painfully in the sunlight, and wondered how Josh could die on a day as beautiful as this.

Bright made Alex sit in Fatima's back seat. He was doubled over like a paper clip looking completely unimpressed, but he had the wisdom not to say anything. I could feel the passionate pull between us in the proximity of the little car, but my body was so numb from agony that it didn't overwhelm me. We drove home in silence. I stared straight ahead, but I didn't see anything. Time disappeared. I was surprised when we bumped into the driveway.

Bright got out of the car and moved her seat so Alex could unfold himself. He stretched out slowly, like crawling out of a box. I didn't move. Bright put her head down and looked in through her open door, "Come on, Grace," she said gently, "time to go in. We have a lot of things to talk about."

That's exactly what I was afraid of. I didn't want to listen to anyone yelling at me for going off by myself. I didn't want to hear their condemnation. My own was already loud enough. Suddenly I felt tired in my very bones. My lack of sleep had caught up to me like a crashing wave. I realized I'd been awake for over thirty hours. No wonder I was weary to my bones.

Bright seemed to understand, "I know you're exhausted, Grace. It won't take long, but it needs to happen. Let's go." She turned, "Open her door, Alex. Help her inside."

Alex swung the car door open and smiled that seductive little smile of his, "Hey, Sweetheart, I'm going to get you in my arms at last." With that, he scooped me up and carried me into the house.

Bright opened the door to the house as Alex swept us in like Superman and Lois Lane. He deposited me gently on the couch, then he ran a finger down my cheek tracing the path of a silent tear and whispered, "You can do it, Grace. You have the power!"

I sat there in a confused daze. My head couldn't capture my thoughts.

My mom and Aglaea came down the stairs and sat on the couch opposite watching me silently. Bright sat next to me, and started rubbing my back gently. Alex stood leaning against the arch at the entrance of the room, as if he was on guard. *Now* he's watchful, I thought spitefully, but then I remembered the fight with Ares and forgave him. Sort of.

Aglaea cleared her throat, "Now that Ares has declared himself, this is war. Before it may have been about malice or retribution, but no longer. This is their last chance, and they're going to pull out everything they have to destroy you, Grace."

"How do you know about it?" I asked wearily. "I didn't know the twins had a brother, why do you know about all of them?"

Aglaea gave me a disgusted look, "It's my job, Grace." She carried on, "If you've gained your power, their evil will not succeed. The war against us will be over."

My mom looked over to Aglaea and shook her head. "Wait a minute Aglaea. You're moving too quickly. Grace isn't ready to process this yet." She turned to me and asked quietly, "Have you read any of the book Aglaea gave you yet?"

I shook my head. I'd forgotten about the book. Maybe I should have been reading instead of walking along the foreshore. I could have been learning about my family instead of causing death and destruction. I sighed. Aglaea gave an exasperated exhalation. Apparently, when she assigned reading, it was to be done immediately.

Mom nodded, unsurprised. "Okay. We know him because Ares is related to us as well, Grace. He's our half-brother."

"So the twins?" My voice trailed away.

"Yes."

Bright interrupted, "Grace, in big families there are always petty jealousies and complicated tangles of relationships. We're just a *really* big, really *old,* and particularly dysfunctional family. Our dad had a lot of…ah…romances." She paused for a moment. "We have so many relatives that even we can't keep straight how we're all related. You'll see in the family history book that there are lots of contradictions." She shrugged. "There are hundreds of us; obviously we don't all get along."

That was an understatement.

I started to cry again then, because there was just too much going on in my head. I was beyond weary. I could not sort it all out. I didn't understand how I had immortal family members who were a little too closely related. I didn't understand how giant mythical creatures could be roaming the woods. I couldn't understand why Josh would even have been in the Shuswap, let alone on an isolated forestry road. *Nothing* made any sense.

Bright rubbed my back absently and asked gently, "What are you thinking, Grace?" Nice of her to ask, since I was pretty sure she already knew. I took that to mean I should ask the others the question burning in my brain.

I looked across at Aglaea and my mom and demanded, "Why was Josh even here?"

Aglaea looked business-like. "He was here doing research for me."

Josh was a researcher? I visualized a tiny guy with glasses perched on the end of his nose peering into dusty books. That picture didn't fit Josh at all.

Bright rolled her eyes and shook her head. "He wasn't researching. He was *spying*, Grace."

Spying. Huh. That sounded a little more like Josh. "What was he spying on?"

"Ares," Aglaea responded promptly.

I pondered that for a moment. That would explain our last, strange visit at Tims. Yet, it didn't explain the need for him to be spying.

"Why?"

Aglaea explained, "Because we knew of Ares' plan to destroy you before you could officially become a Grace, before you gained full command of the power you were born to. He's been working on eliminating you for awhile, as you now know, but Ben was supposed to be keeping you safe."

I nodded. I knew how *that* part of the story had worked out. I did not meet my mother's eyes to see if she was gloating.

I choked a little bit as I asked, "Did Josh get you the information you needed?" I hadn't quite managed to keep the bitterness out of my voice.

Aglaea nodded. Bright gave me a little squeeze across the shoulders.

"So what happens now?"

Before Aglaea could answer in her analytical way, Bright got right to the point and announced enthusiastically, "Now you need to take him down."

I stared at her for a moment, waiting for people to laugh at her joke before I realized that she was serious. Me. I was supposed to *take him down*. Me? Right. Ares the god of war vs. Grace. They were insane. I looked around the room and every face was watching me with a serious expression.

I fought down the panic that threatened to overwhelm me.

I shook my head, and changed the subject. "Why is Ares after me?"

"Oh, a few reasons, I guess. We work for his girlfriend, though these days we're pretty independent. You've probably seen Aphrodite at reunions in Greece?"

I thought back and immediately pictured the stunningly beautiful woman who was fawned over by every man in the room. I nodded. "Yeah, I remember. She's family, too?" I had an idea of the mostly likely scenario and waited expectantly.

Bright smirked, "She's our half-sister."

I grunted. No surprise.

She laughed at my expression. "Anyway, I think he's angry that we're getting more attention on our own these days, and people are not paying enough service to her. It's a crazy testosterone thing though, because obviously we only do what she has authorized us to do. She's the one who set us up in business this way. She wanted a break. But you can't tell that to a man who's got an idea stuck in his head. He circles like a vulture above a battlefield waiting for one of us to slip up. Now he thinks I have, so he believes he has a chance to get Aphrodite to fall back in love with him again." I raised my eyebrow as she added, "They tend to have a rather tumultuous relationship."

"Sounds stupid."

"Oh I agree. There's no reasoning with him at all. So we'll play the game his way. You are strong enough to defeat him if you use your wits. Ares' greatest weakness is his temper. He doesn't think. If you can be calm and cool, then you will have a chance."

I shivered at the idea. "How can I fight him? He is evil, Auntie Bright. I'm just an unathletic girl. This is crazy."

She smiled in understanding.

"Bright, I'm *afraid*."

My mom interjected, "You'd be stupid if you weren't, Grace. But *use* that. Don't let it overpower you."

I caught a sputtering breath, feeling my gut contract.

"Breathe, Grace," whispered Bright. "You *have* the power." She raised an eyebrow meaningfully.

With a flash, I remembered the force that had filled me this morning. Was it still there? If it was, maybe I *could* destroy him. Maybe I could avenge Josh.

"Careful, Hon," whispered Bright, squeezing my shoulders again. "You're a Grace, not a Fury." I had no idea what she was referring to, but I got the gist and sighed, though the sigh morphed into a yawn. I would save vengeance for someone else.

"I think," Bright said to Aglaea, "that Grace is falling asleep. I think we should get everything ready and let her begin her battle in the morning."

Aglaea scowled, but my mother nodded. "Yes, I think you're right."

The sisters were doing a lot of thinking together. I chuckled wearily to myself. It was odd to see them standing up to Aglaea. They were right, though; I wanted my bed more than anything, even though it was only mid-afternoon. I tried to move, but my legs were glued to the couch and I was a giant sandbag. Bright laughed and looked over to the entryway, "Alex?"

He grinned, "Woo hoo! All the way to the bedroom! I'm on it!"

The sisters laughed and smirked, but I was too tired to comment.

As he came close to me, I felt a burning response and my body completely betrayed me when it clung to him as he lifted me again.

The next thing I knew I was waking up in my bed, and there was no sign of Alex or anyone else in my room. Out the window there was a weak sun shining on the lake. It was early morning. I was still wearing my clothes from yesterday. Alex had not taken advantage of his trip into my bedroom, at least. I stretched, feeling my body ache all over. There were muscles I'd never known I had screaming their existence; I caught a whiff of myself. Phew. I'd been in this shirt for two days straight. I was covered in dirt and blood. I reeked.

I crawled out of bed gingerly, feeling the pain. I welcomed it. I deserved it. I had caused the death of a man I loved. My body ached, but my chest was hollow where Josh's loss had burrowed itself. I climbed into the shower and let the water stream down my body. I wished I was washing away the agony, but I wasn't. When I left the shower, I smelled a whole lot better and my muscles weren't shrieking quite as loudly, but I still felt empty inside.

The phone rang and I heard Uncle Jim answering it. There was a murmur of voices, and then there was a knock on my bedroom door. "Grace?"

"Yes?" I sniffled.

"The phone is for you. It's Christie calling from Calgary."

"Oh." I opened the door and stuck my hand out.

Jim smiled gently as he placed the phone into it and I shut the door on him. I still didn't want to talk to anyone out there.

"Hi, Christie," I whispered.

"Hey, Grace. I hear you had quite a day yesterday." Ah. Someone had been talking.

I sniffed and croaked, "Yeah." It was all I could say as the tears began to flow again.

"Grace. I know it's never going to be easy, but you know Josh wanted to be there, right? You know it was his sacrifice to make."

What was I supposed to say to that? I didn't want anyone making sacrifices for me. I would rather have been the one lying in the morgue. It wasn't for him to die for me. I shook my head and whispered, "No."

"Yes, Grace. Ask your mom and your aunts. Ask Ben. Everyone has a role to play. When you accepted him into your life last fall, the end was already in place. He knew then what would probably happen. He understood the ramifications. All of them."

"No," I whispered, "no."

She was silent on the other end of the phone while I absorbed her words. A thought came to me, "Christie, what do *you* know about this anyway? "

"Oh, Grace. Surely you've realized by now?"

I sighed. I didn't have the energy to think. "Realized what?"

"I've been your friend since grade one, Grace."

"Yeah, so?"

"So, I've been your school guardian."

I froze and stared at her. "What? Guardian?" I fought to understand. "So, so you're the one who was supposed to keep me safe? How come my mother wasn't mad at you after the accident?"

"No. I'm not a protector." She emphasized, "I was a *guardian*. I don't fight."

Hmm. "So you've been *spying* on me for eleven years?"

She sighed. "I've been watching. Yes."

"Spying." I felt like I didn't even know her anymore. She'd been spying on me since we were six years old! This was sick. What kind of watching could she have been doing when she was six, for heaven's sake! This was insane.

"Grace…"

I interrupted her, "Don't talk to me like I'm your best friend, Christie."

"Why not? You *are* my best friend, Grace."

"No. I'm your *job*."

"You're my *friend*, Grace. You have been for more years than you know."

I snarled under my breath and she sighed.

"I'm not going to argue with you right now. I know you're upset. I just called to wish you luck today, and to tell you I'm really sorry about Josh. I miss you, and I wish I could be there to help, but, like I said, I just watch…" She sighed again. "Take care of yourself, okay?" Her voice was sincere; she was concerned. Someone else doubted my ability to make it out of this fight alive.

I muttered, "Yeah. Okay, thanks."

"I'm really sorry, Grace. I believe in you. You can do this." She didn't sound very convincing.

"Bye, Christie," I said quietly. "Thanks for phoning."

"I'll talk to you later, all right?"

I snickered at that. "We can hope."

"Yes, we *can*," she said adamantly.

I was silent for a moment as I realized that this might actually be the last time I ever spoke to her. Whatever else had been going on, we had had a lot of fun together throughout our childhood. She wasn't lying; she was my friend, even if she'd been my guardian. "Bye, Christie. You've been great. I've appreciated your friendship."

"Ditto. There's always hope, Grace. Believe that."

"Yeah. I'll try."

I set the phone down and stretched out on the bed, staring blindly at the ceiling. How many others were in on this bizarre secret life I didn't know I'd been living? In how many other ways, unbeknownst to me, had magic and myth intersected my daily life over the years?

I picked up the book Aglaea had given me and flipped through it. So many of these stories I'd half heard at school, but apparently nothing was just a story anymore. This was my family history. Monsters, and chapter after chapter of idiotic games for the gods' amusement. It made me want to scream. I scanned through the story of Pandora's Box. I felt sorry for her; I wondered if she felt guilty for unleashing all the evils into the world. I sighed and put the book back on the night table. This was reality? This was insane.

Half an hour later, I was tempted out of my room by the heavenly aroma of fresh baking. I made my way downstairs to the kitchen then stopped at the entrance. It was *crowded*. Alex took a step toward me with a happy leer, but before he could touch me, I had squealed and raced across the room to embrace Ben who laughingly pulled me onto his lap. Aglaea and my mom scowled, but Bright grinned happily and offered nonchalantly, "Cinnamon bun, Grace?"

"Mmm!" I murmured contentedly. Then I caught myself. It was sick for me to be happy the day after Josh had died.

Bright caught my eye and gave a barely imperceptible shake of her head. "Happiness is always good, Grace. There can be joy amid sorrow." The others looked at her in confusion, but she ignored them, looking at me, waiting for my response.

I understood. I nodded to her, and she turned back to her oven.

The doorbell rang and Alex went to answer it. He came back with Marco in tow. They were both grinning companionably.

Marco doffed his hat in greeting to everyone.

"All right," announced Aglaea in her most business-like voice. "Now that Grace is up and everyone is here, it's time to outline the battle plan and get going. We don't have as much time as I would like."

I was surprised when my mom interrupted her to say, "Aglaea, there is enough time. Don't be so pushy. Let the girl enjoy her breakfast." My mom was defending me to her sister. Huh. It was obviously good to have her hanging around Auntie Bright.

Aglaea dropped a large backpack in front of me. "You'll need this: GPS, head lamp, dehydrated food, water, and some purification tablets. I'm not sure how long you're going to be up there, so you need to be ready to last for a while."

"Up where?"

She took a deep breath, as if trying not to let her temper get the better of her. "Up Bastion Mountain."

"Why?"

"Because Josh was able to identify where Ares has set up his encampment and you need to sneak up there to destroy him." She sighed, and I heard the implied *obviously* in her tone. She was so intense that it was kind of funny. She didn't scare me any more.

Bright caught my eye and winked.

Aglaea had a lot of complicated variations, and everyone had their own jobs to do to prepare various components, but the battle plan as far as I was concerned was fairly simple. I was to go to the coordinates Josh had provided and make my way into Ares' fortress. Once I was there, I could summon my protectors to help me fight whoever was there. Only I could fight Ares, but they could help with others who might be fighting with him. No one offered me any suggestions about how exactly I should be fighting, which was really frustrating. Aglaea rolled her eyes and told me I'd be using my supernatural intuition and strength until Ares surrendered. She didn't say 'Of course' but it was in the tone of her voice. Once I had defeated evil, I was to go to Mount Olympus because it'd be time for me to become a Grace.

Simple.

Yeah right.

I wished I had had a whole lot more training on exactly how this theoretical super strength worked, but they kept telling me to be *tuned into my instincts* and I would be fine. I wished I had their misguided confidence in my abilities. For that matter, I wished I had a clue *how* to tune into my instincts. I didn't believe I could do any of this, and despite the encouraging words said to my face, I saw the anxious looks the others exchanged when they thought I wasn't looking. Plainly, I wasn't the only one who was worried.

By eight o'clock Aglaea stood. "All right then everyone, you have your jobs. Marco, you will take Grace as close to the mountain as you can, drop her off and then continue on. She must travel through the mountain to trigger the magic. And Marco," she added, "try to find the twins. They're bound to be around somewhere to help Ares and it would be a lot easier if they were out of the way early on. Alex, you are to try to find Ares before he goes up the mountain and see if you can do some damage. Distract him if you can, but be prepared for him to disappear, because once Grace reaches his fortress it will summon him. Ben, you are going to travel with a dummy of Grace to try to distract anyone watching the house. When Grace has gone through the mountain and reaches the fortress, all three of you need to be prepared to rendezvous with her. Once she has arrived at the portal, she will be able to summon you. If Ares makes it into the official war zone, it will be Grace's job to take the battle. You can only eliminate others from aiding him; you cannot raise a weapon to defend Grace. If you take up the fight, then management will not grant her Grace Immortality."

Ben muttered, "Graces should not be fighting anything."

Aglaea shrugged her shoulders, "I agree with you, but this is the way management has determined that this game is to be played. We have to follow the rules."

Ben growled, "As if Ares is going to follow any rules."

Aglaea frowned. "You'll all be there to keep him honest."

Alex grunted in agreement. He sounded eager for the opportunity.

I grinned sarcastically at my mom and aunts, "And you'll be here in town composing poetry and music about the epic battle, right?"

Mom laughed shallowly, "Something like that." Her eyes were grieving for me already. It looked like she would be writing an elegy.

"All right then." Aglaea announced, "Enough of this. Time to go."

Everyone rose, hugged, and then headed out the door to a variety of vehicles. I wondered if I would see any of these people again. I wondered what would happen to the world if I failed.

CHAPTER TWELVE

PERCEPTION IS REALITY

Charis is crumbled and broken now; destiny's farce shreds her heartstrings.
No one she loves can be with her, Fury's discordance echoing.
Charis obeys out of duty, follows commands to climb upward,
Facing all history's anguish, summoning, hoping the call's heard.

As Marco and I drove along Sunnybrae Road at the foot of Bastion Mountain, I watched the city on the other side of the lake and remembered my trip along this route under the sweaty armpit of a stinking Sasquatch. Was it only yesterday? How surreal had my life become? I was in some stupid movie. I tried to block Josh's face from crushing my heart; I didn't need the distraction of thinking about him, but I was mourning with every pore. The hollowness was growing.

Despite his own responsibilities, Ben sent me soothing music, flooding me with an uneasy peace. "We will honour his sacrifice, Grace. There will be a time to grieve." It wasn't a sentimental song; it was hopeful. "Be strong, Grace," he murmured in my head. "This isn't finished yet."

He was right, but it still made me angry. I tried to block that from him, but he saw right through, as usual. His comfort showed understanding, but was firm. "I love you, Grace. You can do this."

I hoped so.

Beyond his comforting words to me; however, I sensed something else, something he would have been able to shield from me before. I probed a little and it became painfully clear. With a shiver I thought, "If you're so sure I'm going to succeed, why are you so afraid?"

His answering silence was profound. Obviously, he had thought he was hiding that from me. I felt suddenly giddy with the knowledge that I'd gone through one his barriers, despite the fact that what I was seeing on the other side was rather disturbing. If he was afraid, I was obviously in trouble. "Ben? Tell me the truth. Why *exactly* are you afraid?"

He sighed, "I love you."

"Of course, I already know that. So?"

"Obviously I'm going to be afraid when you're heading off to face an epic battle Grace."

I considered that, searching through his mind. No. That wasn't it. Nice try. "If that was all you were worried about, I wouldn't be asking you the question, Ben." I paused and explained, "I sense a different kind of fear, Love. Be honest with me, please."

Marco coughed beside me, distracting me momentarily as Ben collected his thoughts. The road was winding past summer cabins, houses, rocks, and trees. Canoe was still visible across the lake, windows here and there catching the morning light. It was still weird to be alone with Marco, and have Ben filling my head. You'd think I'd have gotten used to this by now.

Marco glanced over at me, "Talking to Ben?"

I nodded.

He smiled softly and patted my hand. "It's going to be fine, Grace." The certainty of his words was not echoed in his eyes. He was nervous for me, too. Great. I was inspiring confidence everywhere.

I tuned back into my head, "Well, Ben?"

He sighed again. "It's not about the battle, Grace."

"Then *what is it*?" I pushed my question insistently, forcing my will into his head. I could feel a wall, and I pushed against it. There was a glimmer of something and I pushed again, harder. I wasn't prepared for the result as I broke through.

I felt a wave of sorrow gush through him. Unbelievably, it was anguish even more painful than my guilt and loss over Josh; ten minutes ago, I wouldn't have imagined a worse torture than that. He was filled with a soul crushing agony. I recoiled, eyes wide.

Marco looked over in alarm, "Grace? What is it?" He pulled the car to the side of road and turned to me. "Grace?"

I shook my head and put my finger to my lips, as I went back into my head.

"Ben?" I asked cautiously.

He was a shell of agony. How had he managed to keep this kind of intense emotion from me? "Ben? *What* is wrong?"

Finally, he managed to sputter, "They have decided that we will not be together." The agony rolled through him again, and carried me with him like flotsam tossed on waves.

"Oh," was all I managed, as tears poured from my eyes and the pain of loss overwhelmed me. "Oh, no." I had thought I loved him before, but feeling this loss, I realized how profoundly Ben loved me, and had loved me for millennia. I understood how he had ached for any brief life span with me that had been denied to him. I saw how desperately he had fought for me when he'd realized they intended to keep us apart this lifetime. Now he'd been told we'd *never* be together again. His grief was paralyzing.

Marco reached for me then. Pulling me over the stick shift, he wrapped me in his arms. I was crying for Ben in Marco's arms yet again. I sobbed with abandon, soaking the shoulder of his jacket, my body convulsing with spasms of sorrow. He rocked me gently, murmuring, "It'll be okay, Grace. It'll be okay."

He was wrong. It would never be okay again. Josh was gone. They were going to take Ben away. If I couldn't win this battle that I was completely unequipped to fight, all the good things in life would be gone not only for me, but for everyone else, too. This was a burden I was too frail to carry.

He let me sob for a few minutes, but then Marco tilted me back into my own seat, put his hands on either side of my face and forced me to look into his eyes. "All right, Grace. That's enough. Time to pull yourself together."

I sputtered again, but he shook his head. "We don't have time to wallow in self-pity or to let ourselves be distracted by our losses. This is a war. Hard as it is, there are always collateral damages. I'm sorry," he added a little more tenderly, "but that's the way it is." His voice grew firm again. "I'm starting the car again. When I stop in five minutes, you're going to be in complete control of yourself and focused on your obligations. *Is that clear, soldier?*" His voice had a ring of authority, like a general ordering troops. I snapped out of my agony, surprised at his tone.

He gave a chortle of embarrassment, "Sorry," he said, "old habit." He started the car and glanced over his shoulder before pulling back out onto the road. "I'm serious though, Grace. Be ready. Five minutes."

I nodded. Pulling a fast food napkin out of the glove box, I wiped my eyes and tried to clear my head. I opened the window and focused on the sensation of the cool morning air rushing over my face and through my hair. The chill helped. My throat and chest still ached, but I felt determination grow in me. I would do my best. It was all I had.

"I'm putting up the window, now." Marco said quietly a few minutes later, "We're heading onto gravel." The window closed beside me. I focused on simmering a resolute force inside myself.

The gravel road turned out to be the same logging road where the Sasquatch had killed Josh. I fought down the rush of emotions, but didn't stop myself from marking the spot. There was still a strange purplish smear in the middle of the road. I didn't see the beast's corpse, and wondered whether some animal had dragged it off. Marco patted my hand again, but that was his only acknowledgement that he understood the horror of this place.

He pulled into a small side road and looked at me, "Well, Grace, this is it. You're on your own from here. I'll carry on and see if I can lead away anyone following us or find Eris or Enyo."

I nodded, grabbing my pack from the back seat, and swinging it onto my back I said, "Okay. See ya later." I hope.

"Good luck," he wished sincerely as I shut the door. His eyes were haunting. They did not look very confident.

"Thanks." I muttered as he continued up the road in a cloud of dust.

I checked the GPS and started into the trees. There was a small animal track to follow. I wondered if mountain goats had made it because it was hard hiking up the very steep incline. I focused my attention solely on what I was doing, and left the grief behind me at the road. I could not spare a thought for either Josh or Ben right now. I had a job to do. I was hopeful that Marco's distraction had worked should anyone been tracking behind us, but just an hour or so later I caught the distinct sounds of someone following me on the path. More than that, I also had the distinct *sense* of someone. A malevolent someone. I let the sense roam a little out from me and decided it had to be one of the twins. I stepped off the trail for a moment and climbed quickly up a tree to study the panorama below me. A couple of minutes later Eris' short spiky hair came in sight along the path below me. I held very still and pondered my options. I could let her go, but she was obviously hunting for me, and she would inevitably keep hunting for me. She'd probably lay some trap that I'd walk right into. I sighed. I could kill her, but... I couldn't even fathom the thought. I couldn't stand the idea of seeing the light leaving anyone else's eyes, even someone truly evil. That left one option. I would have to incapacitate her.

Well then.

I sat there for a moment trying to figure out how I was going to do that, when I recognized a familiar sensation: a magnetic draw. Sure enough, Alex silently rounded the trail behind my tree just as Eris disappeared around a bend up ahead. As I watched the flawless perfection of him draw closer I felt my body flood with heat as the attraction overwhelmed me.

I fought to regain my focus as I re-arranged myself more comfortably in the tree and waited. As he came beneath me I hissed, "Psst!"

He stopped and looked up. He caught sight of me and grinned seductively as he stepped closer and purred, "I thought I felt you. How far ahead is she?"

"Just a few dozen metres."

He nodded. "Okay. Let's get her. You go up the hill here so you'll be ahead of her on the path. I'll cut through over there. With any luck, she'll try to attack you, and then I'll come up from the rear and ambush her. It's the classic hammer and anvil technique. What do you think?"

I shrugged, "You're the protector. I don't have a clue what I'm doing."

He shook his head with a vague smile. "It'll come when you need it.'

Why was everyone always saying that? "I'm leaving," I said as I leapt from the tree. "See you at the ambush," I added flippantly.

He smiled, calling out quietly after me with a laugh, "Don't die before I get there."

I turned to glower at him, but he'd already turned away and started up the trail, so he didn't see it. It was one thing for me to be facetious about my coming demise, but altogether something else for *him* to be so light about my inevitable death.

Fighting down the feelings of inadequacy and irritation, I hiked up the hill steadily, amazed that I wasn't collapsing from the effort. I was not used to physical exertion, so I should have been panting in agony, but the climb seemed effortless. I could sense Eris' position and I made sure to pull out of woods onto the path just ahead of her. Alex was closing in behind her. I waited for her to come around a bend, and then I stepped out into the trail.

"Hi, Eris. Looking for anyone?"

Her eyes narrowed. "As a matter of fact," she snarled, "I am looking for you. Ready to die?"

"Not quite yet, actually."

She stepped forward growling, "I *will* kill you."

"Promises, promises," I remarked nonchalantly. It would be nice for all this to be over with, but I wasn't going to make it easy for her.

She scowled and lunged at me.

I was actually surprised at her quick action, and I almost didn't get out of the way in time. I slipped to the right so I didn't take her full weight, but she forced me rather painfully into a tree.

She growled in frustration as I spun back to her. "Oh come on, surely you can do better than that?"

She raised her fists and ran at me again, throwing a very impressive right hook.

My left arm flew up to guard the shot from contacting, and I fired off a right hook of my own.

She wasn't expecting it and reacted too late, so my punch hit her jaw, though not as hard as I would have liked. Her eyes narrowed.

She stepped back to grab a large stick, and strode back to me with it extended like a spear. She ran at me, and in trying to dodge out of the way, I stumbled backwards, hitting the dirt hard. She laughed and went to fire her makeshift spear at me when an arm reached out and plucked it from the air. She spun in fury as Alex grinned down at her smugly and said, "This doesn't look like a very fair fight, sweetie."

Her eyes got huge and she snarled again, this time with a note of impatience. She flew at me again where I was still sprawled on the ground, but I was ready for her. I had my fingers wrapped around a rock. As she powered toward me, I raised it and shot it at her as hard as I could. It hit smack in the middle of her forehead. There was a crunch and she dropped to the ground. David and Goliath mixed into hammer and anvil.

"Nice shot," Alex said conversationally. "I'm impressed."

I was shaking. "Um. Thanks." I stood up slowly, brushing off the earth as I rose. I felt nauseous. "Do you think she's dead?"

He shrugged and stepped over to her, reaching down to check her pulse. He concentrated for a moment before he said, "No, her heart is beating." He straightened up and came beside me. "Can you handle it from here? I am going to try to find Enyo."

I nodded. "Yeah, okay. Go ahead. I'll be fine."

He took off up the trail and I turned back to Eris. I had no idea how long she'd stay unconscious. My body was shaking from the adrenaline coursing through it. I concentrated on regaining my breathing as I checked her pulse for myself. Sure enough, her heart was beating steadily. I wouldn't have been surprised if Alex had lied to spare my feelings. He seemed completely immune to violence. I rummaged hopefully in my pack for rope. No luck, but there was a roll of duct tape. I smirked, betting that that was an Auntie Bright contribution. I dragged Eris off the path and behind a boulder, bound her feet, pulled her arms behind her back and bound her wrists. I made a wad of the silver tape and forced it into her mouth, then spread two strips across her mouth. I chuckled to myself as I did. Maybe she'd thank me; when that strip came off, she wouldn't have to pay for lip waxing this month.

One evil sibling down: two to go.

I checked the GPS and adjusted my angles a little bit before I carried on up the mountain. I'd been climbing maybe another hour when I heard distinct voices in the distance. I spread out the radar of my mind. Two this time, but before I could think of what I wanted to do to avoid them, there was a shout, "There she is! Get her!"

I ran. I was astonished at how quickly I could move, and how little it tired me. It occurred to me that I should have tried Super Grace running earlier, considering I was in a hurry. Instead of sauntering up at my slow human pace and practically inviting the bad guys to catch me, I could have been racing all this time! Too bad no one had told me I had this particular power. At least I knew now. I began tearing up fifty-degree angles and steeper as if I was still strolling. It was as if I was in a bad paranormal movie. Wow. I reached an open space and stopped. My radar wasn't picking up any danger. I breathed deeply, studying my surroundings.

I was standing in a lovely meadow, surrounded by evergreens of various sizes; I could see the red swirls like modern art that showed the stands of trees under beetle attack. That particular battle was not my concern at this moment. I listened carefully. The only sounds were the rustle of the leaves overhead, the calls of small birds, and the chittering from a squirrel irritated by my presence in his domain. The air was spiced with the fragrance of the pine and fir trees. The scent made me think of picnics, camping trips and hikes. Such happy memories to recall at this moment. Would these be my last happy memories? I glanced around, straining for any noises that would suggest I was being pursued. Still nothing. Had I really managed to outrun them? Or were they just waiting for me somewhere else?

I checked the GPS again. Conveniently, my wild race up the mountain had brought me very close to the coordinates provided by Josh. A few metres to the left and I would be at my destination. From where I stood, all I could see in that direction was a mountainside, but perhaps there was a path or something. I stretched my awareness to confirm that I was still alone, and then I started walking.

My destination was a wall of slate, as I'd expected. I stepped back to study the options. Bare rock, a tree against a bare rock, or bare rock? I shrugged and stepped up to the tree, pushing it aside revealed a crack just wide enough to slip through. Of course.

I reached into my pack and pulled out my headlamp. I put the elastic around my head, turned the lamp on and centred it on my forehead; then, holding my pack at my side and my head pointing the lamp into the void, I squeezed through the narrow opening in the cliff face.

For a few metres, it was tight. I could hear the rustle of bats over head, and caught an acrid whiff of guano in the air. Glancing to my feet, I could see the nutrient rich white stuff I was walking through. Perhaps if I made it out alive I could come back and gather some for Bright's garden. I giggled in spite of myself as I inched forward. Gradually, the crack widened into a comfortable hallway width. I slipped my pack back over my shoulders.

The path twisted around a corner and I listened cautiously. This would be an ideal spot for a trap if they were watching their entrance.

Of course, they'd be watching the entrance.

I turned the corner and faced a wall. Apparently, this was the end of the line for anyone who had accidentally arrived in this place. I knew there was something more for me. I walked along the wall, studying in carefully, paying attention to each bump and undulation. There was going to be a way to go further; it was not possible that I would be stopped here, even if such a tidy dead end made a perfect place for an ambush.

I inhaled deeply and shook the thought out of my head. There was no place for panic at a time like this. I turned my attention to my feet. Was there something in the ground? What about over my head? I touched, poked, pushed and pulled almost every inch of the dead end. Where was it? There was an entrance; that was not at question. I refused to consider that Josh had been a sacrifice in this game for nothing. If it wasn't here at the end, where was it? I would widen my search. If the entry wasn't in this spot, it was earlier along the passage, but it *was* here. I had provisions for several days of looking. I would find it. Scraping a line in the dirt with the heel of my boot, I marked my new beginning, and then I turned and started scanning the passage about five metres from the end, working back toward the entrance. After three metres on one side, I marked the line where I stopped and then caught up on the other side. After combing carefully until I had gone back about twenty metres, I spotted it.

There was a slight indentation on the side of the wall, about a hand's breadth deep at waist height. It was about half a metre wide. At eye level, it just looked like a slight dip in the wall. Tilting my head back, I watched the shadows play as the beam traveled up the wall. Above my head, it made a deeper cavity that rose to the roof of the cave. It was a perfect indentation for a makeshift ladder, and sure enough, at the top I could see a slight shadow that could be a hole. My light could not penetrate enough to know for sure. There was only one option. It looked like I was going up.

I took my pack off by back and reversed it, so it was sitting across my chest instead: I'd need my back. I anchored my left foot on one side of the indentation and wedged my arms out to the sides as I dug my right foot into the narrow rock at knee height. I shifted my weight up, pushing my back onto the left side. So far so good. I settled my weight to the right as I lifted my left foot up. Even my toes were curled into the rock, gripping to hold me securely as I inched upward into the shadows. Shale flaked off the wall at my feet and fell noisily to the ground as my heart pounded. I regained my footing and kept going. A few metres further up the sides had become deeper and the indent had become a pipe. This was easier to climb because I could use my back as well. If I turned off my headlamp, someone coming along the path would be hard pressed to notice me hanging half off the wall like a bat.

An hour later, I was probably a hundred metres in the air, opposite the shadowy hole I'd seen from below. It was an opening onto a ledge that was a bit more than half a metre square but led into a tunnel that looked quite deep. I could see for a long way in, so I knew I'd be able to crawl in for a while before it narrowed again. It was worth exploring, at any rate. I wedged my hips in place and loosened my pack off, tossing it onto the ledge. I eased forward and stretched out, lowering my shoulder onto the landing. I pulled up my knee, heaved, and I was in the opening. I wasn't going to be able to go forward with my pack on me, so I pushed it into the tunnel. On my hands and knees, I crawled along, pushing the pack ahead of me, wondering if this was what it was like to be born: to force oneself along a tight tunnel and hope there was something at the other end of it. I had only gone a couple dozen metres when I was surprised to see that there was another opening to the right. Hmmm. This was interesting. To go straight or to turn off? I poked my head into the gap and gasped. No doubt, I was going in. I crawled through the opening and stood up looking around at the astounding scene before me.

This was a definite corridor, not a natural cave tunnel at all, but a level, carved creation by some amazing architect. Here and there were carvings in the wall. The letters weren't English, so I couldn't understand the words, but the pictures were clear: battle scenes throughout the ages. From cavemen with rocks and sticks, to grand armies, a history of warfare was unfolding beside me in the dim light. As I passed them, it seemed as I could hear water running on the other side of the wall. Instead of being soothing, the tumbling river brought thoughts of death. First Josh's, and then I saw Ben crumpled and bleeding on a battlefield, Alex's head severed from his body and swinging from a dark hand, and finally Marco covered with gashes and blackened with burnt flesh. "Only my mind," I told myself. I could not afford even to consider that this was a premonition of how today would end. I willed myself forward, and saw another casualty of the battle. My own eyes stared blankly toward the sky before me. My clothes had been torn off my body and the bloody result of another type of warfare was clear. Forever had rape accompanied war. I felt as if I was going to vomit. Swallowing the burning, churning waves, I forced myself onward. Death and despair. Pain and anguish. I was walking toward them and I couldn't understand anymore why I was being forced to do it. I saw my empty eyes and ravished body again in my mind, and I shivered. Then the shiver became shaking and I crumpled to the ground. The nausea overwhelmed me and I vomited beneath a particularly heinous picture of the grey faces of living death.

I could not go on. I lay there shaking uncontrollably, seeing all the people that I loved fallen beside me, their bodies crushed or broken and bloody, their eyes vacant and hollow because of me. I could not deal with this. Evil would always win. Death always claimed its prize at the end. What could joy and love do against such despair?

I lay on the cold stone floor for a long time. I couldn't go forward to face death in battle, but I could not go back the way I had come either. So I would stay here, and wait for death to find me.

A distant sussurance of water echoed my grief as I lay there, remembering my friends and family. I would never see them again. I sobbed uncontrollably for a while, overwhelmed, sad and lost. All at once, like a faint whisper in my memory, I remembered Christie's words. *There's always hope.* When Pandora released all the evils of the world, one thing remained in the box: hope. Did I dare hope?

I tried to summon a hopeful thought, but everything was black. I could see Ben if I reached the end, I could hope for that, but we were not going to be allowed to be together. The sadness overwhelmed me again as I cried out in my anguish, "Ben!"

As if he'd been waiting for me, he answered. Not with words, but with music. It was a slow, melancholy tune in a minor key that captured my feelings exactly. We mourned together for a while, but then there was a flicker of twinkling melody, a staccato of laughter, and hope entered the song. As it danced into the melancholy motif, it wrapped around the dark notes and it created a sparkling joy. Love amid pain. Joy amid horror. Hope conquered despair and flooded my heart

I rose to my feet.

The darkened corridor beckoned me onward. The tiniest light glimmered in the distance and I ran toward it desperately. This was the end. There would be no more waiting. The corridor started climbing. I could feel the strips of grit on the floor meant to keep pedestrians from slipping as I ran steadily forward. I wondered vaguely if there was an easier entrance to warrant that sort of a safety precaution. Small demi-lunes of light shone down at intervals from the wall, offering an antiseptic glow to light the way. It was adequate for the purpose, but barely. I was thinking calmly. That was a relief. I was no longer paralyzed with fear, but I was moving forward purposefully, no thought in my mind but my goal.

The walls began to narrow in. It could have been claustrophobic, had I tendencies that way, but I traveled on without concern along the narrow passage. Suddenly the hallway widened. I had reached a landing. This was the end of the corridor. Four doors were arrayed before me. I stopped to consider my options. The Lady or the Tiger? I laughed to myself, shaking my head. Bright had said that it was always tricks and games with management. They hunted for amusement anywhere they could find it. I understood intellectually; I'd spent enough summer afternoons watching anthills with fascination, amused to put obstacles before the little creatures and marvelling at their ingenuity as they worked out the problems I initiated in their world. Knowing why it happened didn't really remove the irritation. I didn't like being the ant.

I studied the four identical doors. Aglaea had said that once I reached the doors that I could summon the others. Was there a door for each of us? Hmm. I looked around me considering exactly how I *should* summon them. I probably should have asked her about that in the kitchen. There was nothing except the corridor carved in the rock and the four doors. I pursed my lips and held up my arms. A wave of electricity seemed to trickle from my fingers down to my shoulders. I could feel power. In a calmly compelling voice I commanded, "Ben! Marco! Alex! I summon you! Come to me!" My voice echoed along the corridor and I felt a surge of energy travel through me. It felt dramatic, but nothing else happened. They didn't appear.

Oh well. They'd been summoned. There was nothing more for me but to go through one of the doors and let the next component of this crazy day unfold. Which door? I put my ear on each. They were equally silent. Twenty-five per cent chance of success. No point wasting time over thinking it. I arbitrarily chose the door second on the right, waiting for a moment before I actually moved to see if any instinct baulked at the choice. Nothing. Well then.

I reached forward and turned the handle confidently. The door swung open and I stepped through onto the top of a mountain. Of course. I chuckled grudgingly. They were nothing if not thorough.

The rocky crags around me caught the dazzling afternoon light, vivid from the black clouds gathered in the distance, concentrating the bright rays. I was at the tree line. Above was only rock, but I was in an open space surrounded only by a few scrawny trees.

This was not Bastion Mountain.

CHAPTER THIRTEEN

MANAGEMENT GAMES AGAIN

Battleground chosen, war rages. Spears and the swords of the soldiers,
Flashing in glistening sunlight. Friends from the past growing bolder,
Greatest of warrior's welcoming best of his friends to the battle.
Charis finds strengths within herself, fight until death has been settled.

There was a quivering in the light ahead of me and suddenly three men stood before me, each one a classical statue come to life. They weren't the same young men I'd left that morning, but they were undoubtedly here in response to my summons. It seemed so long ago that we were in Bright's kitchen. I shook my head in bemusement. They were no longer in mortal disguises. Instead, their true, immortal nature was clearly apparent. Each one was rippled, carved with hard muscle, tall and handsome. Beyond handsome: they were other-worldly. I knew each slightly modified face, and welcomed their warm smiles of greeting. Alex stood taller and broader than the others. He was bronzed, stunning and perfect, his mouth curved in his usual lopsided, sultry smile. Marco, more slender and slightly shorter, was grinning at me mischievously, his eyes sparkled as his dark brown curls were tousled by the wind. Between them stood my own beautiful blond Ben, his blue eyes glowing with adoration. It was to him that my eyes were drawn longest; an irresistible fondness echoed in my own gaze.

I felt the crackle of electricity in the air and I smirked at them. Distantly, thunder rumbled, shaking the ground where the four of us exchanged conspiratorial grins. We were together for the battle, whatever this battle would be. Their presence took away a little of the overwhelming anxiety that I'd been forcing down all day. Eventually it was going to catch up to me, but I couldn't face it just yet. I needed my wits about me.

A roar in the distance announced a powerful engine barrelling upwards. Over the edge of the cliff snarled a huge off-road vehicle. It was black with gold trim and painted flames burning down the sides. It was the foolishly ostentatious vehicle of someone who liked to show off.

Of course, it was Ares who opened the door and stepped out, grinning deviously.

I thought I heard a rumbling growl coming from Alex's chest. Ares strolled casually to the back of the truck and dropped the hatch. Out jumped a huge hairy dog. It stood to his hips, mostly white but with dark splotches, and it had massive shoulders and jowls. It sat down looking obediently at Ares, then at his command it headed to the edge of the meadow, watching us carefully. I heard Alex snicker quietly behind me while Ares laughed malevolently. His eyes sought mine and his gaze burned with his conviction that victory was moments away. His victory, not mine. I gulped down a wave of panic.

Ares held his hand out to the air. There was a blue flash and a spear appeared in his hand. Cool trick. I was impressed despite myself. He balanced it horizontally, bouncing it up and down until he reached the spot he liked, "Ready for some target practice?" he asked me with a mock pleasantness.

"Of course, Ares, give me your best shot." I said calmly. I took a deep breath and felt for my power. I had no idea how I was going to fight him. It was kind of weird to be in the midst of a battle with strategies that were so mysterious that I didn't even know what they were. I giggled to myself again, feeling slightly hysterical. *Focus Grace*, I reminded myself.

Ares raised the spear to his shoulder level, bounced it again, and then with a glare, he stepped forward and snapped it straight at me. It flew as if fired from a canon, but I saw it in slow motion. I turned my body to the side and it flashed past me with a whoosh. Without thinking, I stretched out my arm and I plucked it out of the air behind me. I spun it so the lethal end was heading in the opposite direction, and fired it back at him. It trailed a comet's tail of sparks, and I gasped in awe at the terrible splendour of it. Ares was as quick as I was though, and he caught it mid-flight as well. He turned snarling at me, rushing with the spear held out across his body as if he was cross checking in a hockey game. I stretched my hands forward in defence, and suddenly there was a spear of my own in them. I didn't have time to be surprised before I was parrying his advance and our spears were clashing against each other, showering us in fireworks with each resounding crash. Marco shouted, "Grace!" and I realized too late that Ares had been backing me into the cliff. I stumbled and fell just as he changed his grip and thrust toward me with the sharp end of the spear. I had nothing to protect myself with, but I rolled quickly over the sharp slices of shale and flicking my fingers toward it, the sparks fired from my fingertips and with a flash, his spear disappeared. Huh. Looked like I had a few cool tricks of my own.

I raised my eyebrows at Ares.

His lip curled and he gave me a nod of grudging appreciation. "Much better. Now you offer a little challenge!"

"Since I'm still alive I'd say obviously I was plenty enough challenge for you before..." I taunted, "Didn't it occur to you that if you couldn't manage to kill me before I got this far, that you weren't likely to be able to do it once I did?"

He glared at me, "What makes you think you could ever be more powerful than me? You're just a little girl, Grace." He scanned the meadow.

"Are you waiting for the twins? Sorry. They're a little tied up at the moment." Although it wasn't strictly true of both twins, uttering a groaner worthy of Lloyd suddenly provided a little of his sunny presence.

Ares scowled angrily at that and then said something in Greek to the dog that set it moving around the periphery with its eyes scanning us, but not coming forward. Something crunched in the woods behind me. He looked over with a smile and said, "You're sure about that, are you?"

I glanced behind me to see Enyo step into the meadow. Damn. I'd hoped she wouldn't catch up to us.

Ben took a protective step closer to me and Enyo smiled cruelly at him, "Hello, Mr. *Butler*. Long time no see." She had some strange long, black, webbed weapon in her hand.

He nodded to her, his expression serious. "Hello, Enyo. I won't suggest I'm glad to see you. New bow?"

She grinned pleasantly, as she lifted the thing in her hand. It was a black bow, with wheels on the tips and wires crossing it. It was constructed of a crazy hollow framework of menacing grids that looked like the weapon of a comic book villain. She reached beside the scope and pulled an arrow from the quiver on the other side of it. She drew the bow and it clicked into place as she twisted her smile and narrowed her eyes ominously. "Yes, it should be quite efficient for killing you."

I shouted, "No!" but Alex had come up beside me and grabbed my shoulders.

It was foolish for Ben to be here. Marco and Alex were warriors, but Ben was just a musician. I knew that he was only here because he couldn't bear to be away from me when I was in so much danger, but it was ridiculous. What would happen if he was hurt or killed because he'd come to this fight? Even my mother knew he was a useless protector. His love was too distracting for him to focus on what had to be done.

Alex whispered, "Your job is to defeat Ares. We aren't allowed to help with that. But we can take Enyo, and we can keep Ben safe."

I nodded. He was right. I knew that. But it still took everything I had to turn away from Ben and focus my attention back on Ares. I could not afford to let *my* love and concern be a distraction. I looked back at Ares just in time, because he had just fired a spear, and it was heading at Ben. At almost the same moment, there was a snap of a released arrow that whistled through the air. I slashed my arm down and shot a bolt of electricity at the spear, which lost its trajectory and fell harmlessly a few metres short of its target at the same moment that I felt Ben's head explode in pain. Enyo's arrow had made it home. *Excellent protection, Alex!* I thought to myself.

I sent Ben love, and whirled around to fire a bolt of electricity at Enyo. She wasn't expecting it and shrieked in pain as it sliced across her face. I caught a glimpse of Ben's face, a marble mask of white, as he lay on the ground with an arrow in his chest. So much for them keeping him safe.

Fury filled me as I shot another bolt at Ares as he was trying to pull himself to his feet. From his knees, he fired a spear at me; I snapped my arm and it exploded into shatters. Before I could fire again, he'd sent another through the air, at Marco this time.

Marco leapt forward with a spear of his own in his hand and a shield over his arm. He raised the shield and sidestepped, deflecting Ares' spear away from him. With a calculating look he remarked, "You're losing your touch, Ares," but he didn't fire his own spear at him. Instead, he took aim across the field where Enyo had her sights on Alex, and let fly.

She caught a glimpse of the coming spear in her peripheral vision and snarled, turning her bow toward Marco and releasing her arrow at him instead. Marco raised his shield and sidestepped, the arrow buzzed by, narrowly missing him.

Ares' dog was circling around us and growling. Ben was lying still. Was he okay? The dog came closer to him, teeth barred, its shoulders low, its tail straight out.

Alex took a step out of his position behind me and shadowed the dog, which immediately set off a low, menacing bark that would definitely be enough to detract most people from bothering whatever it was protecting.

Alex smiled gently at it and spoke in soothing tones. I heard him whisper something that sounded like, "Pretty dog"

Ares snarled and raced forward as if he was going to tackle Alex. Marco intercepted him with a powerful right jab. The punch was magnified in intensity because Ares had been running into it, and his head flew backward, his eyes rolling. An arrow whizzed by Marco's ear. I shot another bolt of lightning at Enyo. Her bow was raised and she let fly an arrow at me just as my bolt hit her bow with a twang. As her arm shook from the concussion, Alex grabbed her and threw her to the ground. The dog sprang at him, teeth barred, but he stretched a hand out with a firm command in Greek. It froze mid-charge, and began to back off slowly, still growling.

I had a second to catch my breath and I made the mistake of looking over to Ben. My heart contracted. He looked like death had claimed him where he lay limply on the edge of the meadow, blood oozing from his chest and down over his arm.

There was a sound behind and I raised my arm as I turned. Ares was in full flight, spear outstretched to impale me. I watched him come in slow motion as my world stretched in front of me, a huge blank canvas of lonely existence without Ben. If I stood my ground for another moment, the razor sharp tip of Ares' spear would rip through my heart and lungs. I'd be free from the responsibility of being a Grace. I'd be free from the agony of life without Ben. A moment of pain as the spear exploded my chest would be all the payment I'd owe for this freedom.

There was another shout in Greek, and the dog leapt forward toward me. I thought it was going for my throat, but instead its jaw snapped shut ahead of me, snatching the shaft of the spear. Its roar was echoed in Ares' screech of frustration.

"Move, Grace!" shouted Marco from the side. I snapped from my reverie.

I heard a loud smack and glanced to see Alex hitting his hip as the dog raced to him.

I turned back to Ares. My arm slashed through the air to release another bolt that he deflected into the air. I recognized that my commitment to the fight was flagging and with it the power. Why go on without Ben?

Marco stood above Enyo who was bound and lying in the dirt, shooting metaphorical arrows at me with her eyes. Those arrows couldn't hurt me, but she'd already fired one that was destroying my will to live.

Ares glanced at me and he laughed with a menacing whisper, "All's fair in love and war, girlie." He spun and fired a spear at Marco. A scream of warning died in my throat as Marco raised his shield a second too late. The spear was deflected but not far enough. It tore through his bicep, leaving a trail of blood and sinew behind it. Marco shouted and went to raise his own spear in retaliation but Alex grabbed it from him. "No! No weapons, Marco!"

Ares laughed and it rang through the mountain, "Grace hasn't a chance against me Alexandros. Haven't you figured it out yet? She is too weak, and too hampered by her useless affection to the inconsequential dead musician."

I bowed my head, defeated, and Alex looked over frantically. "You're not weak, Grace. You have the power!"

Ares stepped closer to me, menacingly spitting out the sad reality, "She doesn't even want to fight. She's ready to surrender right now."

Alex gasped as he saw the truth of it in my eyes.

"Come on, Grace," Ares murmured almost like a lover, "surrender to me."

Before I could raise my arms in acquiescence, I heard music. It was only a soft echo, heard from a far distance, but it was my song. I looked over to Ben with a shimmer of desperate hope. His arm twitched, and ever so slightly he shut his fingers, leaving a thumb outstretched. "Live," he spoke in my thoughts.

"Will *you*? I demanded back, pushing into his mind for the whole truth. He would not lie to me. If he was dying, so was I.

I heard the whispered affirmation inside my head, and echoing in the air around me. "Yes." He was alive, and he would try to live.

Joy coursed through me, and I felt the electricity following.

"You're boring me, Ares." I took a step toward him and the dog snarled and lunged toward me, mouth gaping, ready to take a chunk out of me this time. Before I could react, Alex shouted a command to the dog at the same moment a spear left Ares' hand. Leaving my side exposed to the dog, I waved my hand to deflect the spear. Marco caught it deftly with his good arm and stepped in between the dog and me, but he needn't have bothered because it had dropped into a sit and frozen, its tail wagging and its tongue lolling in a most unferocious manner. I could swear that dog was making goo-goo eyes at Alexander. A flashing hope flew through my brain that I did not look that slavishly devoted when the magnets between us were on. Gross.

Another spear had appeared in Ares' hand and this one was heading for Alex, if that look of grim fury was any indication. I waved my hand and with a flash, the spear exploded in Ares' hand. He yelped, shaking his arm before he stepped forward with a snarl and drew a sword from the air. He raised it above his head as he stepped forward to slice at me.

I jumped as the blade tore through my shirtsleeve, but slashed back with a lightning bolt that left a momentary glow of red on his shield.

Another slice of his blade bore down but my answering slash of light struck his hand and he dropped his sword with a howl of anger and frustration. His eyes had taken on a fiery gleam of determination.

"We could do this all day, Ares. I really think it would be wiser for you just to give up with your dignity intact."

He snarled, raised another spear that had appeared in his hand, and deked me out like a good hockey wingman. He went right and I followed, then he fired and the spear flew past me. I heard a guttural groan and glanced back to see Alex staggering back with the spear through his shoulder just below the collarbone. He met my eyes and his lips formed 'Sorry' as he fell backwards to the ground.

Ares laughed gleefully as he reached out for another spear and fired it off without a thought. My horror for Alex crashed through my gut. I saw Ben lying helplessly, white and still. My thoughts sought his without success. My heart collapsed into my shoes. He was dead after all. Blood was pouring from Marco's wound. I saw them all in a flash, and power rushed through me. Before Ares' spear had advanced more than a few feet, I'd raised my arm and made an X in the air. The first slash immobilized the spear, the second immobilized Ares. He fell to the earth howling with a white smoking gash across his chest. I turned to Marco, "Did you see that? That one was cool!" I was hysterical from pain and joy.

Nursing his bloody bicep, he grinned fondly.

"You want to tie him up?"

"Yes," he nodded, "definitely." He squeezed his fist and grimaced, "Perhaps you had better do it though. I seem to be lacking a little dexterity."

I looked over to where Ben was lying. He had moved. He'd pulled himself over onto his side. He was so pale that he was ghostly, but his eyes were open, glowing warmly at me through his pain.

I beamed at him in astonishment and joy. "I did it, Ben!"

He nodded with a faint whisper, "You did."

Marco went and crouched beside Alex, snapping the spear off so he only had a bit of length straining on the wound. Ares' dog had sidled up next to them and Alex was talking affectionately to it. It was gazing at him in a most undignified manner, attentive to his every syllable.

I picked up my pack and rummaged for the duct tape, trussing Ares as I had his sister.

Ben raised his head. The other two looked at him expectantly. In the sky, black clouds were rolling toward us at a furious rate. Ben nodded and slowly eased himself up. I helped him stand and moved a little away from him. We were roughly in a semi-circle around Ares' bound body as it was propped awkwardly in the middle of a rock. He was groaning.

The lightning slashed down, but none of us moved. Nearby a tree was hit and it shattered with a blinding flash and rumbling boom. The branches began to smoulder until they began blazing. Our smiles grew larger, while as if of one mind, Marco and I spread apart, so that the four of us surrounded the rock while we scanned the sky around us.

Another lightning bolt shot down, precisely to the centre where we'd been standing moments before. It left a charred, smoking hole in the rock where Ares was lying. He was instantly entombed in light. We threw back our heads and laughed. Management games, again.

Another bolt struck unerringly toward me, and instinctively I reached up to it, welcoming the power, foolishly fearless. To my surprise, instead of being unarrestable light, it felt like rope, a white-hot tether, but it didn't burn me. This did not surprise me either. I grabbed tightly and pulled. The light came with me as I spun, gripping tightly so it bowed like an illuminated kite string. I flung it away from me, watching it fly and then spark on the hillside as it fell back to earth. Flames shot up where it landed. The power rushed through me. Perception is reality. I was the most powerful being on the planet.

A thunderous bellow echoed through the heavens, quaking the rocks around us. A deep voice bellowed, "ENOUGH!" and the mountains instantly became silent.

A glowing apparition appeared: tall, muscular and white haired.

I stared as Ben, Alex and Marco bowed their heads to this illuminated being.

He spread his arms wide and announced, "She has the power. She has earned the right."

As the energy coursed through me, I tried to make sense of his words.

My companions stepped back, making a protective arc around me. I knew I didn't need it. I was stronger than the three of them together at this moment, but I was glad of their companionship nonetheless.

The being from the sky spoke again; there was derision in his tone as he said. "Ares, the girl is the victor."

There was a humiliated groan from the glowing rock. I felt a little sorry for him.

"Girl. As victor in this trial you may declare his punishment."

"I'm sorry?" I muttered.

The being scoffed impatiently, "Punishment. What is the cost of your victory? Shall I lock him in a jar? Banish him to an island? Give him a rock to roll uphill for eternity? What?"

I shook my head and looked helplessly between the three wounded protectors. Ben's eyes were shut; he was breathing shallowly. His survival was still tenuous. Alex and Marco stared straight ahead with military bearing. They would offer no suggestions.

"I can choose whatever I want as the price of my victory?"

The being snorted, "*Choose* girl!"

"I choose the life of the one I love."

"We are not speaking of rewards. A consort is not part of this trial. You are to choose a punishment for my weak son."

This was Ares' father? I stared at him, but he was glowing too brightly to register his features.

"Fine. My punishment is that he may no longer wage war; he must live in peace with his love from now on."

There was a gasp from the glowing rock where Ares was imprisoned.

"Fine," declared the glowing being, "so it is. The child gifts you love, Ares. She is worthy of her role in Aphrodite's retinue, wouldn't you say?"

Then with a flash of white that erased all features of the landscape, everything disappeared.

CHAPTER FOURTEEN

THE ARE MANY KINDS OF STRENGTH

Zeus summons Charis to join him, gathering all to the mountain.
Charites beg Aphrodite; Charis needs love she can count on.
Being alone for eternity, takes all the joy from the victory;
Nothing is worth losing Orpheus; joy was the point of her story.

When I opened my eyes, I stood shivering beside a glacier on Washington's Mount Olympus as people gathered around me. Everyone was draped in outfits that would have been at home on Ancient Greek sculptures. I glanced down and saw that I was wearing the same myself.

I studied the crowd around me. Some of the people I knew, like my mom, aunts, and other assorted relatives that I had met over the years on trips to Greece or at so-called 'family gatherings.' Everyone was looking at me proudly. There were a lot of voices conversing in what seemed like happy tones, but if you'll pardon the cliché, it was all Greek to me. They kept smiling as they glanced over and bobbed their heads at me as if I should have a clue what was going on. It was all very uncomfortable. More than that, it was surreal.

I looked around for Ben, Marco and Alex. I spotted Marco and Alex standing together, capes over shining breastplates with leather gauntlets on their forearms, and Roman sandals on their feet. Neither showed sign of the injuries they'd incurred on the mountaintop.

There was no sign of Ben. My heart sought his thoughts, but found no glimmer of them. He had to be dead then. Ben. Dead.

A virile looking older man with youthfully styled white hair and a well-trimmed beard stepped forward. I'm sure it wasn't coincidence how much he resembled the glowing apparition that had appeared to me on the

388

mountain. Everyone around me took a respectful step back. A few inclined their heads in little bows. He was probably six and a half feet tall and he had extremely broad, powerful looking shoulders. His very modern clothes contrasted with the ancient styles worn by everyone else. There were muscles rippling on his arms and his chest beneath his tight, white v-neck sweater. I did a bit of a double take, because his physique was so incongruent with his obvious age. A fat gold chain glinted around his neck with an ostentatious thunderbolt hanging off it. A huge gold watch adorned his wrist.

"Hello, Grace," he said with a smile that showed a hint of a leer. His voice seemed to echo off the cliffs. It rang with a powerful authority that silenced everything around us. Even the birds were suddenly quiet. The wind seemed to have stopped moving. The people were so quiet that I couldn't even hear them breathing. He opened his arms in a warm but strangely dramatic gesture as he announced in his booming voice with a hint of Greek accent, "I am your grandfather! I am delighted to meet you officially at last!" With that, he stepped forward and crushed me to him. Peeking out from under his armpit, I looked warily over to Bright, mindful of some of the comments she'd made over the years about her father.

She looked watchful, but not alarmed.

He pulled back from the embrace and wrinkled his brows. "You are a like a stick, little one! How have you managed to keep a man interested for all these years?" He laughed to himself and some in the crowd joined sycophantically. My stomach rolled a bit.

"That's enough, Papa," interrupted my mother, or my sister, or whatever she was. "Can't you see you're making her uncomfortable?" She was reminding me a bit of a ferocious mother bear. There was a nervous murmur among the crowd at her challenge.

Her father's mouth gave a slight downward turn. He stared at her for a moment and then took a step back from me. He shrugged his shoulders, and announced to the assembly, "She has completed her trial and shown merit. She is worthy to assume the position ordained for her." He nodded to his right, "Aphrodite? Do you accept her?"

The beautiful woman I remembered from trips to Greece stepped forward. With a gasp, I noticed Ares behind her. He did not meet my eyes.

Aphrodite faced her father and announced, "I accept the acolyte to be a Grace."

There was applause around us as she stepped forward and placed a crown of flowers around my head. "Welcome, Alayna the Grace," she said, smiling warmly.

I looked up and her with confusion. I was too overwhelmed with my loss of Ben to speak to her. Her beautiful alabaster brow wrinkled, "What is it child?"

A single tear traveled slowly down my right cheek and she looked at it in astonishment. "Is this a tear of joy, Grace?"

I shook my head.

"Then what?"

Ares stepped forward then. He cleared his throat and said sullenly, "She is longing for a consort."

A consort. I scowled at him. As if anyone would do!

Aphrodite's face lit up in understanding. "Oh, of course!"

My grandfather grinned. "Aphrodite, that's your area of expertise. Who is the best choice?" The two of them looked meaningfully over at Marco and Alex. They studied them up and down.

Aphrodite finally said, "You both have the skills to guard her. Alexander? Is she to your liking?"

Alex smirked that familiar sultry grin as his eyes raked me up and down and he replied seductively, "She holds some attraction, yes."

I felt naked as Aphrodite smiled and turned her gaze to Marco. "Mars? Would she suit you?"

Marco smiled fondly over to me and responded, "I would be happy to have her."

This was ridiculous. I stomped my foot and snarled, "NO!"

Aphrodite looked over her shoulder at me in astonishment. "You don't like Mars?"

I sucked in my breath with irritation and shook my head, "That's not…" then I let the thought trail off. Ben was dead. I remembered Auntie Bright telling me about the pain of losing the heart's first hope. Ben was ancient honey now. He would remain perfect in my memory and I would never forget. Though my heart was bruised and broken, Marco and Alex were willing to help it mend. Why *not* choose one of them? I loved each of them in a way. Maybe this was the smartest solution. I could choose passion or friendship. It was logical, but part of me ached in loneliness at the thought. I understood why Bright had mourned for decades.

"Fine then," Aphrodite continued impatiently, "Alexander is your choice?"

I looked between the two of them, standing like two cuts of meat in a butcher shop waiting for my decision. Each tried to look confident of my favour, while preparing for rejection. I shook my head helplessly and turned to the crowd, scanning for Auntie Bright.

She stepped forward.

I looked at her pleadingly. She would understand.

She smiled at me and nodded. She stepped up to Aphrodite and her father and said clearly, "Grace has already chosen the one who has followed her through time."

Her father scoffed. "Oh *please!*" he groaned. "He's a pansy! What does she want with a poet and musician when she could have a warrior?"

I listened with vague unease. What did it matter that I'd chosen Ben? He was gone forever.

"There are many kinds of strength, father." Bright replied quietly. "The steadfast devotion and the self-control he has shown over the years require admirable strength of will, wouldn't you agree?" She challenged him with her eyes. Her father's lack of devotion and self-control were legendary.

Her father stared back, and then shook his head. "We have already decided against it. You know that."

Bright scowled at him, "She was successful in her trial. She deserves to choose her reward."

Her father glowered at her. The crowd was absolutely silent. "It was a merit trial, not a reward trial. She earned merit and set the punishment for Ares."

At that moment, Ares stepped forward, clearing his throat again. He stepped next to Aphrodite and took her hand, drawing her head close to his. He whispered earnestly into her ear, and then kissed her tenderly before he stepped back into the crowd.

Aphrodite's gaze followed him as her brows wrinkled again. She looked thoughtfully at me, and then at her father. She drew herself up elegantly and asked imperiously, "It's *my* decision, you said, father?"

He nodded once, curtly, clearly wondering what she was thinking.

Aphrodite studied Bright for a moment, and then in a voice that rang through the hillsides she demanded, "Orpheus! Come forward!"

Far back in the crowd, there was a flurry of movement and the way parted bit by bit as if in slow motion.

I leaned over to Bright and whispered, "Who is Orpheus?"

Bright shook her head quickly as if warning me not to speak. There was a ghost of a smile twitching on her lips.

Her father had heard me, though. "*Who is Orpheus?*" he bellowed in astonishment. "She doesn't even know the name of this great love?"

Bright looked vaguely disdainful, "He has another name in this time, Father."

I looked at her in surprise.

Her father lowered his brows. "Orpheus, Demetrius, whoever!" he glowered. "He's changed his name?" he confirmed. At her irritated nod, he grumbled, "Fine, who is he *now*?"

Before she could answer, a golden god stepped forward, gave a respectful bow and said, "Benjamin Butler, sir."

Ben was alive. Ben was whole. Ben was beautiful. My heart took to the sky as I beamed at him in joyful astonishment. Ben. Ben. Ben. Ben. My head erupted in a brilliant yellow glow of euphoria.

Wait. Ben was actually called *Orpheus*? I stifled a giggle, feeling profoundly thankful that he'd changed his name. He would have been laughed out of school with that one.

"Butler?" boomed my grandfather, distracting me from my giddy joy, "Like a common servant?"

"Yes, sir," said Ben, backing up and wrapping an arm around me, "Grace's servant." I nestled into him feeling my world settle comfortably around me again. I looked up at him with my chest so full of elation I thought I would float away.

My grandfather shook his head in wonderment and studied Ben thoughtfully. "Still not tired of her?"

"No, sir."

"So I take it that you want me to make it official?"

"Yes, sir," said Ben, squeezing me more tightly.

"Hmm." My grandfather glanced at Aphrodite who nodded once. He studied me carefully, and then looked over at Auntie Bright for a long time. She met his eyes without blinking. He looked back to me and I could feel my knees begin shuddering against each other. He turned and looked at Aglaea and my mother. With his booming voice he demanded, "Do you approve of this Thalia?"

My mother nodded. She wisely did not bother to tell him she also used an English name.

"Aglaea?"

"Yes, Father," she said firmly.

I wondered why Auntie Bright was not asked her opinion, but maybe hers was obvious.

He turned back to Ben, appraising him for the longest time. The sun glinted off strands of Ben's hair so that it glowed. The light struck the plains and angles of his face and it was clear that he was an otherworldly being. I wondered again how I had ever thought him average that first day in the band room.

Grandfather looked back at me, shook his head, and then addressed Ben, "You realize that this is the face she will keep forever?"

My heart sank at his uncomplimentary tone. I hadn't thought I was *that* unattractive. I felt myself begin to blush. I knew I was plain beside my aunts, no, my sisters. (I wondered if I would ever get used to that). Everyone was plain beside them. Was I that much plainer? I looked around at the crowd of supernatural beauties and muscular bodies and realized, *maybe*.

Ben glanced down at me, his eyes molten pools of blue and he smiled so adoringly into my eyes that I was embarrassed that there were others around. "I wouldn't have it any other way," he said quietly. "This is the most beautiful face of all."

There were some murmurs in the crowd again, and I wondered if people were doubting Ben's sanity. I know I was, but I couldn't help but smile back at him. As his love filled me, I felt like the most beautiful and desirable woman in the world. His eyes grew closer and his lips met mine possessively and passionately. Everything disappeared. A symphony of joy and adoration was playing in my head. When I came up for air, I took a breath and glanced over nervously at my scowling grandfather. He was staring back at me, "And you Grace? Do you choose him?"

I nodded and then looked adoringly back into the depth of the blue eyes I loved.

Grandfather raised his hands into the air as everyone looked at him expectantly. He scowled and demanded, "Come before me, Orpheus."

Ben took a step away from me, and I felt as if my sun had vanished. The side that had been up against was suddenly cold without him. I shivered again.

My grandfather stepped up to stand directly in front of Ben and set a hand on his shoulder. He stared at Ben for an interminable time. His brows were down and he did not look like he was in a positive frame of mind. It would be accurate to say he was glowering. I remembered, with a stab of fear, what Bright had said about his moodiness. Ben stood emotionlessly, returning the gaze with a clear expression.

It was agony waiting for something to happen.

I looked at my aunts and mom; they seemed anxious. My heart began to pound.

"Come forward, Grace!" my grandfather ordered.

I stepped beside Ben, glancing over at him nervously.

We stood while the wind blew around us and the sun seemed to stop in the sky.

Finally, Grandfather threw his arms into the air; turning to face the crowd behind us, he bellowed with a shout that shook the mountains around our gathering. Visions from many lifetimes flooded through me.

393

His voice echoed as if he was speaking through both space and time, vibrating within me like a drug taking over my nervous system. "It is done! As I so ordain!" At his words a bolt of lightning shot across the clear blue sky and thunder rumbled, sounding remarkably like his deep, booming voice. While the rumble faded away he gave Ben a tender smile and then he turned and spoke in an intimate whisper to me, "He is yours."

Ben inclined his head in a bow and said formally, "Thank you, sir."

"I love you," Ben said in my head, wrapping his arms around me again.

"I love you, too," I thought back as I nestled into his chest.

"Forever," he added.

"Always," I agreed.

EPILOGUE

You Can Always Hope

Epic adventures end sometime. Battles are won and the victors
Pick up their lives and carry on. Memories flutter and flicker.
Looking to Aous and the new days, hopeful for joy in the future,
Charis embraces her powers, knowing the music she nurtures.

The sky was absolutely cloudless and Shuswap Lake was
sparkling as waves rippled gently around our houseboat. I watched with
a grin as Lloyd shouted, "Christie! I've fallen for you!" and dropped
over the side of the boat with a loud splash. Christie shook her head and
rolled her eyes as she grinned at me. He called from the water, "Come
in, Honey! The water's fine!" With a sigh she shrugged her shoulders
and headed over to the top of the slide mounted at the back of the boat.

"You realize, Grace," she said, "that you will never be able to
escape Lloyd now that he has experienced house-boating on Shuswap
Lake?"

I laughed as she pushed herself off and sailed down the slide to
splash into the water beside him.

Bonnie and Taylor came around the corner then and headed for the
slide. Bonnie grinned. "This was the best idea ever, Grace. Thanks for
inviting us!" Taylor nodded in agreement.

"No problem. I'm just really glad to have you all here with me." I
was. This was a celebration, whether all the participants were aware of it
or not.

I leaned over the deck watching Dave's boat towing a tube behind.
I giggled to myself when I recognized Rafiq squealing hysterically

9

beside Brittany as the tube bounced over the wash of Dave's boat. My parents were doing their shift in the kitchen that was bigger than the one in our house in Calgary, creating lunch for twenty.

It was wonderful having all my friends together, enjoying the sun and each other. The only dark spot was Josh's absence, but tonight we would hold a floating candle ceremony in his memory. There would be a lot of poetry and music.

Ben came up beside me; I felt him touch the tenor of my thoughts and he wrapped his arms around me and kissed me tenderly in response. In a moment we broke apart and strolled along the top deck to the hot tub. Auntie Bright was just climbing in. Uncle Jim was steering the boat from the upper wheel nearby.

"Coming in, Grace?" Bright asked invitingly.

"Ah, yeah. Sure." I said, because I could tell she wanted me to herself for a moment. I peeled my shirt off to reveal my bikini and climbed up the ladder.

"I'm surprised more of the family didn't come home with us after the ceremony," I remarked casually as I settled into the water. "I thought a few of them looked interested in visiting."

Jim chortled over at the wheel and I looked at him curiously.

"What's so funny, Uncle Jim?"

He smirked at Bright as he said, "After the disaster when Aglaea's old boyfriend showed up, I'm always glad when the relatives are far away!" He stood up and added, "I'm going down to the kitchen. I'll see if David will take the wheel and I can chop vegetables for Blythe."

I chuckled. My dad had been longing for a chance to drive the houseboat, but I was suspicious that he wouldn't find it as exciting as he imagined. It seemed to be a slow progress from bay to bay.

I looked over at Bright as Ben settled next to me in the water. "What did he mean by ex-boyfriend?"

"It wasn't an ex-boyfriend, actually."

I raised my eye-brow as she whispered conspiratorially, "He was her ex-husband."

"What?" I gasped.

Bright was amused and smirked over at Ben who shook his head in silent laughter. Apparently this was old news to him. "Never mind, Grace. It was over a couple millennia ago. Nothing to worry about."

"But there was trouble when he came to visit?"

She glanced up to the southern hills above the city and shrugged. "The town was saved."

I followed her gaze to Mount Ida with its stumble of burnt trees above the new green and raised my eyebrows. She just shrugged again.

Ben settled blissfully into the jets with a happy moan and closed his eyes. He was still sore. There was a line of new pink skin across his belly, but it was healing well.

"How did Josh find Bastion Mountain?" I whispered.

"With difficulty. Naturally, we presumed initially that Ares would build on Mount Ida," she said, nodding toward the scarred hill.

"Naturally?"

Ben spoke, eyes still closed, "She doesn't remember that far back yet, Bright." He paused a moment before he explained, "There's also a Mount Ida in Greece. It was a source of significant events in the old days, so the local one was the logical choice. Obviously it was *so* logical that he didn't go there. He found his own logic and built his bastion on Bastion Mountain."

"It was linked to somewhere else. From the inside it led to another mountain."

Bright nodded, "Yes, through a portal. It simplifies transportation to have a little supernatural help."

"Where was our battle then?"

She shrugged, "No idea. You'd have to ask Ares. I don't think it matters."

"Ah." She was right; it didn't matter. I looked up at the rocky mauve sides of Bastion Mountain. It wasn't telling any tales. No one would duplicate my fight. "Was Ares' fortress destroyed?"

"The entrance was."

I leaned in closed to Ben as I shivered with the memory of the bloody bodies. I heard Marco shout with laughter down at the water. I could feel Alex right below us in the living room; he was sleeping on the couch. The huge white dog he called Perita was curled up on the floor beside him, her head resting on his thigh.

Bright sighed, "How are you feeling, Grace? It's been a pretty momentous time for you."

That was an understatement.

"Bright?" I asked, changing the subject, "Can I ask you a question?"

"Of course, whatever you want."

"Last night I was reading about the three of you in the book Aglaea gave me."

She smiled. "Oh, yes?"

"Well, first I was wondering how you say your original name."

She laughed. "It's Euphrosyne." She said it like 'You-frossy-knee.'

"Hmm. That's...ah...interesting." I paused while she smirked and then continued. "It's pretty, but I see why you would use something a little simpler."

She nodded with a laugh. "Yeah, I know. It's a mouthful and I get tired of spelling it for people." She smiled, glancing at Ben relaxing with his eyes closed facing up to the sun, as she added, "It's better than being called *Orpheus* though."

Ben opened one eye and growled good-naturedly. She laughed and continued, "My name has a meaning I like, so I just adopt the version that is most accessible to the culture I'm living in at the time."

"So Brigit?"

"Ireland, yeah." Her mouth twitched as she explained, "It was the farthest I could get from India at the time. I needed green and blue landscape to erase the orange and gold."

She smiled gently and added. "Anything else?"

"Well, yeah. The book seems to have your birth orders all mixed up."

"Oh, I know." She snickered, as she sipped a bottle of water. "Funny, eh? We're triplets, so it's all a matter of minutes one way or the other, but not having the order strictly correct in public perception drives Aglaea crazy. I always tease her that it's because the historians thought she was the immature one." She giggled.

"So how did that happen?"

"Actually, I was asked the order once a few millennia ago and I lied."

"Why?"

She laughed, "Because I'm the bratty little sister, of course."

I looked at her with my eyebrows raised and she grinned.

"No, I'm actually serious, Grace. One day Aglaea was being her typical irritating self and that was my revenge. Once something is in print it lingers as truth forever. No one has ever been able to correct it. It's the ultimate verisimilitude." She grinned devilishly, "Can you just imagine how Aglaea hates that people think *I'm* the older, responsible one? I think it might actually be why she's the most driven of us all. She's still trying to prove she's the responsible eldest."

I grinned back, because I could see very well how Aglaea was making up for something with all that intensity. "What about my mom?"

"Oh, she doesn't care. I think she thought it was a pretty good joke herself, at the time. It doesn't make any difference to anyone but Aglaea. We still have the same tasks to do regardless."

Tasks. Ah yes. My new job. Right. I sighed, "I have *so* much to learn."

"Yes, that you do," she smiled fondly, "but you have an immortal lifetime to do it in and a good man at your side."

I nodded, smiling over to at Ben. "Yes, that's true."

Not everyone was immortal though. "You'll stick around for awhile? You're not going to go off and die on me anytime soon?" I asked her in a hushed voice.

"I expect I'll be around a long while yet. You can worry after you've made me a great, great aunt." She looked meaningfully at Ben and I blushed.

There was a shout down below and Marco called up, "Grace!"

I pushed myself out of the hot tub and poked my head over the edge of the boat, "Yeah?"

He was sitting at the wheel of Dave's boat with a huge grin on his face. Brittany was sitting behind him. Bonnie and Taylor were encased in life jackets in the tube at the back of the boat secured with a yellow tow rope held tightly by Claire. "Are you guys coming onto the tube? It's your turn!"

"We'll be down later!" I shouted with a wave.

Rafiq stood beside the hot tub dripping from being in the lake. He was tall, dark, and grinning. "Here," he said, holding out a CD. "I thought you might like to play this for that candle ceremony tonight."

"What is it?"

He shrugged, "Just a song I did. My uncle gave me this Indian keyboard thing. I've been playing around with it."

Bright looked interested. "Really? You play harmonium?"

He nodded with surprise, "Yeah. You've heard one before?"

She smiled with a distant look I recognized. "Oh, yes," she said breathily. "It's one of my favourite instruments. Grace has heard harmonium before, too."

I nodded, "That's so cool, Rafiq. They look hard to play, with that bellows part and the keyboard."

He blushed and murmured, "I kind of wrote a song for you. I hope you don't mind."

He glanced nervously at Ben, who smiled benignly, and then pulled himself up out of the hot tub. "Let's hear it." He took the CD and headed down to the stereo by the inside steering wheel.

In a moment the speakers crackled, and the music began.

Rafiq looked at me nervously. The tune was breathy and mournful. The notes echoed like a calling loon across the water. My skin tingled as I listened.

As the notes faded away I sighed, "Oh, Rafiq. It's so beautiful! Thank you!"

Ben joined us, "She's right." He clapped Rafiq on the shoulder. "You've done a good job, man."

Rafiq quivered with the praise, thanking us with a scarlet face as he headed for the slide, to join the others in the lake.

Bright watched him go with a nostalgic smile and glowing eyes.

I settled back into the hot tub and looked over to Bright. "So *am* I a Grace now?"

She smiled. "Officially, yes, but of course you have a lot to learn. I'll keep working while you train and study some more. University might be a good idea, and it looks like you'll need a trip to Paris for Ben to accept his international youth composition prize fairly soon."

"They haven't even voted yet, Bright. It's only if I'm short-listed that I'll have to go perform in Europe." Ben remarked modestly, eyes still closed.

"Don't be silly, Ben. You have Grace; of course you're going to win."

He shrugged. "It's never good to be too expectant. You never know how things will turn out." He opened his eyes with a smile, looked fondly down at me, and kissed my forehead.

"But you can always hope," I whispered.

"Yes," he said, giving me a squeeze, "there is always hope."

Eternity is our Today

The powers that pulled my love away
Are now defeated, left to mourn
The loss of hopes they held that day.

For from the moment she was born,
Her destiny has been entwined
With songs and words of joy, not scorn.

Now laughter guides all those inclined
to share the bliss of song that's tied
To seas and skies and hearts and minds.

My love lies resting at my side.
Her warmth against me as I sleep
Is worth the deaths that I have died.

No longer are there tears to weep.
No more the days are dreary greys.
No sadness 'round my heart can creep
For love of her the end allays
Eternity is our today.

GLOSSARY OF GODS AND GODDESSES
mentioned in *Grace Awakening*

AGLAEA- (Ah-GLAY-ah) a Grace, her name means beauty

ALEXANDER THE GREAT (aka ALEXANDROS MEGAS, aka ALEXANDER OF MACEDONIA) conqueror of Greece, the Middle East and India. Alexander was worshipped as a god by his people.

APOLLO- god of prophecy and oracles, healing, plague and disease, music, song and poetry, archery, and the protection of the young. He is Orpheus' father.

ARES- (AIR-ees) Greek god of war

ASKLEPIOS- (Ask-le-PEE-os) god of medicine and healing

ATROPOS- (Ah-TROH-pos) one of the Moirae. She cuts the life thread at death

AUTOMATON-

CHARIS- (KAYR-iss) Greek term for one Grace

CHARITES- (KAYR-it-ees) The Three Graces, who inspire happiness, joy, beauty, dance and song.

CLOTHO- (KLOH-thoh) one of the Moirae. She weaves threads into a life fabric

CONCORDIA- (Kon-KORD-ee-ah) Roman goddess of agreement and understanding. She is responsible for marital and universal harmony

CYCLOPS- (Sigh-KLAHPs) race of fierce giants with one eye. Cyclops are known for building fortresses and for skilled metalwork. They made beautiful jewellery and weapons

ENYO- (EN-yoh) goddess of war

EPIALTES- (Ep-ee-AHL-tees) -god of healing

ERINYS (ih RIN-iss) Greek name of the Furies, goddesses of retribution

ERIS-(AIR-iss) sister of Ares. She is a goddess of strife and discord

EROS- god of love

EUPHROSYNE- (Ee-oo-FROSS-in-ee) a Grace, her name means charm or radiance

EURYDICE- (Ee-oo-RID-iss-ee) a nymph, wife of Orpheus, who was killed by a serpent

GORGONES- three powerful, monster women

GRACES- in Greek the Three Graces were known as Charites (KAYR-ee-tess) (singular is a Charis (KAYR-iss)

KHARON- boatman on the River Styx who ferried the souls of the dead into the Underworld (also known as Charon)

LACHESIS- (LATCH-uh-sis) one of the Moirae. She measures the life thread and determines destiny.

LETHE- (LAY thay) goddess of forgetfulness and oblivion

LIMNADES- (Lim-NAD-ees) Naiades or spirits of freshwater lakes

MARS- Roman god of war

MNEMOSYNE- (Meh- MOSS-in-ee) goddess of memory

MOIRAE- the Fates who control the destiny of humankind. They weave the lives into a tapestry.

MOUSAI- The nine muses who inspired artists.

NEMESIS- the goddess of indignation against, and retribution for, evil deeds and undeserved good fortune.

ORPHEUS- (Or-FEE-us) son of Apollo, a god of poetry and music.

PERSEPHONE- (Per-SEFF-oh-nee) wife of Hades, Queen of the Underworld, goddess of re-birth, mother of the Three Furies: Megaira, etc

STHENNO- (Ss-THEN-noh) a Gorgon

THALIA- (THAYL-ee-ah) a Grace, her name means joy or happiness

ZEUS- leader of the Greek gods of Mount Olympus

BIBLIOGRAPHY

Atsma, Aaron J. *The Theoi Project*. www.theoi.com. 2000-2008

Buxton, Richard. *Complete World of Greek Mythology*. New York: Thames and Hutton, 2004.

Evslin, Bernard. *Heroes, Gods and Monsters of the Greek Myths*. New York: Dell Laurel-Leaf, 2005.

Graves, Robert. *The Greek Myths*. Wakefield, RI: Moyer Bell, 1988.

Guhl, E. and W. Koner. *The Greeks and Romans: Their Life and Customs*. London, England: Studio Editions, 1989.

Myth Index. www.mythindex.com. 2007.

Petrarch. *Canzoniere*. Anthony Mortimer, trans. London, England: Penguin, 2002.

Toynbee, Arnold J. *Greek Civilization and Character*. New York: Mentor Books, 1953.

ACKNOWLEDGEMENTS

Many thanks to

Mom & Dad for being the most enthusiast cheerleaders

Lenora for all the 'road trips'

Cathy, Julia, Cyndy, & Heather for the many, many years of friendship

Stephenie Meyer for the inspiration of her myths

My student readers, particularly Brittany, Sami, Sam, & Ethan
for their feedback & enthusiastic encouragement

Vikki Sladen for her excellent insight and observations

& of course,

Amin for the melodies, memories, & imaginings-
the catalyst of it all

Shawn Bird has a BA in English from Athabasca University and a Post Baccalaureate Diploma in Education from Simon Fraser University. She is a secondary school teacher in the Interior of British Columbia. She has taught a variety of subjects including English, Drama, French, and Library. She and her husband have two children. Shawn has been writing poetry, stories and articles since she was a child. She is an active member of Rotary and a former Rotary Youth Exchange Student.

Visit her on the web at http://www.shawnbird.com, at her Facebook Fan Page www.facebook.com/ShawnLBird, or follow her on Twitter: @ShawnLBird.

Made in the USA
Charleston, SC
29 September 2013